Carole Matthews is the *Sunday Times* bestselling author of over thirty novels, including the top ten bestsellers *The Cake Shop in the Garden*, *A Cottage by the Sea*, *Paper Hearts and Summer Kisses*, *Christmas Cakes and Mistletoe Nights*, *Million Love Songs* and *Happiness for Beginners*. In 2015, Carole was awarded the RNA Outstanding Achievement Award. Her novels dazzle and delight readers all over the world and she is published in more than thirty countries.

For all the latest news from Carole, visit www.carolematthews.com and sign up to her newsletter. You can also follow Carole on Twitter (@carolematthews) and Instagram (matthews.carole) or join the thousands of readers who have become Carole's friend on Facebook (carolematthewsbooks).

Praise for Carole Matthews

'All the warmth and wit we expect from Carole . . . Perfect'
Bella

'Matthews is one of the few writers who can rival Marian Keyes' gift for telling heart-warming tales with buckets of charm and laughs'
Daily Record

'Witty, funny and incredibly touching, this is perfect for lifting the spirits'
Heat

'Simply brilliant'
Closer

'A feel-good tale, fun and thoroughly escapist'
Marie Claire

Carole Matthews

It's Now or Never

sphere

SPHERE

First published in Great Britain in 2010 by Headline Review
This reissue published by Sphere in 2020

5 7 9 10 8 6

A CIP catalogue record for this book
is available from the British Library.

ISBN 978-0-7515-5138-9

Typeset in Sabon by Palimpsest Book Production Ltd, Falkirk, Stirlingshire
Printed and bound in Great Britain by Clays Ltd, Elcograf S.p.A.

Papers used by Sphere are from well-managed forests
and other responsible sources.

Sphere
An imprint of
Little, Brown Book Group
Carmelite House
50 Victoria Embankment
London EC4Y 0DZ

An Hachette UK Company
www.hachette.co.uk

www.littlebrown.co.uk

Acknowledgements

To our lovely companions on the Inca Trail trip to Peru – including our Canadian sanity and mobile medicine cabinet, Joanne and Brian. Also to Mick the Gadget, Big Mick, Henny, Simone and our guides, Crystal and Lobo. And, as always, to Lovely Kev, who pushed me up most of it and let me have all of the sleeping bag, and came to the loo with me in the night even when he was still asleep. The Andes are flipping steep and don't let anyone tell you otherwise. With hindsight, it was a very wonderful experience. But I am never, ever camping again – and you can quote me on that.

For information and anecdotes about fishing, thanks to my uncle, David Coleman, and to top MX5 mates Craig 'The Hat' Hitchman and The Terrible Twosome – the fearless, the inimitable, the frequently very silly – Mr Richard Markus and Mr Owen Earl.

Thanks also to Jill and Simon at The Pudding Club, the Threeways Hotel in Mickleton for facilitating my research. Would heartily recommend one of their Pudding Club dinners – yum! A lot easier than walking the Inca Trail but, admittedly, with more calories. Just leave the diet at home. For info go to www.thepuddingclub.com.

Chapter One

'Are we really related to her?' I nudge my sister, Lauren, in the ribs.

She looks up from the glass of champagne that she's staring into, seemingly mesmerised by the bubbles.

'I can hardly believe it,' I add.

'Me neither,' she agrees, and tips more champagne into her mouth.

Chelsea is gliding across the dance floor in the arms of her husband while her guests smile on benignly.

It is our elder sister's fortieth birthday party and, as always, she is a vision of loveliness. She's wearing a floor-length Vera Wang gown in white that's drenched in Swarovski crystals which burst into tiny rainbows whenever they catch the light. It fits like a glove, hugging every inch of her tiny frame. Her auburn curls are piled high and her head is thrown back in uncontained and joyous laughter, showing off the delicious creaminess of her throat and her perfect teeth.

Her husband Richard is tall, tanned, and has the rugged-jawed looks of a classic romantic hero. He's something fabulous in the City, is stonkingly wealthy, is kind to small furry animals, remembers to empty the bins and puts the lid down on the toilet when he's finished too.

'What star sign is Chelsea?' Lauren wants to know.

'Gemini.'

1

'And that means you're the luckiest bitch in the world, does it?'

'I think it means you're a good communicator with a sunny disposition.' With a tendency to be two-faced and selfish on occasions if you believe in the stars, but I won't tell my sister that.

Lauren tuts and throws back her drink. 'What are we?'

'Scorpio.'

'And?'

'We're the most murdered star sign.'

Another tut. 'Fabulous.'

This isn't your usual fortieth birthday party. For mine – next year – I was thinking of having an At Home with a few family and friends, a readymade cake from Asda and some balloons – if I could summon up the necessary energy. Chelsea's birthday party – like the rest of her life – is exquisite.

We're at the Dorchester Hotel on London's Park Lane in the main ballroom, along with about 300 other people. Already I've spotted Jodie Kidd, Jamie Oliver and Richard Hammond – just a few of the celebrities that our sister counts among her closest friends.

'Where did we go wrong?' Lauren asks, as she slides down on her pretty silver chair. She sounds a little drunk. In the same manner that Gordon Ramsay uses a little bad language. Oh – and he's here too, somewhere.

I sigh before I answer, 'I don't know.'

Needless to say, Lauren and I haven't gone down the Vera Wang route of haute couture. I have chosen vintage Next – in other words, a dress that's at least three years old. Not even a good vintage, I feel. My sister has opted for a little number from Coast that will be owned by her credit-card company for the next year or more and, I don't like to mention it, but there's some of the raspberry coulis – from our bitter chocolate mousse with raspberry coulis dessert – down the front of it.

I'm Annie Ashton and my sister, Lauren Osbourne, is the one swaying slightly in her chair next to me. Lauren and I are twins. I'm the elder by five minutes and we have now both recently reached the grand old age of thirty-nine years.

Our sister Chelsea didn't buy into the whole Life Begins at Forty thing. Her life started when she slipped effortlessly from our mother's womb and into an existence that has, ever since, been charmed.

Lauren and I, born a scant year later, were breech twins who entered the world bottom first and, somehow, I think that set the tone.

Chapter Two

Lauren stifles a yawn. 'I need to go to bed.'

My sister twirls her long, dark hair languidly round a manicured finger. We have spent our entire lives fighting not to look exactly like each other. That explains my ultra-short pixie crop. Though I did stop short of dyeing it blond – mainly due to the expense rather than a submission of individuality. I'm a little softer round the middle than Lauren – something I blame on my two children, rather than my penchant for cake. Lauren looks more sporty than me – that's because she is. Other than that, we're two peas in a pod. Annoyingly, despite our advanced years, we still find we turn up in the same outfit to parties sometimes. This time, we took the precaution of co-ordinating our limited wardrobes well in advance by the medium of several dozen text messages. We had no intention of committing our usual fashion faux pas at such a splendid do.

'The night's young,' I remind Lauren. 'You can't be tired.' The party is in full swing and the sounds of 'It's Raining Men' pound out from the disco. There's some dishy actor whose name I can't remember from *Holby City* camping it up on the dance floor. The DJ is someone edgy and famous but, as I live my life under a rock, I've never heard of him. 'Let's have a boogie and see if we can bag you a celebrity boyfriend.'

'I've already got a boyfriend,' Lauren reminds me.

I look around, theatrically. 'So where is he?'

'That's mean,' my sister says.

It probably is.

To fill you in, Lauren's boyfriend of five years was invited but couldn't make it at the last minute. This is a regular occurrence. The small problem is that Jude Taylor has the inconvenient encumbrance of a wife and two children, which makes spontaneous socialising with his long-term girlfriend somewhat tricky. Clearly, whatever excuse he'd fabricated to be absent from the marital home on a Saturday night didn't pass muster when push came to shove.

The reason my twin looks so toned is that she spends a lot of time in the gym pounding the treadmill out of sheer frustration.

'I want to go back to the room,' Lauren insists. 'Jude said that he'd call and I'll never be able to hear my mobile in here.'

'That's because we're at the world's most fabulous party,' I tell her. 'And everyone is having a great time.'

'Everyone but us.'

She's right. I'm also miserable due to a lack of male company. And that's because my husband has – point-blank – refused to come. Greg hates this kind of thing. He'd rather have hot needles poked in his eyes than put a suit and tie on outside of office hours. The thought of being in a room filled with beautiful people doing beautiful things would make him go cold with dread. So, instead of coming to my sister's high-end, celebrity-loaded knees-up with enough champagne to float a ship, he's chosen to go night fishing on the Grand Union Canal with his exceedingly dreary mate, Ray. That's all he ever wants to do.

In twenty years of marriage, I have learned more about coarse fishing than I ever needed to. I could tell you the benefits of Dragon Barrel Pellets over Yellow Pop-Ups, if you cared to listen – or the differences between a waggler and a feeder rod. Call me sceptical, but carp, Greg frequently tells me, are very intelligent fish. I do not share my husband's passion for fishing or his views on the tricksy carp – but that doesn't stop him from regaling me with many tales of their wily ways.

We did have a tiny bit of a row before I left. If I remember rightly, I said something like, 'I'm so sick of my small, dull life. This is the only excitement I've had in years and you're not prepared to share it with me. You're a selfish bastard and if you're not coming I'm going to have a great time without you. I have to put up with all kinds of things for you and your stupid fishing, and yet you won't compromise when it comes to my needs. Well, that's it! I'm off.'

And Greg, I think, closed the door quietly behind him as he left. He didn't even tell me to enjoy myself.

'What a morose pair we are,' Lauren says wearily. 'Let's clear off.'

'Chelsea will be upset. We rarely see her these days.'

'Our dear sister won't even notice that we're gone.'

Lauren's right again. Chelsea is too busy socialising with all of her rich friends to notice if we slope away. It makes me sad that we're not closer to her, but Chelsea now lives a crazy jet-set life, splitting her time between the UK and Dubai, where her husband is for most of the year. She's just swooped in for the party – if not on a private jet, then certainly first class.

'Don't drag me away, Lauren,' I plead. 'Let's have some

fun.' I might just find *myself* a celebrity boyfriend. See what Greg would think to that.

'I've got a headache coming on,' my sister whines, and gives me her most pitiful pout.

So we head for the door – Lauren a little unsteadily.

We pass a table groaning with champagne and Lauren grabs a bottle and two glasses and we take those with us to continue the party on our own.

As we stand and wait for the lift, Lauren takes out her mobile phone. 'Damn,' she says. 'I've missed Jude's call.'

Quickly, she checks her voicemail and there's a whispered message that I can just about overhear – even though Lauren tries to press her phone close enough to her ear so that she thinks I can't.

'Sorry, I couldn't make it, darling,' Jude's smooth tones coo. *'But you know how much I love you. I'll speak to you as soon as I can.'*

I don't even bother checking my phone as I know that Greg won't have bothered to call me. He wouldn't coo sweet nothings even if he did. My husband is not a cooey sort of man. I'm more likely to get sweet FA than sweet nothings.

Lauren hangs up.

The desperation in her tired smile makes my heart want to break.

'He said he loves me.'

I just can't help a disbelieving tut at that. It's out before I can stop it. If he loves Lauren so much, then where is he tonight, eh? Answer me that.

'He does,' she insists crisply. 'And one day we'll be together. You'll see.'

7

'I have to admire your optimism, sis,' I say, as gently as I can.

Then, as we wait to be whisked away from the ball and back up to our bedroom, I marvel at how Lauren can be so optimistic despite the odds being stacked against her. I also take time to wonder where my own optimism has toddled off to.

Chapter Three

Chelsea has very generously booked us a suite in this outrageously posh hotel for the night – and paid for it – even though we could have easily gone back to Lauren's flat in a taxi.

The room we're in is truly gorgeous – an understated extravagance of cream linen and dark wood – and is bigger than my entire house. We have two bathrooms, a double bed each and a lounge with four sofas in it and a television the size of a multiplex cinema. The artworks look as if they've been lifted straight from the walls of Tate Modern.

I want to live here. For ever.

Though it's not yet eleven o'clock, Lauren and I are washed, brushed and ready for bed. We're sitting up, dwarfed by our vast neighbouring beds in our jim-jams, a glass of champagne in hand.

Lauren knocks back her fizz and huffs, 'She's like bloody Cinderella and we're the Ugly Sisters.'

'Thanks.' I don't point out that *we're* the ones who have scarpered from the ball before midnight. The Ugly Sisters were the ones who hung around till dawn having a fab time and schmoozing with the Prince, if I remember rightly.

'You know what I mean.'

More's the pity for us that I do know what she means.

'So what are we going to do?' I ask. 'We're both forty

next year and I feel that our lives are slowly slipping away from us.'

'Speak for yourself,' Lauren says as she swigs.

'You can't be happy with your situation.'

Lauren's chin juts out. 'It won't always be like this.'

Unfortunately, this is a song I've heard before. Lauren has been with her married lover for over five years now and he's not showing that he's in any imminent danger of leaving his wife for my sister despite her blind optimism in the face of reality.

Lauren works for Jude Taylor at the web company he owns. That's how they met. It's called *Happening Today* and they send out funky daily missives about what's 'happening today' in London and various cities round the country. Lauren is one of the sales executives who sell advertising on the site. And very good she is at it too.

Jude is as lavish with his money as he is with his love and helps Lauren pay the mortgage on her tiny flat in West Hampstead – primarily, I believe, so that she is close at hand and he can visit her whenever he wants. She has a great car too. The only thing she doesn't have is her man's full-time attention. Which, obviously, is the only thing that she really wants.

Much as it pains me, I have to admit that Jude Taylor is pretty hunky. He has dark and brooding looks, tousled hair and an astonishing line in trendy clothing for a guy. Almost the perfect man. Apart from the resident wife, of course. And the amount of heartache he's caused my sister over the last five years.

'It will all work out just fine for me,' Lauren says as she

glances surreptitiously at her phone again; I can almost feel her willing it to ring. 'Jude and I are soulmates. We both feel it. He will leave. The timing just has to be right.'

Perhaps that's true, but there always seems to be some sort of feeble excuse that keeps him bound to his double life – a school play that must be attended, a visit from one or other set of grandparents, a forthcoming family holiday. Always something that couldn't possibly be postponed or disrupted. As if walking out on your wife and children isn't going to cause enough disruption.

Still, I wish the thought of a phone call from Greg could instil such excitement in me. But then he and I have been married for over twenty years. Isn't it normal for some of the excitement to go? We'd be in a permanent state of exhaustion if love was still a frenzy after all that time. Am I right?

It's just that now I feel like we've passed from excitement, to contentment, to rut. Quite deep rut. Borderline trench, if I'm truthful.

We got out of the habit of going out when the children were young because we didn't have the money. Now we don't have either the money or the inclination. Or one of us doesn't. And I don't think that it's me. Is this grey monotony what I have to look forward to for the rest of my life? I have to do something or I might just go stark raving mad.

'We've got a year,' I say decisively. 'Not quite a year before we're forty. It's not too late for us to turn things around.'

'How are we going to do that?' Lauren wants to know.

'We have to decide exactly what we want first.'

'That's easy for me,' Lauren says. 'I want my man and,'

she turns to look at me, eyes misty, 'maybe I want a baby too, Annie.'

'*A baby?*' This is the first time she's admitted that to me. It could be the drink talking.

'Christ,' she says. 'Let's face it, I'm not getting any younger. It could be now or never. What if I leave it too late?'

I slip out of my bed and get in next to Lauren as we used to do as youngsters. We snuggle up together. It reminds me of when we were teenagers and I get a stab of regret that we don't get the opportunity for all-night heart-to-hearts any more.

Sometimes I wish that we didn't lead such separate lives, that we were still as close as we used to be. But the fact that Lauren is always hanging on, waiting for precious moments should Jude suddenly become available, means that she's impossible to pin down. She only comes to our house at the weekend if Jude is going off somewhere else with his family as she always lives in hope that he might pop by on the off-chance. Not only is he messing up Lauren's life, but I feel he's coming between us and I resent that too.

'I had no idea you felt like that,' I say gently.

'This isn't an ideal situation,' Lauren sniffs tearfully, 'but I'm making the best of it. I love him, Annie. More than I've ever loved anyone. And that means that I want the things that other people have. It's the simple things that I miss the most. I want him home every night so that I can make him dinner. I want to be able to wake up with him every day. And what if I do want his child before it's too late for me? Is that so wrong of me?'

'Oh, sweetie.' I put my arms round my sister while she cries. At the moment, her wish-list seems like a tall order.

'What about you?' she asks, when her tears are spent. 'What do you want?'

I lean back on Lauren's pile of feather-soft pillows and sip at my champagne. 'I want excitement,' I say. 'The kids are about to fly the nest and what will I be left with?' I can't even vocalise the fact that I find my husband of twenty years as dull as dishwater. He's completely happy simply to be at home, watch television, go fishing. He seems to want nothing more than that. But I do.

'These should be the best years of our lives, but we both seem to be making such a bollocks of it.'

'Tell me about it,' my sister agrees.

'I want to grab life by the throat and shake it. I've never been anywhere, done anything. I want to do something different and worthwhile.'

'Such as?'

'I don't know,' I admit with a defeated huff. 'But this year, I promise myself, I'm damn well going to work on it.'

Chapter Four

Lauren and I are having bacon, eggs, sausage, tomatoes, mushrooms, hash browns and toast when Chelsea breezes in. It seems that our late-night turn-our-lives-round decision has given us both a great appetite – for life, of course, and a mega cooked breakfast. Or maybe we're just going down the cholesterol route as a hangover cure. Whichever way, it feels good. Lauren's normally in such a state of high anxiety that she hardly eats, whereas I always prefer the calorie route to comfort.

'Today is the start of the rest of our lives, Lauren,' I expound brightly. 'And we're going to go all out to get what we want from it.'

'Don't speak so loudly,' Lauren complains, head in hands. She's been glued to her mobile since she opened her eyes, but still no call from Lover Boy, so she's irritable as well as hung over.

'Sorry.'

'We need more vitamin C,' she concludes, and pours herself another glass of fresh orange juice. At five quid a throw. But, thankfully, Chelsea is picking up the breakfast bill too.

When our older sister sees us, she makes her way to our table and kisses each of us in turn on both cheeks. Chelsea doesn't look like she's had a night on the tiles – she looks like she's had a full eight hours' sleep and possibly an oxygen facial since we last saw her, so radiant is she. I'm glad that I put on some slap, a luxury that isn't normally seen at breakfast – even though I did it because I thought Jamie Oliver might still be here.

Our sister puts a hand on each of our shoulders and squeezes affectionately. 'I hope that you both had a great time last night.'

'It was wonderful,' I gush. 'I live my life vicariously through you.'

I always look at my elder sister and envy her. She is cool, calm, collected in every circumstance. Her husband is obviously a sex god as she permanently carries the look of the orgasmically sated. Not for her the once-a-fortnight fumble that I've sadly grown accustomed to, I'll bet.

My niece and nephew are model children and are already seasoned travellers. Sophia is six and is an accomplished pianist and a promising ballerina. Henry, at the age of four, is fluent in French, a star at his stage school (he is the cherubic smiling face of Wheety Bites in the television advert), plays the violin and is probably now a Black Belt in karate as well, as I haven't had an update on their progress for the last couple of weeks. Some days, I even daydream that they're my own children. But then Chelsea would never have anything that didn't come up to scratch – particularly not her kids. Even the dog's a naffing top-ranked pedigree.

Yes, our sister's life is perfect in every way imaginable. I don't know why, but Chelsea's never had to try hard like Lauren and I have. And we try very hard not to resent her for it – but we do.

'It was cool,' Lauren mumbles, pushing in more toast.

'Look what Rich bought me.' Chelsea flashes a sparkling eternity ring encrusted with diamonds. The brightness of it makes us both wince.

'Gorgeous,' I say.

'Humph,' Lauren manages.

Chelsea looks across the room to where her adoring husband is reading *The Times* at their table, a contented smile on his face.

Lauren and I were both pretty rubbish at school, whereas Chelsea was always top of the class. She was the straight A student while we, The Terrible Twins, had a permanent appointment with detention. We were both high-spirited and, as twins can, egged each other on. It wasn't that we were naughty, it was that we were particularly bad at not getting caught.

Chelsea went on to university and did part-time modelling to pay her own way as she knew that Mum and Dad were strapped for cash – well, no one really ever plans for twins, do they? After Uni, Chelsea abandoned an academic career – which she would, no doubt, have been brilliant at – and took up modelling full-time. From then on we saw her only on high days and holidays as she flew in from one exotic location or another. She married Richard King at thirty, then after a year or so of the London scene, bought a sprawling country farm in Woburn, Bedfordshire, overlooking the ancestral seat of the Duke of Bedford and its famous deer park, where she and Richard raised pigs and chickens and did sporty things with horses that I don't begin to understand. A few years later and her perfect two children were born to order and, of course, she regained her figure about ten minutes later.

Now my sister spends a large portion of her year out in Dubai rubbing shoulders with the fabulously rich and famous. Not that you'd guess, to look at her. The desert sun hasn't troubled her peaches-and-cream complexion. Chelsea's time is filled both at home and away by organising charity lunches and doing good in various ways while looking effortlessly stunning. As well as their penthouse in Dubai and a country seat in middle England, my sister and her husband also have a six-bedroomed villa in Tuscany and a river-view apartment in Shad Thames for when they're overnighting in Town on Richard's whistle-stop business trips. Unless, of course, they choose to take a suite in the Dorchester instead, as they did last night.

'I can't stay this morning,' Chelsea says apologetically. 'We're lunching with some friends at the Oxo Tower.'

'Nice,' I comment. 'I have to get back, anyway.' I don't, but I'm not sure what else to say.

'Me too,' Lauren chips in grumpily. I know for certain that the only appointment my twin has is with her treadmill at the gym.

'But we must catch up soon,' Chelsea is saying. Does a shadow cross her face? 'We're not going straight back to Dubai. We'll be here for a little while.'

'Wonderful,' I say. 'Are you staying in London?'

'No. At the manor. We'll be back sometime next week.'

'Even better. We can spend some time together. Catch up.'

'Yes, yes. We must,' Cheslea says, but she's clearly distracted. And I'm well aware that she has a dozen other guests to catch up with. 'I love you both.'

I want to tell her about our revelation last night. That all

17

the champagne we glugged was put to good and productive use and that it's given us the momentum to pursue perfection and fulfilment in our lives, just as she has.

But I don't say this as it seems somehow churlish after she's been so generous to us and, if there's one thing that Chelsea is aware of, it's being slightly outside of our tight little unit of two. I wonder if she ever thinks about our lives. Does she know – would she care – that we find them wanting?

Standing up, I hug my older sister warmly. 'I love you too.'

I want to tell her that we – The Terrible Twins – the ones who caused our parents to have a permanent roll to their eyes, plan to do something wonderful before we reach the impending milestone of forty. But, already, Chelsea is backing away, her hands slipping through mine.

She air-kisses Lauren and then turns back to her own table where Rich is beaming happily at her.

'I want her life,' Lauren mutters as she watches our sister go. 'I *so* want her life.'

And, as I'm sure you'll appreciate, I can't help but agree with her.

Chapter Five

Greg sat on the bank of the Grand Union Canal. They'd set up by the busy car park at the Three Locks pub because his friend, Ray, liked to be able to keep an eye on his Mercedes while he fished.

'I've got two and a half grand's worth of tackle in the boot,' Ray boasted as he flicked a thumb towards the vehicle. 'I don't want any of those thieving bastards getting their hands on it. Only last week, Davey Coleman had his back window smashed and his stuff lifted.'

Greg liked it best when he could park up, walk for half an hour into the middle of nowhere and pick a patch where there was no one else around – no dog walkers, no hikers, no courting couples, no people at all, just him, the fish, the birds, the quiet slap of line on water. But he'd been fishing with Ray since they were both boys and his friend was more forceful, more particular in his fishing requirements. And it was true enough that you were more likely to get your gear robbed if you went down the solitary route.

Ray already had three rods set up and in the water, always in such a rush to get the first bite. Whenever they fished together, which was more often than not, his friend would arrive at the bank in an explosion of activity, eager to be filling his keepnet, and his gear would be set up in a flash amid a flurry of expletives.

For Greg, taking his time over setting up was half the pleasure, part of the relaxation, the meditation. Yesterday, he'd been along and had ground-baited this pitch, encouraging the fish to come and feed in preparation for their arrival today.

Preparation. That was what it was all about.

As he always did, this morning he'd headed off to the tackle shop, Fishy Business, with the Tupperware for maggots that he kept in the fridge – much to Annie's disgust. Then he'd spent a pleasant half an hour selecting his bait for the day, listening to Owen Earl who ran the shop enthusiastically prattling on about the very latest rods and gadgets that Greg could never in his wildest dreams afford.

'You want to get one of these, matey,' Ray said as Greg set up his old camping stool. His friend patted his new reclining fishing chair with fully adjustable legs and an extra-padded seat. Ray had all the gadgets. He was probably Fishy Business's best customer. If Ray ever stopped fishing, the tackle shop would go bust. Not only was there the two and a half grand's worth in the boot of Ray's car, but an equivalent sum still stored in his garage in specifically designed cupboards. Greg sighed to himself.

He'd always had to make do as money was invariably tight at home. Not that he resented his friend's equipment – as it were – but that didn't stop him from envying him from time to time.

Greg unpacked his box next, laying out his maggots, sweetcorn, bread that he'd filched from the bread bin and some luncheon meat in pleasing symmetry.

'Come on, come on,' Ray urged, peering into the murky water of the canal. 'Bite, you bastards! We might have to move if we're going to get lucky today, matey.'

They hadn't been there twenty minutes yet.

This was a good stretch of water; there was a bridge over the nearby road and weeds on the far side of the bank. Good places for canal fish – carp, perch, tench and bream – to linger.

Greg slipped his keepnet into the water and then assembled his rod section by section – the same one that he'd had for the last twenty years. Annie had bought it for him as a wedding present and there might be bigger and better rods with fancier names and certainly fancier prices, but this one would do for him. It was like an old friend. His hands fitted it perfectly. He knew all its nuances and it had served him well all these years. Besides, he firmly believed that it wasn't having state-of-the-art equipment that mattered, it was the skill of the fisherman, the patience, knowing the water, learning which bait suited which fish, years of accumulated knowledge and experience. That surely was worth more than having an ultra-light carbon-fibre rod and no patience?

'Where's the missus today?' Ray wanted to know as he slapped at the water with his line again.

'Party,' Greg said, as he clipped on his reel and carefully threaded his line through the rings along the length of the rod. He was fishing a four-pound line today and probably a size 18 hook. Greg wondered what Ray was fishing. 'Sister's birthday.'

'Not your thing?'

'Nah.' Greg shook his head. Annie liked that kind of thing,

socialising, making inane talk to people you didn't know and were never likely to meet again. What was the point in that? 'You know me.'

She was better going on her own. All Chelsea's friends were posh types, bankers, minor celebrities. Annie loved all that. He couldn't stand it – they were all so false. Annie moaned at him, but then he only annoyed his wife when he went along and then didn't know what to say to anyone.

Similarly, Annie never came fishing with him. She used to, once upon a time. He'd fallen in love with her while he was fishing. Annie used to come along regularly then. She couldn't stand to be away from him for five minutes and she'd spend all day happily lying on the bank beside him just to be near him. He liked that, the quiet moments they'd shared.

As the years passed, his wife had come along less. There was always something to do at home, she said. But occasionally, he'd persuade her. Then he'd fish and she'd sit with a book and a bottle of wine. He thought it was a wonderful way to pass time. Annie was, invariably, bored out of her skull after a couple of hours. And, in recent years, she hadn't come along with him at all. Now she preferred spending time with her twin sister when he was out. But it was good for a couple to have separate interests, wasn't it?

Greg hoped that his wife had enjoyed herself at the party and he was looking forward to her coming home today. He might not want to go with her, but he had to admit that he didn't like it when she wasn't there either.

'She's a good woman, that one,' Ray said sagely. 'Fine, fine woman.'

He might have the upper hand when it came to fishing

skill, Greg thought, but Ray knew an awful lot more about women than Greg ever would.

'Yeah,' Greg said with a contented smile. He couldn't agree more.

Chapter Six

Lauren comes to Euston station with me. She clings on to me before I head off for my train. 'You'll be okay,' I reassure her, patting her back. 'We both will.'

'Love you,' she says. 'I'll come up next week – if Jude's not around.' He still hasn't called and one of her fingernails has been chewed ragged because of it.

'Don't you dare forget that this year we're going all out for it.' I clench my fist in determination.

'You too.'

Something is niggling at me. 'I wonder why Chelsea's back so unexpectedly? She never said she was staying on after the party in her emails, did she?'

Lauren shrugs.

'You don't think there's anything wrong?'

My sister harrumphs. 'In Chelsea's life? No.'

She's probably right. Though I make a mental note to phone my big sister early next week.

Lauren and I hug again and I rush off for my train before I miss it. The carriage is quiet at this time on a Sunday and I flop down into a window seat, ready to be jogged back to my home in Milton Keynes.

I suppose I should ring Greg, let him know that I'm on my way back, but I don't. He'll be head down fishing and won't be interested in where I am or what I'm doing. He might even huff when I ask him to collect me from the station. Hang the expense, I'll get a taxi. Spend a little more of the money we haven't got.

I think of Lauren and worry about her going home to an empty flat. But is that any worse than going home to the tail-end of a petty row?

My sister could do with more steadiness in her life and less drama. Whereas I need less of the steadiness and more excitement. It's like the whole curly hair/straight hair dilemma. Whatever you're blessed with, you want the opposite. Straight, you have it permed. Curly, you have it straightened. Hair issues, I'm sure you've found, are invariably a lot easier to fix than your relationship ones.

It would be fair to say that Lauren and I were more of a disappointment to our dear parents than Chelsea ever was. After our sister's shining example, believe me, they had high hopes for us. We let them down, badly. No matter how often they compared us to Chelsea – and they did, regularly – we were always found wanting.

Instead of globe-trotting the world with a fabulous model-ling career, I was married young at the tender age of nineteen to my first 'proper' boyfriend, one Mr Greg Ashton – the man with the all-consuming fishing obsession. It never crossed my mind to question whether this quiet, somewhat staid boy was even suitable for me. Or that his desire to do nothing else but fish would get on my nerves after multiple years of it. And no one else pointed out to me that I should. Perhaps I ought to have wondered if there was more out there, but I didn't. So, naive and gullible youngsters that we were, we married. A year later, before we'd hardly begun to know each other as man and wife, our first baby was on the way, followed closely by a second.

Ellen is now nearly twenty and our son Bobby has just turned eighteen. I don't feel old enough to have kids that age and I like to think that I don't look it either, but I'm not so sure these days.

Even though Lauren and I are twins, my younger sister has always been the more groomed, the more figure-conscious. Lauren has spray tans and regular manicures. I'm lucky if I remember to wear rubber gloves when I'm doing the washing up. My body is always the shade that nature intended. Pasty. Lauren takes after my mother for that side of her, whereas I'm more like my father. So I have nasal hair and holey cardigans to look forward to in a few years. When our parents died, Lauren and I became even closer and Chelsea became even more engrossed in her fundraising and fabulous life.

Forty-five minutes later and I pull into Milton Keynes station. Outside, I hail a cab and it whisks me to Tattenhoe, the pleasant modern estate where our modest house is.

We were all born and bred in a village just outside the new city and I guess I'm the only one who never escaped. Chelsea was off as soon as she could go. Lauren too headed for the bright lights of London, the moment she left school. Not me. I just sort of hung around waiting to see what would happen. And being proposed to by Greg was all that did happen.

There wasn't much here when Greg and I scrimped and saved to buy our first two-bedroomed terraced home; now, however, Milton Keynes is the fastest-growing city in the country. Every week, a new housing estate appears out of nowhere. And I never questioned whether I wanted to live here or not. Rather like I never questioned whether I should say yes to Greg. Why did I do that? Why didn't I think about where I would like to spend my days, whether this place would suit me rather than another? I just accepted that this is where we would be. I've never considered whether I'm more suited to village or town living, or whether I'd like a house near the beach. We moved here and we stayed here. Probably because Greg likes it.

I'd love to be one of those people who has a dream. One of our neighbours yearns to move to France, run an enormous farm in the middle of nowhere and raise whatever it is they raise on French farms – truffle-hunting pigs, *peut-être*? Another friend has the urge to retire young and move to Suffolk, to finish her days with the tang of salty air in her lungs, days of long walks on the beach and traditional fish and chips for tea. Me? I don't even know what my dream might be.

Greg and I did progress to a small three-bedroom detached place in the intervening years, but that wasn't out of a great desire to better ourselves – we just ran out of space for the kids and were forced to upscale. Even so, we've been in the same house for over fifteen years.

Surprisingly, my husband's car is in the drive. Maybe the fishing lost its thrall in the wee small hours – but I doubt it. And, I feel terrible even saying this, but I have a real heart-sink moment when my key goes into the lock. I know exactly the words that Greg will say to me.

'Cup of tea, love?' His voice comes from the kitchen.

I was right.

It's not a bad thing to be greeted like that, is it? But would it hurt, for once, for Greg to cast aside his teaspoon and, with unbridled passion, declare, 'God, I've missed you!'

Throwing down my battered overnight bag, I head towards him. I know too that nothing will be said about my outburst last night. We never resolve our arguments – we just pretend that they never happened. Are there couples who talk openly and freely on a regular basis to resolve their petty differences and keep their relationship fresh? Or are the majority like us, simmering along in unspoken resentment until the petty difference reaches crisis point and we can't discuss anything without it turning into an argument?

Greg is leaning against the back door, gazing out into the garden. 'Nice day,' he says. 'Think I might dig some worms out of the compost heap for tomorrow.'

That is also not a bad thing, but it makes me bristle with irritation nevertheless.

'Fine.' I keep my voice neutral and make my own tea and pour one for Greg too. Would it be too much to ask for him to sweep me into his arms and kiss me? What would it be like to be rushed up the stairs, thrown saucily on to the marital bed and ravished?

I know that there are a lot of ravishings that go on in Lauren's relationship and perhaps that's what keeps her going back for more and more. But then Greg has never in all our married years been one for impromptu ravishing, so why should he start now?

'Good party?' he asks.

Yes, I feel like saying, *I shagged a C-list celebrity from* Holby City *up against the wall*. See what he'd make of *that*.

Instead, I sigh and settle for just, 'Yes. Chelsea sends her love. She looked lovely.'

'Great.'

That's the extent of his interest of my wild night out without him. I hand Greg his tea. 'Good fishing?'

'Yeah.' I never have to worry where Greg is or who he's with. The only thing I have to compete with is the torrid pleasure of tench.

'Where are the kids?'

'Out.' He shrugs to indicate that he isn't party to their whereabouts. They're at the age where every single move is top secret. Even when I text them to check up on them, they pretend they've been lost in the ether. I still worry about them even though they're both, supposedly, adults now.

'Thought I might go fishing again later, if that's okay with you.'

'Fine.' As if Greg would listen if I said I wanted to do something else. What if I suggested a walk instead? An afternoon in bed? Sharing a bath together?

'What about you?' he asks. 'Fancy coming with me? Bring a book?'

I shake my head. Why can't he read my mind? Why can't he tell what I'd really like to do? Why can't he tell that I'm not happy with the way things are?

Besides, I hate sitting by the river for hours gazing into the distance. Gives me too much time to think dark thoughts. And midges love me. I'll get eaten alive as soon as the sun starts to sink. 'I'll probably watch telly.'

Why not? I do it virtually every night. Why break the habit of a lifetime?

29

But what I don't tell my husband is that while I'm watching *Strictly Come Dancing* and *Celebrity Come Dine With Me* and *Lark Rise to Candleford* and whatever other rubbish is on, I'll be planning and plotting how I'm going to change my life. And that it may or may not include him.

Chapter Seven

Lauren let herself into her apartment. Her sister might not be looking forward to rushing into the arms of her dearly beloved husband with overwhelming lust, but at least there was someone there waiting for her. She'd give her right arm for a bog-standard, boring marriage with a husband you could always rely on, she thought as she threw her overnight bag on the lounge floor.

Perhaps she should think about getting a cat so that there'd be some other living presence here to welcome her home. She did once have a goldfish for a while as someone told her they were a low-maintenance kind of pet, but it hadn't seemed to quite reach the spot. You couldn't cuddle a goldfish when you felt alone and miserable. It was unlikely to keep you warm in bed. So when it turned its fishy fins up after a few months she didn't bother with getting another one. Yes, a cat would be nice – but then it might confirm her status as a mad, sad, single person, and she wasn't ready for that. And, anyway, she didn't know whether Jude was a cat person or not. She didn't want to give him any more reasons to stay away.

In the absence of anyone to fuss over, or anyone to fuss over her, Lauren's first job was to check the answerphone messages. The little red light wasn't blinking to tell her that Jude had called. There was always the chance that she might have missed him on her mobile while she was on the Tube and that he'd called here instead to tell her that he loved her. She pressed the button just in case the red light wasn't working properly. The machine whirred and thunked before informing her, 'You have no messages.' The emphasis, unnecessarily, on 'no'.

Her stomach twisted. If only she could speak to him, re-assure herself that nothing had changed, that he still loved her, then she could get through the rest of the day. Maybe she should text him. Something that couldn't be misconstrued, something innocuous about business that would give him a valid excuse to ring her. But then Jude hated it when she became so insecure that she risked exposing him. If she did that, then he backed away from her for a few weeks, as if to punish her, and that made things even worse.

Lauren sighed to herself. Another long, empty Sunday stretched ahead of her. It was the day of the week she hated most. Monday to Friday she could virtually guarantee seeing Jude – even if it was just for a few snatched moments. It was difficult working together, since they had to be discreet. But occasionally, when they were sure they were alone, their fingers could linger in places where they couldn't go in public, and they might steal a kiss in the office kitchen – or Jude might let his hand rest in the small of her back for longer than was considered appropriate for mere colleagues without someone shouting, 'Sexual harassment!'

Sundays were always more difficult. Sometimes on a Saturday he could call into her flat, having concocted some tale about an errand that needed to be run or some work that urgently needed to be attended to. But on Sundays Jude could rarely get away from family duties. And, as a consequence, that was the day that chewed her up the most.

If she wasn't very careful, her mind could stray into terrible territory where she could see images of Jude playing Happy Families with his wife and kids. His children – Benjy, ten, and Daisy, eight, – were at that age where he'd be taking them to the cinema, maybe playing football on the Heath near where they lived. Sometimes she had to stop herself from going over there for a walk, just to try to catch a glimpse of him to see her through the day. Lauren knew that it wasn't what he really wanted from his life – he wanted nothing more than to be with her – but he was a very devoted father and took his responsibilities seriously. She loved him for that too.

He didn't love his wife Georgia, she also knew that. But some days – Sundays – it was hard to see why.

Lauren had met her on several occasions over the years. Work dos, where it was impossible for their paths not to cross. And she had hated her every single time. Georgia was pretty, vivacious and charming company. Everyone in the company was besotted with her. Everyone except Jude, of course. Oh, he put on a good enough show when he needed to, but Lauren knew differently. The attentiveness, the gentle touching, it was all a show, a sham, an illusion. When they were at home alone, things were very different. Georgia wasn't funny or flirty then. At home she was cold, aloof, unresponsive. Jude had told her often enough while he was lying in Lauren's bed. Why would he come to her, if things weren't seriously messed up?

Perhaps she should have gone to the gym today. An hour on the cross-trainer or the Stairmaster was always good for taking out pent-up frustration. But then, it would be Sod's Law, if the minute she went out of the door, Jude phoned or perhaps called round unexpectedly. She'd never forgive herself if she missed him. Besides, she had a crashing hangover and an hour lying on the sofa watching rubbish on the television might be a better idea.

It was always a difficult balance because what she really wanted to do was slip out of her jeans and shirt and slip on her oldest T-shirt and tracky bottoms, but she never did that just in case Jude popped in. It would never do for him to find her here looking scruffy – not when she had the immaculately groomed Georgia to compete with. The only person she could think of who was better turned out than her lover's wife was Chelsea.

It was horrible being jealous of her own sister, Lauren thought, but she was – even though Chelsea wasn't boastful or did anything to rub their noses in her perfect life. It was just a fact that couldn't be avoided. Chelsea had it all; whereas she and Annie did not. It wasn't that she didn't love Chelsea – of course she did! Not as much as Annie did, though. Her twin always managed to see the good in everyone.

Lauren and Annie had always been close. They were twins – wasn't it natural that they'd stick together? 'Two peas in a pod,' everyone said with a chuckle. And there'd always been a distance between the two of them and Chelsea, even as kids. It hadn't improved as they'd got older. The situation had got worse, if anything, as they were all so busy with their lives and she and Annie had so little in common with Chelsea. Plus the latter was hardly ever in the country these days. She hated to ring her sister and have either Chelsea's nanny or housekeeper answer the phone. Unreasonable. But it made her bristle nevertheless. The truth was that Lauren found it very difficult to be around Chelsea as she only reminded her of everything that she was missing out on. Annie's relationship wasn't perfect and that, in some selfish way, was a comfort to Lauren. Her twin tried very hard to pretend that there wasn't a division between the sisters, but they all knew in their hearts that there was.

Annie was right though. Out of the three of them, Chelsea was the only one who'd got her life in control. And Lauren knew that she couldn't carry on indefinitely letting herself be buffeted about by her emotions, waiting on a man who belonged to someone else – if not in his heart, then legally.

Perhaps this year she should issue Jude with some sort of ultimatum. Put a firm date on when he would forsake his family to be with her. The thought of it made her feel sick to her stomach. The children would be distraught, at first, of course. It was only natural. But they would come round in time. They were bound to. Children were very resilient. They'd take it slowly, until they got to know her, but soon they'd be able to stay at weekends and then she'd be like a proper stepmum to them. She'd be the best stepmum in the world – she'd love them as much as she loved Jude – and they'd end up loving her just as much as they did their real mum.

In the middle of her daydream the intercom buzzed and it jolted her back into the real world. As she flew to the door, she checked herself in the mirror. She didn't look too bad. Not too much the worse for drink. It could be Jude having forgotten his key. Heart pounding, Lauren pressed the intercom.

'Hey!'

Her heart sank. It wasn't Jude. But it was a voice she recognised only too well.

'Zak,' she said. 'Come on up.' And she buzzed the door open.

Moments later, Zak Reynolds was in her flat. 'Did I interrupt something?' he asked, watching her pace around. 'You look very edgy.'

Lauren made herself relax. 'I've only just got home,' she explained. 'From my sister's fortieth birthday party.'

'Good time?'

'A blast.' She wasn't going to tell Zak that she'd eschewed the charms of her sister's rich and well-connected friends to slink off early to bed and lick her emotional wounds. Jude had promised that he would come – and he hadn't. It was the first time he was going to officially meet her family and he had cried off at the last minute.

'I got some buckshee tickets for a gig tonight in Camden. Low-key thing. Thought you might like to come along, have a beer.'

'That's really kind of you, Zak.'

He started to laugh. '"That's really kind of you, Zak".' He flopped down on her sofa. 'Who do you think you're talking to? This is your Uncle Zak.'

She ran her hands through her hair and tried a laugh herself. 'I'm sorry.'

'I know that Sundays are usually shitty for you. Thought I might lighten the load, but if you say "That's really kind of you" in that stupid voice again, I might have to kill you.'

This time Lauren really did laugh. 'Oh God, Zakary Reynolds, what am I going to do?' She flopped down next to him.

Zak rested his hand on her thigh and patted. 'Put your gladrags on, come out, have a beer, forget about what might have been. There's a particular low-cut top of yours that helps to ease *my* pain, if you're interested in a reciprocal arrangement.'

'Don't make me laugh.' She gave him a dig in the ribs. 'I'm supposed to be miserable.'

'Life is too short to spend your time pining for someone who isn't here.'

She and Zak worked together and he was one of the few people who knew about her affair with their boss. He'd found her crying in the kitchen one Friday when she'd realised that it would be two whole days before she could see Jude again. Zak had been caring, sympathetic and, from then on, they'd started up a close friendship that helped to get her through the tough times. Whenever she needed a partner and Jude wasn't around, Zak stepped up to the plate. Whenever she had an empty weekend ahead of her, Zak could usually be relied on for last-minute pizza and cheap red wine. He lived in a studio flat off the Finchley Road, less than a mile away, and Lauren always felt secure, having him in the neighbourhood.

There was no doubt that he was a really great guy. He was a few years younger than her and had a boyish face that made him look even more youthful. Zak had a great sense of humour, soft blue eyes that would melt the hardest of hearts and he was always happy and smiling. At *Happening Today* he was a respected web designer and kept the site looking sharp and contemporary to keep up with the competition. It was also nice to know that there was someone she could confide in at work about her relationship with Jude. Zak really seemed to understand what she was going through.

He pecked her on the cheek. 'I'll be back at eight to pick you up.'

'I don't know, Zak . . .'

'It wasn't a question,' he said, standing.

Lauren threw a cushion at him. 'You're incorrigible.'

'Remember . . .' He winked at her. 'Low-cut top.'

Zak let himself out of the flat and, despite her misery, Lauren found herself grinning.

Chapter Eight

I work at an events company called Party Party. About six months ago, I changed my job with the hope of bringing a little more excitement into my life. Since the kids first started school, I'd worked part-time at a building society in the city centre. Nice, steady work but it was dull, dull, dull.

Now I'm a receptionist at a company that puts on corporate events and parties. Is it any more exciting? I don't think the actual work's much different really, but it's surely a step in the right direction. I'm surrounded by fun, creative people who get to do wonderful things and go to wonderful places. I might not be one of them, but I love to hear the stories about the lavish parties that they've created where budgets are unlimited, no expense spared. How I'd love to go along to one. I imagine that they'd be like Chelsea's fortieth birthday party on steroids.

I wonder why Chelsea didn't use my company to plan her event, but perhaps she's forgotten where I'm working now. We don't talk that much about my life on the rare occasions that she phones. That's generally because I don't have anything of any great interest to tell her. I 'ooh' and 'aah' in the right places over the marvellous things that she's done and hope that she doesn't notice that my life is interminably tedious and small.

The front door swings open and I sit up straighter.

'Morning, Sexy.' That's Blake Chadwick. He's one of the partners here. A big-wig.

'Right back at you,' I say cheekily, even though I can feel myself flushing.

He laughs at that. BC, as we call him, has the most luscious mouth. He's as fit as you like and doesn't he know it. All the girls here are mad for him. He's very trendy, wears suits so sharp that you could cut yourself on them and has a shaved head and a diamond stud in his ear that's bigger than my engagement ring. He's what my daughter Ellen would call 'one cool dude'. But then she's young and impressionable – whereas I'm not supposed to be.

Mind you, I hope she never brings home anyone like Blake Chadwick. He'd eat my daughter alive. Confident to the point of arrogance and beyond, he has a different woman on his arm every week, according to the girls who see him out club-bing. I'm sure he only goes out around here to further his contacts, though. The likes of Blake Chadwick would be much happier in London at clubs like Whisky Mist or Chinawhite – wherever the latest, hottest place is. BC is in his late twen-ties and, apparently, he's got one daughter by a previous partner. By all accounts he doesn't see much of her. Every night of the week there's an event on somewhere that he's obliged to turn up at. It must be hard being a father if you're never around.

'How's it looking today, Angie?'

'It's looking good. And it's Annie.'

He waves as he disappears into the offices. 'Catch you later, Sexy.'

I bet BC's not the sort to laze around on the sofa on a

Sunday night with a Chinese takeaway. Like Greg and I did last night.

We always go to the same takeaway. The Hong Kong Garden. Greg always has the same thing. Chicken curry and chips. Not very Chinese. I try to have something different from the menu every week even though I have my favourites. I think it's good to be adventurous. So I close my eyes and just stick a pin into the three-fold menu and have whatever it comes down on. It seems to work for me – even though sometimes the dish doesn't turn out to be quite as nice as you might hope. The Szechuan-style squid and mushrooms with bean curd was a bit of a low point, but I managed it all just to spite Greg who always laughs at the way I choose my meal. You have to try and live a little, don't you?

One of the young girls totters in next. She's wearing heels that must be six inches high. I've no idea how she walks in them. Mind you, Minny's skirt's so tight that I don't think she could actually stride out anyway.

'Hiya, Annie,' she says brightly. 'Nice weekend?'

'Yes.' What else can I say? Minny wouldn't be interested in a download of my sister's fortieth birthday party as she goes to that sort of thing every night of the week. She wouldn't be interested in my life-changing decision either. But what could I tell her? 'I've decided to change my life, but I'm not quite sure how yet.' That doesn't sound terribly dynamic when I say it like that.

'Are you coming to the meeting at lunchtime?'

'What meeting?' First I've heard about it. Because I'm out of sight on the front desk all day, they do sometimes forget to tell me things.

'We're on about doing something for charity, as a company,' Minny tells me. 'Fancy coming along?'

'What sort of thing?'

'Dunno,' she shrugs. 'I'm game for anything.'

That's the type of people who work here. They don't care about what they do or worry about how they are going to pay for it or fret about what others will think of them. They're reckless, creative, funloving and adventurous. They're the sort of people that I'd really like to be.

'Yes,' I say a little breathlessly. 'I'd love to come along.'

Chapter Nine

Jude and Lauren were in the office kitchen. It was early. Lauren had come in before eight o'clock praying that they'd be able to grab a few moments alone before the rest of the staff arrived and the opportunity was lost. Now it was eight-thirty and Jude had only just arrived. Time was tight.

His arms were around her and she felt like weeping with relief. She'd survived another weekend intact. He hadn't suddenly had a fabulous family time and a subsequent change of heart. She was still the one he loved.

'God, I've missed you,' he murmured against her neck. They were pressed up against the cupboard in the corner, out of the view of the window. It was cramped and uncomfortable, but she could feel his body hardening nevertheless. She was aroused too, to the point of distraction. What a way to start the working week! Was it all this sexual tension between them that kept her coming back for more? What would it be like when they eventually lived together? Would the chemistry between them still be as electric? They were five years into this affair and, even now, couldn't get enough of each other. She hoped that it would always be like this for as long as they lived.

'I'm sorry I didn't hear your call,' she told him.

'I could only stay for a minute anyway,' he said. 'Both of the kids have been ill.'

She'd envisaged them playing in the park, Jude swinging them high in his arms, spinning, spinning and laughter, lots of laughter. Now she knew differently. 'Nothing serious?'

He shook his head, his beautiful mop of black hair. 'Colds. Dastardly. I've seen enough snot to last me a lifetime. You don't want to know the details.'

But she did. She wanted to know everything about him, no matter how trivial. It was best not to say that though, otherwise he thought she was being too clingy.

'I'm sorry about the party.' He pulled his little boy's face. 'Did you have a good time without me?'

'No,' she said. 'It was dull. Annie was unwell, so we went to bed early.'

'Poor darling.'

Lauren decided not to tell him that she'd been out to a gig with Zak last night. Sometimes he could be a bit funny about their friendship. It was as if he resented Zak knowing their secret, as if Zak had one over on him. So she thought it was better to keep quiet.

The gig had been surprisingly good – a new singer who sounded like Duffy. Some of Zak's friends had been there too, guys that he used to play in a band with years ago, and they'd made her laugh. And she'd drunk too much. Again. The make-up had been applied just that little bit thicker this morning to hide the ravages.

'Can we sneak out to lunch together?'

'Not today,' he said. 'I've got a meeting.'

'Oh.' She hated it when he fixed lunchtime meetings, but sometimes it couldn't be helped.

The flat where she lived was in West Hampstead, the office

in Camden in a converted warehouse by the side of the canal – not that far apart, but sometimes she wished they were nearer so they could go there for some privacy in the lunch-hour or straight from work. Time always seemed to be against them. But that's what you got for trying to fit two lives into one, she supposed.

Jude glanced at his watch. It was a Breitling – one that he'd lusted after for a while. It had appeared on his wrist shortly after his birthday. He said that he'd treated himself to it as the company was doing well, but she didn't like to think where it had really come from. Had Georgia been the one to buy it for him? It pained Lauren that she could never afford to buy him presents like that. Even though she had a decent salary, a Breitling was still way beyond her price range.

'I'd better be going to my office,' he said.

'I need to talk to you,' she said, laying a hand on his chest. The heat of it almost made her feel dizzy. 'I've been doing a lot of thinking at the weekend.'

'Not now,' he said, 'but later. Later in the week.'

'I don't think that I can keep on doing this,' she told him. 'Not indefinitely.'

'I know,' Jude said. 'And I'll fix it.' He stroked her face tenderly. But she could see him check his watch again surreptitiously. 'You know I will.'

'We've been doing this for five years, Jude. Five years. It isn't right, and it isn't fair. It isn't fair to any of us.'

'I know.' He kissed her briefly and then straightened his sweater. He looked fabulous today in black cashmere, white jeans and black Cuban-heel boots. Like a model in an after-shave advert. Just looking at him made her mouth go dry and other parts of her go very wet. 'Later, my love. Now, I'm outta here.'

The door swung closed behind him and she leaned against the cupboards, trying to stem the flow of tears.

A minute later, and it swung open again. Her heart leaped and she sniffed back her tears, turning to the door with a beaming smile.

'Whoa,' Zak said. 'Wrong guy?'

Lauren's expression slipped back into misery and she nodded.

'Same old song again?' he asked.

She started to cry. Zak slipped his arm round her shoulder and squeezed.

One day he would leave, she thought. One day Jude would keep his promise to her. All this waiting couldn't be for nothing. She just had to bide her time. She just had to believe.

Chapter Ten

At lunchtime we all sit in the staff room. We're a small company with only twenty or so people who work here and we all get on really well. Most days, the offices are deserted as the teams are out on site setting up for events. We have very nice premises on a high-end business park in Milton Keynes. The floors are brushed steel, the desks are frosted glass. All lovely, lovely.

I'm in the corner, quietly eating my sandwiches. Cheese today, as there was nothing else remotely interesting in the fridge. My mind is still in a whirl after the weekend and I can't bring myself to join in the general chit-chat.

The Managing Director, Sarah Bennett, comes in and claps her hands to get our attention. BC is behind her and he gives me a friendly wink.

'Hi, gang,' she says. Sarah is young, trendy, a powerhouse. A woman who runs her own company, makes her own decisions, buys designer labels. She makes me feel old and tired just looking at her. 'My idea is that we should do something for charity as a company. It would be a great way to do some team bonding and raise a serious amount of cash while we're at it.'

See? Why don't I think of things like that? I've become so narrow in my life that I can't even begin to think out of the box.

'We could do the London Marathon together,' someone suggests.

'Passé,' Sarah decides. 'Been there, done that. Got the T-shirt three years on the run. No pun intended.' Everyone laughs at that. 'I thought we'd try something a little bit more exotic, more colourful.'

I put down my sandwich and sit up.

'Blake,' Sarah turns to her colleague. 'Do you want to do the honours?'

Obligingly, he passes round some small brochures.

'The Inca Trail,' Sarah says before the leaflets reach me. 'A two-week trip including a four-day hike in deepest, darkest Peru. Does anyone fancy giving it a go?'

Hands shoot up. Looks like a popular choice. Minny, sitting next to me, passes me a brightly coloured brochure. I'm surprised to see that my fingers are trembling when I take it.

'Where's Peru?' one of the team asks.

'Where Paddington Bear comes from,' someone shouts.

'South America,' Sarah fills in. 'This is an organised trek for charity. The company's called Dream Days and we'd be raising money for them to take terminally ill children to spend time doing something they'd always dreamed of.'

A tear wells up in my eye. I look round but no one else seems so moved, they just look excited at the prospect of doing this.

'We're thinking of going this September, so there's not a lot of time to prepare. You'd need to use two weeks of your annual holiday entitlement as we'll need some time there before we do the trail to acclimatise to the altitude, plus there are some great sights to see. You'd also need to raise two thousand, five hundred pounds for the charity to pay for your place.'

I gasp that in. No one seems to notice. Or to feel that two and a half thousand pounds is one hell of a lot of money. Greg and I don't have cash lying around like that.

Sarah continues, 'The company will give everyone who decides to do the trek a start of five hundred pounds.'

Cheering for that.

'And you'd need to get fit, fit, fit!' She punches the air.

More cheering and clapping. Most of these guys spend half of their week down at the gym, so I can't see a problem there. It's flabby old me that I'm worried about.

'So, team?' Rabble-rousing voice. 'Do you think we can do it?'

'Yeah!' Everyone punches the air. So do I. A minute too late.

'Yeah,' I echo quietly.

'This is the itinerary,' Sarah says. 'We'd be travelling . . .'

Then I zone out as I look down at the brochure in my hand. There are a group of trekkers, grinning broadly on the front. They're wearing a rag-tag assortment of traditional Inca costumes, colourful ponchos, woven in bright reds, greens and yellows topped with gaudy knitted hats.

Behind them is the most spectacular scenery I've ever laid eyes on. My fingers trace the contours of the towering, lush mountains, stark endless deserts, miles of unbroken blue sky. Machu Picchu. The Sacred Valley or Lost City of the Incas. The Nazca Lines. The words blur in front of me. The sky is the colour of sapphires, the trees the colour of emeralds, and the ruins of the ancient Aztec city rise out of the clouds like

49

a diamond. It looks impossibly exotic and alien. I'm mesmerised by its remote beauty. I've never been to a place like that before.

'So,' Sarah's words bring me back from my daydream. 'How many of you are up for it?'

Nearly everyone puts their hands up. They all turn round to look at me. In fact, everyone has put their hand up except me.

'Annie?'

My mouth has gone dry. My heart is pounding in my chest. Sarah is waiting for answer.

'No,' I say. My cheeks are burning with humiliation. 'I can't do it.'

'That's such a shame,' she says with a sympathetic smile that makes me want to curl up and die. Then she moves on to explaining what everyone needs to do next.

And I sit there frozen to the spot, a vision of Machu Picchu burned on my eyes. This could have been my one big chance to do something different, do something worthwhile and I couldn't do it. I'm too frightened, too unfit, too old to go trekking up mountains. I've never done anything like this before. How would I manage? How would I keep up with these energetic young things who'd probably scamper up there like mountain goats? I don't have that kind of cash kicking around either. How would I raise it? Most damningly, I haven't got the courage. I've never done anything like this before – have never dared – and just the thought of it is making my stomach roil.

So while the others plan their exciting journey, I slink out of the staff room and go back to my desk and wonder why, when I was offered my big chance to change my life – maybe my *one* big chance – I was too scared to get out of my rut.

Chapter Eleven

Lauren took off her headset and powered down her screen. The day had been impossibly busy and she'd hardly caught a glimpse of Jude at all. Still, it had given her the chance to catch up with her own work, and what else had she got to rush home for? The rest of the staff had long gone for the night and she was waiting patiently, hoping that he'd come out of his office soon.

She could call Annie, despite the fact they'd already texted each other a dozen times today, but she knew that the minute she got on the phone then Jude would appear and her sister hated it when she cut a call short because her lover had turned up.

Sure enough, minutes later, the door opened. 'Sorry, sorry,' Jude said, raking his hands through his hair. 'Got stuck on the phone.'

It was pushing seven o'clock.

'Do you want to come back to my place for an hour?' Lauren said.

Jude pursed his lips. 'Can't,' he said. 'Not tonight. There's a thing on at Daisy's school. Quiz or something. Promised I'd go.'

'Oh, Jude.'

'I know, I know,' he said soothingly. 'But these are the duties I have. You know that.'

'I feel as if I've hardly seen you in the last week.'

'So you'd like to see some more of me?'

'Of course I would.'

He took her hand and pulled her across the office to the boardroom. 'I can show you *plenty* more,' he said seductively.

Once inside, he shut the door behind them and pressed her up against it, covering her throat with hot kisses.

'Jude . . .' she began to protest. What she wanted was a drink and a cuddle, to talk about his day, his weekend, not sex.

His mouth still on hers, he steered her to the boardroom table and pushed her on to it. 'I love you,' he murmured. 'God, I love you.'

In a well-practised move, he hitched her skirt up and pulled her pants down in swift succession. Then he eased himself into her with a contented moan.

They'd made love this way a dozen times before and, usually, she was lost in the passion of it, the urgency. This time, as he moved above her, the table was digging into her back and she hadn't been quite ready and it all seemed a bit rushed, a bit *forced*.

He came inside her. They never used protection. She was on the pill and he trusted her to take it. What if one day she just stopped taking it and didn't tell him? she wondered. What if she found that she was pregnant? Surely that would make Jude leave his wife?

While she was thinking this, her lover was already zipping up his trousers.

'Have to dash,' he said, smoothing down his hair. 'I'll call you later if I can. See you tomorrow, darling.'

Then Jude pecked her on the cheek and hurried out of the door.

Lauren stared down at herself. It was as if she was having an out-of-body experience. She could see a woman lying on the oak table, legs akimbo with no knickers on, still in her high heels, her lover's semen inside her. But where was he?

Gone. That's where.

She closed her legs, got down from the table, found her underwear on the floor and tugged it back on. Had she had an orgasm? Had she even vaguely enjoyed it? Had Jude even cared? Was this what he thought that she wanted?

This felt terrible. More than terrible.

Dazed, she left the boardroom and went to go back to her desk. Her legs were shaking, unsteady. All she wanted to do now was collect her things and go home.

'Bloody hell, girl,' a voice said from behind her. 'You nearly gave me a heart-attack.'

'Zak?' Lauren turned. 'What are you doing here so late?'

'I could ask you the same thing.' Both of their gazes returned to the boardroom door.

Self-consciously, Lauren straightened her skirt. A body-language expert would have a field day with that.

Zak nodded towards the door. 'I saw Jude leaving,' he said. 'He didn't see me.'

Lauren realised that he could well have seen much more if he'd been there a few minutes earlier. They'd have to be even more careful from now on.

'I'd left my wallet here,' Zak said hastily to cover their embarrassment. 'I was just going to grab something to eat. Join me?'

'I'd better go home.'

'What for?'

Lauren sagged. What for, indeed?

Zak took her arm. 'Come on,' he said. 'I won't take no for an answer.' He flicked a look towards the boardroom. 'I don't know what's been going on in there . . .'

But Lauren thought that he could more than likely give it a good guess.

'Whatever it was,' Zak continued unabashed, 'it's left you looking like you need a glass of wine.'

That was true. Despite trying to put on a brave face, for some reason, Lauren felt decidedly more shaken than she should.

Chapter Twelve

The restaurant in West Hampstead was calm and unusually quiet. The relaxing atmosphere and gentle hum of the chatter helped Lauren to stop thinking. Well, almost. This was a place that she and Jude often came to, but she decided not to share that information with her current companion. It was small, discreet and just down the road from his house and her flat. They always sat away from the window, in the far corner if possible and, if they were lucky enough to bag their favourite secluded spot, they held hands over the table.

This time they were seated front of house and Lauren could watch the people passing by on Broadhurst Gardens. As Jude wasn't her entire focus, she could even take in the elegant white décor, the sparkling chandelier that hung in the centre of the room, the silvery flocked wallpaper, the artfully arranged vases and soothing paintings – all the things she hadn't noticed before even though they'd been here dozens of times.

Zak ordered a bowl of pasta carbonara and a bottle of house red. She ordered a wild mushroom risotto and was now pushing it round her plate.

'Don't you ever eat, woman?' Zak licked cream from his lips.

He had a good mouth, she thought. Strong. Honest. The

thought brought tears to her eyes and she blinked them away. An honest mouth. Is that what Jude had? Or did her lover have a lying mouth?

'You're all skin and bone.'

'I haven't got much of an appetite, to be truthful.' She picked up her glass and slugged back her wine. That was what was hitting the spot. Most of the time her stomach was so knotted with anxiety that it was impossible to eat, no matter how much she wanted the food.

'You could do with more of this,' Zak pointed at her food, 'and less of that.' The glass of wine.

'Since when did you turn into my mother?'

'Someone needs to look out for you,' he said.

'You said a glass of wine would do me good.'

'A glass,' he reiterated. 'You've polished off a whole bottle.'

'I'll pay extra if that's what you're worried about.'

'Of course it's not.' Zak sounded irritated.

Just to be awkward, she topped her glass up again.

Zak's hand covered hers on the table. 'Look,' he said, 'I don't mean to pry. But could I just ask you, do you really think that you're getting all that you need from this relationship with Jude?'

Lauren was taken aback at his directness. She and Zak had become good friends over the last year or so and he knew the issues she had, but they always skirted round the subject, pretending that it didn't exist. He'd never before asked her so directly about her relationship with their boss.

'He's going to leave her,' she said. 'He's going to leave his wife for me. This isn't just a fling for either of us.'

'And is that what you really want? To break up a family?'

'She doesn't love him,' Lauren insisted. 'It's just a matter of time.'

'Is that what he keeps telling you?'

'It's what I sincerely believe.' She swigged her wine again. 'We're not doing this lightly. I know that people will get hurt.'

'And what if the person that gets hurt is you?'

That stunned her to silence.

Zak sighed. 'Sorry, Lauren. That was below the belt. I didn't ask you to come out with me to have a go at you. I just wonder exactly what it is that you see in Jude, that's all.' He held up his hand. 'And no, I don't want you to tell me.'

They both laughed at that and it broke the tension.

'I'm sorry,' Lauren said. 'I'm being a miserable old moo. In my defence, it isn't easy not being able to be with the one you love.'

Zak gave her a wry glance. 'Tell me about it.' He picked at the tablecloth.

She didn't know much about Zak's romantic past and perhaps now wasn't the time to pry.

'You're a beautiful woman, Lauren Osbourne. Don't spend the best years of your life waiting for someone you might never have.'

'Is that what you did?'

Her friend looked at her enigmatically. 'It's what I'm *doing*,' Zak said.

Chapter Thirteen

I go to the library on the way home and take out a travel book on Peru. Just out of curiosity.

I can't *go*. I can't possibly go. I just want to see where everyone else is going. For my own interest.

Finding a quiet corner, I sit on the well-worn library sofa and curl my legs beneath me. The book is filled with glorious colour photographs that bring an exotic world right on to my lap. I stroke the pages lovingly. Here's the Cañón del Colca – a place I've never ever heard of which is twice as deep as the Grand Canyon, and Lake Titicaca, on the border of Peru and Bolivia, the second-largest lake in South America, that still houses people on floating islands made of reeds. I take out the itinerary that my colleagues will follow and flick to the pages covering the places being visited on the four-day charity trek. The charity trek that I'm not going to do.

Next on the list is the Nazca Lines, a collection of drawings etched into the earth as far back as 500 BC – Before Christ, not Blake Chadwick. Some say that the sophisticated drawings were made by aliens visiting the Earth, some say that they're messages to the ancient gods. I don't know what I think, other than I'd really like to see them for myself. I let my fingers follow the mysterious outlines – the humming-bird, the monkey, the spider, the whale.

I could lose myself completely in this book. Already, I've

been here an hour and have just begun to scratch the surface. Glancing at the clock, I think that I should be going home. Checking the book out, I slip it into the depths of my handbag. Then I can follow where my friends will be going. Lucky them, I think bitterly. Lucky, lucky them.

At home and, as soon as I open the front door, I can smell cooking.

'Dinner's nearly burned,' Greg shouts from the kitchen.

I throw down my bag. 'I didn't know that you were cooking.'

'I got home a bit early. Thought I'd start it.'

Greg never cooks. That's my job. I feel like testing the temperature of his forehead, but I resist.

'Where've you been?' he asks.

In Peru, I want to say. *In the Colca Canyon, at the Nazca Lines, lost in the Andes.* Instead, I say, 'I popped into the library.'

Greg raises his eyebrows but asks no more questions. I notice that the table is set for four. 'Are the kids here?'

He nods and goes back to fiddling with his dinner. 'I just did the pork chops that were in the fridge with some carrots and new potatoes. That okay?'

'Fine.' I want something spicy, unusual – what do they eat in Peru? Haven't got to that bit in the book yet. Probably something involving rice and beans and chillies. Something with a fiery bite. I'd like to wash it down with a Pisco Sour or two. Get drunk on the local hooch. Greg has what you might call a 'narrow palate'. He prefers his food boiled or fried and eats no fruit at all and believes that carrots are the only vegetables worth consuming because they'll prevent him from needing glasses as he gets older. Plus, despite being a lifelong, avid fisherman, he hates fish.

'Cup of tea?'

'I'll make it.'

We drink it while we wait for the potatoes to boil.

'Good day?' Greg asks.

'Yes.' I can't bring myself to tell him about the charity trek in Peru. He wouldn't be interested. Wouldn't want to know. Greg has never had the urge to travel to the four corners of the world. His horizons go no further than the Grand Union Canal and his other favourite bolthole, the North Norfolk coast. 'You?'

'Yes.'

Greg has been at the same company since he was sixteen. He started there as a delivery boy in a brown coat and has been promoted steadily over the years as the company has grown. Now he works in the offices scheduling deliveries. He likes it there. He's comfortable. My husband has never had the desire to pursue a career, has never been ambitious for himself. He likes the company because he knows it and, though he might grumble at times that they take him for granted, I can't ever see him leaving.

We dish out the dinner and shout up to the children, who eventually shuffle down to the kitchen table.

My daughter Ellen is working in Monsoon in the city centre and has been for the last four years. All her wages go on clothes and clubbing – certainly none of it lingers in her bank account. Bobby left school at sixteen with very little to show for it and has yet to decide what his future holds. He's drifted in and out of jobs since then. Plumbing, he decided, was the thing for him – he lasted six weeks. Then he tried his hand at painting and decorating – that one managed to enthral him for nearly three months. Since then he's done odd jobs, mainly cash in hand and barely enough to cover his mobile phone bill. I keep nagging him to go to college, learn a trade, do something that will ensure that he doesn't spend the rest of his life living hand to mouth. But what can I do? He's turned eighteen – he's supposed to be a man, not a child any more. What I feel like doing is pinching hold of one of his ears and pulling him down to the college myself to sign him up to do something – *anything*.

They both take after their father. It isn't me they've inherited their inert disposition from. As I've grown older I've become full of unfocused, unrealised desire and ambition. It's just that I've never managed to do much about it. My role as wife and mother has taken priority and has subsumed any natural instincts to strike out and do something different. Well, no longer. This year is going to be my year.

I get a cursory hug from Ellen, and Bobby says, 'All right, Mum?' And they sit down.

They're hardly ever here so that we can have a family dinner together. I've spent the last two years trying to make sure that they're at least home at dinnertime so that we can all eat together, but it's like pushing water uphill. The lure of the latest trendy bar straight from work is often more appealing than my traditional cooking. In the end, I got fed up with throwing dried-up dinners in the bin and now they largely do their own thing – which seems to involve constantly grazing from the fridge when they grace us with their presence. Dinner together as a family normally happens only on high days and holidays, and soon they'll be gone altogether. Then it will be just me and Greg and his fishing rods. What will I do then?

My husband puts a plate in front of me. The dinner looks lovely but, suddenly, I want to cry. I think of everyone going to Peru, except me. I remember both Bobs and Ellen wailing those same words to me as children: 'But everyone else is going . . .' And that's how I feel now. That's exactly how I feel. *Everyone else is going except me!* Does no one hear my silent cry?

I pick up my knife and fork and then put them down again – a bit too abruptly it seems, as I make my family jump.

'Do something with your lives,' I blurt out.

My children and my husband look up from their pork chops and new potatoes, startled.

'Ellen. Bobby. Both of you. Before it's too late. Go to exotic places. Do exotic things. Sow your wild oats. Try parachuting. Dance naked in the rain. Go scuba-diving. Go to work every day loving your job. Live life to the full. You never know when it might be your last!' I look at their terrified faces. 'Enjoy your chops!'

There's a stunned hiatus at the table.

Ellen glances at her brother and father uncertainly and then is the first to speak. Her voice is hushed. 'Are you going to die, Mum?'

'No,' I say. But I burst into tears anyway.

Chapter Fourteen

'Eat your dinner,' Greg says to the kids. 'I'll take your mum outside for a bit of fresh air.'

My husband helps me from the table and steers me gingerly into the garden as if I might break. Ellen comes out with a glass of water for me and then retreats hastily.

I sit on the brick wall that divides the patio from the small lawn. Greg sits down next to me. He looks like he might put his arm round me, but then he doesn't. 'Mind telling me what that was all about?'

I sniff my tears away. 'Nothing, nothing. Just me being silly.'

'You scared the life out of us all,' he says.

'Sorry. Sorry. It was stupid of me.'

'Is there really nothing wrong with you?'

'No.' Nothing that an adventure, a bit of excitement, a trip to Peru wouldn't cure. Then it comes to me. If I can't go to Peru, then I could go somewhere else.

'Why don't we go away this weekend?' I turn to my husband and take both of his hands in mine. They're strong, workworn now. 'Just the two of us. Let's just take off somewhere.'

He looks alarmed. 'It wasn't *you* that wanted to do the parachuting thing you mentioned in that rant?'

'No,' I say. 'No. No. Though would it be such a bad idea?'

63

His expression tells me that it would.

'Let's do something spontaneous,' I urge. 'The kids can see to themselves. They're more than old enough.' Although they might well still burn the house down. I cross my fingers behind my back. 'They don't need us around.'

'I was going to go fishing with Ray.'

That's all my husband ever does. I bite back that particular comment as unproductive if I'm trying to be encouraging. 'Can't you go another time?'

Greg looks uncertain about this clearly seismic change to his preordained timetable.

I recently read a report in the newspaper which said that men are at their most romantic at the age of fifty-three. That's the time of life when they start writing poetry, sprinkling rose petals in the bath and booking romantic candlelit dinners for two in expensive restaurants without weeks of prompting. The conclusion was that by then they've had all the arguments with their spouse, made all their mistakes – a vacuum cleaner for one birthday springs immediately to my own mind – and have finally worked out what it is that their woman wants from life. On that reckoning, I have another thirteen years to wait before I'm whisked away to Paris on a whim.

'Does it have to be this weekend?' Greg says into my musing.

'No,' I say. 'But I'd like it to be.'

'Will it stop you crying?'

I risk a watery smile. 'It might do.'

'Then we'll go. I'll ring Ray.' He goes to stand up, clearly thinking that this discussion is over.

'Where shall we go then?'

He turns back to me, puzzled. 'Cromer.'

'But we always go to Cromer.' I'm sure that I don't need to remind my husband that it has been the destination for our annual holidays since we've been together.

I tell a lie – once when Greg had been given an unexpected bonus at work I persuaded him to go to Spain with the kids. The Costa del Sol. He hated every moment of it. He hated the sun. He hated being lathered in suntan cream every time he moved. He hated the food – though an awful lot of it involved chips. He hated the fact that everyone was foreign, except for all the English there. He hated the airport, he hated flying and vowed never to do it again.

It was such a traumatic experience for all of us that we have never ventured overseas since – either by plane, boat or train. I don't even know if my passport is still valid. Can you understand now why dropping everything and jetting off to Peru seems such a daunting prospect to me? My husband has dumbed me down over all these years. It's the equivalent of a normal person going to the moon.

'Why don't we try somewhere else for a change?'

Greg looks horrified. 'But we like Cromer.'

'We might like somewhere else too,' I suggest.

My husband is not an unintelligent man, but this is seemingly way beyond his comprehension.

Then I look at Greg and get a rush of love for him. He's still a handsome chap. He's tall, in excellent shape for a man coming up to forty. He wears his dark hair cropped forward now to disguise that it's thinning. My husband frowns permanently as if he's carrying the world on his shoulders and I know that he's worked hard and worried for us all of our married life. The tracks of our troubled years are etched into his forehead now. I feel guilty for all the times I've looked at him critically lately. I should give a little. If I can get him away to myself, who knows? A little passion might spark again. What does it matter whether it's the Costa del Sol or Cairo or Cromer? We'll go together and we'll have a great time. We'll be spontaneous and free and have fun.

'Cromer will be lovely,' I say.

I'll make damn sure that it is.

Chapter Fifteen

Lauren drives up from London to have dinner with me. It's Wednesday and I don't often see her on a Wednesday. That's another one of my home alone nights as Greg goes down to the fishing club then. He's been a member since he was fifteen and I could count on one hand the number of times he's missed it. Greg Ashton is nothing if not a creature of habit.

I can't see the attraction of it myself. All they do is stand around with a pint of beer talking about fishing. But then I can't actually see the fascination with fishing either, though I've tolerated it throughout my married life.

Sometimes, when we were first married, before we had the children, I used to go along with Greg and sit by the bank with my book, perhaps a bottle of Blue Nun or some awful cheap wine that was all we could run to. But I didn't like the hours of waiting for anything to happen and then when Greg did catch a fish, I couldn't bear to see it dangling from the hook, flapping for breath on the bank. All I wanted him to do was throw the poor thing back in as soon as humanly possible. It always seemed to hurt the fish so much, though my husband assured me that it didn't. Of course, when the children came along, it was impossible to go – wriggling toddlers and deep water are not a marriage made in heaven. And I became a permanent fishing widow.

Now, after all these years, I've got used to the routine, accepted it. The fact that Greg is out so much does give me time on my own with Lauren though. We might be on the phone to each other all day or texting like mad things, but you still never manage to say all that you want to, do you? Greg can't understand it. He has no idea what we find to talk about.

I wish that my sister lived nearer to me. She likes life in London whereas I can't stand it. Plus I'd never tear her away from being near Jude now. Her place is less than an hour away on the M1, but I still feel it's too far. We do have a sofa-bed in Ellen's room that Lauren uses regularly, but it's not quite the same, is it?

It was always my dream when we were growing up that we'd have houses next door to each other, that we'd get married on the same day – preferably to identical twin brothers – though I wanted to wear a big meringue dress, floor-length veil and tiara and Lauren said she'd wear jeans and a T-shirt. That was our stand for our individuality. I thought we'd have our children at the same time and then we'd all go on holiday together as one big boisterous family and, generally, live happily ever after.

'Let's go somewhere fancy in The Hub,' Lauren says when she arrives. That's the place in town where all the hip and trendy restaurants are. 'I'm sick to death of pizza.'

'I'm game.' So we head to the Brasserie Blanc and order à la carte, not just from the set menu. The restaurant's busy and they put us at a small table by the window, which I like because I can watch people walk by and pick dripped wax off the glittering candelabras as I do so.

'No Jude tonight?' I ask. Usually Lauren hates to tear herself away from London during the week as there's always the chance that her lover might find five precious minutes for her.

'Told him I couldn't see him,' my sister says. 'It doesn't do to make myself available all of the time.'

That'll be a change. She's hung on his every word for the last five years and it makes me sad to think that we never did find our twin brothers to love us. Instead, I found Greg and went my own way and Lauren, after a relentless series of disastrous love affairs, is still not in a settled relationship. She'd disagree, but I don't think that pacing the floor virtually every night on your own is being in a settled relationship – even if you've done it for more years than you care to count.

'Anyway,' she continues with a dismissive wave of her hand, 'I don't want to talk about Jude.'

I have to say that my twin is in a bit of an odd mood. Quiet, but bolshie with it. Perhaps she was more unsettled by Chelsea's fabulous party than she's admitted to and has thought more about how her life is going. I know that I've been brooding a bit ever since.

As if reading my mind, she says, 'Have you spoken to Chelsea?'

'No, but I sent her a thank-you card today.'

'Did you? I should do that too. I'm so crap.'

'Now that she's back for a while, I could have called her and asked her to join us.' When Chelsea is in England, her home is just fifteen minutes away from here. I had every intention of phoning her this week.

'We should have,' Lauren says. 'But then that would have made us feel *really* crappy.'

'You're feeling crappy?'

She nods. 'You too?'

I nod as well.

'We can bitch to each other,' Lauren states, 'but we always have to pretend that everything is all right when Chelsea's here.'

'We don't,' I say, defending our older sister. 'We just *feel* that we have to.'

'Have you done anything towards changing your life yet?' my sister wants to know.

I get the brochure for the Inca Trail charity trek out of my handbag and push it across the table.

Lauren's eyebrows raise. 'You're doing this?'

'I'd love to,' I say. 'But I'm too chicken. The kids at work are planning it.'

'You should go,' she encourages me.

'Do you fancy doing it with me?'

'Not likely,' Lauren says. 'My idea of adventure is lying on a sunlounger deciding which cocktail to have next.'

'It's a lot of money.' I worry at a fingernail. 'Over two grand. And that's without any spending money. Everyone has to raise that for the charity to get a place.'

'You could tap Chelsea for a few quid.'

I know that our sister would be very generous, but I'd feel funny asking her for money even though it's for a cause that she'd adore.

'I'll ask Jude to stump up some money from our company too. I can twist him round my little finger.'

Oh, Lauren, I don't think so. Otherwise you wouldn't be in this situation. But I keep my mouth shut and say nothing.

'You're already halfway there,' Lauren decides.

My fingernail gets another battering. 'It's so out of my comfort zone.'

'Bloody hell, Annie – listen to you. You sound like Greg. Where's your sense of adventure?'

'I'm not sure I ever had one.'

'Well, it's about time that you did.'

'We're going away for the weekend,' I tell her. 'Just me and Greg.'

'Wow. Hang out the flags,' Lauren says sarkily. 'Wonders will never cease. You're actually going to get him away from that bloody canal bank for a couple of days.'

'He's not that bad.' But I know that he is.

'Where are you going?'

'Cromer.'

Lauren pauses, fork to mouth. 'Not again!'

'We like Cromer.'

'I like eggs, but I wouldn't want them for every damn meal. You always go to Cromer.'

'Greg's comfortable with it.'

'I could give you a list as long as my arm of great little weekend getaways all over the country. Name me a place – any place, go on – and I could tell you of a bijou hotel there.' My sister, due to her dodgy relationship, is indeed the doyenne of the dirty weekend destination.

'We'll stick to Cromer, I think.' It's a miracle that I've got Greg to agree to going away at all without three months' notice. I don't want to push my luck.

'I was going to come up at the weekend. I'm sick of being on my own,' Lauren complains.

I nearly invite her to come with us, but realise that it

wouldn't be quite the point for me to drag my sister along. Plus if Greg thought that Lauren was free, he'd try to wriggle out of coming himself.

'Come on Friday,' I say. 'We're only going overnight. We won't leave until Saturday morning.'

'We've got a bit of a bash for work on Friday night. A rallying the troops kind of thing. Jude will want me to be there, partnering him.' That dreamy look has come back into her eye at the mention of her lover.

Do I go all dreamy when I talk about Greg? I suspect not. Though I'm sure I used to, once upon a time. Perhaps that's the difference between being a husband and a lover.

'We'll catch up next week,' I say. 'I can tell you all about my mucky weekend.'

'If you do insist on going to Cromer, then take plenty of sexy lingerie,' she says. 'That's my advice, sis.'

A smile plays at my lips. I think I might well give that one a try.

Chapter Sixteen

Greg attached the float to his line. The water was slow today, so he chose something light. He cast out and let the plumb bob settle on the bottom of the canal to check the depth of the water. Then he adjusted the line until the float popped out of the water and settled serenely on top.

'Woo, hoo!' Ray shouted out. 'Watch this and weep, matey.' He then landed another perch – his second in a matter of minutes. Nice fish. A couple of pounds, possibly three.

Perch were one of Greg's favourite fish. No other fish pulled quite like it – they jagged, swerved and, if it was a particularly good one, made the odd deep dive. On the bank, they were a good catch too. There was nothing that made the heart soar like lifting one in your net with its golden flanks, striped with black like a tiger, and the bright crimson fins. Old Stripey. On a winter's day it was a real tonic.

His friend's customary three rods were fanned out around him. Greg himself didn't like to catch fish after fish, after fish. He liked a challenge. Liked to work at it. He preferred to sit with just his tipping rod and move the bait on the bottom. It usually meant that you waited longer, caught fewer fish, but when you did there was a chance that they'd be better specimens.

'Picture, matey. Picture. I'm saying *cheese*,' Ray instructed, holding his little perch aloft in the time-honoured pose of fishermen, keeping the fish high on the chest so that it appeared bigger. It was a ritual that Greg had long got used to.

He put his rod to one side, lifted his friend's mobile phone from the top of his tackle box and, obligingly, snapped a photograph. Since technology had allowed them, recording every single fish that Ray hooked had become unavoidable. His friend even had his own website gallery to display the photos.

'What d'ya reckon?' Ray grinned at the lens. 'What d'ya reckon?'

'Nice fish.'

Greg could only remember taking a picture of one catch in recent years. He'd been sitting on the bank late one evening with the hot summer sun sinking over the horizon and the fish coming to the surface for a last lazy bite, when he'd hooked a monster Mirror Carp with nothing more than a piece of stale bread and a four-pound line.

It was unusual to see carp above ten pounds in the canal, but this beast weighed in at twenty pounds. He'd played it for two and a half hours, terrified that it would manage to snap the woefully inadequate line before he had a chance to reel it in. Just when he thought he'd won, the fish would power off again on a long, surging run. Greg had tired before the fish and had called Ray down to the canal to come and help him land it. That had been a fish to photograph. The flanks were chestnut brown, fading to a creamy-white belly, and it was thickset, strong and muscular like the prize-fighter it was. Carp were the fish who rewarded the anglers who worked hardest at their fishing, and the variation in their size and colour and scale patterns were as endless as in a fingerprint. Who could fail to marvel at that?

'I'm not going to be around this weekend,' Greg said as he put the camera phone down and picked up his rod again.

'Not around?'

'Taking Annie to Norfolk.'

'Cromer?'

'Yeah.'

'A bit out of the blue,' Ray said. The perch went proudly into the keep net with his growing haul. 'There's a match on tomorrow.'

Greg hadn't forgotten about that. It was one he'd been particularly keen to fish.

'What's brought this on?' his friend wanted to know.

'Annie's acting a bit funny,' Greg admitted. 'Thought it would do her good.'

'Hormones,' Ray said sagely, checking his arrangement of rods. 'This is the thing, matey. Men – we're wired like circuit boards. Every morning, same thing. No surprises. Click on. Click off. Women – they're like a jar of jelly beans. Shaken up every damn day. You never know what colour you're going to get. Or whether you're going to like it.'

Greg nodded thoughtfully. Annie had never been like this before. She seemed so discontented, so out of sorts. Could hormones really do that much damage overnight? His wife had never been overly troubled by those things, but then he had to admit that they never talked about such matters. If she had any problems in that department, she would have gone straight to her twin, Lauren, not him. Their marriage had always worked like that. Sometimes he wished that Annie would share more with him and less with Lauren, but he'd long accepted that her closeness to her sister was unlikely to alter.

But now this sudden change? It was like a perch suddenly behaving like a pike. What was he to do? Clearly, something was worrying his wife. It worried him too – even though he didn't know what it was. And he had to concede that, at the moment, it seemed like Ray had a point.

Chapter Seventeen

Lauren surveyed the buffet nervously. They'd had caterers in who'd put out a lovely selection of finger food on the board-room table. There were tiny blinis with smoked salmon and cream cheese, slivers of pink roast beef with fresh horseradish, puff-pastry horns filled with a light asparagus mousse. It all looked wonderful and she couldn't face a single mouthful.

Despite the tough economic climate, the sales team had pulled in a lot of revenue this year – down, in no small part, to her own efforts. Jude had decided that he'd put on a reception in the boardroom to say thanks to all the staff at *Happening Today*. She closed her eyes, thinking of the last time she'd been in this room. Her emotions were mixed, to say the least.

'Bringing back memories?'

It was Zak.

She turned, arms folded. 'Of what?'

'We did this at the same time last year, didn't we?' There was a twinkle in his eye.

So he must have seen something when she was in here with Jude the other night. 'You're a monster.'

He picked up a samosa from a selection of Indian titbits and she slapped his wrist. Zak popped it in his mouth. 'I won't tell if you won't.'

He then helped himself to a mini poppadom and dipped

it in some mango chutney. Then he lowered his voice as he said, 'You do know that Georgia's coming tonight?'

Lauren's stomach dropped to the floor. 'No!'

Zak pursed his lips. 'Sorry to be the bearer of bad news.'

Why? Why was Jude's wife coming here? There was no need for her to do that. If it was a big party, important customers with their partners, then fair play, it made sense that she should accompany him. It might have seemed strange if she didn't. But this was just for staff. An intimate little gathering. Georgia had no business being here.

Lauren looked down at her dress. She'd chosen this so carefully this morning. A fine balance between looking smart and not too flash. Now it was all wrong. If she'd known that Georgia was coming along, she'd have gone for full-on bling. She'd have had her hair done at lunchtime too instead of staring dreamily at Jude's office watching him on the phone. Damn.

'You look beautiful,' Zak said, as if picking up her thoughts. 'If you don't mind me saying.'

'I look dreadful,' she replied.

'No.' He put his hands on her shoulders. 'You look just perfect.'

'I have to go,' she said. 'Now. I can't stay.'

'No.' Zak held her tighter. 'You'll stay. You'll smile a lot. And you'll be very professional.'

'I can't.'

'This is the price you pay.'

'For shagging the boss?'

'I couldn't have put it better myself.'

'You'd better get that champagne open,' Lauren said.

Zak wagged a finger. 'And not too much of that either. Two glasses max.'

She'd planned on drinking two glasses straight down just to give herself a basecoat.

'How could he do this to me?' Lauren hadn't meant to say it out loud. Now it was too late. 'How could he not tell me?'

'He should have warned you,' Zak admitted, 'at the very least. I only know because I heard him send Stephen out to collect her in his Merc.'

'Thanks for giving me the heads up.'

'That's what friends are for.' Zak popped the cork on the champagne bottle he was holding and splashed some into two glasses. He chinked his glass against hers. 'You are going to be as bubbly as this fizz, Lauren Osbourne.'

'I'll try my best.'

Zak put his arm round her and hugged Lauren to him. For a second, she let her weary head rest on his shoulder. It was at that moment that Jude walked in with Georgia.

Chapter Eighteen

What had promised to be a lovely, fun evening turned out to be truly terrible. Despite Zak's warning, or maybe because of it, Lauren had drunk too much and was now maudlin.

Georgia was beautiful, funny, flirty and she had Jude. It wasn't fair. Life wasn't fair. She'd done her best, Lauren thought. She'd kept her side of the bargain. She'd never wanted to fall in love with Jude, but he'd been so persuasive. *He'd* pursued her, not the other way around.

Lauren had watched, tortured, as the couple had circulated round the room, chatting to the various groups of staff, moving ever closer towards her. She'd tried to keep one step ahead of them, but now there was nowhere to run. Jude was in front of her, holding Georgia's hand. 'Everything all right, Lauren?'

Nodding, she turned on her brightest smile. 'Hello, Jude. Georgia.'

Jude's wife touched her arm gently and Lauren's skin crawled with shame. 'It's lovely to see you again.'

Lauren said nothing, words stuck in her throat.

'I keep saying to Jude that you'll have to come over to our house sometime for dinner, with your young man.'

There's no young man, she wanted to say. *Only your husband.* That would force Jude's hand, she thought. What if she said something right now? Brought it all out into the open once and for all?

Then Zak was at her side again. She wondered if Georgia thought that she and Zak were an item. Did she think that he was her 'young man'? He had been particularly attentive tonight. Telling her stupid jokes to make her laugh. Trying to make her pause between drinks.

She slipped an arm round Zak's waist and leaned against him flirtily. Jude's face darkened. 'That would be nice,' she said, and her voice sounded considerably more calm than she felt. 'We must arrange it.'

'We should circulate, darling,' Jude said, and tugged at his wife's hand.

He and Georgia moved on to the next group of people.

'Come on,' Zak said close to her ear. 'Let's get you out of here.'

'Just as fast as you can,' she agreed and they left. Only once did she glance back to see Jude with his arm round his wife, laughing, having fun.

Chapter Nineteen

Lauren's legs were buckling as they crossed the office and she wasn't sure that it was all to do with the drink. She held on to Zak.

'Oops a daisy,' he said, and hauled her up. She started to giggle when she really wanted to cry.

Behind them, the boardroom door closed and they turned to see Jude striding across the room towards them.

'Here comes trouble,' Zak whispered.

'Are you going home with him?' Jude hissed under his breath as he got close to them.

'Yes,' Lauren answered a bit squiffily.

'Excuse me a moment,' he said to Zak, and then snatched Lauren by the wrist and pulled her across the office and into the men's toilets. He spun her round and pushed her up against the wall. Lauren was instantly sober.

'What *exactly* do you think you're doing?' he asked through gritted teeth.

'Going home.'

'With him?'

'Yes,' she said again. 'What's it got to do with you?'

'How can you do this to me?'

'You're here with your wife.'

'I had no choice,' Jude protested. 'It's not the same.' His expression was bleak. 'Don't go home with Zak.'

Lauren sagged. 'It's not what you think,' she told him. 'Zak's a good friend. He can see that I'm distressed.' She thumped a fist on her lover's chest, weakly. She was so weary – weary of this party, weary of this relationship, weary of her life. 'You brought your wife here, Jude, and you didn't even think to warn me. Why did you do that?' She pounded on him again, harder this time. '*Why?*'

Jude grabbed her wrist again and held it tightly. 'I'm sorry,' he murmured. 'So sorry. It was thoughtless of me. Stupid. You see, I thought you'd know the score, that you'd cope with it. You always do.'

Now she was crying. 'I don't want to cope any more. I can't cope. I just want to get out of here. Let me go.'

Jude pulled her to him. 'I love you,' he said. 'I'll make this up to you. We'll go away – next weekend. Just the two of us. Somewhere wonderful. We'll stay in bed for two whole days. I'll organise it all.' He stroked her hair as she sobbed against his chest. 'Say you'll come.'

'Jude . . .' She began to protest but already her resolve was weakening.

'Say you still love me even though I'm a selfish bastard.' He kissed her face, tenderly. Tiny hot kisses, all over. 'Say it.'

'I still love you,' she said.

'And I'll show you just how much I love you as soon as I possibly can. But now, I have to go back to the party before Georgia misses me.' He kissed her again. 'Tell me you're okay.'

'I'm okay,' Lauren said. But she wasn't, she really wasn't. 'Wait a minute before you follow me out.'

Lauren nodded. It was back to business as usual.

Jude kissed her again, straightened his jacket and left.

She splashed her face with water and, a moment later, as instructed, she followed him out.

Zak was sitting on a desk waiting patiently for her.

'Sorry,' she said. 'You shouldn't have had to witness that.'

'He said he'd kill me if I laid a hand on you.'

'Perhaps you shouldn't get involved in this, Zak. I'd hate to think that it might cost you your job. Jude could get very funny about it.'

Her friend shrugged. 'It's a risk I'm prepared to take.'

Lauren sighed. 'You really are a good friend.'

Zak smiled. 'I keep telling you that.'

'Come back to my place for a coffee,' Lauren said impulsively. 'I don't want to be alone.'

'Only if you have Jaffa Cakes.'

'We'll pick some up at the shop at the end of my road on the way.'

'You certainly know how to please a man,' her friend joked.

'If only,' she said with a sigh.

The night was warm and pleasant, and Zak flagged down a cab straight away. They had the driver stop at the shop near her flat, to pick up the requisite Jaffa Cakes on the way.

Zak followed her up the stairs to her apartment, letting her lean on his arm for support. She fumbled the key from her handbag as he waited beside her.

'I don't feel very well,' she admitted as, eventually, she opened the door.

'I'll do the coffee,' Zak said. 'Though peppermint tea might be better if you've got any.'

'Putrid stuff,' Lauren said, and her stomach lurched at the thought of it. 'Have to go! 'Scuse me.'

She ran for the bathroom and, making the loo just in time, parted with all the champagne and canapés that she'd consumed.

Lauren was kneeling on the floor of the bathroom, her head in the toilet bowl, feeling wretched, when the door opened behind her and Zak was standing there with a glass of water.

'Thanks,' she said gratefully as he handed it to her. 'Go home, please. I can manage. Let me die in peace.'

'Wouldn't dream of it,' Zak said.

'I don't want you to see me like this.'

He sat down on the side of the bath. 'I'm particularly attracted to puking women. I have a fetish for it. Did you know that there's an entire website dedicated to the art?'

Lauren laughed weakly. 'I'm sure there is.' She sipped at the water.

'Feeling better?'

'Yes. Much.' Then she turned to the loo and threw up again.

Zak knelt down beside her to hold back her hair and stroke the small of her back.

When she'd finished, she said weakly, 'I think I really am dying.'

'Clean your teeth,' Zak instructed. 'Then I'll tuck you into bed.'

'You're so kind to me.' Tears were fighting their way forwards.

'Want me to sleep on the sofa tonight?'

She nodded feebly. 'Please.'

Zak pulled her to his chest and she snuggled against him. 'Well, girl, you *nearly* got through that unscathed.'

'I did, didn't I?' Lauren started to laugh at the ridiculousness of the situation. 'I do love him, Zak,' she said, 'but sometimes I can't for the life of me think why.'

'Love can be a fucking awful thing,' he said with a heartfelt sigh.

And Lauren couldn't have agreed more.

Chapter Twenty

Greg and I set off for the North Norfolk coast at ten o'clock leaving strict instructions that neither of the kids are to announce on Facebook that they're having a party at our house while the old folks are away.

It's lunchtime when we arrive and check into the Clifftop Guest House. Mrs Emerson is ready and waiting for us. As she has been for the last twenty years. 'Hello, dears!' she cries. 'So lovely to see you again.'

We must be her best customers. I wonder, idly, how much money I've paid into her pension fund over the years. Our landlady is a woman of indeterminate age – she's definitely over sixty but she could be nearing a hundred. I think she's run the Clifftop Guest House since the dinosaurs roamed the Earth. She's certainly sported the same blue rinse since we started coming here, and may even be wearing the same cardigan.

'I'll show you to your room.'

Frankly, I could get to it blindfolded. The only other guests here now seem to be old-age pensioners and not the ones who think that sixty is the new forty.

Why *do* we still come here? We could be in one of those trendy bed and breakfasts that have wi-fi connections, throws on the bed in shades of chocolate or mink that are fashioned from natural fibres and not polyester, and have complimentary

Molton Brown toiletries in the en-suite bathroom rather than an industrial-size bottle of Tesco's own brand shampoo. Mrs Emerson still hasn't moved away from nylon sheets and honeycomb blankets with floral bedspreads.

We're too young to be staying somewhere like this. It was okay when the kids were young because it was cheap and cheerful and Mrs Emerson was fleet of foot and synthetic fabrics were still considered a marvellous new invention. Now as we trudge after her to the same room we always have, I could kick myself for not getting the name of a romantic love-nest-style hotel from Lauren.

If I was a stronger woman, I'd demand that we leave now and find somewhere to stay that had been decorated since the 1970s. This place makes me feel a hundred and nine, not thirty-nine.

'It's so homely here,' my husband whispers happily. 'Comfy. That's why I like it.'

And I wonder if he's lost his mind.

Still, the fact that everyone else here is probably deaf means that it won't matter if we make some unseemly noise when we have our night of unbridled passion in room number 4 with a view of the sea. Greg could take me up against the picture window while I bare my breasts to the seagulls of Cromer. A thrill runs through me at the thought.

In preparation, the other day I popped into a nice lingerie shop with an Italian name, and paid continental prices for a little lacy bra and matching knickers. It's not often that my underwear is co-ordinated – some days I'm lucky if my outer clothing is – and I think it's something that I must address. A filmy kimono thing came with the set that I can slip on over the undies. Very sexy. Very Marilyn Monroe. I haven't got them on now, of course. I'm saving them for later. We're planning to go for a walk on the beach while the sun is still shining and I didn't want the lacy bits to be scratchy under my jeans. Even femmes fatales have to be practical.

I look out of said picture window with sea view – which is ten pounds extra at the Clifftop Guest House. (If you don't pay it, you get a view of the car park and the *You Win* Bingo emporium.) It's beautiful out there, in a stark way. The sky is milky blue, the sea a more steely shade . . . but it's not quite the Turks and Caicos Isles, is it? There's plenty of sand, but it isn't white and powdery, it's more mustard yellow and damp. The absence of swaying palms is noticeable.

It's not quite Peru either. Speaking of which, I brought my travel guide with me in my handbag, hoping that I'd have time for a more thorough perusal while we were here and, perhaps, be able to raise the subject with my husband. As yet, I haven't had the chance. I get car sick if I read, but my time will come.

Greg comes up behind me and puts his hands on my shoulders. I hear a wistful sigh as he stares out to sea. 'I'm glad you persuaded me to come away for the weekend,' he says. 'We are getting set in our ways.'

A breakthrough, I think. Like me, he's ready to try new things, embrace a new life that doesn't involve Mrs Emerson or nylon in any way, shape or form.

'We can make a booking now for September while we're here,' he continues, before I have a chance to congratulate him on his insight into my frustration.

September? Greg's planning to come back *here*? Why can't he see it through my eyes? Why can't he see the peeling paint, the faded carpet, the chipped Formica furniture? Why?

'Hmm,' Greg says, as if he's immensely pleased with himself for this momentous decision. 'I'm looking forward to it already.'

So, while my colleagues will be hiking in the Andes, exploring Inca ruins beneath snow-capped peaks and amid lush tropical forests, it looks like I'll be coming back to Cromer and the delights of the Clifftop Guest House.

Chapter Twenty-One

We walk down the High Street, arm-in-arm, looking for somewhere to have lunch. My dark mood has been dispelled by the tang of the salty air and the enlivening breeze.

'We could go to the Crown,' Greg suggests when I stop outside a new bistro that's opened since we were last here.

'This looks nice.' I scan the menu. Herb pancakes with mushroom stuffing and creamy Kirsch Gruyère sauce. Roasted butternut squash and parmesan risotto. Chilli crab linguine with coriander pesto.

'I fancy the Crown,' Greg says.

Egg and chips. Ham and chips. Sausage and chips.

'This is a bit different.'

My husband scowls at the menu and wrinkles his nose in distaste at the delights on offer. 'Looks a bit fussy.'

The Crown it is then. We order two lots of sausage and chips – despite my protesting tastebuds. When we've eaten our solid, traditional lunch, I cast a longing glance at the bijou bistro as we jump back in the car and head out to Holkham for the afternoon.

This is my favourite beach on this coastline. Miles and miles of flat, largely empty sand stretch out as far as the eye can see. This is one place I don't mind coming back to again and again.

We walk along the beach. It's virtually deserted today, bar a couple of hardy dog-walkers as the weather is less than conducive to sunbathing. I snuggle close to Greg as the wind threatens to blow me away. The sun is trying its best, but it's no match for the howling gale. Even the seagulls are being blown backwards.

I tuck my arm into Greg's, asking him, 'Do you never get the urge to do anything different?'

He shakes his head, and that's just as I suspected.

'Not ever?'

'I like our life,' he says. 'We've got a nice house, good friends, great kids. And I enjoy my job.'

'You moan about it all the time.'

'I know, but that's what people do. It's okay really. Pays the bills.'

'Have you never wanted anything more?'

My husband looks genuinely puzzled. 'Like what?'

I realise that this is a pointless conversation as Greg is never happier than when he has a fishing rod in his hand or is talking about the joys of catching carp. Nothing else really matters to him.

Should I be pleased that my husband has no desire to ski down the slopes of Gstaad or own a flash yacht moored in St Tropez? Would I like to have a ruthlessly ambitious husband who was a workaholic and never at home? Or is there a fine line between being contented with one's lot and becoming a sloth? At what point does being laidback tip into downright laziness?

'What's all this about, Annie?' he says, his expression troubled. 'We're okay, aren't we?'

'I just feel . . .' What can I say? Stifled? Suffocated? As if life is passing me by without me being involved in it? Would

Greg even begin to understand how squashed, squeezed and suppressed I feel?

'Is there anyone else?' he asks bleakly.

I laugh out loud at that. 'God, no! How can you think that?'

My husband looks relieved. I take his hand in mine and stuff them together into his pocket as it's bigger than the ones in my jacket. I've never had to question Greg's fidelity. I've always known where he is at all times. He's always at the canal. With Ray. Any woman who wanted to entice Greg away from me would have to dress up as a fish.

'I just want to *do* things,' I confide.

'What kind of things?'

'Anything.' I break away from him, twirling around, letting the wind tangle my hair. 'I don't know.'

He spreads his hands, beseeching. 'Then how can *I* know?'

'Hey – remember that this is a naturist beach now?' I shout to Greg as I spin away from him – although today there are no hardy souls baring their wherewithal to the bracing sea air.

My husband wrinkles his nose again. 'That's horrible.'

'It's natural,' I correct. 'Come on – how much to get your kit off and sprint to that sand-dune thingy?'

'I wouldn't do it for all the tea in China.'

'A hundred quid,' I tease. 'If you strip off and run along the beach I'll give you a hundred quid.'

'No,' he says. 'No way.'

'Give me a hundred quid and I'll do it.'

Now he looks cross.

'No,' Greg says sternly. 'This isn't funny, Annie. What's the matter with you? Is this about your hormones?'

I put my hands on my hips. 'Leave my hormones out of it. You men! That's always your answer to everything.'

'Let's go and get a cup of tea.'

'I want to *feel something*, Greg!' I'm shouting now. 'Wouldn't it be nice to feel the wind on your skin?'

'It's freezing.'

I pull off my anorak. He's right.

But I can't stop now. I've been gripped by a frenzy, an urgency. If I don't take all my clothes off, I think that I'll die of frustration or boredom or something else that I don't quite understand.

'Annie,' Greg says flatly as if he's speaking to a small child. 'Put your anorak back on now.'

'Shan't,' I say. Then to my own surprise, I peel my sweater over my head too.

My husband gasps.

And I fight the urge to cover myself up again. I don't think I've ever been on a beach in my bra before and I'm torn between feeling liberated and terror.

'Annie. Stop this right now.'

I kick off my boots and socks and let the wet sand tickle between my toes. 'I'm going to paddle.'

'That's stupid. You'll catch your death of cold. It'll be about minus five in there.'

'Come with me,' I beg.

'You're mad.'

Running to the sea, arms spread wide, I leave a trail of anorak, sweater, boots and socks behind me.

As I reach the waves, I stop and yank off my trousers.

'Annie!' Greg shouts. 'Now I'm really cross!'

94

I splash about in the sea in my bra and knickers, almost hyperventilating as each wave breaks over me. A man with a sheepdog stops to watch.

Shivering, I launch into a version of Cyndi Lauper's 'Girls Just Want to Have Fun' as I try to jump the waves and mistime all of them. I yell the words pointedly at Greg over the sound of the surf. 'GIRLS. JUST. WANT. TO. HAVE. FUN.'

The sheepdog barks.

Greg puts his hands in his pockets and stomps off.

Then a big wave comes and knocks me flat on my face.

Chapter Twenty-Two

I get back into the car. Greg starts it up. I'm soaking wet. The sexy lingerie stays in the overnight case. We lie back-to-back in Mrs Emerson's lumpy bed. And the seagulls of Cromer never get to see my breasts.

We drive home in silence.

Chapter Twenty-Three

Greg had been fishing since he was a boy. His parents used to take him on holiday to Cromer as a kid and he was never happier than when he was at the end of the pier, hauling crabs out of the sea on a line with a basic hook and filling a bucket. When it was brimming he'd stagger back to the caravan site where they always stayed and he'd spend another hour joyfully releasing the wriggling crustaceans, one by one, into the saltwater boating lake. It was a pastime that was as pointless as it was pleasurable.

'If I was Prime Minister,' Ray was saying, 'I'd use criminals as road cones on the motorways – when they were doing repairs and the like. If you survived a year without getting killed, you went free. Sentence served.' He glanced at Greg to check that he was listening. 'That'd create some space in the prisons.'

'Yeah,' Greg said, and reeled in his line. He hadn't had a bite for a while. Perhaps it was time to try another type of bait.

From crabbing once a year, he'd then progressed to a warped piece of bamboo stick with a bent nail on the end for a hook and had fished for slippery grey-brown gudgeon in the local river. Rice Krispies had opened a whole new world to him when they'd run a special offer of a fishing rod and reel on the back of their packets. He'd lived on the cereal for weeks, eating an extra bowl every night before bed just so that he could cut out and save enough tokens to bag himself one. By the time he'd got his shiny new rod in his hands he never wanted to look at a Rice Krispie ever again. But it was a sacrifice that was worth it as it set him on a lifetime of unceasing pleasure as an angler.

His very first cast with it had caught him a small tench, and Greg had been so excited that he'd struck too fast, flicking the fish off the line and high into the air where it disappeared over a hawthorn hedge behind him, never to be seen again. He'd calmed down a lot since then.

After that, he'd fished with his dad for years, many hours spent in companionable silence. When his dad had passed away, Ray had slipped seamlessly into his father's place. They too had spent many companionable hours, but never in silence.

'Matey,' Ray said, breaking into his thoughts. 'What's on the menu for lunch today?'

Greg got out his plastic box. 'Cheese sandwiches.'

'Me too. A gourmet delight that cannot be surpassed,' Ray concluded. 'Though Marla does make me eat that bloody fancy granary stuff. Why do women not know that cheese sandwiches should only ever be consumed when they're made with white bread?'

Greg grunted. He quite liked granary bread.

'They are different creatures from us, Gregor, my dear friend. Never let us forget that.'

'No.'

Greg opened his lunch box and took out his sandwiches, and he and his friend worked their way through their snack, gazing out over the canal.

His only disappointment had been that his son Bobby had never shared his passion for fishing. He'd brought him along once or twice when he was about eight, but his son had been bored to tears. Greg had tried again when his son reached eleven, but the joys of angling never did catch Bobby in their thrall. He was into football – a sport that Greg didn't understand at all. Perhaps he should have taken more time to learn to like it, as he felt that he didn't know Bobby as his own father had known him – and that saddened him.

'You're a bit glum today,' his friend observed. 'Even for you. All well in the Ashton household?'

Greg never normally confided his problems in Ray. Primarily because he never normally had any problems. Nothing outside of the work environment, anyway. He'd had twenty years of relatively trouble-free marriage with neither his wife nor his kids giving him any grief. Now it seemed that times were changing and it weighed heavy on his heart. Who else could he talk to this about? He wasn't a talking man, but he couldn't keep all this to himself, hold it all in his head which felt as if it was fit to burst.

'When we went to Norfolk,' Greg ventured slowly, 'Annie took all her clothes off and ran into the sea.'

'Bloody hell.' Ray spluttered some of his cheese sandwich into the canal and a brave duck scuttled up to make the most of it. 'She did *what*?'

'She took all her clothes off and ran into the sea.'

'What did she do that for?'

'She said she wanted to do something different.'

Ray spluttered again. 'That's *different*, all right! The woman's lost the plot.'

'That's what I said. And now we're not speaking.'

Annie – good, reliable, uncomplaining Annie – was frightening him with her strange behaviour, and Greg didn't know what to do. She seemed so unsettled, so discontented, and he didn't know what had brought it on. Nothing in their lives had changed. There'd been no upheaval or upset to unbalance the status quo. Their life pottered along as it always had. So what had brought it on?

'Do you think that I should talk to her about it?'

'No,' Ray said, aghast. 'No, no, no. You don't want to be doing that. You'll open the floodgates. Next thing, you'll be down at Relate and unpicking all your dark secrets in front of some posh counsellor in pearls.'

Greg didn't have any dark secrets, but he didn't want to be doing anything in front of a posh counsellor in pearls.

'Has she started reading *Woman and Home* recently?'

'No.'

'That is the publication of the devil, matey. If you check round your house you'll probably find one secreted somewhere.'

'I don't think so.' Greg racked his brains but he didn't recall seeing Annie reading *Woman & Home*. Or any other magazine.

'Trust me.' Ray was adamant. 'It's the *Cosmopolitan* for the over-thirties. Puts ideas into their pretty little heads.'

'What if it's not *Woman & Home*?' Greg wanted to know. 'What if it's something else?'

'Just ignore it,' Ray advised. 'It'll be her hormones, like I said before. Pound to a penny she's having an early *change*.' He mouthed the word *change*. 'They all go funny then. Trust me – I'm speaking as one who knows. Marla's hormones are all over the place. She's a different person every hour.'

That certainly sounded like Annie.

'Ignore it and it will all go away,' his friend said sagely. 'The more time you can spend out of the house fishing, the better.'

It was sound advice, Greg thought. Best to just keep quiet and keep his head down. When had talking ever got anyone anywhere?

Chapter Twenty-Four

Lauren woke up with a monumental hangover. She peeped into her living room and, sure enough, Zak was sprawled out on her sofa. That bit wasn't a bad dream then. He looked suspiciously naked beneath the blanket that was barely covering him.

His kindly face was soft in sleep – the perpetual smile that he wore still there. His hair was messy and, for one mad moment, she wanted to go and run her fingers through it.

Instead, she pulled her dressing-gown around her with a groan. As if her life wasn't complicated enough.

Trying not to wake her impromptu guest, Lauren slipped into the bathroom, locking the door behind her. In the shower, she let the hot water stream over her in a vain attempt at reviving her body. Then, when she did begin to feel better, she didn't want to get out of the shower as she couldn't bear to face Zak. He'd been so kind to her last night. How many other men would be so chivalrous when faced with a snivelling, puking drunk?

When she did venture out of the bathroom, the sofa had been vacated and there were clinking sounds coming from the kitchen. Zak was up and making breakfast.

'You've nothing in the fridge,' he said. 'So I've put a brew on. There's a bit of stale bread.' He banged it on the work surface and it reverberated as bread shouldn't.

'I meant to go shopping yesterday,' Lauren lied. She probably would have just eaten the stale bread and not noticed it.

'I'll just have a cuppa and get out of your hair,' Zak said. 'It's best if I don't hang around. If I was Lover Boy then I'd be popping by first thing to apologise. I'm sure he wouldn't be too happy to find me here.'

'I don't know if Jude will swing by,' she told him honestly. 'I never know.'

'How can you live like that?' Then he held up a hand. 'None of my business.'

'Thanks for being so great last night.'

'I couldn't leave you alone,' Zak said. 'I'd never have forgiven myself if something had happened to you.'

Then suddenly, Lauren felt overwhelmed with loneliness. Annie had gone away for the weekend; if she went to see Chelsea she'd only end up feeling more inadequate, yet there was no way that she wanted to spend another Saturday and Sunday on her own.

'I suppose you've got plans?' she said.

Zak shrugged. 'Nothing pressing.'

'I could stump up for breakfast by way of thanks. There's a great greasy spoon down the road.'

'You must be feeling better.'

'Want to?'

'Can I use your shower first?'

'Sure.'

She went into the bedroom and pulled on her clothes and scraped her hair back into a pony-tail.

From the shower, she could hear Zak whistling 'Torn

Between Two Lovers'. At least, that's what she thought it was. It was terrible, tuneless, and it made her smile when she had wondered at one point last night whether she'd ever smile again. Then Lauren had a momentary image of Zak's taut, toned body in her bathroom, covered in soapsuds and rivulets of water.

An involuntary gulp travelled down her throat. Bacon and eggs. That was *definitely* all that was on the menu.

Chapter Twenty-Five

I'm in the office first thing on Monday morning. Greg and I still aren't speaking. Blake Chadwick's Lotus Exige roars into the car park and moments later he breezes through the swing doors.

'Morning, Sexy.'

'Hello, BC.'

Clearly, he's on a mission this morning as he's through the next set of doors before I can say anything else. He looks like a man who wouldn't mind getting his kit off on a nuddy beach.

I pick up the phone and dial Lauren's number.

'Hi, sis,' she says when she answers. 'Ringing to fill me in on all the sordid details of your dirty weekend?'

'The sexy lingerie was a waste of money,' I tell her with a pained sigh. 'I didn't even get it out of the bag. I'm taking it back at lunchtime.'

'Oh, Annie.'

'Don't "Oh, Annie" me,' I tell her. '*I* was fun. *I* was spontaneous. *I* ran into the sea in my bra and knickers.'

'In Cromer?' she asks incredulously.

'In Holkham, to be accurate.'

'Wow,' Lauren says with a raucous laugh. 'Good on you!'

'Well, Greg didn't think it was very funny. He stormed off in a huff. He's still not really talking to me. He thinks it's either my hormones or another man.'

'Chance would be a fine thing,' she chips in.

'That's pretty much what I said. Please tell me that you had a better time than me.'

'Not really,' Lauren confesses. 'Jude brought his wife to the office do. I was mortified.'

I bet his wife wasn't too impressed either, but I say nothing. After all this time, can Mrs Jude really be completely unaware of what's going on between her husband and one of his employees?

'Zak took me home and I ending up spending the rest of the weekend with him.'

'Oh, really?'

'In a purely platonic way,' my sister adds hastily.

'He's the web-designer guy?'

'The very same,' she says. 'He's lovely. So kind.'

'Does he have a wife and two children?'

'Don't even go there,' Lauren warns. 'This was going to be our year to get what we wanted, Annie. Change our lives for the better. For me, that involves being with Jude.'

Pulling the travel guide to Peru from beneath my desk, I gaze lovingly at its cover and the image of Machu Picchu peeping out of the wisps of swirling cloud. And for me it involves having an adventure. One that's a little more life-affirming than taking off your togs on a blustery Norfolk beach.

Chapter Twenty-Six

I hang up just as my colleague Minny totters through the doors. 'We're having a planning meeting tonight for our trip to Peru at All Bar One,' she tells me. 'Sure you can't come?'

'I can't,' I say. My heart flutters. 'It's just not me.'

'It'll be a blast. Everyone's going,' she wheedles. 'Sarah's going to shut the offices for two weeks. There'll be nothing for you to do here anyway.'

Someone has to hold the fort, I think.

'We'll be there from seven o'clock,' she tells me. 'Hope to see you later. It won't be the same without you.'

And then she's gone.

That's me unsettled for the day.

I have some figures to input into the computer but I can't concentrate. I take messages on the phone, then before I put the calls through, I forget who I was talking to and about what. My mind is a churned-up mess. It drifts from the azure waters of Lake Titicaca, up to the towering peaks of the Andes, beneath the marshmallow clouds of the endless Peruvian sky.

I don't know how I get through the rest of the day. I have to fight the urge to get my travel guide out every five minutes and I swing between desperately wanting to go with the rest of my colleagues and being too terrified to admit that I do.

When it's time to go home, I feel exhausted – though I've

done nothing more demanding than wrestle with my own conscience.

I swing my car into the drive and then sit there with the engine turned off. This is the first time that I've ever felt like this, but I can hardly bring myself to go into my own home.

Everything that is familiar, the things I've always loved now seem to be a source of discontentment. I look at the garden and think that it's in serious need of a revamp. At the weekend, I might pull everything up and start again.

When I eventually haul my reluctant arse indoors, Greg's in the kitchen.

He doesn't look up when I walk in, but says, 'Dinner's nearly ready. I got home a bit early, so I thought I'd start it. There were some lamb chops in the fridge. I've done them with some carrots and new potatoes.'

Then something screeches in my head or maybe I do it out loud. Isn't this the same conversation we had last week?

My husband shoots me a worried glance when there's no response from me. 'That okay?'

I sit down heavily at the kitchen table. 'No,' I say. 'It's not okay.'

That takes him by surprise.

'I need to talk to you.'

Now the grill gets an anxious glance. 'The chops are just about ready.'

'Turn them off,' I say. I don't care if they end up as charcoal discs.

He does as I say and then sits down opposite me. 'If this is about the Norfolk thing,' he says, 'then I'm very sorry. I overreacted. I was thinking about it when I was fishing, and bra and pants aren't that much different from a bikini really. It was just the way you did it.'

'I want to go to Peru,' I blurt out.

Greg's jaw hits the floor.

'My colleagues at work are organising a charity trek doing the Inca Trail. Everyone's going.' I'm aware that I sound like a petulant child. 'I want to go too.'

Then Greg starts laughing and it's not the reaction I expect. Tears roll down his cheeks with hilarity. 'You?' he says. 'Doing the Inca Trail? You can't walk for five minutes on the flat without getting out of puff.'

'I admit,' I retort crisply, 'that I'll have to do some training.'

'You'll hate it,' Greg assures me when he has his laughter under control.

'But I want to try,' I plead. 'If I hate it, then at least I'll know that. I don't want to let this opportunity go by, to do something different. I feel as if I'm stuck in a dreadful dreadful rut that I can't climb out of.'

Now Greg stops laughing completely and the smile falls from his face. 'I didn't realise that life with me was so awful.'

'It isn't.'

My husband stands up. 'You've been acting very strangely lately, Annie,' he says. 'I just don't understand you.'

'Come with me,' I beg. 'I'm sure you could. We should do it together. You might enjoy it. Don't you ever want to do something crazy?'

'I don't need to prove that I'm happy by climbing up a mountain in a foreign country. I'm happy with a beer in front of the television.'

Or a bloody fishing rod in your hand, I think bitterly.

'I'm frightened that we're becoming old before our time. I want to do something to make me feel alive. I don't want to spend the rest of my life never going out of this road, this country. I need some freedom and fun.'

Greg's face darkens. 'What you need is to get a grip on yourself, Annie.'

'Thank you for your support.'

'How much is this trek going to cost?'

Another sticking point coming on. 'As it's for charity, you need to raise two and a half thousand pounds to secure your place.'

Greg laughs again, but it's clear that he doesn't find it funny. 'Two and a half grand?'

'The company are giving us five hundred pounds towards it.'

'That still leaves two grand to find. We haven't got money like that lying around, Annie. Things are always tight. You know that.' He runs his fingers through his hair.

I bet if he needed new fishing tackle we'd somehow find the cash.

'We've only got a small amount of savings to our name. I can't let you squander it on this.'

Squander it?

'I'm not going to use our precious savings, for goodness' sake.'

'Then how on earth do you think that you're going to pay for it?'

'I don't know,' I admit, head bowed. 'I haven't thought it through properly yet.'

Greg snorts. 'That's fairly obvious.' Then he heads to the door. 'I'm going fishing.'

'Let's talk about this some more,' I entreat to his back. 'I'd really love to do it together.'

Another snort.

'What about dinner?' I shout out.

'I've lost my appetite,' Greg says, and then he bangs out of the door.

I sink to the table, head in hands. That went well, I think.

Chapter Twenty-Seven

It was always so peaceful by the canal. Six hours of fishing flew by in what felt like a single hour. Sometimes Greg could just focus on the gentle movement of his float on the water and completely forget about everything else.

Today, it was proving more difficult. And it wasn't simply down to the fact that Ray was unable to keep his mouth shut for five minutes.

'If I was Prime Minister,' Ray began, as he cast out again, 'I'd never go into the Euro. It's all right for those foreigners. Very handy when you're going on holiday. But we certainly don't want it here. No, no, no.'

Greg kept his eyes on his float. 'Annie wants to go to Peru.'

Ray's head snapped up. 'Do what?' he said.

'Peru.'

'They don't use the Euro there.'

'No.' Greg didn't know what currency they used. He didn't know much about Peru at all. 'She wants adventure.'

'Skinny-dipping in Norfolk not enough eh?'

Greg shook his head.

'I take it that you *don't* want to experience all the sights and sounds that South America has to offer, Gregor?'

How could he tell his friend that the very thought of it terrified him? He didn't want adventure. He preferred things exactly the way they were. He liked his home. He liked this country. Why would he want to go anywhere else? All the excitement he ever needed was right here on the canal. What got his heart racing was landing a nice fat chubb or an unexpected bream.

'What should I do?'

'This is the thin end of the wedge,' Ray warned. 'Next thing, she'll be wanting to try strange sexual positions. Then it will be dancing lessons.'

Dancing lessons?

'Remember Sandy Whitman? We used to bump into him down here sometimes.'

Greg nodded. Sandy was a sixteen-stone brickie who was a demon with a carp rod.

'Salsa dancing – three nights a week. Never been here since. Rod's gathering dust in the garage.' Ray shook his head ruefully. 'Mind, he has lost three stone. But what a way to go.'

'It's for charity. A trip with colleagues from work.'

'Even worse, matey,' Ray shrugged but failed to explain why. 'You need to nip this in the bud before it gets out of hand.'

Then the end of Greg's fishing rod quivered and dipped. The reel sang out: he'd got a bite. Quick as a flash, he whipped up the rod and started to reel the fish in. He caught a glimpse of it as it came closer. The enticing golden flanks of a perch.

It was a reliable fish, a perch. You always knew where you were with them.

Then, all of a sudden, the line went slack and Greg's heart sank as he found he was reeling in nothing but a piece of weed. His bait was gone. The fish had slipped away from him and he had a feeling that his wife was doing the same thing.

Chapter Twenty-Eight

Jude arrived at the office shortly after Lauren did and before anyone else.

He crouched down next to her desk and rested his head on his hands. 'Sorry,' he said, looking up at her with sad eyes. 'That was so thoughtless of me.'

'Yes, it was.'

'I've been frantic all weekend.'

'Not frantic enough to phone me.'

'I couldn't get away,' Jude said. 'Not for a minute. Georgia was watching me like a hawk.' He walked his fingers towards her hand and took it. 'All I wanted was to be with you.'

Despite her vow to toughen up, harden her heart, Lauren could feel herself weakening.

'Every minute I was there with Georgia, I was thinking of you, darling. You know that.'

'I can't go on like this, Jude. It's horrible to everyone concerned.'

'I know, I know. And I need to sort it. I'm going down to Brighton this afternoon on business. I'm planning to set up a team for *Happening Today* down there. Come with me. I've booked a lovely hotel on the seafront – we can stay there tonight and travel back tomorrow together. That'll give us a chance to talk.' He glanced round the office. People were starting to arrive in dribs and drabs. He let go of her hand. 'We can't get five minutes' peace here.'

'What will people say?'

'I'm the boss,' he expounded. 'I can give you the afternoon off if I want to.'

Lauren giggled. She loved him when he was like this, reckless and spontaneous.

'Say yes,' he implored. His fingertips tugged playfully at the sleeve of her blouse. 'I can't last the week without you.'

'Don't complain if the revenue figures are down on Friday.'

'It's the last thing I'd do,' he promised as he stood, deal done. He winked at her as he went to his own office.

Her heart was still pounding in her chest when Zak came in and put a takeaway coffee down on her desk. 'Because the lady loves her latte,' he drawled seductively.

'Thanks, Zak.' She smiled up at him.

'I bought a skinny lemon muffin too.' He plonked a brown bag down on her desk. 'Now that I've spent the weekend with you, I realise that you really don't eat.'

'I had a lovely time,' she said honestly. They'd hung out together for the rest of the weekend after the Friday Night Disaster. Nothing too drastic. They'd had a walk on Hampstead Heath, gone to the pub in the evening. On Sunday they'd wandered round Camden Market together and had eaten noodles outside a cheap Chinese place in the sunshine. It was just relaxed. Zak didn't try to hold her hand or jump her bones. He was cool.

'I'm thinking of going to the cinema later in the week. That new Tarantino is showing. Fancy it?'

It was one thing having some fun with Zak when they were both at a loose end at a weekend, but this felt more like fixing up a date. 'Not really my thing,' Lauren lied. 'Maybe another time.'

Zak shrugged. 'Catch you later, then.'

'Sure. And thanks for the breakfast.'

Lauren sipped at her coffee and smiled. A trip to Brighton with Jude. What a great way to start the week.

Chapter Twenty-Nine

I put on my trendiest top and trousers and head off to All Bar One for the planning meeting about the proposed Peru trip.

Greg hasn't yet returned from work. I'd have liked to discuss this further with him before I went out. I want him to support me, to encourage me, maybe even to come with me – but it looks like it's not to be.

Tonight it's raining and parking in the city is a complete nightmare. I trail round for nearly fifteen minutes looking for a vacant space. To be honest, I nearly give up at one point and go straight home. So much for being up for a challenge!

Eventually, I find a spot, throw the car in and scuttle to the bar under my umbrella. All Bar One isn't too busy as it's a wet and miserable Monday night, but it seems that everyone else from the office is already here. They're sitting in a cosy huddle round a group of sofas, itineraries spread out on the low coffee-tables between them.

Several of my colleagues turn when I approach, umbrella dripping on the floor. I stand there shivering and uncertain.

'Is there room for one more?' I say nervously.

'On the sofa or on the trip to Peru?' Blake Chadwick challenges.

'Both.'

A cheer goes up and the girls jump up and come to hug

me and haul me round in a happy dance. Minny comes over and gives me a kiss. 'We'll have great fun, Annie. It'll be fab. You wait and see.'

They all budge up and I squeeze on to the sofa with them. Blake Chadwick pours me a glass of wine and hands it over, giving me a wink. 'Nice one, Sexy.'

Shaking, I take the glass. I've said it. I've said it out loud. There's no going back now.

I'm going to Peru.

While I shake and shiver and sip my Shiraz, Sarah Bennett runs through the practicalities of our expedition, but I barely hear her I'm still so shocked by my momentous decision. I have to call Lauren just as soon as I can.

Our trip takes us into Lima, out to the Nazca Lines, then into the Atacama Desert – all of the places I've been dreaming about from my travel guide. Then we move on to Arequipa, the Colca Canyon, Cusco and Lake Titicaca. When we've had time to acclimatise to the thin air of the Peruvian Andes, the second of our two weeks is spent hiking the Inca Trail through the ruins of Llactapata, Sayaqmarka, Puyupatamarka, Wiñay Wayna and up, up, up, up, up to the magnificent pinnacle, the lost city of Machu Picchu!

The names, exotic, unfamiliar, sing in my head. Sarah talks about the practical aspects of our trips – the equipment we'll need, the money side of things. But already I'm lost in the mountains of Peru. I can see myself swathed in a traditional poncho, striding along the ancient pathways of the Incas, breathing in the rarefied air, taking in the vast, expansive landscape. I'll be an explorer, an adventurer, treading the historic trails of ancient people.

Then Blake Chadwick stands up and I switch back to the present. 'I suggest that we all do some training before we go as it's quite a tough hike. I'm planning to go running three times a week around Furzton Lake,' he says. 'It's a circuit of about a mile and you're all welcome to join me.'

Training, I think. I need to do training. Lots of it. 'I'd like to do that,' I say to BC when he sits down.

'I'll be there from tomorrow,' he tells me. 'See you there straight after work, Sexy?'

I nod. It's years since I've done any running. Years since I've done any proper exercise, to be honest. Unless you count opening packets of Revels as exercise. I should be panicking but I can't keep the silly smile off my face.

I've done it. I'm going. No looking back. This is the start of the rest of my life. This is the new intrepid me. Let the adventure begin!

All I need to do is raise the money. And, of course, tell Greg.

Chapter Thirty

The hotel was beautiful. Lauren had to hand it to him, Jude had exquisite taste when it came to booking the perfect destinations for romantic trysts.

They'd quickly collected an overnight bag from her flat before driving down to Brighton. She'd thought that they might find a few moments to talk about their situation in the car on the way down, but Jude had been forced to spend most of his time on the phone sorting out a problem back in the office. So she'd dozed and listened to the radio and planned their future together by herself.

Now he was at his meeting. He'd booked her a treatment package in the hotel's luxurious spa and she'd enjoyed a relaxing facial, a back massage and a pedicure which had taken up most of the afternoon.

Lauren checked her watch. Jude had said that the meeting wouldn't take long and it was five o'clock already. Soon he'd be back.

The room was just so chic. The vast king-size bed was upholstered with black plush velvet, as was the chaise longue at its foot. Two black leather chesterfield sofas flanked the grey marble fireplace, while the walls were covered in a silver-grey metallic paper matched by the thick carpet. The view of the sea was magnificent and the sun sparkled on the water.

She felt mellow, warm and very loved. This is how it would be when they were married, when she was the next Mrs Taylor. In the grey marble bathroom, Lauren took off her fluffy dressing-gown. When packing, she'd taken care to include some of Jude's favourite underwear. It was a set he'd bought her from Agent Provocateur at Christmas – though being tied by family duties over the holiday period, it had been days before she'd been able to wear them for him.

Now they had hours stretching ahead of them. Maybe they could make love before going down for dinner. The thought thrilled through her. So she slid the underwear over her skin. Small, black lacy bra, French-cut briefs, a matching suspender belt and stockings. To complete the look, she stepped into her black-patent high heels. Obvious, but very effective.

Lauren had already ordered a bottle of champagne from room service and it was now chilling nicely in an ice-bucket. She decided against the dressing-gown. Let Jude find her just like this. He was an Alpha male – he'd like that.

She opened the champagne, poured herself a glass and reclined on the bed, striking a pose. Half an hour and another couple of glasses later, and Jude finally came through the door.

'Sorry, I've been longer than I planned,' he said. 'My God, look at you.' His eyes travelled over her. 'You're stunning.'

He threw down his briefcase and loosened his tie before coming over to the bed. His mouth found hers and he kissed her deeply. The now familiar bolt of electricity shot through her, but every time the power of it amazed her. She knew that Jude felt it too. Perhaps that's what kept him coming back for more.

Lauren broke away from him. 'Here.' She poured him a glass of champagne.

'Hmm. I need this,' Jude said. 'But not as much as I need you.' He pulled down her bra, exposing her breasts, then he drank deeply from his champagne and covered her with his mouth. The chilled bubbles danced on her nipples and Lauren threw her head back, gasping.

Then Jude's mobile rang.

'Let it ring,' she begged.

Her lover frowned. 'Can't,' he said. 'It's home.' The precaution of a married man with a mistress – a different ring tone for every aspect of his life.

Lauren flopped back on the bed and pulled her bra back into place.

'Hi, darling,' Jude said.

She wanted to block her ears.

'He has? When was this? How is he? Let me speak to him.' He turned to Lauren, his handsome face concerned, his hand covering his phone as he whispered, 'Benjy's come home from school feeling unwell.'

His voice softened as he spoke to his ten-year-old son. 'Hi, Ben,' he said. 'Mummy said you've got a temperature. Did you go to the nurse at school?'

Lauren zoned out while the private conversation continued. This was part of being in love with a family man, she told herself. These things happened.

'Put me back on to Mummy.' He mouthed to Lauren, *'Sorry.'* She filled her glass again and knocked it back. 'I think you should take him down to the walk-in centre,' Jude advised. 'He sounded very listless.'

Then more at the other end from Georgia.

Jude stood up and paced to the other side of the room. 'Don't cry, darling. I know you're worried. I'm worried too.' He glanced anxiously at Lauren. 'I'll come back right now. Straight away – I promise. Give me an hour, maybe a bit longer.' He hung up.

Lauren sighed. She finished her champagne and got up from the bed. 'I'll get dressed,' she said.

Chapter Thirty-One

The mood at work is so exciting. There's a real buzz about the place and everyone is talking non-stop about Peru. I wish the same could be said about my home.

The atmosphere here is so tense that you could cut it with a knife. Even a very blunt one. It's fair to say that my husband does not share my enthusiasm for the exotic delights that South America might have to offer.

However, that's where I'm going, whether Greg likes it or not. I've got my sponsorship forms in hand and that's what I'm going to do next. Lauren is coming up tonight to see me for a couple of hours and I want to make a start on my fundraising before she gets here.

Greg is stomping about, looking very unhappy. He had nothing to say – well, not very much and certainly nothing encouraging – when I told him that I had made my decision and that I was, indeed, going to Peru. When I told him that I was also going to raise the necessary money all by myself, he snorted and disappeared into the garage to do whatever he does with his fishing tackle. I haven't seen him since.

I leave my travel guide and my itinerary overtly displayed on the kitchen table. If by chance he pops back in and picks them up, then he might find that he's interested after all. And, he could, if he makes a reasonably quick decision, still change his mind and come along with me.

Ellen wanders in as I'm putting my shoes on. 'I can't believe you're doing this, Mum. It's not like you.'

'That's what your father says.'

'He probably thinks you've cracked.'

I take Ellen's hand as she passes and pull her to me. 'I've loved being a mum,' I say, 'but you two don't need me any more. Now it's time for me to do something for me.'

'Don't women of your age normally take up Pilates or join a book club or something? I don't know many of my friends' mums who go trogging up the Andes.'

'Doesn't that make you even a bit proud of me?'

'I just think you're completely barking,' my daughter reassures me.

'Ellen, I want you to do something wonderful with your life,' I tell her with a sigh.

'I wouldn't know what to do.'

'The world is literally your oyster,' I point out. 'You're a bright girl. You could go back to college, study to do something exciting or worthwhile.'

She shrugs. 'I like working in Monsoon.'

'I want more for you,' I say. 'I wish you wanted more for yourself.'

Another shrug. 'I want a cuppa,' she jokes. 'Do you?'

'No, thanks. I'm going out to start my fundraising. I need to raise at least two thousand pounds to pay for my place.'

'*Two grand*? And you've got to pay? I'd need someone to pay *me* to go. You're bonkers.'

'Thanks for your support.' I slip on my jacket.

'You're giving Dad a lot of grief over this, you know,' she says. 'He thinks you'll be applying to go on *Big Brother* next.'

'I might well do,' I tell Ellen. 'Or I could audition for *X Factor*. What a good idea. My version of Chaka Khan's "I'm Every Woman" is unique.'

And then, leaving my daughter with a gaping mouth, I flounce out.

Chapter Thirty-Two

I start with my next-door neighbour, Pat.

'I'm going to Peru,' I say. 'Doing the Inca Trail for the Dream Days charity. Would you perhaps like to sponsor me?'

'Greg told Terry about this.' She flicks her thumb towards her husband indoors as she throws back her head and guffaws. 'Are you mad, girl?'

I feel my lips tighten and I hope it looks like a smile. 'I thought it would be a fun way to raise money for a good cause.'

'Fun?' My neighbour snorts at that. 'I'll sponsor you,' she says. 'Too right I will.' And she writes down a pound on the form.

A pound? Her expression tells me that she thinks she's Rockefeller's daughter for stumping up that much.

'Thanks,' I say. Pat closes the door and, muttering, I head for the next house.

'Peru?' Mr Manley says. 'You can't drink the water there.'

'Possibly not.'

'*Definitely* not.'

'Would you like to sponsor me?'

He huffs at that, clearly not enamoured at this unexpected request for expenditure, and looks at what else is on the form. As Pat has written a pound, so does he.

Next house. 'Why would *I* want to pay for *you* to go to Peru?'

'It's not actually for me, it's for the Dream Days charity.'

'And how much money does the charity get out of this lot?'

'Er,' I say. 'I'm not exactly sure.'

Sighing. 'Put me down for a pound.'

It seems that none of my neighbours in Goldstone Road are high-rollers as I spend the next hour working my way along the road in a very depressing manner. By the time I've visited twenty houses, I've received fifteen pounds in pledges, four people didn't come to the door even though I know that they're in, and one person slammed the door in my face without even offering me a measly pound for my efforts. They won't get a Christmas card this year.

It's accurate to say that my soul has been destroyed. I decide to give up for the night and trudge home. I'm slightly alarmed that this makes me breathless and our road is as flat as the proverbial pancake. How am I going to tackle the Andes puffing like this?

By the time I get back home, my confidence has departed and Lauren has arrived.

My sister's sitting at the kitchen table with my darling daughter, and a bottle of wine is open. I kiss her when I come in and Ellen slopes off – presumably before I try to tell her how to run her life again.

Lauren pours me a glass of wine. 'You look knackered.'

I flop into the chair next to her with a heartfelt huff. 'Fifteen quid,' I say. 'It's taken me a whole hour to raise a measly fifteen quid. Times are clearly hard in Goldstone Road. I'm never going to get my money at this rate.'

'Early days,' Lauren reassures me. 'I'll get you some cash from Jude. In fact, the way he's just treated me, I'll ask him for double.'

'Is he being difficult?'

'He's being *married*,' she sighs.

'Oh, Lauren.'

'Never mind that now.' She waves away my concern. 'Chelsea will be ridiculously generous to make up for the fact that she's incredibly wealthy and we're povs. And I'll give you a hundred quid even though I'm skint.'

'Thanks.' Tears come to my eyes.

'No crying,' Lauren admonishes. 'What's that for?'

'I don't know if I'm up to this. Now that I've said I'll go, I'm really frightened.'

'You'll raise your money. You'll go. You'll be fine.'

'Greg's not happy.'

'Hard lines,' is Lauren's verdict. 'He shouldn't be such a boring old fart.'

Greg is standing at the door.

'Sorry, Brother-in-law,' Lauren says with an embarrassed giggle. She gets up to hug him.

Greg glowers at me over her shoulder.

'You should go with her.' Lauren digs my husband in the ribs. 'Have a laugh, a bit of excitement in your twilight years. What harm would it do?'

My husband has no answer to that. But the hurt in his eyes makes me want to curl up and die.

Chapter Thirty-Three

Greg liked to start with maggots. Always. Three on the hook, cast out. Then he'd catapult some more maggots on to the surface of the water around the same area. Fish had very short memories and would feed constantly. Perch preferred a red maggot. White for bream.

If he hadn't had a bite in half an hour, he'd change his bait. Perhaps go for a cocktail – a worm and a piece of sweetcorn. If that didn't work, then he might change to what Ray was using if his friend was being more successful. Ray always had the widest range of bait with him – boilies, hemp, cat meat, dog biscuits, floaters in a stunning variety of bizarre flavours, such as tutti-frutti and strawberry split, pellets, groats, bog standard bread, breadflake and magic bread.

If a shark had wandered, unsuspecting, through the Grand Union Canal, Ray would have had something to hand to tempt it with.

'Where have all our fishy little friends naffed off to today?' Ray asked, exasperated. 'We'll have to move in a minute, matey, otherwise I'll be getting some dynamite out of my box to blow the buggers out of the water!'

Greg looked over to his friend. 'Do you think I'm a boring old fart?'

'No, no, no,' Ray said. 'You like what you like. That's a quality to be admired.'

He thought so too. Greg was a creature of habit, that was for sure. He liked his food plain. He liked his tea from the same mug. He liked the same toothpaste. He liked a certain regularity of mealtimes. But did that, per se, make him boring? Was old-fashioned steadiness a virtue that was currently overlooked?

How would Annie cope if, after all these years, he suddenly changed overnight into a person she didn't recognise? Suddenly decided he didn't like fishing? Suddenly started eating curries or staying out late? Began dressing like one of those daft forty-year-old blokes who wear teenagers' clothes? Maybe got a tattoo?

But he was no more likely to do that than he was to . . . well, to suddenly announce that he was going to Peru.

Greg had always steered a steady course and it had served him well. He didn't see any reason now to turn away from it.

At work, he'd watched some of the managers who came and went through his office. They wanted to do nothing but trample over everyone else on their fight to the top. And for what? A few extra pounds in their pockets, a bigger motor in the drive, a house that cost an arm and a leg to run that they never saw?

He'd never wanted to be like that, and if it meant that money was a bit tight, did that really matter, at the end of the day? They didn't go hungry, their kids had never been barefoot. Okay, Ellen and Bobby didn't always have the latest computer games or the trendiest trainers, but they'd had a good, solid family upbringing with two parents around who cared for them and their tea on the table at the same time every night. That's more than could be said for most kids.

Greg had never put his work first. He'd never thought to chase after any of the secretaries who had given him the eye. He'd only ever thought of Annie, Ellen and Bobby. If they were happy, he was happy.

Now it seemed that Annie wasn't happy and he had no idea what to do about it.

Chapter Thirty-Four

I take my trainers and tracksuit into work. Then sit and stress all day. Exercising will be fun. Won't it? I could do with losing a few pounds anyway. Plus I want to be powering up the hills with the rest of the young things in the Party Party expedition and not lagging behind at the back.

At five-thirty there is a steady trickle of people departing, all wearing their jogging gear. They look undeniably keen. And undeniably better than I do in a Lycra ensemble. I nip to the ladies' loo, slip into my ratty old stuff and, heavy of heart, drive the couple of miles to Furzton Lake for our running rendezvous.

In the car park by the large leisure lake, the team are assembling. I can't say that I've ever exercised in public before and I'm not that enthusiastic about starting now. Blake Chadwick is summoning everyone together, so I get out of my car and go to join them, trying a little half-run as I do. Good grief, that's unpleasant.

'Hi, Sexy,' BC says to me as I approach.

I try to pretend I'm not panting and gasp out a, 'Hi.'

'Ready for this?'

Not so that you'd notice.

'Okay, team,' he shouts in a particularly encouraging way. 'Let's do this!' And he sets off at breakneck pace, jogging around the lake.

I love this part of Milton Keynes. The sun's sparkling on the expanse of water, herons glide gracefully through the air, a throng of ducks, coots and Canada Geese shadow our progress. The lake is bordered on two sides by a luxury housing development and I'd like to live here, sitting out on my balcony with a beautiful view of the water and of hyper-ventilating receptionists trying to get fit.

We're not a quarter of the way round and, already, I wonder why I'm doing this. My heart is banging against my chest so hard that I think it might burst out. Everything feels like it's jiggling too much and I realise that I should have bought an industrial-strength sports bra. Everyone else shoots ahead, but Minny stays back, jogging along with me. This is the first time I've seen her without her high heels. She's a tiny little thing, very pretty, very young, very girly.

'I'm really pleased that you're coming with us,' she says as we run along together.

'Thanks,' I manage to pant. 'That's nice.'

'We all are,' she continues. 'We think it's great that you're doing something like this at your age.'

Not quite so nice. I'm only thirty-nine, but maybe I do seem like the Old Woman of the Sea to these bright young things.

A moment later, Blake drops back to join us. 'How are you doing, girls?'

'Okay.' Minny picks up her step and I do likewise.

'One lap of the lake or two?' BC asks.

'One,' Minny says. 'I'm going out.'

'Undoing all this hard work?'

'If I'm lucky,' she teases.

'Angie?'

'Annie,' I puff. 'I'll try two.' If I haven't had a heart-attack by then.

'Good girl.' Then Blake sprints to the front again.

'He's well fit,' Minny says approvingly, and I couldn't possibly disagree with her.

Chapter Thirty-Five

By the time we start the second lap, I am beyond pain. My face is glowing like the setting sun. Everything hurts. All of it. I can't even be specific.

I don't notice until we start running again, but it seems to be just Blake Chadwick and my good self. Everyone else has faded away into the car park, even my companion, Minny.

'Just the two of us,' Blake says, noticing the absence of our colleagues at the same time as I do. 'Lightweights.'

I laugh at that and we fall into step together. I might be imagining it, but I think he slows down to my pace. Well, put it this way, I'm damn sure that I'm not keeping up with him.

This may sound silly, but I think his easy style is helping me. I seem to pick up a rhythm that blocks out the pain and, this may be a shock, but I actually start to enjoy it. Well, that may be stretching it. I just don't feel like I'm dying. Thankfully, BC doesn't tempt fate by trying conversation as this might test my theory too far, but we jog along together quietly in pleasant harmony.

When we've finished our second lap, I stand in the car park wheezing like a forty-a-day smoker.

'Well done,' Blake says, and I hold up a hand in thanks, talking still being a little tricky. He gets a towel out of his car and rubs himself down with it. 'Fancy a celebratory drink?'

'I couldn't touch alcohol,' I say. 'I'd be flat on my back.'

'We wouldn't want that, Sexy,' Blake says. One of his winks again. 'I was thinking more along the lines of a cola or something.'

There's a pub by the side of the lake – one of those big, impersonal family affairs with plastic food at credit-crunch prices. But there are benches and tables outside and, for some reason, a canal boat stranded afloat in a fake bit of canal which makes quite an attractive area.

'Yes,' I say without panting too much. What am I rushing home for, except to be met by stony silence? 'That would be nice.'

We walk the hundred yards or so to the pub at a – mercifully – sedate pace.

'Sit here,' Blake says, as we reach a table by the narrow-boat. 'I'll get the drinks.'

So I sit there fanning myself with a plastic menu, trying to cool down until my colleague returns with a glass of cola for me and a pint of orange juice for himself. We drink in silence as we look out over the lake.

'Do you run here often?' I ask.

He laughs. 'Is that a pick-up line, Sexy?'

I feel myself colour up and, thankfully, Blake steps in to rescue me. 'Yes, in fact I run here nearly every day – usually in the morning before I come to work. When you enjoy as much corporate hospitality as I do, you have to do something to keep in shape.' He pats his washboard stomach fondly. 'What about you?'

'The only exercise I've had for the last twenty years is picking up dirty washing that my children have left on the floor.'

It was meant to be a joke but, for some reason, it makes my eyes prickle with tears.

'What age are your kids?'

'Ellen's coming up twenty and Bobby's just turned eighteen.'

'You don't look old enough to have kids that age.'

More blushing.

'I bet they're really proud of you.'

How can I tell Blake that they probably couldn't care less? That ambition and adventure are words that aren't in their vocabulary? That the only thing they're bothered about is spending all their money on booze at the weekends?

'They're thrilled,' I lie.

'And your husband?'

Ah. Can't even force a lie about that one. 'Less so.' I hang my head.

'Then it's even more brave that you've decided to go without his support. That's tough.'

My throat has closed. 'Yes.'

Blake fixes me with his baby-blue eyes and a smile curls his lips. 'Well, I think you're a very feisty woman, Annie Ashton.'

My heart bangs in my chest again even though I'm not exercising and it's not just because Blake Chadwick has actually remembered my name.

Chapter Thirty-Six

It was after eleven o'clock at night when the intercom buzzer at Lauren's flat sounded. Most people, she thought, would be worried by that, someone calling so late. For Lauren, it sent a bolt of anticipation through her.

'It's me.' Jude's voice sounded urgent. 'Can I come up?'

He had a key, of course, but mostly, out of courtesy, he didn't use it.

She buzzed him in and seconds later was in his arms. His hands roved over her body as he kissed her deeply.

'I can't stay long,' he whispered into her hair. 'I've just popped out to get some petrol.'

Instantly, Lauren felt herself deflate. There'd been no chance for them to speak in the office at all today and the rash of emails she'd sent to Jude had gone unanswered. Now it was going to be just a few snatched moments when she always, always yearned for more.

She'd given up any thoughts of seeing Jude at about nine o'clock that evening and had settled for a long bath and a night watching television instead. Lauren pulled her dressing-gown around her, aware that it was past its best.

'How's Benjy?' she asked.

'Better,' Jude said, with a look of relief on his face. 'You understand, I had to come back the other day. I couldn't stay away when my son was ill.'

'Of course,' Lauren said, but it came out more crisply than she would have liked.

'I said I'd make it up to you,' her lover continued, 'so I've booked a hotel for this weekend. Gorgeous place. Just you, me, long romantic walks and lazy hours in bed.'

'Oh, Jude.' He held her to him again. But somewhere, in the back of her brain, there was a nagging thought. What if she'd been busy this weekend? What if she'd decided to do something else for once?

'It's down in Bath.' Jude was animated now. 'I know you love it there.'

She swallowed hard. 'I've never been before.'

'Oh.'

Sometimes he got her likes and dislikes mixed up with those of his wife.

'Well, you *will* love it,' he said, recovering his composure quickly. 'Bath's a wonderful city, and the hotel has a great spa.'

Despite her joy, Lauren wondered who he'd been there with in the past. It didn't take much imagination to work it out.

'I'll have to meet you there,' Jude said. 'But I should arrive by lunchtime.'

'Can't we go together?'

He tsked. 'No can do.'

Lauren remembered now – Georgia's mother lived down that way. Was Jude taking his wife and children to see their in-laws on the way to visit his mistress? She knew that his whole relationship with her was based on lies, half-truths and manipulations, but that somehow seemed too cold, too calculating.

'Are you happy, darling?'

She nodded, pushing away any doubts, any fears.

'Two whole days together. Though I'll have to leave after lunch on Sunday.'

That wasn't two whole days, she thought, it was barely twenty-four hours.

'What am I this time?' she asked. 'An urgent business meeting or a conference?'

Jude looked taken aback.

And even Lauren was surprised at how bitter she sounded.

Chapter Thirty-Seven

Greg and I are having dinner. At home. On our own. Goodness knows where Ellen and Bobby are. As their parents we're not privy to such vital information. I used to insist on knowing their every movement, but I gave up when they both turned eighteen and I realised that they'd rather I didn't know where they were. The mood at the table is sombre and, without the kids here, there's nothing to distract us.

I've been running twice more this week with Blake Chadwick and my complaining muscles are currently struggling to keep me upright. My calves feel like they've got two tennis balls forced inside them.

Tonight, I've made us chilli con carne. Greg hates chilli, yet is forcing it down without complaint. He's not even picking out the kidney beans like he normally does. The silence is stretching between us and I realise that we've turned into one of those couples you see in restaurants who never speak a word to each other throughout their dinner.

My husband clears his throat and takes a sip of his water.

I'm now feeling bad that I've made the chilli so hot.

'Is Lauren coming up tomorrow?' he asks, his voice gruff.

'No. She's having a weekend away.' I don't add that it's with Jude although it's implicit in the statement. Greg doesn't agree with her relationship with a married man. As well as an old-fashioned view of most things in the world, he has old-fashioned morals too.

'Thought we could do the same. The two of us. Together.' He looks embarrassed by the thought. My heart twists. I should have done boiled potatoes. 'Last time was a bit of a disaster,' he adds sheepishly.

Hit the nail on the head there. 'It was my fault as much as yours,' I say. We give each other tentative smiles and, I guess that's as near as we're ever going to get to apologising to each other.

'The weather forecast is good,' Greg continues.

'That would be lovely. Where to?'

If he says Cromer, I'll scream.

'It's a surprise,' he says, and concentrates on his chilli.

Greg doesn't do surprises. Not in twenty years of marriage have I ever been swept off my feet by him or whisked away to an exotic destination. He's never even turned up with a bunch of flowers from the local petrol station – and most men manage that at least once in a lifetime.

'A surprise?'

He nods. 'Yeah.'

That *is* a surprise.

So that's why I'm up early and in the car before seven o'clock on a Saturday morning. I was going to go running with Blake this morning and that gives me a flutter of guilt. Maybe I should call him or text him. I have his number for work purposes. It was only a loose arrangement, but I don't like letting people down. What should I do?

'Ready?' my husband asks.

'Yes.' And I let my mobile phone fall into my handbag and try not to think of Blake Chadwick waiting for me.

Chapter Thirty-Eight

By lunchtime we're in the Lake District. The sky is an unbroken blue. The sun is working overtime to reach Mediterranean proportions. There is no sign of the low-slung, penetrating rain for which this area is so famous.

Greg and I wind our way through narrow roads of ever-decreasing size, squeezing through the drystone walls that line either side until we eventually reach the gravel car park at Wasdale Head, a deep valley nestling at the foot of Scafell Pike. We climb out and gaze up at the peak's dark, immense contours.

Scafell Pike is the highest mountain in England. It's still so remote and difficult to access that it has managed to escape the worst excesses of the Lakes tourism. You'll not find coachloads of Japanese tourists here with the very latest in digital-camera technology clicking away. Today, there is just a scattering of cars parked up and it feels like we have the place pretty much to ourselves.

'Walking boots are in the back,' Greg says.

Our rucksacks are in there too and both have sandwiches in them. Looks like my husband has thought of everything.

It's years since we did anything like this. Once upon a time we used to enjoy going out hiking together – short four- or five-mile circuits in the soft, rolling countryside of Buckinghamshire – but we've never done any serious hillwalking. In front of me, Scafell Pike looms mountainous and challenging. This is a relatively small lump of rock compared to the towering slopes of the Andes and already I'm looking at it and thinking, I'll never get up there. The guidebook tells me that the ascent is nearly 1,000 metres and, to me, that sounds like no mean feat.

In the car park we change into our hiking gear. I'm amazed that my boots still fit me as they only get an outing now once a year on our rare days of snow at home. Greg must have had to venture into the depths of the loft to dig the rucksacks out, too. They were probably behind the cot the kids used to sleep in that I can't bear to part with, and the Christmas decorations which needed binning years ago.

'This is a really great idea,' I say. 'Thank you.'

The valley is also home to the deepest lake in England – Wast Water – and the scree-slopes climb steeply from its edges, mirrored perfectly in the still surface of this three-mile stretch of water.

Greg takes my hand and we set off at a steady pace, walking up through the fields, across trickling brooks, scattering skittish sheep as we go. As we start to climb higher, the peaty waters of Wast Water shimmer below us in the midday sunshine. Even this bit's steeper than it looks. As a novice, my breathing's already hard and laboured, but I'm determined to do this. This has to be fabulous training for the Andes and I'm really grateful to Greg for bringing me up here.

'All right?' he asks.

I nod in lieu of speaking and we continue higher. Even my husband is panting now. The rough stone path steepens and we climb in silence, only the sound of our breathing disturbing the air. The crystal-clear waters of Lingmell Gill cascade alongside the rocky trail. We splash across the gill and climb steadily up Brown Tongue. Ahead we can see the towering peaks of Pikes Crag and Scafell Crag, joined by the impressive col ridge of Mickledore.

We pause and look down the valley. My lungs are crying out for release and I think that if I slipped now, then surely I would slither all the way down to the bottomless pit of Wast Water with nothing to stop my fall.

We press on to the summit. My thighs are burning with the exertion and we reach a steep gully known as Lord's Rake. The rough scree grabs at my feet, making them slip and slide as we scramble slowly upwards. From the top we stop to catch our breath. Mine is hot and ragged in my chest. The view from here is stupendous. The mighty Wast Water looks like nothing more threatening than a large blue puddle.

The terrain is rough and boulder-strewn now, and the clouds come down to meet us, but I feel a spring in my step as I can see that we've nearly reached our goal.

When we finally ascend to the pinnacle of the peak my soul soars and I feel as if I can see the whole world from here. The rocky crags and the soft, verdant curves of the Lake District are spread out before us – and the beauty of it brings a tear to my eye.

I hug Greg fiercely. 'Thank you,' I say. 'Thank you so much.'

We're both flushed, unaccustomed as we are to such exercise and I haven't felt this alive in years. The blood is zinging in my veins and, although I could do with a lung transplant and my poor muscles are wondering quite what's hit them, I'm feeling fan-flipping-tastic!

I throw my arms wide and breathe in the sharp air. 'Imagine what the Andes will be like compared to this. I can't wait!'

Looking at my husband, I see that his face has darkened. My arms drop to my sides.

'What?'

'I hoped,' Greg says tightly, 'that by showing you *this* –' he makes an angry little dismissive wave at the stunning landscape of the Lake District – 'you'd realise that you can have adventure in this country. There's no need to pursue some harebrained scheme to go to the other side of the world with kids half your age to prove yourself.'

I'm open-mouthed. 'Is that what this is about?' I say when I eventually regain the power of speech. 'To try and show me that I'm an idiot to dream?'

Greg, jaw set, stares out from the summit.

'I thought you'd done it to help with my training,' I tell him. 'To encourage me.'

'You don't seem to need any encouragement,' he spits out. My husband looks hurt, confused and more than a little angry. 'It's quite obvious you've got your mind set on it.'

'I have,' I say. 'I'm going to Peru. I'm going to do the Inca Trail. I'd like it even better if it was something we could do together. But it's quite obvious that *you've* got your mind set on remaining a boring old fart for the rest of your life.'

'Go,' Greg says. 'Go on your own.'

Hands on hips. 'I will.'

My husband shakes his head sadly. 'I don't know what's got into you recently, Annie. But I don't understand it.'

And, with that, he stomps off down the mountain, leaving me behind.

I sit, stunned, and pull out my sandwiches. I'm aghast at Greg's reaction – as he clearly is at mine. All I want to do is go on a small adventure. I'm not declaring that I intend to sail the world single-handedly. I've not announced a major lifestyle upheaval such as moving a long-term toy-boy lover into the marital home. I haven't suddenly broken the news that I'm carrying George Clooney's love-child.

I want to go to Peru. For charity. I'd love Greg to want to come with me. Is that really too much to ask?

My stomach is in knots and the last thing I want to do is eat, but I force my sarnies down really, really slowly, chewing and chewing each bite, and even though they taste like sawdust in my mouth, I make them last a really long time.

Chapter Thirty-Nine

I stomp down the mountain. I fall into a brook on the way. I get back into the car. Hours later. Soaking wet. Greg starts the engine. We sleep back-to-back in the lumpy bed in the Mountain View Guest House. Which is equally bad, if not worse, than Mrs Emerson's Clifftop Guest House. The sexy lingerie has already been returned to the sexy lingerie emporium, so no worries on that front.

We drive home in silence.

Chapter Forty

Lauren drove down to Bath with the wind beneath her wheels. As much as she wanted to feel cool towards Jude, to punish him for being married, for being only available to her on a part-time basis and entirely on his terms, her heart had other ideas.

The hotel, as he'd promised, was magnificent. Set high on one of the hills above the centre of the city, it was a grand Georgian mansion of mellow stone and splendid proportions. A quintessentially English destination for lovers. Another marvellous addition to the dirty weekends diary.

Jude hadn't yet arrived. For once, it would have been nice if he'd been waiting here to meet her, if she was the one running into his arms. Still, he'd be here soon enough and then the loving and the laughing could start.

At this hotel, they even had their own appointed butler dressed in black tails and striped trousers. Lauren was shown to their suite by him. Jude had surpassed himself. Champagne was already waiting on ice.

The rooms were elegant, traditional. They were decorated in a tastefully understated way – cream walls and bedlinen, silvery green and burgundy soft furnishings. Lauren could have written the definitive guide to hotel rooms, since she'd seen the inside of so many during her relationship with her boss.

This time she wouldn't get the saucy lingerie out until

later. It wouldn't do to tempt fate. Maybe they'd walk into Bath, have lunch there. Take a look at some of the sights. With the day stretching ahead of them they could afford not to rush straight to bed as they usually did.

She sat in the living room of the suite, flicked through a magazine – *Country Living*. The property on offer for the discerning and loaded purchaser was mouthwatering. Perhaps when Jude left his wife they could move somewhere like this. A nice barn conversion or restored Georgian manor house with five or six bedrooms on the outskirts of the city would suit just fine. It wasn't absolutely essential for the offices of *Happening Today* to be tied to London. They'd need to have easy access to his children for when they came to stay for weekends, of course, but there was no real reason for them to be there every day. They could look to live in the country. Somewhere not too far away from Annie either. Lauren smiled. She could quite see herself as the Lady of the Manor – finally give their sister Chelsea a run for her money.

Lauren glanced at her watch. Lunchtime. She hadn't been able to eat breakfast for excitement, but now she was more than peckish.

Jude, she thought, should have been here by now. Time was getting on. She'd been on the internet this week to have a look at some of the touristy things they might do. It was always wonderful to be able to walk through the streets, the parks, wherever, arm-in-arm and not be forever dreading that they might bump into someone that Jude knew.

The magazine she was flicking through was starting to lose its thrall. Should she text him? He always hated her doing that in case Georgia was by his side and, at the moment, there was every chance that they were driving down here together. Her stomach growled. Lauren didn't want to start lunch without him. That would be rude. And if she went out for a walk, then the moment she left the room, Jude was bound to turn up. Didn't it always happen like that? She drummed her fingers on the arm of the sofa. Maybe she should have brought a book with her, but Lauren hadn't imagined that there would be much time for reading this weekend.

Channel-surfing the television produced no joy. In the end, she cracked and texted Jude. *Where r u?*

Then she paced the room. The view from the full-length Georgian windows was wonderful. It looked really warm out there. Perhaps they could take an open-top bus tour round the city this afternoon. What was left of it. That would be fun. Or they could try the new rooftop spa today in case the weather turned colder tomorrow. Lauren just couldn't wait to get out and get at it.

Ten minutes passed. Then twenty. Maybe she should send the message again in case it had got lost in the ether somewhere. Just as she was about to try again, her phone beeped. She snatched it up and scanned the message.

An hour, it said. *Maybe more. J xx*

An hour. It was a ridiculous amount of time. Too short to take a swim in the health spa or to walk into the city. Too long to sit here twiddling her thumbs. She would normally have phoned Annie but – miracle upon miracle – her sister's stuck-in-the-mud husband had decided to take her away again on a whim. The second time this century.

Far be it for her to interrupt her sister's romantic interlude to moan about her own. Besides, what if she was busy chatting on the phone and Jude was trying to get through?

There was nothing for it. She opened the champagne, kicked off her shoes and put her feet up. Surfing through the channels on the television again, she settled on a programme called *Animal Park* which seemed marginally less dull than *Live Snooker*.

A rare deer had just got its antlers stuck in the perimeter fence of its compound and Lauren was beginning to feel very anxious about how its keepers would release the poor thing, when her phone beeped again. Her heart leaped at the sound. That surely would be Jude letting her know that he was about to arrive? Lauren switched off the television and laughed to herself. It would be just like him to be standing outside the door.

She threw open the door to the suite. Just in case. But he wasn't there. Then she saw that the text message read: *Can't make it. Forgive me. J xx*

Chapter Forty-One

Lauren drank too much – she knew she did. But it stopped the pain. Well, mostly. She was curled up on the bed, mascara tracks down her face. One bottle of champagne had been drained and she was about to call the butler to ask him to bring her another.

There was no way she could drive home now, she was too far gone. Besides, Jude had paid for this extravagance for the weekend, so why shouldn't she enjoy it? If only she could stop crying, then she was sure that she would.

His family won all the time. Whenever it was her versus them, they won. She was the one who was always left alone. She was the one who suffered. They didn't even know that she existed.

Her fingers played over the keys of her phone. She wanted to call him. She wanted to rant and rave and cry and beg for him not to leave her here alone. This should have been their weekend together. This should have been him making up for a thousand small hurts. Where was he? Why did he care so little for her feelings?

She shouldn't call Jude – she knew she shouldn't. But it was tempting, so tempting. Instead, she called Annie. She was desperate. Annie would understand. Her dear, dear sister always did. But Annie's phone went straight to voicemail and, dismayed, Lauren hung up. She cried on her pillow some more.

Chelsea would never understand her pain. Her elder sister disapproved of her relationship with a married man. She never came out and said as much, but Lauren could always sense it. Perhaps it was because her sister secretly worried that one day her little life might be turned upside down by another woman. In her perfect world, perhaps Chelsea preferred to pretend that these things didn't exist. Anyway, she'd be out and about on a Saturday doing important things to make the wheels of her family's life turn smoothly.

Then, before she realised what she was doing, she'd pressed Zak's number. A second later, he answered.

She sniffed her tears away. 'Hi.'

'Ooo,' he said. 'Someone doesn't sound too good.'

'No.' More sniffing.

'Are you hurt?' His voice was concerned now.

'Yes,' she said. 'I'm in the world's swankiest hotel in Bath all alone. And I shouldn't be.'

'Ah,' Zak said. 'A no-show from Jude?'

Lauren nodded even though she was on the phone.

'Oh, Lauren,' her friend sighed. 'What are we going to do with you?'

'I don't know.'

'Where is the main man?'

'I don't know that either,' she admitted. 'Not with me. With his family.'

'Come on,' Zak said. 'You have to be strong. Dry those eyes.'

She pulled a tissue out of the box next to her and blew her nose into it.

'Don't sit there by yourself,' her friend advised. 'Take

yourself out, see the city. Pick up a hot guy, take him back to your hotel and shag him senseless at Jude's expense.'

Despite her tears, she laughed at that. 'If only it were so easy.'

'Actually, that's a really bad idea. You should scratch that last suggestion.'

'I have a bit of a downer on hot guys at the moment,' she reassured him.

'You sound as if you've been hitting the bottle.'

'Just a little champagne,' Lauren said. But she might have slurred. 'I'll stay here. Entertain myself.'

'Now that sounds *too* kinky.'

Lauren laughed again. 'Now I know why I phoned you.'

'I'm glad you did,' Zak said.

'I'll be okay.' Lauren put on her bravest voice. 'I'm cool.'

'You are a *very* cool lady, Ms Osbourne. Don't ever forget that.'

'Thanks, Zak,' she said. 'You're a good friend.'

'Don't ever forget that either,' said Zak, and then he hung up.

Now, for some reason, she felt even more lonely than ever. Lauren curled up into herself and cried and cried and cried until the tasteful cream linen was black with her tears.

Chapter Forty-Two

In the end, Lauren had sent for another bottle of champagne. She couldn't face going out sightseeing or finding a hot man to shag as Zak had suggested. The butler might have been an outside possibility, if he hadn't been a slender boy of about twenty-six. But, as she'd said to Zak, finding a replacement man was the last thing on her mind.

She'd poured herself another glass or two, had languished in a long, hot bath, sobbing intermittently about the unfairness of falling in love with someone who belonged to someone else, and had let herself get all wrinkly. Then she'd tortured herself by putting on her sexy black underwear and the high heels especially brought for the purposes of seduction.

Lauren stood in front of the mirror and posed provocatively. Who wouldn't want to have sex with that? Did Jude realise what he was missing doing whatever he was, wherever he was with his wife? Georgia probably wore big, comfy pants and tights. She stared at her reflection. Look at her. She was hot. Hot and alone. As the tears flowed again, she wrapped herself in the fluffy bathrobe provided, lay on the bed and wished for sleep – even though it was only four o'clock.

Lauren hadn't yet returned Jude's text. What could she

say? That it was okay? That she didn't mind? She wasn't inclined to send a forgiving note. Instead, she hugged the phone to her chest and sobbed a bit more.

The next thing she knew, there was a soft rap at her door and Lauren woke with a start, not even realising that she'd dozed off. It would probably be the butler wanting to see if she needed her drink replenished. She'd long since given up hoping that Jude would still turn up unexpectedly.

Pulling her dressing-gown around her, Lauren went to the door. When she opened it, she smiled.

'I came to entertain you,' Zak said. He was holding out the board game *Scrabble*.

'Where on earth did you get that?'

'I'm a wicked master of the manipulated word,' her friend said. 'This has been gathering dust in my cupboard for too long.' He tapped the game's box. 'You're going to have to think of some tricky words to get them past me.'

'What are you doing here?'

'I was worried,' Zak said, leaning on the doorframe and fixing his puppy-dog eyes on her. 'I couldn't stand the thought of you being here alone.'

'You drove all the way down?'

He nodded. 'As soon as you hung up.' Then, lowering his voice, he said, 'Jude didn't turn up, did he? I'm not interrupting anything?'

Lauren held open the door to the suite. 'Nobody home but me.'

Zak came into the room and glanced around appraisingly. 'Very flash.'

'And too big for one.'

'We could go out for dinner. The night is young. So are we. Allegedly.'

'I can't face putting the war paint on.' Or leaving this room ever again, Lauren thought.

'I assumed you wouldn't want to go out,' her friend said. 'I have extensive experience of love-lorn women. Therefore, as well as a fiendishly distracting board game, I have brought along a selection of rubbish girly DVDs for your delectation too.' He opened the man bag that was slung over his shoulder and from the inside pocket pulled the promised bunch of DVDs. Slapping them down on top of the nearest coffee-table, he reeled off the titles. '*27 Dresses*, *Sweet Home Alabama*, *Enchanted*, *Sleepless in Seattle* – bet you can't get through that one without crying – *Bridget Jones's Diary*, *Pride and Prejudice*, and, last, but certainly by no means least, the inimitable *Mamma Mia*!'

'They're all pretty rubbishy,' Lauren concluded. 'Perfect viewing.'

Zak scooped up the DVDs and tossed them on to the bed. 'You can't beat a bit of Colin Firth or Tom Hanks for a broken heart.'

'You have a point there. *Sleepless in Seattle* is, indeed, my favourite film. And I *will* need the Kleenex to hand.'

'Wonderful.' Zak pointed at the champagne. 'You can pour me a glass of that and we can begin our evening's entertainment in earnest.'

Lauren touched his arm. 'Thanks,' she said. 'I warn you though, I might be rotten company.'

'You always are,' he told her brightly, as he stripped off

his jacket. 'That's why I like you. The more miserable you are, the more fun I seem.'

And Lauren couldn't help but laugh at that.

Chapter Forty-Three

Grabbing another glass, Lauren curled up on the bed and poured out more champagne. She kicked off the fuck-me shoes, pulled the dressing-gown around her and tucked her legs under her. Zak tugged off his Converse trainers and tossed them to the floor. He sat sprawled out in front of her.

'You look very drunk,' Zak noted.

'I am,' she admitted.

'I bet you haven't eaten either.'

'Not a thing.'

'Then may I select something for you from the room service menu, madam?'

'I don't—'

Zak held up a hand. 'I'm going to stuff my face at your boyfriend's expense and I suggest you do the same thing.'

'I have a butler,' Lauren giggled.

'Then let's force him to bring us burgers and fries.' She rang the bell and, sure enough, the butler appeared to take their order.

When he'd gone, Zak spread out the films on the bed. 'Close your eyes and pick one.'

She did.

'*Enchanted*. Oh, yes. A fine choice. Particularly cheesy, Ms Osbourne.'

He slotted it into the DVD player and then set up the

Scrabble on the bed, climbing on so that the board was between them. 'Have you played this before?'

'Not for years.'

'It's like riding a bike – the minute you get back on, you remember how to do it.'

'I never had a bike.'

'Now you're being pedantic,' he warned and Lauren giggled.

Zak rolled up his shirt-sleeves and flexed his fingers and did some neck circles. 'Ready?'

Lauren nodded. She waggled her fingers at him. 'Bring. It. On.'

They selected their letters. Seven each. 'Ladies first,' Zak said graciously and Lauren took the opening turn.

She slapped her letters down on the board, enthusiastically.

'S.H.I.T.B.A.G.' Zak raised an eyebrow. 'An interesting opening gambit.' He studied her word. 'I don't mean to be a stickler but the words are supposed to come from the Oxford English Dictionary. I don't think you'll find S.H.I.T.B.A.G. in there.'

'S.H.I.T.B.A.G.' Lauren pointed at the board. 'Lots of points.'

'I see,' Zak said. 'We're going to play dirty *Scrabble*.'

He countered with S.E.X.Y.

'Pathetic.'

'Eight points for the X alone, I think you'll find.' He cracked his knuckles.

The butler brought cheeseburgers and chips and they ate them from the tray he put between them. Lauren couldn't remember the last time she'd had chips or had enjoyed them so much. She dipped each one in ketchup.

Lots of it. Between chips, she clinked her letters down on the board.

'B.A.S.T.A.R?' Zak queried. 'That's definitely not a word.'

'You get my drift.'

'I put it down to you being inordinately drunk and will let you have the points anyway.'

'It's not easy being one D short of a bastard,' she said, and laughed uproariously. *Enchanted* played away in the background. It was at the point where the fairytale princess landed up in New York in the hands of a cynical lawyer. It was a beautiful, optimistic film in a harsh world. And, of course, Giselle finds her handsome prince in the most unlikely of men. Lauren sniffed away a tear.

'Don't cry,' Zak instructed sternly. 'It's nowhere near the sad bit. Concentrate on the game.'

Lauren helped herself to a tissue and focused on the *Scrabble* board.

Her friend tried A.D.O.R.E.D.

'Hmm,' Lauren said. 'Lame.'

'Sixteen points. Double word score,' he shrugged.

Lauren slapped down B.I.T.C.H.

'You're technically not allowed to put that there.'

Lauren shot him a look. 'Why?'

'Your pieces are butted up against another word, rendering it nonsensical.'

Lauren folded her arms and stared him down.

Zak held up his hands in surrender. 'But I'm not arguing with you in your current state of mind.'

'Good move.'

'Want to tell me who we're talking about?'

'No one,' she insisted, feigning innocence. 'I wanted to make C.A.R.D.I.G.A.N. but I didn't have enough letters.' Then she picked up the champagne bottle again.

'Are you sure you want more?' he asked.

'Just a little.'

When they'd finished the bottle and were all Scrabbled out, they leaned back on the pillows and watched the end of *Enchanted* and Lauren cried again when the fairytale princess ended up with the uptight, pinstriped city slicker who was really a softie, because in real life no one really ended up with who they should be with.

It was getting dark outside now and they watched *Sleepless in Seattle* because it had to be done. She had a little cry again because it was so sad and Tom Hanks had been the cutest person alive at that time and Zak dabbed tenderly at her cheeks with a tissue.

Lauren rested her head on his shoulder and her eyes started to roll with tiredness and she snuggled down on the bed next to him.

It felt nice having Zak here with her. More than nice. She let her hand wander to his chest. The heat of it made her mouth go dry. Her dressing-gown fell open and she made no move to cover herself.

'I have to assume that's not the sort of underwear that you put on every day, Ms Lauren Osbourne, otherwise I'm never going to be able to look at you in the same way again.'

'What if I said it was?'

'Then I'd be lost.'

'There are worse things to be,' she murmured, her mouth against his neck.

Zak sat up abruptly. He swept the *Scrabble* letters from the board at their feet and then started to rearrange them. A moment later, he held it up to her. C.O.L.D.S.H.O.W.E.R. it said.

'That's what I'll need, if we go any further,' he told her.

'Double-word score and it goes over the middle star thingy,' she informed him. 'I reckon that gives you forty points.'

'Whooping your arse at *Scrabble* is no longer my major consideration.'

'Zak.' Her voice faltered. 'We could spend the night together.'

He shook his head. 'You're with Jude.'

She held out her hands. 'Not that you'd notice.'

'You know what I mean, Lauren. Two wrongs don't make a right. There's nothing I'd like more than to spend the night with you. But you've had a lot to drink, you're with another man and you might well regret this in the morning. I'm happy to *Scrabble* you within an inch of your life but that's as far as it goes. I'll stay here tonight if you want me to. I'll curl up on that rather comfortable-looking sofa over there.'

Lauren ran her fingers down his chest. 'Sure?'

'If you hear the shower running in the night then you know that I'm having second thoughts,' he said with a laugh.

'You spend a lot of time on sofas on my behalf,' she reminded him.

'You're worth it.' Then he stood up and briskly moved the food tray and the *Scrabble* from the bed. 'Settle down,' he said. 'I'll tuck you in.'

When she was snuggled between the mascara-stained sheets, Zak kissed her softly on the lips. His mouth was warm on hers, soothing, and she didn't want it to stop there.

Lauren watched Zak pottering round the room for a few minutes, then he lay down on the sofa and pulled the throw from the bed over him. Lauren realised that she hadn't thought of Jude for hours.

'Goodnight, Ms Osbourne,' he said.

'Goodnight, Mr Reynolds.' She blew him a kiss.

Zak put his hands behind his head and stared at the ceiling. Lauren pretended to go to sleep, but she didn't. Watching him in the dark made her smile.

Chapter Forty-Four

'I missed you on Saturday morning, Sexy,' Blake Chadwick tells me when he swings into the office on Monday morning.

The colour floods to my cheeks as it always does when he talks to me. 'I'm sorry.'

Blake shrugs. 'No worries.'

'My husband took me away for the weekend,' I tell him. I don't mention that it was an utter disaster on every level.

'Nice.'

It wasn't. But I don't say this either.

'I hiked up Scafell Pike.'

BC's eyebrows rise. 'I'm impressed.'

What I also don't tell him is that none of my muscles will now move. My thighs scream in protest with every step I take, my knees throb with pain and my shins feel like I've been kicked in them by a particularly bad-tempered donkey. Even my neck hurts from unaccustomed rucksack carrying. This does not bode well for scampering up the Andes like the proverbial mountain goat.

I had to hobble in here like an old lady and, frankly, I have no intention of putting one foot in front of the other any more than I possibly need to today. I'm even going to cut down on my caffeine intake to ensure that I minimise my trips to the loo as that would involve walking to the other side of reception.

'Coming running with us again tonight?' Blake asks.

'I think I'll give it a miss,' I say. 'I'm meeting my sister for a coffee this evening and I need to get straight back.'

'Wednesday then?'

I nod. 'Wednesday.' Two days away. Hopefully, I'll be able to walk by then, maybe even run.

'Catch you later,' BC says, and waves as he heads to his office.

Sighing to myself, I log on to the computer to check today's diary.

Greg still isn't really speaking to me and I feel very unsettled. There was a lot of banging around in the kitchen this morning as we both made our respective sandwiches. We've never been like this before in all our years of married life. But then there's never really been a time when we've been pulling in opposite directions. Any adversity that we have faced – and it usually centred round the kids or money – has made us grow closer together to work through it. I'm not sure why he feels so threatened about me going off to Peru or why he won't sit down and talk to me about it. But there you have it. He won't.

I felt such joy, such liberation on top of Scafell Pike that I don't know why it's not something that we've done as a couple before. If we'd got on better we could be making regular trips to the Lakes or the Peak District, hiking boots in hand – or on feet. You know what I mean.

Then Minny totters in and breaks my train of thought. 'I've come back to work for a rest,' she declares. 'I've never done so much damn exercise.' My colleague leans on my desk. 'How's the fundraising going?'

'I haven't done much yet. You?'

'I've just press-ganged all of my Facebook mates. I'm pretty much there.'

I don't have any Facebook mates to press-gang.

'Mum and Dad will give me the rest.'

Ah, good old Bank of Mum and Dad.

'Coming running tonight?'

'Can't,' I say. 'Things to do.'

'See you at lunch then,' she says and totters off.

Then I pick up the phone and call Chelsea and invite her to meet me and Lauren for coffee tonight. She sounds delighted and I feel mean for not having contacted her before and even meaner for having an ulterior motive for wanting my big sister to be there.

When I hang up, I pull my travel guide of Peru out of my handbag and immerse myself in it, gazing at the pictures of the walnut-brown women who live a life that's a world away from mine with their black plaits, their bowler hats and their pipes, and dreaming of when I can visit places like Tambomachay, Puca Pucara, Salapunco, Qenko, Ollantaytambo. I won't think of Greg or how difficult he's being. I'll only think of what a great adventure this will be.

Chapter Forty-Five

To show that he wasn't boring, that he could be flexible, exciting even, Greg had borrowed one of Ray's top of the range, ultra-light poles today to fish with. The sixteen-metre pole weighed next to nothing and was probably worth about two grand, maybe more. It felt strange, uncomfortable in his hands. He liked what he liked, as Ray said. And he liked his own rod. He knew the feel of it. With his own rod there were no surprises. He didn't know what to expect with this one. However, he was prepared to give it a go.

They were still fishing in the same spot that they always went to – it didn't do to change too many things all at once.

He'd been sitting, deep in thought, without a bite for half an hour now.

Carp were tricky fish to catch. You had to be wily. They were smarter than your average fish. Carp learn by their mistakes. Once they'd been caught by one type of bait, they wouldn't go for it again. So you had to think of different ways to keep them keen.

He was thinking that if Annie were a fish, she'd be a carp.

'How did the trip to the Lakes go?' his friend enquired as he slipped the hook from the two-pound perch he'd just landed.

It had been Ray's idea to take Annie hiking in the Lake District. The idea was that it would be a three-pronged attack. Annie would be impressed that Greg wanted to go somewhere other than Norfolk – and, specifically, Cromer – she would see that there was wonderful walking and adventure to be had in this country, something that he would be happy to do with her and, most importantly of all, would realise that she wasn't capable of going to the Andes and would give up this whole, harebrained idea.

It had seemed like a grand plan at the time.

And, for a brief moment, it had looked as if it might work. As they'd summitted Scafell Pike, all was harmonious in the world. Then Annie had taken umbrage at something, some misplaced word or sentiment, and hadn't appreciated the entirety of the scheme or its subtle nuances. He frowned. Or maybe she had? Whichever way, it had all been, literally, downhill from that moment.

'Not well,' Greg told his friend.

He pulled the pole in to allow a woman walking her dog to pass by on the path. The constant hauling in and out drove Ray mad, but it was part of the deal with this kind of fishing and Greg viewed it as a kind of meditation in itself.

While Greg had the rod in, he changed the bait on the end of the hook before he let the pole out again.

There was something to be said for using a pole which could stretch over the width of the canal and tantalise the fish hiding in the weeds on the far bank. When you used a float it was buffeted about by the wind, by the movement of the water, by canal barges passing by – but with a pole you could be more accurate, less affected by outside influence. With a rod you needed to play the fish, to tire it out. With a pole, the elastic fitting on it did the job for you. Did that take the skill out of it? he wondered. There were infinite possibilities and permutations to fishing. No day was the same. Each time you dipped your hook into the water, you never knew what would be on the end – if anything. The anticipation of it was what kept him coming back for more. How anyone could ever think that fishing was dull was beyond him.

'She's still thinking of going to Peru?' Ray asked.

'Definitely.' Why couldn't Annie want to do something that didn't take her so far away from home? Why couldn't she have wanted to run the London Marathon or something? The usual things that people did for charity. Why couldn't she do something that he could go along with? They'd enjoyed tackling Scafell Pike together – at least, the going-up bit. To be honest, he was surprised at how much she'd enjoyed it. Would the old Annie have been interested in Lakeland walking if he'd suggested it? Why couldn't the new Annie be happy doing something like that?

Ray tsked. 'You're going to have to slap that down, matey.'

Greg didn't think that he could. He didn't think that he wanted to either, not really. It was just that she frightened him, this new Annie who'd become headstrong, determined, focused – and very fed up with him.

Chapter Forty-Six

Lauren and Zak decided not to tell Jude what had happened. Not that anything did happen. Not really.

When Zak had woken, they'd had a lovely breakfast together in the hotel restaurant and then they'd gone out in the sunshine of Bath for the day. That was all.

Lauren had got her trip on an open-top tourist bus, then they'd gone to the Roman Baths together and, finally, they'd visited the new rooftop spa and had a lovely long soak, luxuriating in the warm, restorative waters. She had missed a text from Jude while they'd been bathing telling her that he loved her and, strangely, it hadn't made her stomach churn to have been unavailable to reply immediately.

She and Zak didn't hold hands, there were no lingering looks over the cappuccinos they'd enjoyed, nothing like that. Still, it was cosy, friendly and a lot of fun. Then they'd driven home, separately, after a chaste kiss. And Lauren didn't want to share that with Jude.

In fact, she wanted him to believe that she'd had a thoroughly miserable time by herself while he was busy being married and duty bound. Besides, it wasn't fair on Zak. She didn't want Jude to think that there was anything in it and possibly jeopardise Zak's career prospects at *Happening Today*.

On Monday morning, Lauren was deliberately late for work. She knew that Jude would be in early, looking for her, trying to snatch some time alone. It was a pattern she was well used to.

Defiantly, she kept herself busy and surrounded by other people all morning and she hadn't answered Jude's emails either. It was childish, but there was no doubt that it gave her a certain sense of satisfaction. Whenever she looked up, just to glance in Jude's direction, it seemed that Zak was looking at her.

She couldn't thank her friend enough for coming to her rescue this weekend, and the Sunday they'd spent together was, Lauren was sure, more relaxing than it would have been with her lover. Jude would have been constantly checking his phone and watching the clock, anxious not to miss his appointed departure slot.

At lunchtime, she'd dashed out to the sandwich shop on the corner and, just as she entered the door to join the queue, she'd felt a hand on her arm.

It was Jude and he was out of breath. 'I've been calling you,' he panted.

'Really?'

'You didn't hear?'

'No.' She hadn't. To be honest, Lauren had been back on that open-top bus in Bath with Zak.

Jude hung his head. 'I thought you were deliberately avoiding me.'

They joined the queue.

'Would you blame me if I was?' Lauren asked.

'Forgive me,' he said. 'I'll make it up to you. Anything. All you have to do is ask.'

'Leave your wife,' she said flatly. 'That would work for me.'

'I'm trying to,' Jude insisted. 'It's not that easy.'

'If you can't get away for a weekend, how are you going to leave for ever?'

'I have to choose my moment carefully,' Jude said. 'Georgia's very fragile.'

'You forget that I've met her,' Lauren reminded him. Fragile, Georgia was not.

Jude looked exasperated. 'I am putting things in place, Lauren. Please believe me. One day we *will* be together.'

'Don't leave it too long, Jude,' she warned. 'Or I may not be waiting.'

'Tonight,' he said. 'I'll come round tonight.' Then, lowering his voice, 'God, I want you.'

They'd reached the counter in the shop and Lauren browsed the menu. They ordered and Jude pulled out his wallet and paid.

'Before you put that away, you need to give me some money,' she said. 'My sister's doing the Inca Trail for charity and you're going to sponsor her.'

Jude peeled off a twenty.

'More.'

He gave her another.

'Several more.'

Her lover handed over all he had in his wallet.

'A hundred pounds – that's it? She needs two grand.'

'You've cleaned me out.'

Lauren tutted. He might be sorry, but clearly he wasn't *that* sorry.

The woman behind the counter handed her a brown bag with her sandwich in it.

She always had the same thing in here. Every day. Prawn mayonnaise on brown with salad. It was a habit. Yet there was a whole array of unusual and varied fillings to be had. It was a habit that she should break.

Maybe one day she'd surprise herself and have a complete change.

Chapter Forty-Seven

I arrive ten minutes early at the big Borders book-store in the city where I'm meeting my sisters, so I head straight to the travel section and South America in particular.

My mouth waters as I read about the exotic dishes I can hope to sample while I'm out there. Ceviche, chunks of fish marinated with lime juice, more than 1,000 different varieties of potato (good job we're doing a lot of walking to counteract that) roasted *cuy* or guinea pig – think I might give that one a miss – chillies, avocados and 100 different types of corn on the cob.

I'm on a sofa with a stash of books open by my side when, a few minutes later, Lauren swings in between the shelves. 'I knew I'd find you here,' she says.

'Just browsing.' I close the books and return them to their rightful place. We head up to the coffee shop and order. Then, having made myself hungry and with my tastebuds crying out to be tantalised, I get a blueberry muffin to go with my coffee. Admittedly, it's not that exotic, but it's the best that Starbucks can offer.

'Chelsea's coming along too,' I tell Lauren when we sit down.

'Noooo,' she complains. 'She'll arrive looking all beautiful and elegant and make me feel like a right old skank. Why didn't you tell me?'

'She's our sister. Be nice.'

Lauren looks down at her jeans. 'I'd have dressed up if I'd known.'

'Chelsea's not like that.'

'She is.'

'How was the weekend?' I ask as a distraction technique.

'Crap,' Lauren says. 'Well, sort of. Jude didn't turn up.'

'Oh, Lauren. Again?'

'I know. I know. I know.' She puffs out an unhappy breath. 'I ended up phoning Zak and he came down to Bath to hang out with me.' My sister tries to shrug off her disappointment, but I can see the pain in her eyes. 'All's well that ends well.'

'Why didn't you call me?'

'Of course, I called you. But you were up a mountain somewhere without a phone signal.'

I'd forgotten about that. Or maybe I'd just decided to blank it as an unpleasant experience. But then, it wasn't unpleasant – not the walking bit: I loved it. Only the falling-out-with-the-husband bit put a damper on it. 'You seem to be spending a lot of time with Zak.'

'He's cool,' Lauren says. 'A lot of fun.'

'And available?'

'Don't go there,' Lauren warns.

Then Chelsea arrives and I can't interrogate her any further. Oh, God. Lauren is right. Our big sister is looking beautiful and pristine and already my inadequacy levels are rising.

'Hello, girls,' she says, and then kisses us both on the cheek. Chelsea isn't an enthusiastic kisser. Her lips are cool, dry, and I bet she hasn't left a lipstick mark either.

Chelsea is wearing a baby-pink cashmere sweater and

179

black wool trousers and looks a million dollars. None of it, I know, will have come from George at Asda. The shoes, I suspect, are Prada, Jimmy Choo or something. The handbag is one of those oversize ones that celebrities use.

I pull out a chair for my big sister and generally fuss round her, earning myself a glare from Lauren in the process. My twin looks miserable. Taking Chelsea's order, I scuttle off to the counter and get it for her.

'One skinny latte,' I say, when I bring it back. What else?

Lauren – whom I've persuaded to eat – puts down her slab of Rocky Road and gives me another pointed and black look.

'It's great to see you both,' Chelsea says. 'We don't do this often enough. The three of us, I mean.' A tacit acknowledgement that Lauren and I get together more often without her.

'We should,' I gush. 'Now that you're back for a while. Is it nice to be in your own home again?'

'Yes.' Again, I'm sure I see a shadow cross her face. Then my sister sweeps back her luxuriant hair and smiles and I'm convinced that I imagined it.

'How's the boyfriend?' Chelsea asks.

'Great,' Lauren takes up the gushing. 'We've just had a fabulous weekend in Bath together.'

Chelsea's lips tighten almost imperceptibly. Lauren's eyes challenge me to spill the beans on her lie.

'Lovely,' Chelsea says and then turns to me. 'What have you been up to, Annie?'

I take a deep breath. This is my moment. 'I'm planning to trek the Inca Trail,' I announce. My sister's jaw hits the table. Just like my husband's did. I soldier on, regardless. 'In

180

aid of Dream Days. I need to raise two thousand pounds by September.' I don't mention the measly fifteen pounds I've cajoled out of my neighbours.

When she has recovered from the shock of her useless sister doing something useful, Chelsea claps her hands together in approval which makes me glow. 'Oh, Annie. That's wonderful!'

Strike while the iron's hot. I whip out my form. 'I was hoping that you might sponsor me.'

Behind our sister's back, Lauren winks.

'Of course. Of course.' Chelsea reaches into the depths of the voluminous handbag that's probably set her back over a thousand pounds. She pulls out a chequebook. Coutts account.

I sit feeling embarrassed as she fills in the cheque in her painstakingly immaculate script with her Mont Blanc pen. She won prizes for that writing at school. Lauren and I would make great GPs on the writing front. Chelsea signs with a flourish. It's only then that I notice that her nail varnish is chipped, her manicure long overdue. And that's not like my sister at all. Perhaps she's not had time with the party and moving back into her house in Woburn.

Then, folding the cheque, my sister hands it over. I take it gratefully.

'Thank you, Chelsea.' I feel quite teary. *Peru, here I come!* 'Thank you for helping make my dream come true.'

Lauren, behind Chelsea's back, sticks her finger down her throat and makes vomity mimes at me.

'Nonsense,' my sister says with a tinkling laugh. 'It's the very least I could do.'

'Let me get more coffee,' I say. 'My treat.'

So I scuttle up to the counter again.

As we sip our second cups, Chelsea tells us all about our niece and nephew. 'Their performing arts school has a performance on Saturday afternoon. You'd both be most welcome.'

We nod our heads enthusiastically, knowing that Chelsea will forget to tell us when and where, and that we probably wouldn't go anyway. I wish our children had been closer in ages, then perhaps they'd be closer as cousins. When Ellen and Bobby were young, Chelsea was jetting off all round the world and rarely saw them. Now I try to be a dedicated aunty when the children are in the country, but I always feel that I'm being looked down on by Chelsea's highfalutin friends when I turn up to their concerts or parties.

'Sophia has a ballet solo and Henry will be playing the violin and reciting poetry in French. In fact,' Chelsea glances at the Rolex watch her husband bought her last Christmas (I got a new frying pan from Greg), 'I'd better be going as Sophia wanted to go through her steps with me.'

Lauren and I stand to kiss our sister goodbye. We get the cheek treatment again. I want to hug her, kiss her, but Chelsea isn't that kind.

'Thanks, Chelsea,' I say. Teary once more. 'I really appreciate this.'

'Enjoy yourself,' my sister tells me. 'I'm sure it will be wonderful.'

Chelsea's idea of wonderful is a sunlounger on a white sand beach with cocktails on tap. The Kings went to Necker Island last year for their holiday.

'I can't wait.'

'We'll speak soon,' Chelsea says. And she glides away from us to her waiting top-of-the-range whatever.

We watch our sister leave. 'Yes, she is,' Lauren says.

'Is what?'

'Related to us.'

'I didn't say anything.'

'You were about to.'

Lauren's right.

My twin sighs. 'We are Dot Cotton and Pauline Fowler to her Krystle Carrington.'

And I'd like to disagree, but I can't. 'She's lovely,' I say defensively. 'We should be kinder to her. We always leave her out of things, and look what she's done for me.'

A tear slips through my lashes.

'For goodness' sake,' Lauren admonishes. 'Get a grip on yourself, Annie.' She snatches Chelsea's cheque from my fingers. 'She's bloody loaded and I want to see how much she's coughed.'

Then Lauren gasps. 'Oh, God.' She thrusts the cheque back at me.

I look at the number written on it. Then I double-check that I've got the amount of noughts right. I gasp too.

'A hundred pounds!' Lauren shrieks. 'Mrs Five Grand Watch gave you a hundred quid?'

A hundred pounds. The figures swim before my eyes.

'I thought she'd stump up the lot,' my sister says, aghast.

So did I, if I'm brutally honest.

'This is very generous.' I force the words out of dry lips.

'Is it hell,' Lauren says. 'I'm going after her. She's right. This *is* the very least she could do.'

'No.' I put a hand on Lauren's arm to hold her back. 'No. Chelsea's given me what she thought was right. It's very kind of her.'

183

'Pah,' from Lauren.

'The rest is down to me.'

Lauren flops in her chair. 'I got a hundred quid out of Jude today.' She pulls a bunch of notes out of her bag. 'I thought *that* was being miserly. Well, I still do.' My sister stares at me mystified as I try to fight back my tears. 'I thought Chelsea would come good.'

Me too. But I say nothing.

'I can bung in a hundred too,' Lauren says gently. She puts her arm round me and gives me a comforting hug. 'What does that give you?'

'Three hundred and fifteen pounds.' Not a huge tally. My heart sinks. 'That leaves me sixteen hundred and eighty-five pounds to raise myself.'

'Bugger.' Lauren puts her head in her hands.

'Bugger, indeed.'

But I will raise it. Come hell or high water. You just watch me.

Chapter Forty-Eight

A car-wash. A charity car-wash! This lightbulb moment comes to me while I'm puffing round Furzton Lake side-by-side with Blake Chadwick on Saturday morning. That's what I'll do to raise my cash.

I expressly forbade Lauren from phoning up and berating Chelsea about the meagre amount of her donation to my good cause. I think my twin thought that our elder sister would stump up whatever money I needed. In my heart, I can secretly confess that I did too. It looks like it's now going to be all down to my own efforts. Just when I was hoping for an easy ride.

The lake is quiet today. Only the overnight fishermen are up and about, pottering outside their bivouacs making tea, fussing with their fishing gear. Greg isn't here today – he doesn't often fish overnight now. He prefers to look the fish in the eye or some such – but I recognise a few of his mates. There's a wisp of mist in the air. The early chill disguises the fact that we're in for a bright, sunny day. I wonder why I haven't discovered the joys of early-morning running before. I've begun to really look forward to these sessions and am quietly proud of how much I've improved in such a short time. When I put on my trousers for work yesterday, I'll swear there was a bit more room around the waistband too.

My other co-workers have dropped out of the running circle more quickly. They try to make the evening sessions, but rarely appear at the weekends. When most of them are out on the tiles on a Friday night then perhaps it's a bit optimistic to expect them to be here first thing on a Saturday morning. Still, Blake's here, as always. No wonder he looks so fit.

I hate to say this, but my stomach knotted with something that felt suspiciously like excitement when I saw him waiting here for me in the car park this morning. Bad, bad feeling.

Greg turned over in bed as I tried to slip out quietly and I'm sure he was awake, but pretended to be asleep. If he wants to play that game then let him.

'You're quiet today, Annie,' Blake says as our steps pound the perimeter pavement together.

'Sorry. Deep in thought.' I must be getting fitter as I can now do running and speaking at the same time.

'Anything I can help with?'

'Just working out ways to increase my fundraising efforts.'

'I contacted all my old girlfriends,' Blake tells me. 'I told them I'd put all the compromising photographs I took of them on Facebook if they didn't cough up.' He laughs at that.

I think he's joking, so I laugh too.

Greg is due to go out fishing today, as usual, and I've got the day to myself. This is the time for action.

I could set out my car wash at home. Paint a bit of a sign to stand at the front gate. The road is quite a busy thoroughfare at the rush hour and weekends. Perhaps I could entice both my stingy neighbours and the passing traffic. Surely someone would be prepared to pay a fiver for a superb hand car wash in aid of charity? It's not yet eight o'clock so I've plenty of time to implement my plan, wash a couple of dozen cars and have everything packed away by the time my husband comes home.

The thought of it puts a spring in my step.

'Whoa,' BC says. 'What's got into you, woman? I'm having trouble keeping up with you this morning.'

I know that he's teasing me, but it makes me feel good anyway.

'Come on, slowcoach,' I shout at him as, from somewhere, I find a veritable sprint and leave him behind. Blake picks up his pace and drops in beside me again as we race past the trees, the houses, the ducks, a lightness in my spirit.

I am a resourceful, powerful woman and nothing can stop me now.

Chapter Forty-Nine

In the depths of the loft I find a massive piece of white cardboard that'll do just nicely. From the back of the kitchen drawer comes a black magic marker that's not too dried up.

CHARITY CAR WASH, I write in my biggest, boldest script. ONLY £5!

As I imagined, I have the house to myself. Greg has gone fishing. No note left. Once upon a time he would have left a little endearment scribbled on the Post-it notepad, but not now. Ellen works every Saturday and my son spends most of it at the pub squandering the meagre wages he's spent all week earning on Magners cider.

In the garage I find the bucket, some Halford's car shampoo, a sponge and a chamois leather. It's fair to say that my car-washing skills are a little rusty as that's normally Greg's job, but I'll soon get my hand in again.

I'll practise on my own car – a silver Corsa that's more than a few years old now – while I wait for my first customers to roll up. I dig out my old paint-spattered jeans and purloin one of Greg's tatty polo-shirts that he uses for decorating. Donning my flowery wellies, I head out into the drive and set my sign up by the gate.

Filling my bucket up with warm, soapy water. I then set about giving my little car a wash. It doesn't really need it as Greg did it during the week, but it might encourage business.

I put in some serious elbow grease so that passers-by can tell that I'm not just tickling the car. This isn't bad exercise too. It will certainly help with my Get Fit programme. I must remember to thank my husband more fervently in future when he does this for me. I realise with a pang that I do sometimes take him for granted.

When the car's all washed and clean, I take my time with the chamois leather, polishing off all the streaks so that it dries with a shine that's like glass. I stand back and admire my handiwork. Not a bad job even if I do say it myself.

Then I wait. And I wait a bit more. There's a steady stream of traffic this morning zuzzing past the end of my drive, but none of the cars have yet stopped and taken advantage of my offer.

I go indoors, make myself a cup of tea and linger hopefully by the back door. No one even slows down. There's nothing else for it. When I've downed my tea, I fill up my bucket again and rewash my car. It must wonder what on earth has hit it.

An hour later and it's looking even more sparkling. Still no one has stopped. What am I going to do now? I can't keep washing my own car as I'm going to take a layer of paint off it. And I can't really reduce my price as it's not going to be worth the effort. While I have time on my hands, I even contemplate *selling* my car to raise the money. But it's so old now that I'd probably only get a few hundred quid for it and my precious bit of independence would disappear.

A few minutes later and my heart lifts as a car slows down outside the house. Then I see that it's Lauren and I'm torn between disappointment that she's not my first bona-fide customer and joy that my sister has turned up unexpectedly. Clearly no chance of Jude visiting this weekend.

'Hi, sis.' She kisses my cheek. 'What in God's name are you doing?'

I point to my sign. 'Charity car wash.'

Lauren frowns. 'Going well?'

My shoulders sag. 'No.'

'Can't say I'm surprised,' is her verdict. 'I wouldn't want my car washed by a bag lady.'

I look down at my attire. 'I'm doing a great job,' I point out. 'Does it matter what I'm dressed in?'

'I take my car to a load of fit Polish blokes every couple of weeks. I can tell you that I don't do it for their car-washing skills. You need a unique selling point.' My sister purses her lips in thought.

'A theme or something, you mean?'

'Hmm.'

'I know!' I'm excited now. 'What if I bake some homemade cakes to give away with each car wash?'

'Get a life,' Lauren says.

'What then?'

'Shush. I'm thinking.' She swings her sunglasses between her fingers and chews at her lip.

I shrug. 'I could probably borrow a costume from work.'

Lauren's eyes light up. 'What a great idea.'

'Is it?'

'Can we get in there now?'

'I've got a key,' I tell her. 'I'd better phone one of the bosses, Blake Chadwick, and ask his permission. But I'm sure he won't mind.'

'Don't just stand there, then. Do it.' Lauren can be very bossy.

I punch in BC's number. 'I'm sorry to bother you,' I say, my heart fluttering ridiculously at the sound of his voice, 'but I'm doing a charity car wash and it's not going all that well. Could I possibly borrow a couple of costumes from the office store to spice it up a bit?' Now that Lauren's here she might as well help. If my sister had any objections she would have punched me by now.

'I like the sound of that.' Blake laughs down the line. 'Of course you can.'

'Thanks.'

'No worries.' He hangs up.

'Let's get down there,' I say, and we jump into Lauren's car and speed away. But she makes me take off my flowery wellies first.

Chapter Fifty

'We can't wear those!'

'We can,' my sister insists.

'I'll never be able to hold my head up in Goldstone Road again.'

'What nonsense.'

The costume store at Party Party is vast. There's everything you could possibly want in here for a great night out. Racks and racks of fancy dress outfits stretch out ahead of us. You can be anything from Napoleon to Elvis Presley.

We, it seems, are going to be Bunny Girls.

Lauren waggles the fluffy pink ears at me. 'What sells?'

'Sex.'

'Exactly.'

'We're thirty-nine years old,' I remind her. 'Past our prime.'

'You speak for yourself.' Lauren holds up the bunny outfit against her and preens in the mirror.

'Who in their right minds will want to see us dressed like this?'

'Plenty of jaded middle-aged men. We'll bring a bit of fun to their otherwise dull weekends down at the DIY superstore.'

'I hope you're right.' I have grave misgivings about this.

'Come on then. Let's not hang about. We've work to do.'

We also need to have every trace of our venture cleared

away before Greg comes home as he'll have a blue fit if he even gets a whiff of this.

Less than an hour later and my sister and I are in black stilettos, fishnet tights, black satin Bunny Girl corsets and pink fluffy ears. I feel ridiculous. And long for my wellies. Thank goodness it's a warm day otherwise I'd be freezing my butt off out here. As it is, I'm a bit hot under the collar with embarrassment.

Self-consciously, I smooth down my corset. 'I feel really stupid.'

'Do you want to go to Peru?' Lauren snaps.

'Yes.'

'Then shut up whining.'

I shut up whining.

As well as my car-washing dress sense, my informational sign was also deemed inadequate and Lauren has produced another one.

LET THE BUNNY TWINS RUB YOUR BUMPERS!

Let the bunny twins rub your bumpers? I shudder.

HAVE A HAND JOB FOR ONLY A FIVER!

Hand job! Oh, my word. Are we really only offering car washing services?

'Are you sure this is a good idea?' I ask Lauren for the hundredth time.

'Positive,' she says. 'And may I remind you that raiding the costume store was your suggestion.'

'I didn't imagine kitting myself up like this though.'

'What were you going to do, to draw in the punters?'

'We could have done Elvis,' I say, trying to suck my tummy in. 'That would have been funny.'

'We don't want funny,' Lauren points out. 'We want money. And fast.' Then she nudges me. 'Look sharp. Looks like we've got our first punter.'

And, sure enough, a sleek black Jaguar pulls in.

Lauren teeters over to him as the man gets out of his car. I have to admit that my sister looks hot, hot, hot and it's clear that our first customer thinks so too. Picking up my bucket, I follow her.

'Can we give you a rubdown?' Lauren asks.

'I wish I was ten years younger,' Jaguar Man says with a chortle.

Make that twenty, I'd say.

'The sight of you two lovely ladies has made a happy man feel very old,' he jokes. And that pretty much sets the stage for the rest of the day.

So, while I leap into action with my sponge and soapy water, Lauren flirts shamelessly and wiggles her tail. The man grins from ear to ear. He chortles particularly loudly when I bend over to reach the middle of the bonnet. I sigh as I try to enter into the spirit of this and waggle my tail too as I do it. Jaguar Man gets so excited that I think he's going to have a coronary.

My sister has our customer by the tie and is making pouty faces at him. I am the oily rag to her mechanic. Or, perhaps, I am the monkey here as, clearly, my sister is happy in her role as the organ grinder. I decide not to share that thought with her, but concentrate on getting a streak-free finish instead.

When we've finished he hands over twenty quid and tells us to keep the change. He takes a photo of us both on his camera bent over his bonnet in a seductive manner for another fiver. He also wants to know whether this will be available every weekend.

'Not on your nelly!' I want to say, but smile sweetly as Lauren does instead. This is one step nearer to Peru for me and if this is what it takes to get me there, then that's fine by me.

Jaguar Man jumps in his spruce car and speeds away. I'm not even sure that he's noticed how brilliantly it's been washed. Then I look up and notice that there is a little queue of three cars forming.

'We'll split them,' Lauren says. 'Let's do a great job, but remember we don't need to be able to eat our dinner off the damn things.'

'Right.' And two more male customers grinning broadly roll into my drive.

By five o'clock we've done fifteen cars and have had the same number of commemorative photographs taken. We turn away five who are waiting, promising them that business will resume tomorrow morning at ten o'clock.

I glance anxiously at my watch. 'We need to get this cleared up before Greg comes back.' If I could have done this somewhere else I would have, but the logistics of getting water to car stumped us. I'm just hoping that Greg sticks to his usual routine – and there's no reason why he shouldn't.

'He'll definitely go fishing tomorrow?'

'Hail, rain or shine.'

'Good,' Lauren says, and I couldn't agree more. I have been a fishing widow all of our married life and, finally, some good is coming of it.

All of our satisfied customers have given us more than

our suggested five pounds. I count out our booty. 'A hundred and ninety-five pounds.' I'm open mouthed.

'In one afternoon,' Lauren reminds me. 'We'll have a good crack at it tomorrow. We could do another four hundred pounds if business is as brisk.'

'Fingers crossed,' I say.

Lauren puts her arm round me. 'Then you're halfway there, Annie.'

Constricted by my bunny corset, my heart pounds with excitement. Halfway there!

Chapter Fifty-One

My husband comes home from fishing. When he walks through the door, my sister and I are sitting in the kitchen – fully clothed – innocently drinking cups of tea.

'What?' he says as we turn to look at him.

'Nothing.' I smile sweetly.

'You both look guilty.'

'No.' I shrug. 'Had a good day fishing?'

'Yes. Thanks.'

'How big was the one that got away?' my sister asks.

'Very funny,' Greg says.

'Are you going again tomorrow?' I sound too bright.

'If you don't mind,' my husband says, still regarding me suspiciously.

'No. Of course not.' How can I tell him that I have plans that don't involve him being here? 'I always encourage you to do what you want to do.'

My husband's face darkens. 'There's no need to be sarcastic, Annie.'

'I wasn't!'

But with that, he bangs out to the garage.

'Hmm,' Lauren says. 'Touchy.'

I sigh. 'He's like that all the time now. I can't say anything without him biting my head off. I spend my life walking on eggshells.'

'No wonder you want to get away.' I say nothing to contradict that sentiment. Frankly, the more stubborn Greg becomes, the more it makes me want to disappear to Peru and, preferably, not come back. 'Did you put the costumes in my room?'

I nod.

'Thank goodness. We don't want him finding out about this.'

I'll second that.

So at nine o'clock on Sunday morning we're rushing Greg out of the door, off for his day of fishing. If my husband is perplexed by my haste to shoo him out, then he says nothing. He probably just thinks that Lauren and I can't wait to get to the shops or something. In his wildest dreams he wouldn't imagine what the 'something' might be.

By ten we're booted and suited in our bunny gear and back in business in our drive. By noon we've done six men – or more accurately their vehicles – and have a queue of six more which stretches down Goldstone Road. I'm also almost another hundred pounds nearer to my target.

Then just as I'm getting into my stride and I'm starting to relax, the sight of the next car freezes my blood. Blake Chadwick's black Lotus Exige pulls into my driveway and stops right next to me.

'I hope you haven't waited long, sir,' I say as coolly as I can manage as he steps out.

BC takes off his shades and lets out a long low whistle. 'I'd have waited all day and more for this privilege.'

My heart bangs and my cheeks burn. Lauren sashays over. His eyes rove over both of us.

'I had no idea you were a twin,' he says. 'Now my nocturnal fantasies will go into overdrive.'

My sister is looking intrigued. BC is looking not just hot, but scorching today in black jeans and a white shirt.

'This is Blake Chadwick,' I tell her. 'My boss. The person who agreed that we could borrow these costumes.'

'And very glad that I did.'

'We'd better make sure that we give him an extra special service,' my sister says flirtatiously, and I wish she wouldn't. I'm flustered enough already.

I pick up my bucket and start to wash his car. He grins at me. 'This is very enterprising, Annie.'

'I'm determined to get to Peru.'

'I like that kind of focus in a woman,' he says, and makes my hormones go all silly. I drop my bucket and then fall off my heels and, in righting myself, knock my bunny ears all askew.

'I think we're going to have great fun on this trip, me and you.'

BC doesn't stop watching me all the time I'm washing his car. When I'm done he gives me a lazy smile and says, 'Great job. Ever thought of turning pro?'

Then, before I can come up with a suitably witty answer, he hands over a hundred pounds.

I just about stop my mouth from dropping open. 'I . . . I . . . I can't take this,' I stammer. 'It's way too much.'

'Worth every penny.' He winks. 'Believe me.'

Then he slides smoothly back into his Exige and purrs away.

'Wow,' Lauren says. 'And he's going to Peru too?'

I nod. 'All of the company are.'

'I bet they don't all look like that.'

'No,' I agree.

My bunny twin punches my arm. 'You dark horse,' she

says. 'Are you sure you're doing this entirely for the benefit of the poor kiddies?' Lauren waggles her eyebrows at me. 'Or is there an ulterior motive?'

'Don't be ridiculous.' And, as I try not to think of BC and his sleek curves, my heart-rate returns to normal and I wave in our next customer.

Chapter Fifty-Two

On Monday morning, Jude signalled to Lauren to come into his office as soon as she arrived. He closed the door behind her. 'I've been here since seven,' he said pointedly. 'Waiting.'

She'd thought about getting into work early as she normally did in an attempt to snatch a few moments alone with her lover, but today, instead, she'd turned over in bed and had enjoyed another half-hour's snoozing.

To be honest, Lauren was thoroughly exhausted after the weekend's exertions. All the hours she spent in the gym were nowhere near as energetic as the car-washing adventures with her sister had turned out to be. All of her muscles ached. When they'd finished last night, Lauren thought she might never lift her arms again. But it had been fun and she always loved spending time with her twin whatever they did.

As a bonus, by the end of the two snatched sessions, she and Annie had earned just over five hundred pounds to put towards her trip. If they could make sure that her brother-in-law was well out of the way and do the same thing next weekend, then that would pretty much sort out Annie's fare. Another one or two and that would be her spending money and any clothing or equipment she needed sorted too.

'Missed you this weekend,' Jude said softly, breaking into her daydreaming. He checked out of the window to the office before he risked stroking her arm.

She dragged her attention back to him. 'I went to see Annie.'

'Did you have a good time?'

Lauren nodded. She couldn't be bothered to tell him that they'd spent a very profitable weekend giving great car-wash. 'You?'

'Family stuff,' Jude said. She didn't really want to know that. 'I still need to make up for the weekend before,' he continued. 'I haven't forgotten.'

The strange thing was, Lauren kind of had.

'I could get away tonight,' he said. 'For an hour.'

'An hour.' A few weeks ago, that would have made her heart soar with joy at the thought of an illicit hour with him. Now, surprisingly, she just thought that she couldn't be bothered to make the effort if he was going to dash off.

'Maybe longer.'

'I'm tired.' An involuntary yawn escaped just to prove it.

Jude frowned. Was this the first time that she'd said that to him? Lauren wondered. She couldn't remember another occasion. For the last five years she'd always wanted to be bright, bubbly, enthusiastic – make him realise what he was missing at home. At the moment, she just couldn't be bothered.

Jude lowered his voice. 'I could come to the flat and give you a back rub, run you a hot bath.'

Now her resolve was weakening. Her lover had magic hands and that was just what her tired body needed.

'I'll make you feel good,' he wheedled.

Her smile softened. She liked a man who knew when to beg. 'Okay.' She turned to go back to her desk. 'I'll catch you later.'

'Lauren,' Jude called after her. 'What did you do in Bath last weekend?'

'Do?' she asked. 'You mean apart from cry myself senseless?'

'Ouch.' Her lover clutched his heart. 'I deserved that.'

'Yes,' she said. 'You did.'

'You didn't put any expenses into the company.'

'I wouldn't have dreamed of it,' Lauren told him. 'I wasn't on business, as far as I was aware.'

'Put the bills through,' Jude said gently. 'I feel like such a heel. It's the least I can do.'

'It doesn't matter.'

'I insist,' he said. 'Just give me the receipts.'

Maybe there was a knowing look in his eyes or maybe it was her belated guilt kicking in. Her mouth went dry as she thought of Zak and what a great time they'd had. It would be just like Jude to sack him out of spite if he found out that her friend had slipped into his place.

Which meant that if she put in her expenses for the weekend then Jude would see that there were two meals on each bill, not one. And she had no intention of explaining to him that it wasn't down to comfort eating.

Chapter Fifty-Three

I'm behind my desk on Monday morning poring over my travel guide to Peru, as usual, when Blake Chadwick swings in. I close the pages on the floating Uros Islands made of nothing but reeds and slip the book into my drawer.

'Morning, Sexy,' he says with a twinkle in his eye. 'Hardly recognised you with your clothes on.'

'The old ones are the best,' I retort cheekily.

'That's what I'd heard.' He gives me another saucy look. Now it's Blake who's being cheeky. Just because he's seen me in my fishnets, he clearly thinks he can get away with murder.

I fold my arms across my chest, defensively.

'Joking aside,' BC says quickly, 'I really admire your ingenuity. I don't know many women who'd have the guts to do something like that. Good for you, Annie.'

I don't like to tell him that it was back-breaking work and that by the end of Sunday my body was begging me to lie down and die. As it still is.

'Can I hang on to the bunny costumes for another few weeks, please?' I ask.

'For recreational purposes?'

'No.' I can't help but laugh. Greg would faint if he saw me dressed up like that. 'Lauren and I want to try to do the car washing again next weekend if we can.' If my husband disappears off fishing, as I pray that he will.

'Your sister seems really nice. Very supportive.'

'Yes, she is.'

'And you two are really twins?'

I blush. 'Yes,' I admit. 'We are.'

'Wow.' There's a vaguely dreamy look in his eye.

Typical male reaction.

'Annie,' BC says, suddenly serious, 'we've got a big event coming up in a few weeks in London. Launch of a new tropical cocktail mix. No expense spared on this one. You never get out of the office. Fancy coming along to it?'

No one has ever asked me to go along to a company do before. I'm nearly speechless. Nearly. 'I'd love to,' I manage to squeak out.

'Bring Lauren along too. If you like.'

'That'd be great.'

'Cool.' He grins at me. 'Think I'm going to have to drive through some very muddy puddles this week.'

I give him a puzzled look.

'I want to make sure I'm first in the queue next Saturday morning.'

'You can't afford me,' I quip, thinking of the hundred quid he gave me. Then, 'Thanks so much for the contribution to my fighting fund.'

'I told you,' he says, and our eyes meet. 'Worth every penny. And I meant it.' He leans on my desk and suddenly the temperature shoots up in here. 'You'll do this, Annie. You'll get to Peru. And I'll be there for you, cheering you on.'

Then he goes. Which is just as well because there's not a lot I can think of to say to that.

Chapter Fifty-Four

It was seven o'clock by the time Lauren got home. Jude followed her minutes later. He tossed his jacket on to the sofa, making himself at home. What would happen, she mused, if they split up, as a considerable part of her mortgage was paid for by Jude?

He came and twined his arms round her, holding her tightly. 'God, I love you,' he murmured against her neck.

Why was she even thinking like that? This year was going to be her year. By the time she was forty, she'd be with Jude if it was the last thing she did. Though she was coming to realise that it was going to be a much more tricky achievement than raising two thousand pounds for Annie to do the Inca Trail.

'I love the curve of your neck, the scent of you. All day long I've wanted to make love to you.'

'I thought I was getting a back rub?'

'Would you like it before or after?' He grinned at her and took her hand and led her through to the bedroom.

Moments later she was naked in his arms. As he moved above her she wondered how often he made love to his wife. Never, if she believed Jude's account of their non-existent love-life. But did she really buy into that? Did they reach the heights of ecstasy that Lauren and Jude did? She'd never had a lover as good as Jude and that was a hard drug to give up.

Her mobile phone rang. 'Leave it,' Jude instructed, but she picked it up and looked at the display in case it was her sister.

It wasn't Annie, it was Zak. She let the call go to voicemail. Lauren felt a mixture of elation and irritation. On the one hand she really wanted to talk to Zak as she hadn't seen him all day and she knew that he'd be interested in her car-washing activities – much more than Jude would ever be – but, on the other hand, she felt irritated that he'd called at a bad moment. Did Jude, she wondered, ever feel like that when she phoned him? Acid swirled in her stomach at the thought. Had she ever interrupted him and Georgia while they were in the throes of passion? More acid. What was wrong with her these days? She knew the score. This was what she'd bought into. But did that mean that she always had to like it?

She turned back to her lover, but the mood had gone.

'Anything wrong?'

Lauren shook her head. 'No.'

'Who was on the phone?'

'Just a friend.'

Jude sighed and rolled off her.

Stroking his chest, she said, 'You could give me that back rub now.'

Her lover looked at his watch. 'I've run out of time. I'll have to go.' He winked at her. 'I'll put it on account for you.'

Lauren pulled the sheet over her body, her skin cold now. How much more had she accrued on account over the years? Several spoiled birthdays, too many Christmases alone, the best years of her life spent waiting.

Jude was already up and dressing. How many times had

she lain in bed watching him shrug on his shirt, smooth down his hair where she'd ruffled it and then walk away from her and back to his wife and family? Tears welled in her eyes.

'I'll see you tomorrow at work,' he said.

If he noticed that she was crying, he didn't mention it. Her lover probably didn't have time to get involved with any unnecessary emotion – Georgia would be wondering where he was.

Chapter Fifty-Five

'I think I'm coming down with a cold,' Greg says, giving a tentative sniff. 'I might give fishing a miss today.'

'*Miss fishing*?' My husband never misses fishing.

I'm already out of bed, but he's still lying there. Looking very comfortable, I might add.

'I'll give Ray a ring.'

'You can't let him down,' I say.

I'm panicking now, as Lauren and I had planned to don our Bunny Girl outfits again and take up our chamois leathers with a vengeance. If Greg's here, moping around with Man Flu, then my fundraising efforts will be severely hampered. 'You always go fishing with him on a Saturday. It just sounds like a sniffle to me.'

He gives me a look that says, 'Thank you for your sympathy, dear wife.'

'I'll make you some breakfast,' I offer. 'That will make you feel better.'

'I don't think I could eat.'

Now he's just trying to wind me up.

I glance at my watch. I'm due to meet Blake Chadwick for our regular Saturday-morning run, and then Lauren is coming here with the aim of washing the dirty cars of Milton Keynes and relieving our customers of vast sums of money for the privilege.

Perhaps I should just come clean and tell Greg of our super wizard scheme to raise the money for my trip to Peru, but then I remember that he doesn't want me to go to Peru at any cost and he certainly wouldn't want me dressed as a Bunny Girl in pursuit of my dream.

'If you don't want anything to eat, then I'll be off,' I say.

'Where are you going?'

'Running.'

'Again.'

'Yes.' And my training is coming on marvellously, thank you for asking.

Though I have to admit that the added incentive of seeing Blake Chadwick in a muscle top always helps me with my motivation. My mouth is starting to go way too dry when I think of Mr Chadwick and his taut, toned muscles. I've started to put on mascara and lipstick to go running. That's bad, isn't it?

Now, I don't want to be late. 'I'll see you when I come back.'

'I might go fishing after all,' Greg grizzles.

I don't say the, 'Whatever,' that's on my lips. Instead, I pick up my water bottle and head for the car.

Ten minutes later and I swing into the car park. My eyes nearly pop out of my head. I wind down my window. 'What are *you* doing here?'

'Morning,' Lauren says. 'Thought I'd give you a surprise and come running with you this morning.'

That certainly is a surprise.

'Great.'

'You don't sound very enthusiastic,' my sister snaps. 'I hauled myself out of my pit at the crack of dawn to get here to support you in your quest. The least you could do is look bloody grateful.'

I laugh. 'I am grateful. Of course I am.' Jumping out of the car, I say, 'We might be thwarted in our fundraising attempts today. Greg's got a cold.'

'Heaven help us,' she says.

'I know.' I shrug. 'We'll have to play it by ear.'

'If he's still hanging around we'll have to go shopping and do lunch. Hmm,' she adds, 'that doesn't sound *too* bad.'

'But it won't get me to Peru,' I mutter.

Then Blake Chadwick's car growls into the car park and slots into a space right next to me.

'Oh,' my sister says, 'isn't that your boss? I remember his car from last week.'

Now I know that I'm looking sheepish. 'Oh, yes,' I say too brightly. 'So it is.'

Lauren frowns. 'Did you expect him to be here?'

'Er, I, er . . .' I may just have given Lauren the impression that I am struggling manfully with my punishing training schedule alone.

BC is out of the car and next to us. 'Morning, ladies,' he says. 'I'm glad you can make it this morning, Annie. I was lonely last week.' He puts his arm round my shoulders and hugs me.

'Er, I, er . . .' My cheeks go pink even before I've started to run. I wonder how much he missed me. As much as I missed him?

'Glad you could join us,' BC says to my sister. 'Lauren, isn't it?'

Lauren nods grimly.

211

'Let's do it then.' Blake sets off at a gentle jog. Lauren and I fall into step behind him.

My sister gives me the evil eye. 'I will be talking to you about this situation when we've finished, Annie Ashton.' It's a half-whisper, half-hiss.

Knowing my sister, it won't be a talk, it will be an interrogation. She may even inflict on me one of the Chinese burns she was so good at as a child – and I'm not sure that she'll like the answers I'll give her.

Chapter Fifty-Six

We finish our run, towel down and say goodbye to Blake Chadwick. Lauren and I stand and watch his Lotus roar out of the car park.

'So?' she says immediately.

'There's nothing to tell.'

'Why didn't you mention that he was going to Peru before we washed his car last week? Why didn't you tell me that you were meeting him here every Saturday morning to run together?'

'And Wednesday evening,' I add. 'But then we're joined by about another ten people from the office.'

'You tell me everything and yet you've never mentioned this?'

I sigh guiltily. My sister is right. I've kept my crush on Blake Chadwick all to myself. It's been my little secret. And I've loved having it.

'Are you in love with him?' Lauren wants to know.

I start to laugh at that. 'You can't be serious.'

'You go all goo-goo ga-ga when he looks at you.'

That stops me laughing. 'Perhaps it's because no one else looks at me in that way any more.' Then I burst into tears.

'Oh, Annie.' Lauren puts her arm round me and steers me to the nearest bench. We sit on it and stare out at the ducks on the lake while I have a cry.

'Are you sleeping with him?'

A teary laugh. 'Of course I'm not.'

'But you want to.'

'Of course I do,' I say. 'He's fit, he's fabulous and he's an outrageous flirt.'

'He certainly seems to like you.'

Lauren pulls a tissue out of the little bag at her waist and hands it to me. I dutifully blow my nose.

'I think he does,' I admit. 'He's asked me to go to one of the work's events next week.'

'Are you going?'

I nod. 'He said would you like to come along too.'

'You know,' Lauren says, 'you need to tread very carefully here. He is a young, single guy.'

'Not that much younger than me,' I point out. 'He's about thirty-four.'

Lauren puffs out an irritated breath. 'I can't believe that this is you talking. What if you go to this dinner or event or whatever it is – what then? What if he wants to take it further? Do you really know what you're starting out on?'

I don't remind her that she has provided a very good role model for adulterous affairs over the last few years.

'What if Greg was to find out?' my sister goes on, warming to her theme. 'You're willing to risk breaking up your family for someone like that?'

'This is the pot calling the kettle black.' I fold my arms defensively. 'Aren't you currently in the process of trying to break up someone else's family?'

Lauren's face darkens. 'That's different.'

'It is,' I agree. 'Jude's children are only young so it will be completely devastating for them, whereas mine are about to

214

fly the nest anyway. It will be easier for them to adjust to their parents living apart.'

'So you've really thought about this?' she says, mouth falling open.

'Yes, I have.' Whereas I think my sister has not.

'Georgia doesn't love Jude like Greg loves you.'

'Open your eyes, Lauren. If . . . *if* . . . anything happens with Blake, then I'll be walking into this knowing exactly what the risks are. Just as you did.'

My sister puts her head in her hands. 'Don't do it,' she says. 'I beg you.'

I say nothing.

'I didn't think it would hurt like this, Annie,' she confesses, tears in her eyes. 'When I first got together with Jude, I thought I could handle it. But I can't. I thought I wanted him at any cost, but this is ripping me apart.'

'And if you win . . . if *you* get what you want, then it will rip his family apart.'

The tears roll down her cheeks at that.

'There are no winners in this, Lauren,' I go on inexorably. 'If Jude comes to you then he'll leave a horrible gaping mess in his wake. One that you'll spend years trying to patch up.'

She wails now as if in agony and rocks herself back and forth on the bench. 'What am I going to do, Annie?'

'Walk away,' I say. 'Come to your senses and walk away.'

My sister looks at me, eyes over-bright and red rimmed. 'And what about you, Annie? Will you do the same?'

Chapter Fifty-Seven

We go to the Co-op on the way home and buy chocolate croissants to cheer ourselves up and to undo all the good we've just done in one fell swoop. We don't mention Jude Taylor or Blake Chadwick again.

When we get back to my house there's no one else home. On the work surface is a Post-it Note from Greg, saying, *Gone fishing. Back at 5*. No endearments, no kisses, no nothing.

'Great,' I say. 'We can put Plan A into action.'

So we eat our croissants quickly and down a swift cup of coffee with them while we are gearing up in our bunny costumes. Today, I don't have quite so much enthusiasm for this.

'Think of Peru,' my sister says when she sees my long face. Then she hugs me. 'I didn't mean to nag you. You've got to do as you want to do. It's your life.'

Yes, it is, I think miserably as I trudge downstairs with our saucy advertisement board. Lauren goes to the garage to get the buckets. During the week she's bought two big pink sponges for us to use. For some reason the sight of them makes me smile.

'Come on,' she says encouragingly. 'Let's wiggle our bunny tails for the good residents of Milton Keynes.'

So I put the sign out and stand by the gate waving cheekily at the cars that pass. Within minutes, our first customer has stopped.

'It's always the men in cars on their own who take up our services,' Lauren mutters as we hose down the Renault in a suggestive manner. 'I should have got my friend Zak to dress up as a fireman to attract the women drivers.'

And Blake, I think. But then I'm not entirely sure that I could have coped with seeing BC in a fireman's uniform. My hormones might well have self-destructed.

Like last weekend, we have a steady stream of clients. We take turns to grab a sandwich at lunchtime and then the next time I look at my watch it's nearly three o'clock. We've already done fifteen cars and have banked nearly £150 pounds. That takes me just over halfway to my target and that lifts my heart. Another hour or so and then we'll need to clear up before Greg comes home.

Then I glance down the road at our queue. Three more cars. Perhaps we should call it a day after that. As I turn back to my current customer – a Mini that just needs a wash and brush-up – a car screeches up to the front of the queue. It's a vehicle that I know only too well.

A moment later, the driver's door slams and the driver – who I also know only too well – stamps up the drive. His eyes pop out of his head when he sees my Bunny Girl outfit.

'What's all this about?' my husband says. His face is red and he is frothing at the mouth.

'It's about raising money for my trip to Peru,' I say calmly. 'And we're doing very well.'

'It stops now,' Greg says, and he kicks over our sign declaring, LET THE BUNNY TWINS RUB YOUR BUMPERS!

I don't think I've ever seen him so cross.

'I knew you'd be unreasonable,' I say quietly. 'That's why I'm doing it while you're out.'

Our waiting customers are out of their cars now and are watching with interest our developing domestic crisis.

'Except I'm not out now,' my husband points out. 'I'm home. I came home because I'm feeling dreadful with this bloody cold. And I come home to this. *This*. I had no idea what was going on when I saw the queue outside our house. What will the neighbours think?'

I put my hands on my hips and shout back, 'Some of them obviously like it. They've already had their cars washed!'

With that, a dark cloud comes over him and he grabs hold of my bunny ears, snatches them from my head and throws them to the ground. Then he jumps on them. Three times.

Now he has gone too far.

'I don't know who you are any more,' Greg spits. 'You're not the wife I've been married to for the last twenty years.'

'No, I'm not,' I spit back. 'I'm glad you've realised that.'

Greg and I square up to each other, me armed with my pink sponge covered in suds, Greg armed with the moral high ground. My sister comes over.

'Greg,' she hisses, 'calm down. You're showing us up.'

'*Showing you up?*' My husband's eyes bulge alarmingly. I should imagine that his blood pressure is currently off the known scale. 'You're the ones in Bunny Girl get-ups! You're middle-aged women. What do you think you look like?'

A posse of men with folded arms have gathered at our gates. 'We think they look great,' one ventures.

My husband wheels on him. 'Who asked you?'

'It's for charity,' our brave champion continues recklessly. 'Give them a break.'

Greg's response is to stomp across the drive and kick over our buckets.

Lauren and I stand there impotently. There is a disapproving grumbling from our customers. Mutters of 'Killjoy' and 'Spoilsport' are heard.

I sigh deeply. 'I think that our car-wash is closed for this evening,' I tell them sadly.

Greg is sulking at the side of the house, hands wedged in his pockets.

I take a deep breath. 'It will, however, recommence at ten o'clock in the morning.'

A cheer goes up. Placated, our customers go back to their cars.

'See you tomorrow, darling,' one of them shouts.

'That was an outright declaration of war,' Lauren whispers to me. 'Are you sure you want to do this?'

My chin takes on a determined little jut. 'Oh, yes.' Picking up my bunny ears, I straighten them out and plonk them back on my head. I will not let anyone, not even my husband, crush my dream.

And I wonder what the chances are of me persuading Greg to don a fireman's uniform and help us out tomorrow. None, I think the answer is to that.

Chapter Fifty-Eight

I take off my bunny outfit. For dinner, I open a tin of Heinz tomato soup. Greg has a Lemsip. We sit glued to the television avoiding eye-contact with each other. My husband stomps up to bed at nine o'clock. Half an hour later, I follow him.

We lie on our backs staring at the ceiling in silence.

Chapter Fifty-Nine

The next morning, Greg is up and gone before I'm awake. His fishing equipment is missing too, but then I could have hazarded an educated guess as to where he'd be.

My sister, very sensibly, made herself scarce last night. She hightailed it back to London when she could sense that trouble was brewing.

I sit at the kitchen table in my dressing-gown, brooding. When I decided to embark on this trip, this adventure, I had no idea that my husband would be so dead set against it. At best, I imagined that he'd want to come with me. At worst, that he'd give me as much support as he could without actually accompanying me. Shows how little I know him after all these years of marriage – and that makes me feel incredibly sad.

My mobile phone is lying on the kitchen table and I stare wistfully at it. We haven't had a disagreement like this in all our years together. We might never have reached the passionate heights of Burton and Taylor, but we've rubbed along together well enough. I could call him. Make peace. I can picture exactly where he'll be sitting on his favourite spot on the canal. Or I could text him.

In the end I do nothing.

Neither of the kids are home. Ellen is probably staying with her boyfriend as she does most nights. As for my son, who knows where he is? He seems to pick up a different girl every weekend but, thankfully, he doesn't often bring them home. At least he picks up girls who have their own place or more accommodating parents. What is my purpose here any more, I wonder, home all alone on a Sunday?

Making some tea and toast for breakfast, I take my time over it. I should be donning the bunny outfit and getting out there with my bucket to whip the men of Milton Keynes into a veritable frenzy of giving with my pink sponge, my winning smile and my cute little pom-pom. But I lack the enthusiasm today. I'm taking no pleasure in my victory, and without Lauren here to chivvy me on, be my partner in crime, I'm finding the prospect of a day's car washing in little more than my underwear quite daunting.

I could call my sister and ask her to come back to help me again, but my heart just isn't in it. Yesterday's post is still waiting, unopened, on the table. All we ever get is bills, bills, bills – so no one is ever in a rush to check out the contents. As I eat my toast, I slit open the first envelope. Gas bill. Ghastly. Then the second. Credit-card bill. Deplorable. The third is clearly from the bank, and I hope that we're not overdrawn yet again. But no – inside the envelope is a cheque. I get a bit excited for a minute, thinking that I might have come into some money, but when I look closely it's Chelsea's cheque for £100. The letter with it tells me that the cheque has been refused due to 'insufficient funds'. Chelsea's cheque has *bounced*. It can't have! The bank must have cocked something up. It wouldn't be the first time. God, that means I'm going to have to give it back to her. How embarrassing. Why is none of this straightforward?

Dragging my feet, I go back upstairs and get the Bunny Girl outfit out of the back of my wardrobe. I throw my middle-aged mum's towelling dressing-gown on the bed and pull on the fishnet tights, then the snug corset with the ridiculous white fluffy tail. Slipping on my stilettos, I take a long, hard look at myself in the full-length mirror.

I look stupid. Utterly stupid. Greg's right. Why did I think that it was a good idea to humiliate myself in this way? Is this trip really worth putting my marriage under this terrible strain? What am I trying to prove?

Pulling the travel guide out of my handbag by the bed, I browse its pages once more, stroking the glossy coloured pictures of locations too achingly exotic to contemplate – Isla Ballestas, Puerta Inca, Chala, Cahuachi, Puno, Moquegua. Places that are so vivid, so vast, so far removed from my ordinary life, that I can barely imagine myself in that landscape. My eyes prickle with hot tears and the towering mountains, lush valleys and sparkling rivers blur until I can't see them any more. Will I ever get there? Should I even be trying? Should I not just be happy with my lot and let this silly notion of adventure and independence go, for the sake of my family?

Sitting by myself on the bed, I cry, miserable, self-pitying tears, letting them roll down my face and wet the bare skin of my chest.

'What shall I do?' I howl out loud to no one. 'What shall I do?'

But no one answers me and I don't know what to say to myself.

Chapter Sixty

Greg had long nurtured a love affair with tench. There was nothing better in life than sitting by the canal watching the dawn break, the rays of sunshine peeping tentatively through the trees and over the hedges, warming the waters of the canal, stirring the slothlike nature of the fish in to slow, languorous movement.

They had a lovely feel to them too, tench. Leathery, firm skin, fat, round and smooth with a shiny, iridescent green body that glistened in the sun. Their crimson eyes kept a soulful watch on you as you disgorged the hook from their mouths and released them to swim another day. Fine-looking fish, a tench.

He looked at the specimen in his hands with pride. They never struggled either, tench. They were the most placid of all the homely well-loved fish. When all else in life was falling apart, you could depend on the relaxing nature of the tench.

'If I was Prime Minister,' Ray said as he ferreted deep in his tackle box, looking for his box of weights or his floats, 'I'd send all these Polish blokes home. They're taking all our jobs. Send 'em back – that's what I'd do.'

'Didn't you get a firm of Polish builders in to do your extension?'

Ray busied himself in his box. 'Yeah, well. They came in at a good price. All the builders round here are thieving bastards.'

'And don't you get your car washed at that Polish place up by the golf club?'

'They do a good job there,' Ray admitted reluctantly, 'and it's only five quid.'

'You could have had it done by a Bunny Girl yesterday,' Greg said.

'I wouldn't mind that,' his friend said with a raucous laugh. 'My wife would have obliged.'

Ray's eyes bulged like a carp. 'You're kidding me?'

Greg sighed. 'I wish.'

What was it the sign had said? *Let the bunny twins rub your bumpers?* Greg shuddered. *Have a hand job for only a fiver.*

He thought that his wife had lost her mind. This was the woman who swaddled herself in a sarong on the beach on holiday so that no one would see her in her bikini, the one who wore thick, fleecy pyjamas in bed and didn't possess one shred of sexy lingerie. Now she was skinny-dipping in the North Sea and prancing up and down their own drive in a Bunny Girl outfit. What would the neighbours think? What did *he* think?

Greg had packed in fishing early yesterday not just because he was feeling terrible with his cold, but because he was feeling terrible in general. He hated them falling out. They'd never been the sort of couple who thrived on regular fisticuffs, like some did. He'd wanted to go home early so that he could see Annie, eat some humble pie or whatever it took to try to get them back on track.

He had no idea that their relationship would be so summarily derailed when he got there. Would she even have mentioned her escapades at all if he hadn't happened upon them *in flagrante delicto*? He'd even called in at the garage on the way home to buy her some flowers on Ray's advice, but they'd run out. Thank God for small mercies. He'd have probably felt like ramming them down the throat of one of the guys who were queuing up to ogle Annie and her twin bunny.

'Are you sure that she's not got another man?' Ray said into his dark musings. 'Even taking into account the unbalanced hormones of a woman of a certain age, she's behaving very strangely.'

'Another man?' It was something that had crossed Greg's mind, but he hadn't seriously considered it as a possibility. Annie wouldn't do that. Not his Annie. No way.

'I'd keep an eye on her if I was you,' his friend advised sagely. 'Take it from one who knows.'

Ray should know. He was much married, much divorced and, through bitter experience, was much wiser in the ways of the world than Greg ever hoped to be.

The tip of Greg's rod dipped and he watched as his float bobbed and a circle of telltale bubbles puttered around it. His heart raced. A tench – he was sure. He made a strike and hooked the fish. Definitely a tench. They might look like placid fish, but when push came to shove they could be powerful fighters. Greg wondered whether, if push came to shove, he'd be the same.

Chapter Sixty-One

Lauren sat in front of *Country File* on the television, her legs curled under her, a bowl of stale muesli on her lap. The programme was very informative regarding the festive prepartions that were taking place in the Cotswolds ready for Christmas. Lauren assumed that it was a repeat from last year as it was still the height of summer, but you could never be quite sure.

She should call Annie, make sure that she was all right. As she left her sister's home yesterday, it looked like World War Three was about to erupt. She hesitated to pick up the phone in case Greg answered. No doubt she'd be in the firing line too and she just wasn't feeling strong enough to deal with that. Annie's husband would be more than happy to blame her for leading his wife astray.

Lauren could fully understand why her sister wanted to go off on this jaunt. Greg was such a stick-in-the-mud, getting old before his time. Annie had never been given the chance to try her wings. Now was her time.

Instead, she settled on texting Annie. *R u ok?*

Her sister replied. *Fine. Greg out.*

All well?

So so.

Want me 2 cum up?

No. C u in week?

Luv u Lauren texted back.

Luv u 2 from Annie.

Lauren clicked off her phone. So that was it. Another Sunday stretching ahead of her. Jude hadn't phoned yesterday and there'd been nothing from him this morning even though it was nearly ten o'clock. Some days he feigned going for an early-morning run so that he could pay her a fleeting visit, but that clearly wasn't on the cards for today.

Country File was failing to hold her interest. Who, these days, had time to collect their own branches to fashion a Christmas wreath? Lauren sank back on the sofa. She hadn't liked to ask Annie whether she planned to do the cheesy car wash on her own or whether she'd abandoned the idea.

Her fingers toyed with the buttons of her phone. Should she text Zak, see what he was up to today? It was wrong of her to keep using him as her fallback plan, she knew that. She should spend the day at home, catch up with some chores, clean the place, go shopping for some food. But that sounded duller than dull. Before she could think better of it, she speed-dialled Zak's number.

'Hey,' he said a moment later. 'I was just thinking of you.'

'Yeah?'

'I thought you were up at your sister's place this weekend.'

'Slight change of plan,' she admitted.

'So you're phoning to see what Uncle Zak's doing?'

'Do you mind?'

'No. In fact, that's why I was thinking of you. I have a very exciting day ahead of me which is just up your street. Or several streets, to be more accurate.'

Lauren smiled. Talking to Zak always soothed her, made her feel less neurotic. 'Tell me more.'

'You know that I normally don't encourage you to drink to excess. Well, today I'll make an exception. If you can get your gladrags on in the next half an hour, I'll reveal all to you. Make sure you've had some breakfast too.'

Lauren looked down at the half-finished bowl of stale muesli. 'I've already eaten.'

'Good. And wear shoes that you can walk in, not those ridiculous heels you like so much.'

She hadn't realised that Zak was paying so much attention to her choice of footwear.

'Go and get ready,' her friend said.

'Tell me,' Lauren said, a frisson of excitement running through her. She was already off the sofa and scraping the remains of the soggy breakfast cereal into the bin. 'Tell me where we're going.'

Zak sighed. 'You're so impatient.'

'A girl needs to be able to dress appropriately.'

Another sigh. This time perplexed. 'A bunch of us are doing the Monopoly Board Pub Crawl.'

Lauren laughed. 'The what?' She was already in her bedroom, shrugging off her dressing-gown. It was a good job that this wasn't a videophone.

'Twenty-six pubs, one in each of the locations listed on the Monopoly Board. One drink in each.'

'Wow. That's a lot of drinks. Even for me.'

'Then we won't make them doubles,' her friend said. 'We're starting at the George on the Old Kent Road.'

'At this time in the morning?'

'They're opening up early for us. I'll be with you soon.'

'Thanks, Zak.' She hung up. Now she wasn't a sad and

lonely single mistress, she had a fun day to look forward to in good company.

Lauren pulled on her jeans and a T-shirt. There was no time for a shower if she was going to be ready in time. She fluffed up her hair and tied it in a scrunchy, then slicked some make-up round her face.

Not five minutes later, the doorbell rang. 'Bloody hell,' she muttered. 'That was quick.'

Lauren flung the door open and was surprised to see not Zak standing there, but Jude.

Chapter Sixty-Two

I don't do the car wash. You'll probably think that I'm pathetic. I know that Lauren will. Instead, I sadly strip off my Bunny Girl outfit and pull on my old tracksuit bottoms and a skanky T-shirt.

I know that there are a thousand things that I could do round the house this afternoon, but I don't fancy any of them. If, for the sake of marital relations, I can't carry on with the car wash for fundraising, then I need to think of something else – and quick. Or – also for the sake of marital relations – do I need to drop this silly idea altogether?

I decide to go and pound the pavement around Furzton Lake; not only will it help with my training, but it might also get rid of some of my anger and frustration. It could clear my head and help me to think of a new and dastardly money making scheme.

I jump into my car – which looks washed and polished to within an inch of its life – and head off to the lake. Minutes later, I'm in the car park. The air is fresh today and the cool breeze does much to lift my spirits out of the doldrums.

The lake is a little busier on a Sunday morning with a few joggers already out in the sunshine.

As I do some cursory warm-up stretches, I see a runner coming round the corner and, frankly, I'd recognise that physique anywhere. While my brain still tries to process the information, Blake Chadwick is on me.

'Annie,' he says, pulling up in surprise. 'Didn't expect to see you here today.'

His face is flushed. Clearly he runs at a more determined pace when he's alone, unencumbered by me.

'Hi. Didn't expect to be here myself,' I admit. 'I'm home alone today. At a loose end. Thought I'd do a bit of training.'

'Me too,' BC says. 'I normally have my daughter on a Sunday, but she's not well with a cold today. I'm kicking around the house too.'

I hadn't imagined Blake with time on his hands to fill. I thought he was an all-Action Man with every second lived in the fast lane.

'You going to run with me?'

'No, no,' I say. 'You look like you're in your groove. I don't want to hold you up.'

'Don't be silly,' he laughs. 'It's good to have the company.'

Am I imagining it, or does BC look a bit bashful after saying that?

'Okay.' *Be nonchalant*, I counsel myself. *Otherwise he'll hear your heart thumping*. 'If you're sure you don't mind.'

I fall into step next to him and we set off together, Blake at his modified pace.

'No car wash today?'

My face reddens. 'My husband put a stop to it. Wasn't very keen for the neighbours to see me in my bunny outfit.'

'Very fetching, I thought,' BC says with a laugh. 'Your husband should be stoked that he's got a hot wife.'

He's not. But I don't share that information. I do, however, gulp at the thought of BC finding me hot.

'And enterprising,' he continues. 'It looks like you were doing good business.'

'We were.'

'I thought he would have been proud of your money-making skills.'

But he wasn't, was he? 'I could have done with a few more weekends like that.' I sigh. 'I still have nearly a grand to raise for my place. Now I'll have to think of something else.'

'You will,' he assures me. 'You have to find that money, Annie.' He glances across at me. 'It won't be the same in Peru without you.'

And I wonder whether anything in my life will be the same if I *do* go to Peru.

Chapter Sixty-Three

'I have two hours,' Jude said. He was breathless from running up the stairs. In his hand there was a fancy carrier bag. 'I have a picnic breakfast. Croissants straight from the baker's oven, freshly squeezed orange juice. Some fresh fruit. One or two other treats.'

Her lover had obviously forgotten that she wasn't available, that she was supposed to be away all weekend at Annie's house.

Jude caught Lauren round the waist and pulled her close. 'We can go to Regent's Park and sit in one of the deckchairs in the sunshine and eat it there. Or . . . ?' He let the suggestion hang in the air.

'. . . we could eat it in bed,' Lauren finished for him.

'What a marvellous idea!' Jude agreed. 'I like a woman who's on the same wavelength.'

Now she was torn. She was so looking forward to her day out with Zak and his mates, but now that Jude was here she wanted to spend time with him too. If she blew Zak out of the water in favour of Jude then she'd have the rest of the day to kill by herself once her lover had gone back to the bosom of his family. But then how could she tell Jude that she'd just had another offer? Another offer which also sounded very appealing.

Jude took her hand and tugged her towards the bedroom. In jeans and a white T-shirt, hair still damp from the shower, he looked sensational today. What she really wanted to do was go to the park, be out in the sunshine together, hold hands, take a walk through the Rose Garden, be seen with this fabulous-looking man. Do the things that every other couple took for granted. But then if they went out, she couldn't lie in Jude's arms and let him kiss the doubts away.

'Wait,' she said. 'I just need to text Annie.'

'Now?'

'I'll be two seconds.'

'I'll be waiting.'

As her lover disappeared into her room, Lauren quickly texted Zak. *Something came up*, she wrote. *Can't make it. Catch up with u l8tr?*

Shame, Zak texted back. *C u at work tomorrow. Say hi 2 Jude.*

As she snapped off her phone, a wave of sadness washed over her. Of course Zak would realise why she was turning him down. Now she felt terrible. It wasn't fair of her to treat her friend like that – especially since she'd been the one to call him. Lauren sighed to herself. How many great parties/picnics/pub crawls had she missed over the years because she'd chosen to wait around for Jude instead? Lauren pushed the thought to the back of her mind, her heart heavy. Frustration and disappointment had become an integral part of this relationship. Still, the decision had been made. She'd just have to stick to it.

'Come on, darling,' Jude shouted from the bedroom. There was a note of irritation in his voice. 'I haven't got long.'

Lauren sighed. She might have known that the clock was ticking on her already.

Chapter Sixty-Four

'Have lunch with me,' Blake says as we finish our run.

I laugh breathlessly at the suggestion. 'I can't do that.'

'Why not?'

Why not? Er . . . Let me think about that. 'I look a mess.' I'm standing in the car park feeling all sweaty.

'You look fabulous,' he says, and there's a sincerity in his tone which takes my breath away more surely than all that jogging.

'I look like a woman who's just huffed and puffed five miles.'

'Let's go somewhere low-key,' BC suggests. 'We can sit out in the garden in a shady corner well away from the designer-label crowd, if that'll make you feel better.'

'Okay,' I say, with an attempt at a casual shrug. I should be used to Blake's company by now – we've done enough running together. So why does he still make me feel like some gauche teenager?

'Leave your car here,' he instructs, as he opens the passenger door of his Lotus Exige for me.

With some difficulty and no elegance whatsoever, I deposit myself inside, trying to look as if I'm not a novice sports-car passenger. Blake slips in beside me and, with a smile, he roars away, pinning me back into my seat.

I try to look cool and unflustered as we zoom through

the streets, lower to the road than I've ever been before. My sister would kill me if she could see me now after her stern warning. Well, perhaps Lauren – or anyone else for that matter – doesn't need to know about this.

True to his word, Blake pulls up outside a bargain-basement family pub.

'I didn't think you knew about places like this,' I tease, as I clamber out of the low-slung car in an equally ungainly manner.

'My daughter, Leona, likes the ball pond.'

'Oh. How old is she?'

'Just three. She's an angel and a demon all rolled into one.'

'They all are at that age.'

He flicks out the latest iPhone as we go into the bar. There's nothing bargain basement about that. 'This is her.' BC holds it out so that I can admire the photograph of his child. A little girl with dreads and milk-chocolate-coloured skin looks back at me.

'She's beautiful.'

'Yeah.' He grins as he looks lovingly at the photo himself. Gone is the brash, boastful bloke that I know from work. 'Gets that from her mother,' he adds. 'Just hope she hasn't got her temper, too.'

'You're not together now?'

'We'd split by the time Leona was born,' he says sadly. 'I don't get to see enough of my little girl. I can't have her in the week because half the time I'm away. Sunday is my only day.'

'That's a shame.'

He shrugs. 'It's life now. We just have to make the most of it. My relationship with my ex is okay.' He gives me a wicked grin. 'Usually.' BC slips his phone back into his pocket. 'I just want Leona to have the best life that she can. Do wonderful things, go to wonderful places.'

'That's great,' I say, but there's an unbidden lump in my throat. Are my own two children completely lacking in ambition because I didn't have big dreams for them or for myself? Should I have urged them from an early age to want more for themselves than either Greg or I did? Perhaps it's not too late. For them or for me.

Then BC slips his arm casually round my shoulders but that doesn't stop my heart from beating triple time. He steers me towards the bar. 'Let's see what delights this place has to offer. I'm famished after our run.' Blake turns to me and winks. 'We make a good team, you and me.'

I like this softer side of Blake Chadwick. In fact, I think I might like it a bit too much.

Chapter Sixty-Five

The early part of the week has passed without event. It has also passed without Greg and me resolving our differences or me having raised any more money for my trip.

Still, I don't want to think of any of that now. Tonight my mind will be filled with nothing but thoughts of fun.

Lauren and I are going to this utterly *fabulous* Party Party event later this evening and I just can't wait. My knees might even be shaking a bit.

This is the first time I've ever been invited to attend one of our company's dos and it looks like this is going to be lavish beyond my expectations. The only flash parties that I've ever attended have been at Chelsea's behest, and it's nice to have a marvellous affair to go to that's all down to my own efforts.

Tonight's bash is the launch of a new ready-blended cocktail called Totally Tropical. *An intoxicating blend of warm Amaretto, smooth cherry brandy, zesty lime and the sweetness of pineapple juices created on the island of Hawaii that'll make you think of long, hot days beneath the Caribbean sun and soft, sultry nights beneath the Caribbean stars.* All that from a drink, eh?

It sounds a bit sickly for my taste, but I'm sure that if I get to sample enough of it then I'll become a convert.

The party's being held on an enormous boat, a river cruiser

on the Thames, and there's a guest-list of over 200 people and a seemingly unlimited budget. I feel like clapping my hands in glee. All the costumes and props have been packed into a lorry and sent down earlier in the day – I could just about see from the reception windows as a veritable forest of palm trees was loaded into the back.

Now, at four o'clock, a mini-bus pulls up outside for the staff and we all pile inside, chattering excitedly. I sit next to Minny at the front.

'Wow,' she says. 'You look amazing, Annie.'

'Thanks.' A warm glow goes through me.

'New dress?'

'Yes.' I have to confess that I slipped out of work at lunchtime to have my hair done and, shame on me, I couldn't resist a flirty little number with a tropical design which I thought would be perfect for this evening. My credit card was less impressed and the dress will have to be hidden at the back of the wardrobe as Greg would have a fit if he knew. But it's so rarely that I get the chance to go to anything like this that I really wanted to look the part and enjoy it to the full.

The bus sets off and we're heading towards the M1 and the bright lights of London. Someone has put a CD of sunshine hits in the player to get us in the mood. Lauren is joining us down there at the dockside and I'm sure she'll be surprised to see me looking so spruce. As I sing along to 'Club Tropicana', I'm trying to convince myself that I haven't just done this to try to impress Blake Chadwick.

He's already down at the boat and has been since early this morning, along with several members of Party Party staff who are setting up the event. I haven't seen BC that much this week since our lunch on Sunday, so I'm not sure how things lie between us. Nothing was said, or anything like that. Don't get me wrong. There was no impropriety at all. Though BC did give me a peck on the cheek as I left him back at the car park that might have lingered a *little* too long.

As he left this morning, he did say, 'See you tonight.' And then he winked at me. My stomach swirls with nerves at the thought of it.

What will I do if he wants to . . . *progress* . . . things this evening? Is that his ulterior motive for inviting me? I guess that I'll have my sister there to look out for me and prevent any mischief from happening. I don't even know how I can be thinking like this. Greg and I have been happy for so many years. I've never looked at another man in this way before. I've never looked at another man and thought, What if? What if I wasn't married, what if he wants me to kiss him, what if he wants us to be together?

I realise that Minny is talking to me and pull myself back to the present.

'How's the fundraising going, Annie?'

'Great,' I say. 'My sister and I have been washing cars at the weekend dressed as Bunny Girls.'

'Fabulous,' she cries. 'And at your age!'

'Yes.' Has Minny been talking to my husband? I wonder.

Relations are still very strained between Greg and me, and I wonder if we'll ever get back to the way we were. Then I wonder if I would ever want to.

Chapter Sixty-Six

Zak had been cool with her for a couple of days. And it bothered her. Lauren didn't want to lose his friendship. He'd been really good to her, particularly over the last few months, and she realised that you could push a friendship too far – even a good one.

She vowed to make amends, so at lunchtime she wandered over to Zak's desk. 'Come for a sandwich with me?' she said. 'My treat.'

Zak looked up from his computer. 'Jude not available?'

Her lover was busy in his office.

'That's not the only reason I wanted to see you, Zak,' she said, stung. Although he'd had every right to bowl a low one at her. 'I felt bad about Sunday and I wanted to hear how it went.'

Her friend sighed. 'One of the reasons I'm cranky is that I still have a monumental hangover.'

'Three days later?'

'The *Monopoly* board is a lot bigger than you think.'

She laughed at that and Zak managed a smile. 'And the other reason you're cranky?' she asked.

'You missed a *monumental* event,' Zak said. 'And I nearly did too.' He ran his hand through his hair in an exasperated way. 'When you decided not to come, I thought about not going either. Then I realised that I was doing exactly what you do with Jude. I was going to hang around and wait to see if you called again, had changed your mind. I don't want to be like that, Lauren. I don't want to miss out on life while I wait around for the pleasure of your company.'

She sat down heavily on the edge of his desk. 'I had no idea that you felt like that.'

Zak shrugged. 'Well, now you do.'

'Does that mean you don't want ham and mayo on granary with me?'

'I think it's best if I don't see you,' Zak said. 'Other than in the office. It's just too . . . difficult.'

'But we're mates,' she insisted. 'We should talk about this. I don't want to lose your friendship.'

'And I'm not sure that I want to be one of your friends, Lauren.' He looked at her sadly. 'You don't treat them very well.'

'I'm sorry, Zak. I hope that you'll reconsider.'

He shook his head. 'I need to get out, start dating again. See other people.'

'I've never stopped you from doing that,' she said.

'No.' He sighed. 'I stopped myself.' His eyes returned to his computer screen. 'I'm busy, Lauren. I should get on.'

'I hope that you find someone wonderful out there.'

'And I hope that you won't wait around for Jude for ever,' Zak said. 'But I think that we'll both be disappointed.'

'He loves me,' Lauren heard herself say. 'It's not like you think it is.'

'Whatever.' Zak turned back to his computer. 'I won't call you again, Lauren.'

'But—' Then she stopped. What could she say to him? In so many ways he was right. Her shoulders drooped and she walked away from his desk.

In his office, Jude was also tapping away at his computer. Lauren popped her head round the door. 'Lunch?'

'Can't.' Jude barely looked up. 'Busy.'

'Don't forget I'm leaving early tonight,' she said. 'I've got that party with Annie.'

'Oh. Right. Have a great time.'

She wondered if she could sneak Jude on to the guest-list too. There were bound to be some spare invitations kicking around. There always were at that kind of thing. 'You don't fancy coming along, do you?'

Jude shook his head. Finally, he looked up at her. 'I'm stacked out,' he said, raising his hands at his computer. 'I'll be burning the midnight oil here.'

'Another time,' she said.

'Yeah,' but his attention had already drifted away from her.

So lunch alone it was, Lauren thought miserably. She couldn't wait to get out of this place. Tonight she was going to make sure that she had a thoroughly splendid time!

Chapter Sixty-Seven

Lauren is already waiting on the jetty when we pull up in the mini-bus. All the staff burst out, exuberant after a rousing chorus of 'Caribbean Queen'. The pontoon has been strung with colourful lights and the enormous shiny white boat that's moored there looks very luxurious. There's a hive of industry with people rushing up and down the gangway taking packages on board. I'm almost beside myself with joy.

I rush over and hug my sister. 'I'm so excited,' I tell her. 'I've been looking forward to this for days.'

'Me too,' Lauren agrees. 'I need something to cheer me up.'

'What's wrong?'

'Usual,' she says dismissively, then holds up her hands. 'But I'm not going to talk about any of my problems. Tonight, I'm going to forget all about Jude and have some fun.'

'Spoken like the sister I know and love.'

'You look great,' Lauren says. 'We are *so* shaggable. Let's go and find two unsuspecting men and give them hell.'

'Why not?' But I don't tell my sister that I already have my beady eye on one particular man.

So we link arms and follow the rest of my colleagues up the gangway and on to the boat.

When we enter the main salon, the sight that greets me nearly takes my breath away. A tropical jungle has been created on board. The palm trees that I saw being loaded on to the lorry this morning are all in situ and, at one end of the huge room, there's a silver sand beach where a steel band are warming up for the evening. A bar has been created in the style of a beach hut and already the glasses are lined up waiting to dispense shots of Totally Tropical.

'This looks amazing,' Lauren says, and I'm so proud that my company has created this breathtaking tropical island.

Waiters in Hawaiian shirts are starting to drift in with trays of exotically colourful canapés. Young and impossibly slender nubile women dressed in skimpy straw hula skirts and flower leis bring more food.

'I can't wait to get stuck in,' I say to my sister.

'Me too,' she says and, to start the ball rolling, she picks up two shot glasses and we down them.

'To us,' I toast belatedly.

'To us,' my sister agrees, and picks up another two glasses.

Blake Chadwick approaches us, grinning. 'Hey,' he says. 'No drinking on duty.'

We laugh at that.

He sweeps an arm round the room. 'How do you think it looks?'

'Marvellous.' I'm a little too breathy when I reply. 'Is this all your handiwork?'

His smile widens. 'Modesty prevents me.'

'I've never been to anything quite like this before,' I say. 'Thanks for asking us.'

'No worries.' BC shrugs away my thanks. 'Later, there are hula dancers and a couple doing limbo. It'll be a blast.' My boss checks his watch. 'You've got about fifteen minutes to get into your costumes.'

There's an abrupt screech in my head. *Costumes?*

'Minny's in charge of them,' he continues. 'She's at the back of the boat – in the stern. They're going fast though.'

Lauren gives me the blackest of black looks. When I say nothing, she nudges me in the ribs. Hard.

'Costumes?' I venture.

'All hands to the pumps,' Blake says briskly, and claps his hands in a manner that says he means business.

'You wanted us here to work?' My voice is small and uncertain and very disappointed.

BC stares at me, then bangs his forehead with the heel of his hand. 'Oh God,' he says. 'You thought you were here as a guest?'

My cheeks flush with embarrassment.

'That's why you're all dressed up like that?'

I look down at my beautiful new sunshine island dress. I'm so humiliated that I can't speak. Lauren looks like she's about to clobber me.

'I feel terrible,' Blake says. 'This is such a big event that we needed everyone's help. I'm really sorry, Annie. I don't know how this misunderstanding happened.'

I do, I think. It was me being stupid, silly, optimistic. 'Can't you manage without us?'

My boss sucks in a breath. ''Fraid not. You don't mind, do you?'

'No, no.'

'Yes, yes,' Lauren mouths behind his back.

'We'll go and get our costumes then,' I say miserably.

'Good girl,' Blake says, and claps me on the shoulder before striding away to attend to something else.

'This is the last time I'm ever coming out with you,' Lauren says when he's gone.

'I'm sorry, Lauren.' My spirits are in my strappy shoes. 'I had no idea. I don't know how I can have got it so wrong.'

'Bloody men,' Lauren mutters.

'It won't be so bad.'

'They'd better be paying us.'

'I'm sure they will,' I assure her. 'And we can still have fun.' I put my arm round my sister and steer her in the direction of the stern and the costumes that await us. 'Wait and see.'

Chapter Sixty-Eight

'Ooo,' Minny says when she sees us. 'I was starting to get in a panic. I didn't know where you were.'

'There was a slight misunderstanding,' I tell her. 'I didn't realise we were working.'

'Oh no.' Minny's face is full of pity. 'That's why you had your hair done and bought a new dress.'

Yes, I think. Don't need reminding of that one.

'All the hula outfits have gone now,' she says regretfully.

I laugh at that. 'Not sure that I'd have wanted to show so much skin.'

'Oh, the costumes that are left won't show any skin,' my little friend assures us. 'You don't need to worry about that.'

'Thank goodness!'

'I'll get them,' Minny says, and she totters off to the far side of the room. After a moment, she shouts, 'Perhaps it would be easier if you came over here.'

Lauren and I exchange a puzzled glance, but do as we're told and go over to where Minny is.

I gasp, loud and involuntarily, when I see what she's holding up.

'No,' I say. 'No way.'

'It's all that's left,' Minny tells us. 'Besides, they're great.'

'You wear one then,' I challenge.

She looks shifty at that. 'BC wants me doing other stuff.'

'I'm not wearing that,' Lauren chips in.

'Please,' Minny begs. 'Pretty please. The customer has paid a fortune for these and there's no one else left to do it.'

Out of the window I can see stilt-walkers entertaining the guests who are streaming up the gangway and on to the boat. They're all wearing summery, tropical clothing.

'I'm out of here now,' Lauren says.

'Wait, wait.' I pull my sister to one side out of Minny's earshot. 'If I refuse to do this, it could cost me my job.'

'They can't sack you for not wanting to dress up in a hideous costume,' Lauren points out.

'But suppose I get a name for being difficult – it might make things uncomfortable for me on our trip to Peru.' I tut – which doesn't go anywhere close to expressing my frustration. Not within ten miles of it. 'Do it,' I urge Lauren. 'Please do it. For me.'

She sighs unhappily. 'For you,' she says. 'I'll do it only for you.'

I turn back to Minny. 'Okay,' I tell her. 'We'll do it.'

And, with that, she hands us two big orange plastic pineapple costumes.

Chapter Sixty-Nine

Lauren and I regard ourselves in the full-length mirror which Minny has brought along, then wish we hadn't. Dearly wish we hadn't.

'Fucking hell,' Lauren puffs out with feeling.

I couldn't agree more.

Our outfits are beyond awful, beyond hideous, beyond a joke. My lovely dress is on a hanger beside me, looking forlorn. My new hairdo is squashed flat.

'Whatever they're paying us,' my sister snarls, 'it isn't enough.'

The pineapple costumes fit tightly round our neck and then the rigid plastic goes right down to our knees. It's like trying to walk while encased in a great big orange barrel. Beyond that there are thick beige tights like surgical stockings. My strappy shoes look ridiculous at the end of them – *if* I could actually look more ridiculous than I do already.

On our heads we have a sprout of green plastic leaves like a pineapple top, held on by strong elastic under our chins. In no way, shape or form is this a good look. Not by any stretch of the imagination.

We can poke our arms out of the sides of the pineapple, but moving them about is another matter. Minny hands us orange gloves and we reluctantly pull them on for each other.

'You owe me for this,' my sister snarls as I yank her glove

in place. 'Big time. I don't know what and I don't know when, but you will pay me back for this.'

'I will,' I promise. 'I'm so sorry, Lauren.' Misery is raining down on me. 'And I thought we were going to have such fun tonight.'

'You thought you'd be snogging Lover Boy under the swaying palms,' she huffs.

It's better to say nothing.

On cue, BC appears. 'Ladies, ladies,' he says, rubbing his hands. 'You look fab-u-lous!'

We don't.

'You're needed in the main room,' he continues. 'Chop, chop.'

Lauren and I shuffle towards the door. 'I'd like to bloody well chop, chop him,' my sister mutters darkly.

I want to cry. And when I find that we can barely squeeze through the doors, I want to cry more. Lauren pushes while I pull and then, like a cork out of a bottle, we both shoot out.

The boat is already in the middle of the Thames and, even with a slight sway, it's hard to stay upright in these damn suits. We shuffle into the palm-treed paradise, both grumbling in a manner that's probably not fitting for a pineapple – which is generally, I would assume, considered an inoffensive fruit.

The steel band are in full swing and there's a great party atmosphere in the air. Across the room I can see two bananas, a cherry and a lime. We're clearly supposed to be the ingredients of the drink. I wonder if they feel as depressed as we do. But then perhaps they realised that they were coming here to be large fruit and not on an illicit date.

The fit waiters and sexy ladies move round the room offering canapés. Oh, why couldn't we have had skimpy costumes! Already the outfit is chafing at my neck and I'm bathed in sweat inside it. We don't seem to have a particular role – other than to be jolly – so we move round, smiling at the guests through gritted teeth and trying to act like tropical fruit.

'I'm sure they could have managed without the pineapples,' Lauren complains.

'Customer has ordered pineapples,' I say tightly. 'Customer gets pineapples.' But I have to agree with her. We just seem to be getting in the way, barging and barrelling through the crowd of partygoers. I can only thank the Lord that the customer hadn't ordered *dancing* pineapples.

'I'm sure this must be against my human rights,' Lauren whines, and she grabs a shot of Totally Tropical from a passing hunk in a Hawaiian shirt and downs it. 'Pineapple or not,' my sister growls, 'I plan on getting slaughtered.'

'Please don't tell Greg about this,' I plead. 'I'd never live it down.'

'Your secret's safe with me.'

'I'll never tell Chelsea either, if you won't.'

'Good plan,' she agrees. 'If we never speak about this again in our entire lifetime, then we can pretend that it never really happened.'

'Can I gasp "pineapple" on my deathbed?' I want to know.

'Not funny,' my sister says. 'Do we have a deal?'

'Deal,' I agree.

'At least I'm not likely to bump into anyone I know,' Lauren says with a relieved puff. 'That's one saving grace. The *only* saving grace.'

It's then that I see my sister's lover, Jude Taylor – complete with his wife, children and a Hawaiian shirt – heading directly for us.

Chapter Seventy

It is him. I'm sure it is. I've only met him fleetingly over the years at Lauren's workplace, but I'm convinced I'm not mistaken.

I steer my pineappled sister towards the beachside bar hut and grab three shots of Totally Tropical for her and line them up.

'Drink that,' I instruct.

'Hmm. Lovely, lovely,' she says, taking one in her little orange-gloved hand. 'I need this.'

'You will,' I tell her.

'What?' Now my sister has picked up on the alarm in my voice.

'Don't hyperventilate,' I say. 'But Jude is over there.'

My sister starts to hyperventilate.

'With his wife and children.'

Lauren gasps at the air for breath. 'What? *What?* WHAT!' She swallows the other couple of shots.

I'd normally try to stop my sister from drinking so much, but this stuff is probably not much stronger than fruit juice. I knock another shot back myself – it certainly tastes harmless enough.

Her eyes lock on to her lover. Jude currently has his arm round his wife and is holding his daughter's hand. They're all laughing. They look like a family off a cereal advert or something. All wholesome and scrubbed and perfect.

'What the hell's he doing *here*?' Lauren wants to know. Her voice is laced with anguish. She would probably wave her arms about – if she could.

And, in my defence, if I hadn't been so distressed at being kitted out as a pineapple, I might have noticed her slurring earlier.

'This can't be happening to me,' my sister continues, sounding crazed. 'It's a nightmare. Any minute now I'm going to wake up and be in my own bed. And oh, how I'll laugh!'

I pinch her.

'Fuck,' she says. 'This is reality.' She puts her green-leaved pineapple-top head in her hands. 'And all I was thinking was that I should lay off the cheese before bedtime.'

'We can avoid him,' I assure her. 'All we need do is to keep one step ahead of him.'

'I might remind you that we're dressed as pineapples,' Lauren snaps. 'We're not exactly *in-con-fucking-spicuous*.'

She has a point.

'Why is he here?' she wails miserably. 'He told me he was working late. He couldn't even tell me the truth.'

I think that Jude probably has general issues with the truth, but realise that this isn't the time to raise that.

'Why would he bring his wife here?'

That's generally how it goes when you're married, I think, but decide that it's best not to remind Lauren of that either in her current state of mind. Instead, I say, 'I'm sorry, Lauren. So sorry.'

'He has his children here too.' She looks at me, pained. 'Oh, God. Why would he bring his children?'

'There are a few kids here.' Not that many of them, admittedly. Most adults, I'm sure, would rather have the opportunity to get blotto on free booze without the kids in tow. 'I don't think it's restricted to adults.' Perhaps the kids were actually invited too. Or perhaps their babysitter let them down at the last minute. Perhaps they just wanted to be here as a family. Plus there's more than enough to keep children entertained. There are jugglers and fire-eaters and dancers. And where else can you go to see life-size fruit these days?

'They do a non-alcoholic version of this stuff too,' I tell Lauren as we down another pair of shots. 'The kids can drink that. Perhaps we should move on to it too?'

'What is the purpose of drink without alcohol?' my sister snaps, and polishes off another glass as she eyeballs me. 'Tell me that.'

'I'm sorry,' I say again, because I don't know what else I have to offer. Maybe Lauren is better off drunk. Maybe I am too.

'He'll have come here under protest,' she says. 'Because *she* made him.'

At which point Jude, smiling broadly – as far away from the picture of a man who's miserable in his marriage could be – pulls his wife to him and kisses her warmly. If he has been dragged here, it seems that he's putting a brave face on it. Very brave.

'That's it,' Lauren announces as she downs two more shots.

Clearly, my sister has no intention of considering the no-alcohol idea. 'I can't stay here.'

And with that, my big, orange, distraught twin sister waddles away as fast as she can.

Chapter Seventy-One

I catch up with Lauren in the ladies' loo. I can't actually see her, but I can hear her sobbing.

'Lauren.' I knock gently on the cubicle door. Renewed sobbing. 'Lauren, open the door. Please.'

A moment later the door opens. Lauren, with some difficulty, is sitting on the toilet seat.

'Oh, love,' I say and, also with some difficulty, wrap my arms round her. Sort of.

The heartfelt crying is racking her body, making her pineapple shake up and down. 'Don't. Don't.' I stroke her plastic leaves tenderly. 'He's not worth it.'

'I have a pain in my heart.'

'It could be the pineapple suit,' I venture.

'Annie!' my sister snaps.

'I'm trying to make you laugh.'

'I want to die. I want to lie on this toilet floor and never get up again. I have given him five years of my life,' she cries bleakly. 'How can I walk away? How can I leave? If I do, it will all have been for nothing.'

'Oh, Lauren,' I say. 'You always knew that this could end in pain.'

'He doesn't love her,' she sobs, slurring her words. 'He tells me all the time. He has to stop himself from calling out my name in his sleep. Did you know that?'

'No,' I say. 'I didn't know that.' But how can I tell my sister that it sounds like a terrible, clichéd line to me?

'He *will* leave her.'

'When, though?' Perhaps this is the time for tough talking. 'He's been stringing you along for years with empty promises.'

'What's a few months, a few years when we're planning to be together for ever?'

Then I hear the door open and my heart jumps to my mouth when I see who comes in.

'Shut up,' I say to Lauren and I try to get into the cubicle with her, but there's no chance. This is a one-pineapple toilet.

Instead, I make myself as big as I can and fill the door.

Jude's wife Georgia and her daughter come in. I remember Lauren telling me that the child's name was Daisy and I think she's eight. She's certainly as cute as a button.

'Oh,' Daisy says when she sees me. 'A pineapple.'

I give them both a big, fake smile and a pineappley wave and pray that they can't hear the desolate sobs coming from behind me.

Georgia smiles sweetly at me. 'Don't I know you from somewhere?'

I shake my head frantically.

'You look exactly like someone who works with my husband. If you don't mind me saying.'

Damn being a twin! I try to shrug nonchalantly in my pineapple suit which may not translate that well. No matter how hard I try, I can't find the words to explain our predicament to my sister's lover's wife.

'Her hands are all sticky from the fruit juice,' Georgia says, smiling at her daughter.

I nod. My voice still stuck fast in my throat.

Daisy puts her hands under the tap that her mother has turned on for her.

'This is a lovely party,' the little girl says.

'It's just like the Caribbean island where Daddy took us on holiday last Christmas, isn't it, sweetheart?'

That would be the fifth Christmas that my sister spent alone.

'Oh, yes,' Daisy says with a happy sigh. 'That was lovely.'

Georgia hands her daughter a paper towel to dry her hands. I try to block Lauren's view.

'You must be very hot in that costume,' Georgia says sympathetically.

I nod again. If she wonders why I'm jamming myself in this cubicle door, unmoving, then she doesn't reveal it.

This woman has no idea who I am. She has no idea that my sister, right behind me, has been sleeping with her husband for five years. That I know intimate details of her life while she knows nothing of mine. We are, as far as she's concerned, strangers passing pleasantries.

Jude's wife studies herself in the mirror. She's a slender, stunningly attractive woman. Not the limp loser or the clingy control freak Lauren has described to me. Tonight she's wearing a lemon strappy top and a colourful beaded sarong with delicate jewelled flip-flops on her pedicured toes. It is just the most perfect outfit. She runs a lipstick over her full, sensuous lips.

'Do you need to use the bathroom while we're here, darling?'

Daisy shakes her head.

261

'We'd better get back then or Daddy will be wondering where we've got to.'

'I'm having such a lovely time at this party,' Daisy declares.

'Me too,' Georgia says. 'Daddy thought you would like it.'

Daisy sighs contentedly and then announces, 'I have the best daddy in the world.'

Georgia chucks her daughter under the chin. 'Yes, you do,' she agrees.

My sister's lover's wife smiles in my direction again. She looks like a happy woman, a woman in love, a woman who would never suspect that her husband was cheating on her. Looks, so they say, can be deceptive. But I'd bet a pound on that being wrong in this case.

Georgia gives me a friendly wave. 'See you later,' she says.

Another mute wave from me. Then, as the door closes, I sag against the doorpost with relief.

'It was her, wasn't it?' Lauren asks as if she needs my confirmation. 'They're so happy together, aren't they?'

I can't deny that's how it seems.

'She's wonderful. Did you see her?'

I did.

'How can I compete with that?' she says sadly. 'How can I even want to?'

'Oh, Lauren.'

'He's never going to leave her, is he?'

Do I tell the truth here or do I encourage my sister in her misplaced fantasy of life with her married lover? I opt for the truth. 'I don't think so, honey.'

Lauren lets out a keening wail. 'Why did I have to be dressed as a pineapple?'

Would any other fruit have been better?

'A bad hair day I might have been able to cope with. But a *pineapple*? Why couldn't I have been wearing some chi-chi designer outfit like she was?'

'It's no good thinking like that, Lauren.' I need to try to cheer my sister up before she descends into the gloom of depression. 'That way madness lies.'

'This *is* making me crazy, isn't it?' My sister's face is as white as the driven snow when she looks up at me. 'I have completely lost my mind because of this man. I have to call an end to this, Annie, don't I?'

I take Lauren's horrible orange-gloved hand in mine. 'Yes, darling, you do.'

My sister's tears fall again. And I cry with her.

Chapter Seventy-Two

Eventually, Lauren comes out of the toilet cubicle. 'My bum was getting numb,' she complains as she waddles forth.

My sister takes off her gloves and splashes her face with water. 'What are we going to do now? I can't go back in there, Annie. It would kill me.'

'Stay in here until I can find somewhere quiet for you to go. I'll tell BC that you're not feeling well.'

'Seasick,' Lauren says. 'Tell him I'm seasick.'

To be honest, my stomach is rolling too as if I have got some kind of sympathetic travel sickness.

'I'll be back in a minute,' I tell Lauren. 'Don't move.'

'I *can't* bloody move in this!' she howls after me.

I scuttle off down the corridor in search of Blake Chadwick, but I don't have to go very far. As I turn the corner, or whatever the nautical term for it is on a boat, I find who I'm looking for.

Stopping in my tracks, I'm transfixed.

There, pressed up against each other in a little nook, are BC and Minny. His tongue is down her throat, one hand is on her breast, the other up her skirt. Now I do feel like I'm going to be sick. Nausea smashes into me, heaving up to my chest.

I reel back against the wall and practise deep-breathing techniques.

How can I have been so stupid? How can I have ever believed that this man was interested in me? To think that I had my hair done for him. And bought a new dress. To think that I could have – *may well have* – jeopardised my marriage for him?

'Someone might see us,' Minny murmurs.

'Who cares?' Blake says back, and continues his tender assault.

Who cares, indeed?

I do. I care. Fool that I am.

'What if Annie sees us?' Minny says, mouth still on his. 'She'll be upset. She's got a crush on you.'

Blake presses against her. 'She's old enough to be my mother.'

I only just stop myself from gasping out loud or jumping out of my hiding-place to protest. For the record, I am *so* not. Though how could I, a plain, boring mother of two grown-up children, think that someone like Blake Chadwick could have looked at me with a twinkle in his eye? Of course he's going to want a younger, slimmer, more available girl, rather than a middle-aged woman with a spare tyre and stars in her eyes.

The taste of bile fills my mouth and there are tears in my eyes as, blindly, I stumble back to the room where the party is in full swing. I catch sight of Jude grinning like a loon and dancing to 'Hot, Hot, Hot' with his arms round his babe of a wife. He glances up and, for a moment, I think he catches my eye as a stricken look flits across his face. Then it's gone and I duck out of sight.

When the Hawaiian-shirted barman moves out of the way, I slip behind the beach hut and swipe two unopened bottles of Totally Tropical out of a cardboard box. I double-check that it's the alcoholic version. There have been enough mistakes tonight and that's one that I really don't want to make. Back on my way to Lauren I pass the kitchen, so pop in to liberate a tray of canapés.

I find her still in the loo, looking dazed and confused and not a little drunk.

'Come on,' I say, grabbing her by the arm. 'Let's get out of here.'

'But you're working,' she says.

'Not now.' I stop and sigh. 'I just saw Blake Chadwick snogging one of my younger, more beautiful colleagues. He can stuff his job up his bottom.'

'All men are bastards,' Lauren declares.

'Yes,' I agree. 'They are. So let's go and get stupidly drunk on this rubbish.'

Out on deck, and the cool breeze hits us like a slap in the face. We head towards the stern, where I see a ladder going up to another level. We'd be well out of anyone's way if we can get up there. No one would ever find us. With much huffing, puffing, pulling and pushing, Lauren and I climb it.

As I suspected, there's no one else up here. No one else foolhardy enough.

It's some sort of flat roof with rails along the side, but other than that it's blissfully empty. We can still hear the steel band playing its heart out on the deck below. The inky black waters of the Thames are far beneath us. I help Lauren to sit down, then she reciprocates. Our costumes are ridiculously uncomfortable but I quickly realise that if we were to take them off then we'd succumb to hypothermia within minutes. It may be summer, but out here on the river in the night air, it's not overly warm.

I undo Lauren's pineapple leaf hat and she does mine. I feel like throwing them into the Thames, but sense prevails and I put them down next to us so that someone else in the future can be humiliated by dressing as a tropical fruit.

'I'm never going to eat pineapple again,' my sister says.

'Me neither.'

The sun is just setting, casting a pink glow over the magnificent London skyline. I crack open the bottles of Totally Tropical and hand one to my sister. We swig in unison.

'This stuff tastes better, the more you drink of it,' she decides.

The water rushes below us. The wind lifts our hair. We tuck into the canapés that I've purloined.

'This was going to be our year,' I remind her.

'Fine fucking mess we're making of it.'

I sigh and it's snatched away from my mouth. 'What are you going to do about Jude?'

'Leave him.'

We drink from our bottles then wipe our mouths with our orange gloves.

'What are you going to do about Greg?'

'Love him,' I say.

'And Peru?'

'I don't know,' I say. Is there any point in having a dream when no one else cares whether you achieve it or not? At this moment, I'm too drunk, too dazed, too disorientated to be able to come to a conclusion.

Chapter Seventy-Three

We're nearly at the bottom of our bottles of Totally Tropical and, to be honest, it's not true that you can never have too much of a good thing.

'I feel sick,' Lauren says, just as I'm thinking exactly the same.

Surely this torture will be over soon. The boat turned ages ago, so we must be coming near to the dock again before long.

'We should think about getting down from here and finding our clothes,' I say to my sister. Do I sound a little slurry too?

I can't even stand up in this damn suit. My feet scrabble on the floor and, try as I might, I can't get the necessary leverage.

'Here, let me help,' Lauren says.

'I've got it.' I tip myself over until I'm on my knees on all fours. Then I take a bit of a breather, before hoisting myself upright. 'Is it me or are these costumes getting heavier?'

Grabbing Lauren's hands, I haul her to her feet, both of us panting alarmingly.

'Think we can tackle the ladder again?' Oh, it seemed like such a good idea when we climbed up here! Now it seems to be swaying alarmingly.

'I'll go first,' Lauren says, and she waddles towards the edge of the roof in a slightly unnerving and wobbly way.

'Be careful,' I say. I might only be a couple of minutes older than Lauren but I still think of myself as the big sister.

She swings her legs over the side and starts down the

ladder. There's a lot of huffing, puffing and swearing. I peer over the side anxiously until she's nearly at the bottom, out of harm's way.

The boat sways enthusiastically as I make my way towards the vertical ladder, holding on tightly to the railings. I can see the dock coming into view now – thank goodness!

Lauren is at the bottom, down below, when she suddenly shouts out, 'You bastard!' and launches her barrel-shaped body across the deck. It can only be Jude.

Sure enough, her lover is standing there, trying to grab hold of Lauren's arms as she pounds her orange gloves against his chest. Then she clocks him round the head with her pineapple hat.

Hastily, I swing my own legs round and ease my pineapple-clad bottom to the edge. I need to get down there before blood is shed. As my feet hit the first rung, I feel very unsteady. Ooo. I think I've had way more to drink than I imagined. I thought this Totally Tropical stuff was as weak as gnat's wee. Maybe I was wrong.

I try to hurry down the ladder. But hurrying and being dressed as a pineapple are not, it seems, compatible.

Chapter Seventy-Four

Lauren whacked Jude again with her pineapple-top hat. He held up his hands. 'Ouch!'

'How could you?' she wailed. 'You said you were working late. You said you couldn't get away. *You lied to me!*'

'Lauren, Lauren,' he cajoled. 'Calm down. People are starting to look.'

It was true that a small but very interested crowd had inched nearer to them.

'What else have you lied to me about?' she sobbed.

'Nothing.' Jude was now gripping her by the arms. 'Nothing, I promise you.'

'Are you ever going to leave her?' Lauren cried, all semblance of dignity gone. How could she conduct a dignified argument dressed like this? She might as well give her lover both barrels while she was fortified by a bottle of Totally Tropical. 'Five years, Jude. I have waited five years for you.'

'Not much longer,' her lover swore. 'Just calm down. Please, Lauren, you're making a scene.'

'I want to make a scene,' she shouted. 'I want you with me. Permanently. Not just two or three times a week for a rushed hour. It's not fair to me and it's not fair to your family.'

'I will sort it out.' Jude looked stricken and glanced round at the crowd. 'Financially, this is a really bad time for me to leave. But I will do it. The timing just has to be right.'

'No.' Lauren stood back from him. Suddenly she sounded a lot more sober and sensible than she had. 'Stay with your family. Make this up to them. I don't want anything more to do with you.'

'Don't say that, Lauren,' Jude begged. 'You know you don't mean it.'

'This time, I do,' she insisted.

'I *will* leave.'

'No,' Lauren said. 'This is over. It's gone on way too long. I should never, *ever* have got involved with you in the first place, Jude. It was insanity.' The pineapple suit made her feel as if she had the weight of the world on her shoulders. 'Well, now I've had enough. Stay with your wife and your children. I don't want you.'

Then a small voice came from the crowd. 'And I don't want you either.'

Jude's wife Georgia stepped forward.

'I can explain everything,' Jude said in time-honoured fashion.

'I don't want your explanations,' his wife said, her voice calm and level. 'And I don't want you to come home tonight. Book into a hotel or go to her. It doesn't matter either way to me.'

'This is all a dreadful misunderstanding.' Jude tried a laugh. No one joined in.

'I'm surprised at you, Lauren,' Georgia said. 'I always liked you. I thought you were a friend.'

'I'm so sorry, Georgia,' Lauren offered. 'I can't apologise enough for what I've done.'

'I don't want your apology. I just want you to keep away from me and my family.'

With that, the children ran up behind their mother. 'We didn't know where you'd gone, Mummy!' Benjy said.

'I came to look for Daddy.' Her eyes met Jude's. 'And I found him.'

'Are we going home now?'

'Yes,' Georgia said with a glance behind her. 'The boat's about to dock.'

'Come on, Daddy,' Daisy said.

'Daddy's got things to do,' Georgia said. 'He's not coming back with us.'

'Oooh,' Jude's daughter whined.

'Georgia,' Jude pleaded. 'I beg you not to do this.'

'Come on, children,' she said. 'Let's make our way downstairs. You go ahead of me. I want a word with Daddy. But don't run.'

When the children were out of earshot, she lowered her voice and said, 'You're welcome to him, Lauren. He's not fit to be my husband.' With that she turned on her heel and walked, head held high, after her children.

Jude turned to Lauren. 'What have you done?' Then he chased after his wife, barging through the open-mouthed people who barred his way. 'Georgia,' he shouted as he chased after her. 'Georgia, wait!'

Lauren sank to the deck. Her heart was breaking, not for her, not for the fact that she'd lost Jude, but for the pain that it had caused – would cause – to his wife and children.

Annie had always warned her that this would end in tears, she thought – and it looked as if her twin sister had been right.

Chapter Seventy-Five

I'm halfway down the ladder, frozen with shock at the devastation that's unfolding on the deck beneath me. My hands are white fists as I grip the metal.

This is all my fault. All my stupid fault. If I hadn't been so keen to come here in pursuit of Blake Chadwick, then none of this would have happened. My sister will never forgive me for this. I'll never forgive myself.

I watch as Jude storms after his wife and my sister slumps to the deck. As fast as I can, I scuttle down the last of the rungs. I have to go and comfort Lauren.

'Lauren!' I shout. 'Don't move – I'm coming.'

And then I'm not sure exactly what happens, but I think the boat swings hard into the dock – maybe even hits against it – and the next thing I know, I'm sailing through the air. My arms are flailing in lots of empty space and I can hear a gasp from the crowd. They're certainly getting a great deal more entertainment tonight than they bargained for.

It's true that your life flashes before you in moments of terror. As I fall, I see Greg and me at our wedding, my kids being born, me and Lauren and Chelsea playing together as kids – even Blake Chadwick gets a flicker. And I realise that, just as I suspected, there's nothing in there of particular note to take with me to my grave.

A second later and I land heavily on the deck with a heartfelt, *'Ouff!'*

My pineapple costume helps to break my fall – and I never thought that I'd be grateful to be wearing it, but right at this moment I am – but all the wind is knocked out of me and I bang my head. More worryingly, there's an unhealthy sounding snap from somewhere in my foot. The pain is excruciating.

My vision seems to be all swimmy, but I can still see Lauren bending over me, her face white with anxiety.

'Annie,' she says in an urgent way. 'Annie, stay with me!'

But I don't think that I do.

Chapter Seventy-Six

I wake up in a hospital bed. And I'd like to be able to say that I remember nothing about what happened, but I remember it well. Only *too* well. I consider pretending that I have amnesia. Believe me, the temptation to blot out the events of this miserable evening is very appealing.

On one side, Lauren is next to me, *sans* pineapple. That I can cope with. The concerned face of Blake Chadwick on the other is a different matter altogether.

'Okay?' he asks, when he sees my eyes open.

Not that you'd notice, but I make a valiant attempt at a nod anyway.

'God, Annie,' he says with a sigh of relief. 'You had us worried there.'

My mouth is dry, my throat closed. I manage to croak out, 'Where am I?' Which is a bit clichéd, I know. But, hey, I'm clearly traumatised.

BC, his face the picture of sympathy, offers me a drink of water and then helps me to lift my head while I take a sip.

'You knocked yourself out when you hit the deck.' My sister, eyes red-rimmed, kindly fills in my missing moments.

That would go some way to explaining the throbbing pain that's got my skull in a vice-like grip.

'They're just keeping you in overnight for observation.'

I always wondered what that involved. Now I know. It

involves me lying in a bed feeling pitifully sorry for myself while being ignored by hospital staff.

Still, no harm done if it's only my head I've injured, I think. Then I realise that there's a throbbing pain in my foot too and I remember the rather ear-splitting crack that came from that region as I hit the deck. It feels like there's some kind of splint on it.

'Is it broken?'

BC nods and Lauren bursts into tears – not for the first time, by the look of her. I lean back against the pillow and close my eyes. My dream of going to Peru has just evaporated before my very eyes.

'Metatarsal fracture.' Blake reads my thoughts. 'They said it could mend in time. Six weeks, if all goes well. It'll be close, but it's not impossible.'

Six weeks. But is it really likely either?

BC bites his lip. 'It could be eight though.'

Eight weeks.

'They've put a removable plastic cast on so that you can start physio early.'

So, some good news then.

'What on earth were you thinking of, Annie, climbing up there?' Blake wants to know. 'When you were drunk.' He sounds so disappointed in me.

How can I tell him that I was thinking of him kissing my little colleague, Minny, of hearing him say I was past it, and that I too have disappointments of my own?

'It's my fault,' Lauren butts in. 'It's my fault we were up there.' But, quite wisely, she offers Blake no further in-formation.

'Where's Jude?' I croak.

She meets my eyes. 'Gone home.'

A nurse bustles along to my bedside. She looks irritated at having her night-shift disturbed by someone dressed as a pineapple getting drunk and falling off a ladder. 'How's the patient?'

'*Disappointed in love, life and luck*,' I want to say but, of course, answer politely, 'Not too bad.'

'Hmm,' she says.

Blake strokes my arm tenderly and I want to pull it away, but I can't. All of my limbs feel weak and feeble.

'Are you the husband?' the nurse asks.

'No,' a familiar voice says. 'I am.'

I may be hallucinating, due to having a bang on the head, but it looks to me as if that's Greg standing there at the bottom of the bed. And he doesn't seem best pleased.

Chapter Seventy-Seven

Greg is still in his fishing gear and I can tell where he was when he got the call. My husband must have come straight here.

'I rang him,' Lauren admits, plucking at her lip. 'I was worried.'

I see Greg glance at BC, his hand on my arm, stroking softly. Then my husband looks at me. His lips form a tight white line. Perhaps I should introduce my boss to my husband, but I can't summon the necessary energy, to be honest. I should just like everyone to go away while I slip into the pleasant oblivion of sedation once more.

'I should be going,' Blake says, standing up to vacate his seat for Greg. He looks uncomfortable now that my husband is here and I don't know why. 'We've got to strip down the boat overnight.'

'I'm sorry to put you out,' I say.

'Don't be silly,' BC chides. 'As long as you're all right.' He looks like he might go to kiss me on the cheek, but thinks better of it. Then he strides off down the ward, head fixed forward, not looking at the other people in the rows of beds.

Greg takes up his place in the chair. I notice that he doesn't kiss me.

'Okay?' he says.

Why does everyone say that to people who are patently

ill or in pain and lying in hospital beds? *'Of course I'm not okay,'* I want to scream. 'Fine.'

'I'm going to get off too,' my sister says. 'If that's okay?'

'You go ahead,' I tell her. 'You must be exhausted.'

Lauren gathers her things. 'I'll call you in the morning.' She kisses my cheek. 'Will you be all right?'

'Yes, yes.' Once everything stops hurting.

'Try to get some sleep,' she advises.

'You too.'

Lauren smiles at that. 'As if.'

'You'll be okay.' I squeeze her hand.

'So will you.' Then she kisses Greg briefly and disappears.

Now my husband and I are left alone. And it seems as if he doesn't know what to say. And neither do I.

'Thanks for coming,' I say, as if he's a stranger.

'I was worried,' Greg says. I notice that he's wringing his hands. 'The nurse says you were drunk.'

Thanks for that, Nursie. 'Tipsy,' I correct. 'Lauren and I got tipsy on Totally Tropical. It was much stronger than it appeared.'

'And you fell off a ladder.'

'Yes.'

'I suppose this means that the Inca Trail is off the agenda?' Is there a note of smugness in my husband's voice? Maybe there's even a glimmer of a smile at his lips. I could be imagining it, but perhaps I'm not.

'No,' I say calmly. 'I could well be recovered in time.'

His face clouds over. 'You can't seriously *still* be thinking of going?'

My dander rises and, you know, I'm not even sure where my dander is. 'Absolutely.'

'I don't know what's got into you. Or who.' He glances in the direction where Blake Chadwick has recently exited. 'You're completely mad, woman.' And it's not said in a fun, teasy way. My husband really does think that I'm mad.

'I'd be mad to give up my dream,' I tell him stubbornly. And, at this moment, if I have to hop all the bloody way, then I damn well will.

Chapter Seventy-Eight

Greg took the bottle that Ray was offering. They both sipped on chilled beer from the cooler that his friend had installed in the boot of his car.

'This is the life,' Ray said, smacking his lips.

Greg's rod twitched, his float bobbed and he could feel a little pull on the reel. Not much – maybe a perch – light, a pound, nothing more. Then, as he reeled it in, he saw the menacing wide head and tooth-filled jaw of a pike come up and snatch the fish from his hook with deadly efficiency. The ultimate predator had struck.

'Bloody pike,' Ray muttered in sympathy. 'They'd eat their own granny if they could. No morals.'

The pike wasn't a fish Greg would normally seek out. He usually only encountered them when they were snatching his own fish from beneath his nose while he was powerless to do anything about it. They looked like trouble and they were trouble.

They were a prehistoric fish, old as time itself, and their behaviour and appearance hadn't changed much in all that time. If you hooked one they'd fight like fury to defeat you. The pike was the most fearsome and fearless of all the freshwater fish.

Its camouflage was perfect, allowing it to move unseen alongside an unsuspecting fish before striking. It was enough to send shivers down the spine of any angler. The pike had a frightening turn of speed and explosive power. Underestimate him at your peril.

Greg turned to his friend. 'I think there is another man,' he said. 'I can't be sure.'

'No smoke without fire,' Ray warned.

'Annie fell over. Broke her foot.' Greg decided not to mention the pineapple costume. The Bunny Girl, he thought, had been a step too far. Now this. 'There was a bloke at the hospital. A bit too close for comfort.'

He couldn't believe it. His Annie. How could she do this? The old Annie would never have dreamed of cheating on him. But this newfangled, unrecognisable Annie? This strange, unfamiliar woman seemed to be capable of anything.

Chapter Seventy-Nine

Lauren didn't go to work. She stayed in bed with the curtains closed. The phone had rung constantly and she'd put a pillow over her head to block out the sound, but still it continued. Finally, she'd hauled herself out of her pit and had pulled the plug out of the wall. Then her mobile had started, so she'd switched that off too.

It was Jude. She knew it was. His ring had a certain tone to it. And this tone was cross. And getting crosser.

She didn't want to speak to Jude. She didn't want to speak to anyone. Not even Annie, if she was truthful, and yet she knew she should phone her sister and see how she was now.

Her head throbbed and she'd spent an hour puking up a strange lemon fluid which tasted of rancid pineapple and which she assumed was regurgitated Totally Tropical. Then she ate a piece of dry toast and threw that up too.

Perhaps she'd never eat again. Perhaps she'd just lie here and let herself wither away to nothing. Who would care? Who would notice?

So. It was over. Just like that. All those years gone to waste.

She should feel good that she had at least called a stop to all that subterfuge, deceit and downright lying – but she didn't. There was just a big hollow bit inside her where feeling was meant to be.

Lauren couldn't go back to work at *Happening Today*. She

could never face Jude again. Never be in the same room as him again. That was the end of her career as she knew it.

It wasn't one final lie that had tipped her over the edge. It was seeing Jude with his family, his children. She'd always managed to avoid that in the past. If he'd hosted a company barbecue at his home where children were invited, Lauren had always managed to find some excuse to dip out of it. She'd never had to confront the fact that they were actually all very happy together – that both his wife and his kids were blissfully unaware of their father's duplicity, or her part in it.

They looked like great kids – the sort of kids that she would like to have herself one day. That made her cry again. With pity for herself and with sorrow for the damage she'd caused.

What would she do now? Another job would be the first thing. Then another place to live. This mortgage would, she was sure, be too expensive for her to pay off on her salary alone. Perhaps she could move further north, out of the Smoke and nearer to Annie. Maybe she could get a house in the same road as her sister, as they'd always planned as kids. Say goodbye to London completely. That way, she'd be sure never to bump into Jude ever again.

Even the thought made her stomach roil. How on earth would she begin to fill that gap in her life?

It was over. It had to be. But that didn't stop it hurting. It didn't stop her loving him.

Chapter Eighty

As a supposed compromise, I continue with the car wash in order to raise my funds but, as I'm on crutches, I don't do it in the bunny outfit. However, Greg continues to look at me with disdain – as if I'm still in the Bunny Girl get-up.

To be honest, it's not a great success. Hopping around is uncomfortable, and I should be resting my foot, not putting my weight on it. It takes me ages to do each car and there's very little interest in my services now that, to put it bluntly, my tits aren't hanging out. What does that say about the human race? Or the male of the species in particular?

After a miserable, long day and a measly fifty pounds, I call it quits. It would have been so easy to have carried on as I was. Another couple of weekends and I would have had my sponsorship money. As it is, I'm going to have to do it the hard way. But I haven't quite worked out what that is yet.

I can't rope my sister in because she's in no fit state to do anything. I'm so worried about her. She's not eating and she's drinking way too much – although not Totally Tropical, which I doubt either of us will ever touch again.

Despite the Ashton twins embarrassing themselves royally at the disastrous Party Party boat event, I managed to keep my job. Perhaps if I hadn't so roundly injured myself, it might have been a different story, but apparently, there were some Health and Safety issues surrounding dressing people as fruit without adequate training, and it was decided not to sack me in case I sued the pants off them. It's the first time in my life that I have felt grateful for the ridiculous rules of the EU.

So, my 'embarrassing incident', as it will be referred to, has been swept under the carpet – at work, if not at home – though I'm sure it will go down in the annals of company folklore once the pain has subsided. At Chez Ashton, however, the matter will clearly not be forgotten quite so quickly.

I can't remember a time in our entire marriage when Greg and I have been at such odds and it's depressing me immensely. He's out fishing even more than normal, and when he is at home he tries to avoid me completely. Which in a house our size, is no mean feat. Most of the time he's hiding away in the garage doing things to his fishing equipment that I just don't understand, and am not interested in enough to bother to learn.

I'm hopping about, tidying away my bucket and my pink sponge – even that looks sorry for itself – when my big sister's posh car pulls up outside our house.

It's weeks since I've seen Chelsea and I feel bad because I should have made more effort now that she's at home in Woburn. To be honest, I've been avoiding her because of the Bounced Cheque Situation. How am I going to raise it with her? I know Chelsea will be mortified. My sister slips out of her car and comes towards me, arms outstretched. 'Why didn't you tell me?' she cries.

'I forgot,' I apologise. 'I've had a lot on my mind.'

'I had to find out from Stephanie,' she tuts.

I have no idea who Stephanie is and, obviously, that registers on my face.

286

'You know, Annie.' Chelsea pulls a face. 'Mrs Drew-Phillips' daughter.'

Still none the wiser. I do not know and have never known a Mrs Drew-Phillips. And I'm definitely not sure how Stephanie, Mrs Drew-Phillips' daughter, got to hear about my misfortune. 'Oh, yes,' I say. '*That* Stephanie.'

If my sister has also been told by Stephanie the way I came about my injury, then she doesn't let on. I'm hoping to take that particular secret with me to the grave.

Chelsea lifts my bucket and puts it away for me. Her nose gives an involuntary crinkle when she sees the state of our garage. Chelsea's garage has a painted floor and white walls lined with useful storage cupboards. Ours doesn't.

'Don't you two ever think of involving me in your lives?' she asks suddenly, in a tone that I've never heard her use before. 'Why didn't Lauren phone me?'

'Lauren has troubles of her own,' I admit, even though Lauren would rather do something unpleasant to her face with a blunt knife than let Chelsea know that things aren't perfect in her world.

Chelsea waits for further explanation. Which, after a short tussle with my conscience, I give. 'She's finally broken up with Jude.'

'About time,' is my sister's verdict. I agree. But I also know that not everything in this life is black and white. Nor does it fit into little boxes as Chelsea likes it to.

I hop into the kitchen and Chelsea follows.

'Sit, sit,' she instructs and I do, while she swans serenely about my untidy kitchen making tea.

'No Greg?'

'He's fishing.' And while I'm in confessional mood, I add, 'Things aren't all that great here either.'

'Oh, Annie. You've always had such a good marriage.'

A *good* marriage, I'll agree. But not a *perfect* marriage like Chelsea's, with a wealthy husband who knows the meaning of the word 'romance', and a big house and two model children.

'He doesn't want me to do this charity trek to the Inca Trail.'

'I'm surprised that you're still thinking of doing it.' She casts a pointed glance at my gammy foot.

'I can't just give up my dream at the first hurdle,' I protest. Even though I think there might actually have been more than one hurdle, if I were to count them. 'My foot should be better by then.' I decide to go for broke. 'My main problem is money. Lauren and I had been doing car washing.' I opt to miss out the Bunny Girl aspect. There are several things that Chelsea is best not knowing. Though it's possible that Stephanie whatever-her-name-was could rat on me again. 'That's obviously out of the question now.'

'Obviously,' Chelsea agrees.

'There's one other thing.' My cheeks redden. 'That cheque you gave me – for a hundred pounds.' I sort of grind to a halt.

'Yes?'

'Well, it bounced.'

Chelsea looks taken aback, as I knew she would. 'There must be some mistake.'

'That's exactly what I thought. Bloody banks.'

'Indeed. I'll give you another one.' Chelsea's cheeks have coloured up too, and she avoids my eyes by delving into the depths of her handbag. I could bite out my own tongue for having raised it with her. She'll be mortified.

'Damn,' she says. 'No chequebook. Can I give it to you another time?'

'Any time,' I say. 'I'm just really grateful for any donation.'

Then we sit awkwardly for a moment and I can't help myself as I ask, 'Everything is okay, Chelsea?'

'Of course,' she assures me briskly. 'Some glitch at the bank.'

'I didn't just mean that. You never told us that you were coming home. It's all a bit unexpected. Is everything else all right?'

'Fine. You shouldn't be worrying about me. You've got enough on your plate.'

And with that reminder, my worries rush back. 'I hate being tight for cash.' I wish I had an enormous bank account that I could just dip into, but I don't. 'I'm not sure what else to do to raise the money.'

'Have a trawl through your wardrobe,' my sister advises as she hands me my tea. Cup, not mug, I note. *I'm* not even sure where I keep my cups. 'Put some of your old designer gear on eBay.'

'I don't have any *old* designer gear, Chelsea. I don't have *any* designer gear.'

'Oh.' My sister looks slightly confused by this concept.

'Perhaps you've got some lurking that you could donate to a good cause.' Despite the cheque bouncing, I know that Chelsea will give me £100 towards my quest, but as Lauren pointed out, it's hardly generous for her. Chelsea would think absolutely nothing of spending £100 on a T-shirt.

'I'll have a root through my things,' she says, 'but surely you have stuff in the house that you could sell at a car boot? Things that you want to get rid of?'

My sister is eyeing the white china hen that I keep my eggs in with something approaching loathing while I am thinking, Is there much of a market for second-hand unwanted husbands?

'Bake cakes,' Chelsea continues, 'put them in a pretty basket and sell them at work. There's all kinds of inventive things you can do to raise money.'

I realise that I have possibly been colluding with the wrong sister. Chelsea could give Bree Hodge from *Desperate Housewives* a run for her money. We chat about nothing in particular and then Chelsea says, 'Do let me know if there's anything I can do for you. Anything at all.'

I want to say, 'Write me a cheque for a grand rather than a hundred pounds and, this time, make it a pukka one.' But I don't. Instead, I say, 'I'm fine, thanks. Nothing I need.'

My sister looks relieved. Perhaps, like Lauren, she's better at reading my mind than I'd like her to be. 'I have to go,' she says, and stands up. 'Things to do.'

Marvellous things, I have no doubt. As much as I love my sister, she does have a knack of raising my inadequacy quotient quite considerably.

But, as soon as she's gone, Plan B will be put into action. I'll be hauling myself into the loft to furtle out all manner of tat that is surplus to requirements and I'll be getting out my cookbooks to see if I can remember how to bake.

Chapter Eighty-One

It had been three days. Three days without answering the phone. Three days without replying to text messages. Three days without food. Unless you counted neat vodka.

Lauren's stomach burned with acid. She knew that today she would have to go out and buy food. Real food. Not alcohol-based sustenance. But facing the world seemed to be such a difficult prospect. Being here for the rest of her life with the curtains closed was a much better option.

She wasn't sure that she'd showered or washed her hair, but she did know that she'd slept a lot, and when she hadn't been sleeping, she'd watched a lot of mindless television in the dark. *Countdown* was a particular favourite – even though the new girl wasn't a patch on old Vorders.

There had been a lot of banging on her front door, but she hadn't responded. Jude might have been shouting through the door too, but with a pillow over her head and the duvet pulled up, she could almost block it out.

Annie also texted her constantly to make sure that she was all right – and Lauren assured her that she was. It was the good thing about texting. No one could tell if you were lying.

Lauren lay in her bed. She had to get up. This was bad – she knew that much. It was just such an effort.

There was more banging at the front door and she pulled the pillow round her ears, holding it tightly in place.

Jude had a key, but she'd put the security chain in place and he could do nothing but rattle impotently at the lock.

The next thing, she heard the door bang open and footsteps in the flat. Clearly the bang had been the demise of the security chain. Or perhaps it wasn't Jude at all. Perhaps she was being burgled. Let them take everything, she thought. There's nothing of value here.

A figure came into her bedroom, a shadow looming in the darkness. But it was a shadow she recognised.

Jude flicked on the light and she shielded her eyes against it.

'Why have you not answered my calls?' her ex-lover shouted. 'Why are you being like this?'

Lauren abandoned her pillow and hauled herself upright. 'I'm being like this because I'm upset.' 'Upset' was a long way short of what she was.

Jude came and sat on the edge of her bed. 'I wanted to sort everything out with you,' he said more quietly. 'I have been going insane.'

Me too, Lauren thought, but she said nothing.

'I've rented a flat,' Jude told her. 'It's a terrible place. I didn't know where else to go. I tried calling you . . .'

Yes. He'd certainly done that.

'I thought that I might come here.'

She shook her head. 'No.'

Her ex-lover took her hand and held it tightly. His eyes were brimming with tears. 'I don't want it to be over between us,' he said. 'I'm sorting everything out, just as I said I would. We can be together.'

'Stay with Georgia,' Lauren urged. 'Make it up to your wife – if you can. Make it up to the kids. They're young,

292

they need you. Start being a good husband and a good father.'

'I love you, Lauren,' he said.

'And I love you too,' she said. 'That's why I'm letting you go.'

She worried that if he kept coming round, kept working his way back into her good books, kept protesting his love for her, then she would not have the strength to resist him. And, this time, Lauren so wanted to.

Before she could put this into words, Jude glanced at his watch. 'I have to go. I've got an appointment with the bank.'

There was always somewhere else that her lover needed to be. She should remember that. Put that at the forefront of her mind and forget how wonderful he could be when he wanted to. Was it an appointment with the bank, Lauren thought, or was Georgia sitting waiting for him somewhere? She realised that as long as she was with Jude, she'd never be entirely free of those thoughts.

'Come back to work,' he begged.

'I can't. I need time. I'll take a couple of weeks' holiday until I decide what to do.'

'I can't live without you,' he said.

And Lauren only wished that he'd decided that much, much earlier.

Chapter Eighty-Two

Following Chelsea's advice, I now have a growing pile of rubbish – sorry, saleable items – to take to a car-boot sale. I'm sure there must be a dozen round here. I'll have a scan through the local paper and pick my pitch.

I did also discover, to my surprise, that I do, in fact, have a pretty basket lurking in my loft. So I bribed my dear son to nip down to the local Co-op supermarket for me to buy a few groceries. Now I've spent over an hour, propped on my good leg, making a range of sandwiches, chocolate chip muffins and pretty iced cup cakes to sell to my colleagues for their lunch tomorrow. Making sandwiches on one leg, rather than washing cars is, I have to admit, infinitely easier. If not as profitable. Though if I manage to sell twenty sandwiches at two pounds and twenty of the cakes at fifty pence each, that should net me around fifty pounds – which isn't too shabby and doesn't involve me wearing ridiculous costumes. And, frankly, I feel that I've now developed a severe allergy to silly outfits.

Talking of silly outfits brings my sister to mind. I've called Lauren a dozen times today but she's still not picking up. She does, however, reply to all of my texts. She tells me she's perfectly fine and I don't believe a single word of it. If I can't talk to her today then I'm going to go down to her flat after work tomorrow to see exactly what's going on.

I'm sure that she's finding this break-up with Jude

incredibly hard, but I'm equally sure that it's the right thing to do. I know that she'll need my support if she's going to get through this.

Greg comes into the kitchen and eyes my tray of cakes. 'They look good,' he comments.

'Good enough to eat?' I tease.

He laughs at that, and I realise that I haven't heard the sound of my husband's laughter for some time – and I also realise that it's all my fault. How bad does *that* make me feel?

'Help yourself. You can do a consumer road-test for me.' I hand him a chocolate chip muffin. 'I'm making sandwiches and cakes to sell to my colleagues – Chelsea's idea.'

'I might have guessed,' Greg says.

I find myself gripping the sides of my bowl more tightly. 'I don't want to argue about this.'

'Me neither.'

I notice that my husband looks very miserable. I'd like to put my arms round him and give him a hug, but we're too far apart for that.

'It wasn't meant as a criticism, just an observation,' Greg says. Then, as he tries the cake, he tentatively asks, 'What happened to the car wash?'

'I dropped that idea,' I shrug. 'It was too difficult on crutches.' Frankly, the excuse of my broken foot gives us both an out, and my husband is wise enough not to say anything further.

He nods at the muffin in his hand. 'This is wonderful.'

'Thanks. I'm a bit out of practice. You think I'll sell out?'

Greg nods, his mouth full. 'I'd make another batch.'

'Perhaps I will.'

My husband sighs at me. 'You're still intent on going to Peru?'

'Of course.' I fail to meet his eyes. 'If I can raise enough money.'

'I wish you wouldn't go.'

'And I wish you'd be happy for me.' I tip another load of flour into my mixing bowl and splash in some milk. 'Better still, I wish you'd come with me.'

'I'm worried about you,' Greg says. 'What if your foot isn't right? Who'll look after you?'

He regards me with an expression that might or might not be loaded.

'I'll have to look after myself,' I say firmly. 'I know that you're against this and that it's going to cost a fortune and I'm not fit enough. But I want to get there by hook or by crook.'

My husband sighs again. He's doing a lot of it recently. 'Then I should probably help you.' We exchange a wary glance. Is this what's called a truce? Greg risks a smile. 'Give me that mixing bowl.'

Is this mixing bowl our equivalent of a white flag? In case it is, I release my death grip and hand it to Greg. 'Thank you,' I say.

As my husband stirs the mixture thoughtfully, my heart softens towards him. He's not a bad man. He could be a lot worse. What if I had a husband like Jude? Greg has always been steady, faithful, and I could trust him with my life. It's so easy to overlook these qualities when you live with them every day.

'This doesn't mean I approve,' Greg goes on. 'Or even that I understand. But it means that I will support you.'

I come and wrap my arms round his waist. He puts down the bowl and I lay my head on his chest. And we don't speak, because we don't need to.

Chapter Eighty-Three

An hour later and Lauren was still lying in bed, mind whirling. She wanted to phone Zak but she couldn't. It was like an itch prickling at her skin. He'd know what to say, what to do.

Then she heard a knock at the door and she let out a groan. It couldn't be Jude, surely. He'd not long gone and there was very little left to say between them.

A voice shouted out her name.

It wasn't Jude. It was Zak Reynolds, who must have added mindreading to his seemingly endless list of skills.

'Lauren,' he shouted as he rapped again. 'Let me in. I'm going to camp on your doorstep until you open up.'

Groaning once more, Lauren dragged herself out of bed and went to the door. She leaned against it. Not a lot of imagination was required to picture Zak leaning on the other side – his untamed hair, his winning boyish smile.

'Lauren!' Zak shouted.

'Ssh,' she said. 'I'm here. Be quiet or you'll annoy the neighbours.'

'She lives!' Zak whispered back through the door.

It was a close-run thing, Lauren thought. 'I can't open the door,' she said, 'because I'm a complete mess.'

'I like a skanky bird,' Zak assured her. 'I'm Amy Winehouse's biggest fan, and you can't get much skankier than that.'

'I'm *very* skanky,' she told him. 'But you've been warned.' Then she opened the door.

'Whoa,' Zak said as he came into her flat. 'You're right. On the skanky scale you're way up there.'

'Thanks.'

'Fortunately, I come bearing lovely things to remedy that.' Lauren had already noticed the box of groceries in his hands. 'When did you last eat?' He clocked the half-empty bottle of vodka on the table. 'I bet there are plenty more where that came from.'

'One or two,' she admitted.

'Go and have a shower,' Zak instructed. 'Your hair smells like chip fat.'

Lauren laughed at that. 'It so does not.'

'No,' he agreed, 'but it will do if you don't wash it immediately.'

'Anything else?'

'Uncle Zak has brought chicken soup from the deli to set you back on the road to recovery.'

Tears welled in Lauren's eyes. 'You heard then?'

Zak stopped and smiled sympathetically at her. 'You know what office gossip is like.'

'Only too well.'

'Plus Jude is stomping around the office like a bear with a sore head and you're inexplicably not there. It's not that hard to put two and two together.'

'He's left his wife.'

Zak purses his lips. 'I thought that was the plan.'

'It's a long story.' Lauren hugged herself. Involving a pine-apple suit and too much drink, she recalled miserably. 'I'm trying to stay away from him, Zak, but it's not easy. He's ringing me constantly.'

'Hence the reason you've unplugged your phone.' He strolled over to the phone and plugged it back in. It rang immediately.

'Shall I answer?'

Lauren shrugged.

Her friend picked up the receiver. 'Hi, Lauren's unavailable at the moment.' He spoke in the style of an answerphone message. An American one. 'This is Zak, her virtual message-taker. Please speak after the tone.'

He made a tone.

'You're a very silly person,' Lauren said.

Zak turned to her. 'Whoever it was hung up.'

Straight away, the phone rang again. Zak pulled the plug out of the wall. 'Now I can see why you did that.'

'Jude doesn't want it to end, but I do,' Lauren said, a mixture of desperation and determination in her voice. 'I want it to end now. I just pray that I'm strong enough, because right now it really hurts.'

'Just as well I'm here,' Zak said chirpily. 'In addition to nourishing food, I've brought you a ghastly-tasting herbal tonic to set you on your feet again and a book – *Detoxifying Your Relationships*. That should help with your emotional pain.'

'What would I do without you?'

'I don't ever want you to find out,' he said.

'Friends again?'

'A friend in need,' Zak said in a wise manner, 'is a friend indeed.'

'Who said something like "a woman can only become a

man's friend in three stages – first an acquaintance, next a mistress and only then a friend"?'

'I have no idea,' Zak admitted.

'It might have been Chekhov.'

'I loved *Star Trek*,' he joked, 'but I don't remember Mr Chekov saying that.'

'I was thinking more of Anton Chekhov,' she said, 'rather than the Starship *Enterprise*.'

'Ah, then that's way out of my league,' Zak said. 'But I think the concept would work for me.'

She was laughing again. Years and years of crying with Jude and, despite feeling wretched, within minutes Zak was making her giggle. There was probably a wise proverb in that too.

Chapter Eighty-Four

Lauren showered, washed her hair, slipped on clean jeans and a T-shirt, pulled back the curtains, opened the windows, stripped the bed, put the vodka bottle back in the cupboard and began to feel human once more.

While she had been busy, so had Zak. There were baguettes warming in the oven and the scent of fresh bread made the small kitchen feel homely. Her friend was stirring the chicken soup on the hob.

'That smells delicious.'

'When did you last use your oven?'

Lauren looked sheepish. 'I don't think I ever have.'

'You don't look after yourself properly, woman,' Zak scolded.

'I know.' She was embarrassed to admit it, but her friend was right. 'But I will do from now on, I promise.'

She risked turning on her mobile phone. It rang immediately. Lauren clicked it off. 'Jude,' she said.

'You're going to have to face him,' Zak pointed out as he poured the soup into two bowls. 'Be firm with him.'

'I have,' she said. 'He's trying to wear me down. Whenever I've tried to break away from him in the past, he just keeps pursuing me until I give in.'

'Except this time his wife knows about it.'

Lauren nodded.

There was a small bistro-style table in the kitchen with

two chairs opposite each other. She sat down and Zak put a bowl of soup in front of her. Lauren's taste buds tingled for the first time in as long as she could remember.

He then took the bread out of the oven and laid that before her too. 'There is butter,' he said, getting it out of the fridge. 'It looks like it's been there a while, but I think it's one step short of botulism.'

'It'll be fine,' Lauren said, waving away his concerns. 'I've eaten a lot worse.'

The soup was delicious and she ate ravenously, like a woman who hadn't seen food for days. Which, come to think of it, she hadn't.

'Good?' Zak wanted to know.

'Delicious.' She put her hand on his arm and their eyes met. 'Thanks. Thanks for this.'

'It's what friends are for.'

She wondered why Jude hadn't turned up with groceries or trashy self-help books or some hideous vitamin concoction. She wondered why he hadn't bullied her into the shower or cajoled her to eat.

'I need to get away from here,' Lauren said. 'For a few days, at least. I want it to be over this time, and I want to be strong enough to stick to my resolution. I'm sure Annie would be glad to have me.'

Zak looked bashful. 'I've got a place in the Cotswolds. It's small, nothing fancy. I could take you up there for a long weekend?'

Lauren looked up from her soup, spoon paused. 'Why don't I know about this?'

'I bought it with my last long-term girlfriend,' he confessed.

'She was a real country freak. We both loved the area, going for bracing walks in the winter, having candlelit dinners, the whole log-fire thing. When we split, I bought her out of the cottage. I thought it would work as a bachelor bolt-hole. But then it just didn't have the same appeal. Trekking up there to spend the weekend on my own seemed just too much of a sad bastard thing to do. Now all I do is go to check on it every few months. I'm even thinking of getting rid when the market picks up.'

'I didn't know that.'

'You don't know everything about me, Lauren Osbourne,' he said with a laugh.

She wondered what else she didn't know about Zak. 'Do you have any other dark secrets, Zakary Reynolds?'

'Oh, I have lots of skeletons in my closet,' he said with an air of the macabre. 'But I'll clear them all out so that you can hang your clothes in there if you insist.'

Suddenly, Lauren realised that she *would* like to know a lot more about this man. She drummed her fingers on the table. 'How would you get away from work?'

'I'll take some leave.'

'Jude will know,' she said. 'He'll sack you.'

'What will be, will be.'

'Is that Chekhov too?' she teased.

'No. I think that was Doris Day.'

'Could we really just disappear?' A thrill of excitement ran through her exhausted body.

Her friend shrugged. 'I don't see why not. We could be there in a few hours. Far from the madding crowd.'

And persistent ex-lovers. Lauren grinned at him. 'Then let's do it.'

Chapter Eighty-Five

Every day I sell out of my sandwiches and cakes. Every day I take more in. I never realised how hungry these people were. That's the youth of today for you – no thought of their middle-aged waistlines.

By today, Friday, at close of business I should have made the grand sum of two hundred and ninety-five pounds and I'm almost delirious with joy. I've around five hundred pounds to raise now and, if I can avoid giving my colleagues food poisoning, it should take me just a few weeks more. In fact, this is such a lucrative side-line that I'm thinking of carrying on so that I can raise my spending money too. Even when I'm back from Peru, the extra cash would certainly come in handy at home.

It does mean that I'm spending two or three hours every night making sandwiches and baking cakes – Chelsea, of course, never pointed out the downside to me. But what else would I be doing but watching mindless television and letting my brain turn to mush? By the time I've finished though, all I can do is fall into bed in an exhausted heap. Which is not a problem as Greg and I are hardly swinging from the chandeliers at the moment. Despite a distinct thawing in our frosty relations, we are still doing non-contact sleeping. No bouncy cuddles for me yet.

Still, I'm sure that me wearing a blue plastic boot isn't a big turn-on anyway. And, if it was, I'd be worried.

I give Blake Chadwick his cheese and chutney sandwich and try not to think about sex. He hands over his cash with a winning smile. 'Keep the change,' he says. 'Put it towards the fighting fund.'

'Thanks.'

Things are a bit awkward between us now. I think he feels bad about the whole pineapple thing and I feel bad that I witnessed him snogging Minny when I thought it might just have been me.

'How's the foot holding up?'

I glance down at my attractive blue boot. 'It's okay. I have to make sure that I rest it at night.'

And, of course, our cosy little running sessions have been curtailed. Which is perhaps just as well.

'You'll still make it,' he says encouragingly.

'That's the plan.'

But, to be honest, I'm not so sure. I have become a demon on my crutches, but as I lay in the bath last night, foot up on the side, reading my Peru guidebook, reality hit me. And it was a cold, hard slap. I'm never going to be fit enough to do this. My dream now seems so unreal, so unattainable. Sacsayhuamán, Tambomachay, Pikillacta, Rumicolca . . . will I ever see any of these places with my own eyes? Or has this trip just become a pipe dream? I may well manage to raise all my money in time, but can I possibly hop the entire length of the Inca Trail?

My heart feels too heavy to think of that now. I just need to focus on raising the money and religiously doing my physiotherapy exercises.

At five o'clock, Greg picks me up from work. He helps me to the car and I mutter about my day while he pretends to listen.

Blake Chadwick comes out after us and shouts across, 'Want a hand?'

'No, thanks,' Greg says back, more crisply than he needs to. 'I can manage just fine.'

Then instead of starting up the engine straight away, we sit in the car and my husband's eyes narrow as he watches Blake get into his flash sporty number and drive off.

'That's Blake Chadwick,' I offer. More to fill the silence than anything else. 'One of the bosses.'

'Yes – I saw him at the hospital,' he says, and gives me a quizzical look.

I often think that Greg notices nothing unless it involves fish. Now I'm not so sure.

Chapter Eighty-Six

Lauren threw a few things into a bag. She couldn't really concentrate, so she'd probably packed all the wrong things. But, hey, they had shops in the Cotswolds, didn't they?

All she wanted to do was get away, flee this place. Be as far away from Jude as she could possibly manage. She realised that a small corner of the rolling English countryside might not count as 'far away', but it was certainly a great start and about all she could handle at the moment. The fact that Zak was coming along with her was adding to her feelings of comfort and joy. She'd spent too many days being alone.

And her friend was wonderful company, relaxing to be with and funny in his own silly way. That was just what she needed now.

Zak had gone home to get his own stuff together and then he was coming back to collect her. She'd switched on her phone again and had already ignored more than two dozen calls from Jude.

She'd phoned Annie and told her that she was escaping London and Jude's clutches for a few days until the heat died down, and her sister sounded relieved to hear that she was still alive, let alone anything else.

An hour later, there was a knock on the door and, for a moment, Lauren held her breath. Then Zak shouted, 'It's only me!'

Her body relaxed again as she opened the door. 'I'm ready,' she said. 'I just need to get my bag.'

'Let me,' Zak said, and he swept through to her bedroom and hoisted up her bag. 'This weighs a ton! How long do you think we're going for, woman?'

'Travelling light has never been my style.'

'I can't imagine what you've got in here. You are planning on coming back?'

'I don't know,' Lauren said. 'I might not.' And she wasn't sure if she was joking.

Zak dropped her bag on the floor and came and hugged her. 'You'll be fine,' he said. 'Absolutely fine.'

She nodded. 'Let's get out of here.'

Outside and the bright light hurt her eyes. Lauren put on her sunglasses. It looked like it was going to be a lovely weekend. A beam of lightness pushed into her bruised heart.

Zak threw her bag in the back and slipped into the driver's seat.

'I'm a rubbish navigator,' Lauren warned him.

'This old car knows her own way there. Sit back, relax, enjoy the in-flight movie. We'll be there before you know it.'

'I can't thank you enough for this,' Lauren said earnestly.

'It's not entirely altruistic. A break won't do me any harm either.' Zak slid the car into gear and pulled out into the traffic.

'This is going to be great,' Lauren said with a happy sigh. 'I can't wait.'

And neither of them saw Jude standing on the other side of the road, watching them.

Chapter Eighty-Seven

Greg drives me to Chelsea's house in Woburn. Or country pile, should I say. The tyres of our knacky old car crunch on the gravel – my sister probably has a man in to rake it every day – heralding our arrival.

I'm still struggling out of the car with my crutches when Chelsea appears at the front door. Her hanging baskets are blooming effusively and, unlike me, she clearly doesn't forget to water hers. Chelsea, as a person, exudes perfection and her home is merely an extension of that. I do wonder every single time I see her how we came to be related. Why couldn't Lauren and I have inherited the loveliness gene too?

Greg decides to stay in the car. He doesn't really like either of my sisters that much – Lauren for one set of reasons, Chelsea for another. My husband, as you may have gathered, is far more comfortable with relationships with fish rather than people.

'I can't stay long,' I say as I hop towards Chelsea. 'Greg's got to get back.'

She knows that this is sister-speak for, 'My husband is being an anti-social bastard again.'

'I have some clothes sorted out for you. There's not much,' she says apologetically. 'There was a Designer Rail Sale event at the Swan Restaurant recently which I was involved in and I had a major clear-out then.'

I'm grateful for anything. This Sunday morning, I'm planning to do a car-boot sale. A hideous thought. But needs must.

Then when I've hopped through to her vast hall and I've stopped focusing on simply staying upright, I look up at Chelsea. 'Oh.' I'm taken aback that there are dark shadows under her eyes. 'Is everything all right?'

'Fine, fine.' My sister waves away my concerns.

My nephew and niece barrel out of the kitchen and into my legs with the cry of, 'Aunty Annie!'

'Mind you don't knock me off my crutches, you two!' That would be all I need, two broken legs as well. That would well and truly put paid to my Andean adventure. I kiss them both. 'How's my favourite nephew and niece?'

'I passed my ballet exam yesterday,' Sophia tells me, giving me an exemplary twirl.

'Good girl. That's lovely.'

'I want to dance for the Ballet Rambert when I grow up.'

And, if my sister has anything to do with it, then I'm sure she will.

'And I want to be Harry Potter,' Henry announces.

And, if my sister has anything to do with it, then I'm sure he will too.

'Come in and say hello to Rich while you're here,' Chelsea urges. 'He'd love to see you.'

'He's at home? Now?' My brother-in-law is one of those who go out to work at six o'clock in the morning and is never home before nine o'clock every night.

Chelsea nods towards the kitchen. I go in and, sure enough, Rich is sitting at the farmhouse-style table, a glass of whisky in his hand.

'Bit early for that?' I joke. But no one laughs.

As I hug my brother-in-law, I notice that the atmosphere between my sister and her husband is a bit strained. Again, I ask, 'Everything okay?'

'Yes, yes.' Richard also waves away my question. 'Never better.'

He and Chelsea exchange a wary glance and I'm no psychic but I can tell that all is not well in the King household.

'How are things with Lauren?' my sister wants to know.

'Oh, she's doing all right.' Though it was touch and go for a minute. 'She's gone away for a few days with a friend. To the Cotswolds.'

'I could do with a bit of that myself,' Chelsea says, and the accompanying laugh is tired. This is the first time I've ever heard her voice the fact that there might be a chink in her perfect life.

Perhaps they've had a row. Goodness only knows, it's normal in most marriages. Just not Chelsea's.

Guiltily, I glance out of the window at our car. We're hardly the picture of marital harmony. Predictably, Greg is drumming his fingers on the steering wheel. 'I'd better go.'

I was going to raise the matter of the bounced cheque again, but decide that this isn't the right time.

'I'll help you carry the bags,' Chelsea offers.

I follow her back to the hall. The feeling of disquiet just won't leave me. 'Sure everything's fine?'

'Tickety-boo,' she says. But her smile is tight.

She picks up the two carriers and I notice that the contents are rather more meagre than I'd hoped. Still, I'm grateful that Chelsea has even bothered, and my sister's cast-offs will be a

312

million times better than anything I can drag out of my wardrobe. She carries the clothes out to the car, and Greg gets out and kisses her briefly on the cheek. Then Chelsea put the bags in the boot.

'Call me,' I say to her. 'Let me know if there's anything that you need.'

'I will,' she promises. 'I'm fine. Don't worry about me.'

But now I am worried, and I don't know why.

Chapter Eighty-Eight

Lauren and Zak exited London at warp speed. At least, it felt like it. In truth, it was probably more like sixty miles an hour in Zak's old car. They headed up the M40, skirted round Oxford and then wound their way slowly into the heart of the Cotswolds.

Coldplay serenaded them on the journey and Lauren relaxed back into her seat, watching as the narrow streets of mellow stone houses replaced the motorways. She was sure they'd been to this part of the world as children with Annie and Chelsea, maybe for a family holiday. She'd have to ask Annie, as her sister was always better at hanging on to memories of that kind of stuff. If they had been here before, Lauren didn't remember it being quite so pretty or so soothing to the soul. Perhaps she just hadn't been stressed enough to appreciate it way back then.

A while later, they arrived at the small village of Mickleton, just beyond the clutches of the main thrust of tourism in Broadway and Chipping Camden.

Zak steered his car into a quiet lane by the old church and they trundled along the pot-holed lane, trying to miss the worst of the dips. At the end was a row of three tiny terraced cottages built in traditional golden Cotswold stone.

'Left-hand one.' Zak pointed at it. 'Home Sweet Home.'

'It's beautiful. You can't get rid of this!'

He shrugged good-naturedly.

In front of the houses was a shallow stream, and each of the houses was reached by an individual stone bridge just wide enough for one person. The front door was painted white, and a rambling pink clematis wound its way round the frame.

'It's more homely than glamorous,' Zak warned. 'But it has all mod cons.'

He hoisted the bags out of the car and set off across the bridge to open up the cottage. Lauren followed, gazing wistfully at the scenery. Behind the houses it looked as if there was nothing but open fields, nothing to spoil the view.

Inside, the ceilings were low, beamed. In the living room was a comfortable-looking sofa and a plump armchair by the fireside. The fireplace and chimney were of plain brick and housed a wood-burning stove that looked much-used. The stripped floorboards were partially covered by a colourful rug that co-ordinated with the soft blue upholstery of the chairs.

Through to the kitchen, which was small but had clearly been recently refitted with Shaker-style units. A bright conservatory had been grafted on to the back of the house, and in there was a small pine table that would seat four and another squishy sofa. Lauren wandered out in the garden, which was long and narrow and remarkably well maintained.

'The man in the next cottage looks after it for me,' Zak said as he came outside too, as if reading her thoughts. 'I don't know what I'd do without him. His wife airs the place and makes up the beds when I'm coming here too. All I have to do is phone them in advance.'

The garden was well stocked with pretty flower borders. By the conservatory was a small patio which held two chairs.

There was a shed near the bottom which looked as if it had been newly painted in a soft green colour. In the field beyond, a few sheep wandered aimlessly, plucking at the grass. Birds tweeted happily.

'Idyllic,' Lauren said, hugging herself.

'Think this will give you some space to breathe?'

'It was a wonderful idea to come up here. Thank you.'

'It's nice to have company. You can't really have a romantic weekend here on your own.' Then Zak tutted at himself. 'Not that I'm suggesting . . . that wasn't why I brought you here . . . Oh damn – you know what I mean.'

'Yes,' Lauren laughed. 'I do.'

'There are two bedrooms and a small bathroom upstairs,' Zak told her. 'I'll put your bag in the front room.'

'That sounds great.'

'You might not think so come Sunday morning. I warn you now that the vicar does like to ring the church bells *very* early.'

'Clearly has no consideration for the stressed townies up here for some R and R.'

'Strange country folk with their strange country ways.' Zak laughed. 'You settle yourself in. When I've whipped the bags upstairs, then I'll make us some tea.'

As he disappeared inside again, Lauren lowered herself into one of the garden chairs with a contented sigh. This was the life. Being here was like being in another world. The sun was warm, but not too hot, a gentle breeze taking the edge from it.

She switched on her mobile phone. Missed calls – twenty-two. All from Jude. Lauren switched it off again. And that, she thought, would be the very last time she looked at her phone while she was here.

Chapter Eighty-Nine

Ellen has split up with her boyfriend. As far as I know, she hasn't cried. She doesn't seem overly bothered at all, even though she's been with him for a long time. Another product of the easy-come, easy-go society.

Instead, she seems to be hell-bent on finding another boyfriend. Tonight.

'You can't go out looking like that,' I gasp, horrified.

As well as being horrified at Ellen's outfit, I'm also horrified that I'm saying the same thing to her that my mother used to say to me – the same thing that I vowed *never* to say to my daughter.

'Shut up, Mum.' Even now, at the ripe old age of twenty, Ellen sometimes reverts to the stroppy fourteen-year-old she used to be.

I have accosted her in the kitchen just as she was about to go out. 'Please, love. Look at yourself in the mirror.'

'I'm cool,' she whines. 'Leave me alone.'

The difference between me and my own mother is that I have a valid point. Whereas my mother did not.

Frankly, my child looks like she's on the game. Her top is little more than a bra and her ample bosom, not inherited from her mother I might add, is spilling out of it. Her skirt is what would have been called a pussy pelmet in the 1960s. It sits low, low, low on her hips and, at the other end, barely skims her bottom. It is hardly worth wearing. I have belts that are wider. How old does that make me sound?

'Greg,' I entreat. 'Say something.'

My husband looks up at my daughter. 'Do as your mother says,' is his token effort. Then he returns to studying *Angling Weekly*, but I see him give a secret shudder.

'You were the one dressed as a Bunny Girl last week.' Ellen's hands are on her hips. 'At least I'm not doing it for money.'

But you could be, I think. You so easily could be.

'She has a point,' Greg chips in, looking up from his magazine.

Who asked you? I think. But instead say nothing. This is one argument that I know I have lost.

I turn to my son. My last hope. Bobby shrugs. 'Everyone dresses like that now.'

'Then everyone should have better taste,' I tell him.

'Whatever,' Ellen mumbles.

'Besides, what I was doing was for charity,' I announce loftily to the back of the stalls.

'And that makes a difference?'

'It makes a *world* of difference.'

Ellen snorts.

'I'm trying to do something with my dull little life. I'm trying to be a role model.'

More snorting.

'I'll be late,' she says, which is the equivalent of 'fat chance'.

'I just wish . . .'

'Everyone's hanging on me,' my daughter says, cutting me off in mid-flow. 'Don't wait up. And don't pull the bedroom curtain back when you hear the taxi.'

I stand guilty as accused. I don't want to worry about them both, but I do. Constantly. They're both adults – even though they never, ever behave like it. They should live their own lives as they see fit. I just don't want them doing it in my house.

'Give us a lift, bro,' Ellen cajoles.

'No worries,' Bobby says, and picks up his car keys.

Ellen flounces out of the room.

'Keep an eye on her, Bobs,' I beg.

'As if,' my son says with a hopeless shrug. 'Laters.'

The back door slams and my stomach tenses as I hear Bobby's old banger roar up the road.

'Why don't they want to do marvellous things with their lives?' I complain as I stomp up and down the kitchen on my crutches. 'Why are they happy to settle for mediocrity? Why do they have no ambition for themselves? Why do we not expect more from them?'

'*You* do.'

'Then why are they happy to do nothing but drink and go to nightclubs in unsuitable clothing?'

'Perhaps it makes them happy,' my husband suggests.

Greg could at this point remind me that I got my injury by drinking whilst dressed in an unsuitable manner. But he doesn't. I'm sure if he'd thought of it then he would.

'Then it shouldn't make them happy,' I retort in full rant mode. 'It should make them miserable. They shouldn't be content with dead-end partners, dead-end jobs and dead-end lives. They should want to . . . *fly*!'

My husband looks at me as if I'm mad. Which, perhaps, I am. 'Stop trying to make them discontented.'

'I'm trying to make them ambitious.'

'It's the same thing.'

'Okay then, maybe a bit of discontentment is necessary to get people off their backsides and achieve something with their lives. When did you ever see a content person rule the world? Does the person who is happy to sit on the riverbank of life ever scale the dizzy heights of Everest?'

'That sounds like it came from one of those fortune cookies that the Hong Kong Garden give away.'

'I'm trying to think more deeply about my life.'

'That's fine, but don't expect the rest of us to do it. We're not all like you.'

'Well, you should be.'

'If you're such a great role model, what were you doing getting blind drunk and falling off a ladder just the other week?' He looks pointedly at my cast.

Ah. He hasn't forgotten that, after all.

'That was a one-off,' I mutter, wind gone somewhat out of my sails. 'I don't do it every weekend.'

'And neither do your children.'

But they do. 'Don't you want more for them? Don't you want more for yourself?'

'I'm going to get my tackle ready for tomorrow.' Greg shuts his *Angling Weekly*, causing a disgruntled draught, and with that he bangs out of the room.

The discussion, it seems, is closed.

Chapter Ninety

Lauren spent the rest of the afternoon dozing on and off in a garden chair, enjoying the warmth of the gentle sun on her face.

Zak pottered about inside the cottage and, occasionally, brought her out a drink of orange juice or a welcome cup of tea. It was a very pleasant way to while away the remains of the day. They'd be going frantic at the office without her, but that was the least of her worries now.

If it was finally over with Jude – and this time she really wanted to stick to her guns – then a new job and a new place to live would have to be her top priorities. She saw Zak coming out into the garden again and smiled at him. But she wasn't going to dwell on her impending homeless and jobless status now.

'I've booked dinner at a local hotel tonight, if that's okay,' her friend said as he sat down next to her.

Lauren was surprised to find that she was hungry again. But then, it had been a long time since her chicken soup earlier today.

'We only have to stroll down the road.'

'Sounds perfect.'

'I thought we could go and have a drink first.'

'Even better.'

'Then you go and freshen up while I take up deckchair duty.' Zak closed his eyes and settled into his garden chair.

It was nice for someone else to take charge of her life, as her brain was too exhausted to think. She looked at his face while his eyes were closed. He was a very handsome man, there was no doubt about that. Had she noticed that before? *Really* noticed it?

'What?' he said, opening one eye.

Lauren smiled. 'I'm just thinking that you're a very nice man.'

'I'm a complete bastard, actually,' Zak informed her. 'This is a carefully constructed façade that could shatter at any moment.'

'I bet you're kind to small children and furry animals too.'

'Nah,' Zak said. 'Eat them for breakfast.'

'And here was me thinking you liked nothing more than a bit of toast.'

'Shows just how easily you're fooled,' he teased. He closed his eyes again.

Zak might only be joking, but it was true. She had been fooled by the man in her life. For years.

'I won't be long,' Lauren said. The promise of a strong drink was calling her.

Upstairs, the cottage was small and neat. Her case was on the bed in the room at the front. There was an old-fashioned wrought-iron bed with crisp white linen on it. An oak dressing-table and a tall wardrobe flanked it. The room was cool, welcoming, like a safe cocoon.

Lauren sat on the bed and tested it. The springs creaked, just as she knew they would. It made her smile.

Zak was being so kind to her that she felt like weeping. No one had ever cosseted her like he did. She looked at herself in the mirror on the dressing-table and was shocked. A gaunt white face stared back at her. Blue shadows ringed her eyes. She looked like a giant panda minus the cuteness. Lying down on the bed, she cried what she vowed would be her last tears for Jude into the soft pillow.

Lauren had reached rock bottom. The only way from here was up.

Chapter Ninety-One

'The Pudding Club?' Lauren laughed incredulously.

She and Zak were sitting in the pretty garden of a small hotel in the centre of Mickleton, a slow ten-minute stroll from Zak's cottage.

Lauren was wearing a white, strappy summer dress that she didn't even remember packing, and Zak was looking handsome in a dark linen shirt, his hair freshly washed.

'You do eat puddings?' Zak frowned.

'I'm sure I used to, once,' she said. Though she couldn't quite recall when.

'Well, it won't do you any harm,' he told her. 'You could do with a bit of meat on your bones.'

'And sticky toffee pudding will do that?'

'Most definitely.'

The Three Ways House Hotel, as Zak explained, was the home of The Pudding Club. The couple who ran it had grown tired of going to restaurants where all that was on offer for dessert was frozen cheesecake or Black Forest Gâteau, and had decided to do something about it. Thus The Pudding Club was born – nearly twenty-five years ago. Now there were regular dinners where good, old-fashioned traditional British puddings were the mainstay of the menu.

Zak clinked his champagne glass against hers. 'To you,' he said.

'I'm not sure that I've got anything much to celebrate.'

'To a new start.'

'A new start,' Lauren echoed, and sipped at her fizz. She felt as if she was a million miles away from London, in a different country almost. And it was a nice place to be.

An old school bell was rung at the door to signal the start of dinner.

Zak took her by the hand and, smiling, said, 'Let's go and have some fun.'

They sat at large communal tables in the dining room – a young couple on a romantic weekend away on one side and an older couple celebrating their twentieth wedding anniversary on the other. She thought with a sharp pang that it was quite a surprise that Jude had never brought her to this place. It was just his sort of thing.

The light main course was dispensed with efficiently before the serious business of introducing the puddings got under way. By the time all the different traditional steamed puddings were brought in, both she and Zak had knocked back quite a bit of wine. Lauren was feeling decidedly merry and better than she had in a long time.

The couples next to them were full of fun and she realised that virtually every restaurant meal she'd had with Jude had been spent huddled at a corner table with them avoiding eye-contact with anyone apart from the waiter. What a delightful difference this was!

Each pudding was introduced in turn and everyone in the room banged their spoons on the table to herald their arrival. Gargantuan puddings with clouds of sweet, aromatic steam rising from them were paraded before them – sticky toffee pudding, spotted dick, jam roly-poly, golden syrup sponge and chocolate pudding.

The mood was uproarious, good-natured and exactly the tonic she needed.

'The only rule,' Zak said, 'is that you have to finish all that's in your bowl before you can go back for another pudding.'

The heavenly scent of them was making her salivate. 'I can tell that you've done this before,' Lauren said.

'Just once or twice.'

'Any tips from the maestro?'

'Start with the heaviest and work your way towards the lightest.'

'They all look equally rich.'

'That is the slight downside of my cunning plan.'

Lauren picked up her bowl. 'Let's get this started.'

'I have to warn you that my own personal record is ten puddings,' Zak boasted. 'You have a lot to live up to.'

She grinned at her friend. 'That very much sounds like you're throwing down the gauntlet, Mr Reynolds.'

'Are you woman enough for the challenge?' he teased.

Lauren strode towards the pudding buffet, glad that she'd worn a loose-fitting dress. 'We'll see, shall we?'

Chapter Ninety-Two

An hour later and Zak sat back in his chair, massaging his stomach. 'Oh, that was so good.'

Lauren massaged her tummy too and groaned contentedly.

'Though I do have to point out that you're a total light-weight, my dear Ms Osbourne.'

'One measly pudding more than me. That was all you managed.' She inspected his bowl carefully. 'And I question whether you've eaten all of that one. I'm sure that I can still see traces of sticky toffee pudding.'

Zak ran his spoon round the bowl again and scooped them up. 'You are a ferocious competitor.'

'This time I've been beaten by a better man.'

'Want a chance to redeem yourself?'

She shook her head. 'I couldn't eat another thing.' This was the most she'd eaten in years. And, though she might well regret it in the morning, she now felt very pleasantly satiated. Food seemed to have become a substance that had lost all of its pleasure for her.

'One more for the road,' Zak challenged. 'Equal portions. First to finish.'

'What are the stakes?'

Zak pondered, then said, 'Breakfast in bed for the victor.'

'I won't be letting another morsel of food pass my lips for about a week!'

'I don't believe it. You can't live on fresh air, woman. You have to start eating properly.'

'I'm not sure that devouring five puddings in a row counts as eating properly.'

'It's a start,' her friend said, and he picked up her bowl and carried it to the buffet table. Lauren followed behind him, eager to see that he didn't cheat.

'This is a very serious competition,' Zak explained to the chef. 'Honour is at stake. The portions need to be exactly equal.' He turned to Lauren. 'Choose your pudding.'

She mulled it over. They had all been delicious. 'Chocolate, please.'

'And I'll take the golden syrup sponge again.'

'I think you'll find that's lighter than mine,' Lauren joked.

'I think you'll find not.'

They poured on equal amounts of creamy yellow custard, checking the levels in their bowls carefully and then returned to their table. The couples they'd been seated with were long gone, and she and Zak sat at the table alone, facing each other.

'Spoons at the ready,' Zak said, and they both held their spoons above their bowls. 'On your marks, get set . . . go!'

They tucked into their final pudding with gusto, giggling between spoonfuls.

Lauren got halfway down the bowl and pushed it away from her, holding up her hands in surrender. 'I'm done,' she said. 'I give in. The man with hardened arteries wins.'

Zak laughed. 'I could eat another one!'

'You liar.'

He finished another spoonful and tapped his bowl, saying: 'There! Breakfast in bed for me.'

'It will be my pleasure,' Lauren conceded. 'It's been such a great evening. I don't think I've laughed so much in ages.'

'Come here.' He beckoned her towards him. 'You have custard on your lip.'

'Here?' Lauren tried to wipe it off with her napkin.

Zak shook his head. 'Let me.' He lifted her chin with his thumb. Then their eyes locked and time stopped and all the silly things that only happen in the movies happened.

He leaned forward and kissed her mouth tenderly.

'All gone,' he said when they parted. They were both breathing unevenly.

'That last pudding nearly tipped us over the edge into gluttony,' she laughed, in an attempt to add levity to the situation.

'Ah, one of the Seven Deadly Sins,' Zak said.

'Yes,' Lauren breathed.

And the way she felt right now, she wouldn't mind indulging in one or two more of them.

Chapter Ninety-Three

At midnight, the phone rings. I'm not asleep. I'm awake staring at the ceiling. One of my favourite pastimes these days.

Greg grumbles to himself, but doesn't quite wake. I pick up, heart pounding. It can only be one of the kids.

Sure enough, it's Bobby. 'Mum,' he says, 'can you come and get us, please? We've had a bit of bother.'

'Bother?'

'Ellen's been mugged and I nearly had the bloke, but I think I've busted my hand.'

'What? Is Ellen all right?' I'm already half out of the bed.

'She'll be fine.' But my son doesn't sound like he thinks she'll be fine.

'Let me speak to her.'

'My battery's about to run out.' Always a popular one.

'Where are you?'

'Up at the city centre. Outside Nitebox.'

A notorious club. A notorious trouble spot. What were my children doing there?

'Give me fifteen minutes.' I hang up. As I head to the wardrobe to find my jeans, my husband turns over, arm across his face. 'What's wrong?' he mumbles.

'That was Bobby. Ellen's been mugged and he thinks he's broken his hand.'

'*What?*'

'Ellen's been—'

'I heard. I just didn't believe it.'

'Believe it.'

A groan. Now Greg is awake and getting out of bed. 'I'll go. You can't drive.'

I look down at my foot. I'd forgotten about that.

'We'll both go,' I say. 'We're both awake now anyway.' Not that I'm likely to rest until I can find out what's been going on.

So, minutes later, we're up, dressed, and jump into my car and speed off towards the city centre to rescue our children.

When Greg pulls up outside Nitebox, Ellen is sitting on the pavement, head in hands. We struggle to pick her out at first as there are so many similarly attired drunken women slouched by the roadside in the same state of disarray. Her feet are bare, her shoes nowhere to be seen. Bobby, beside her, is nursing his hand. A group of youths are having a fist-fight not far behind them.

There's a police van parked up there, but no sign of any policemen.

Greg and I are out of the car in seconds. I can now see why they couldn't get a taxi home. A pool of vomit is at my daughter's feet. My anger rises.

'Is that why you couldn't get a taxi?'

'Yeah,' Bobby admits. 'No one would take us. I've not had that much to drink.'

'But still too much to drive?'

My son doesn't grace that with a reply. Nearly every weekend he ends up abandoning his car here and we're the mugs who have to come and get it with him in the morning. But, I suppose,

I'd rather him do that than drink and drive. Though, if I had my way, he wouldn't drink at all.

'Let's take you straight to hospital.'

'I'll be all right,' he insists.

'Don't be silly.' I realise that I'm speaking to him like he's a five-year-old, but at the moment, I feel he deserves it. 'Get in, get in.' I usher him towards the car.

Greg puts his arms round Ellen and scoops her up from the gutter.

'God, she smells like a brewery,' I complain.

Her skirt is torn and her hair is all over the place. To think that this is someone who prides herself on her appearance.

Greg lowers her into the front seat of the car and she's promptly sick in the footwell.

I get in the back with Bobby. 'Care to shed any light on this?'

'Ellen got a bit lashed.' We both look at my daughter, her mascara-streaked face, her make-up all smeared, clown-like.

I'm disappointed, angry, frustrated. I should take a photo of her on her mobile phone and paste it up on Facebook – that might make her think just how she looks. What is wrong with young girls these days? Why do they behave like this? Why do they think this is what having fun means?

As I'm unlikely to get any sense out of Ellen, I turn on my son. 'I thought you were supposed to be looking after her?'

'I'm not her keeper,' Bobby whines. 'You know what she's like.'

Only too well.

'I saw her going outside. Her mates said she was getting some fresh air.' My son avoids my eyes. 'When I got out, there was some bloke pawing her. I shouted at him to leave her alone. When he saw me, he lifted her handbag and legged it. I chased after him, but I've had a few too.'

That's also rather obvious.

'I managed to land a punch on him, but he pulled me over and I fell on my hand,' Bobby continues. 'I didn't get the bag back. Don't know whether it was lumping the bloke or the fall that did it, but my hand is killing me now.'

'You're lucky that the police didn't get involved.'

'They're not bothered,' he says with a quick glance at the police van. 'Turn a blind eye to anything that goes on up here. They just want a quiet night.'

'It's a shame that the pair of you don't.'

Greg's found some old towels in the boot of my car that I keep for wiping muddy shoes and he's mopping up the aftermath of my daughter's drinking binge. When he's made the best job of it that he can, he slips back into the driver's seat and looks at me in the rearview mirror. 'Hospital?'

'Where else?' I reply tightly but, in fairness, my temper isn't directed at my husband.

He eases the car away from the pavement, dodging broken glass in the road. A kid staggers across the street, bare-chested. 'It feels like the flipping Wild West up here.'

And I wonder what's happened to our society that this is considered a good night out.

'I just want to go home,' Ellen wails, suddenly coming round.

'Well, instead, you're going to be spending the rest of the night in A and E with your brother.'

'Get a life, Mum,' Ellen mutters under her breath, but just about loud enough for me to hear.

Well, I won't swallow it this time and I round on her, snapping, 'Has it ever occurred to you that it's *you two* who need to get a life?'

Then we all fall into a tense silence and stay like that until we get to the hospital.

Chapter Ninety-Four

Lauren paced the floor of her bedroom in Zak's cottage. She'd tried sleeping but it just wasn't happening, and it was nothing to do with the sugar rush that all of those scrumptious puddings had given her. It was mainly down to the rush that Zak's unexpected kiss had given her.

They'd kissed again when they'd said goodnight and she'd watched him disappear into his own room.

She was drunk. Too much fizz and too much wine had been consumed for her to be thinking straight. Lauren wrung her hands together. It would be a really bad idea to go to Zak, to offer herself to him. She was too raw, too emotionally vulnerable. Too soon out of one relationship to consider another one.

She could go downstairs, make a cup of tea, watch something rubbishy on the television. That's what she'd do at home when she was frustrated and restless. Or should she risk their friendship by making an approach to Zak?

What if he wasn't interested? What if she'd misread the signs? What if he was already fast asleep? What if his kiss had really just been a slight overstepping of the mark between friends? What if he was now regretting getting carried away?

Her mouth was dry. There was only one way to find out.

Tugging off her comfy pyjamas Lauren slipped her kimono on. Unlatching her door as quietly as she could – strange when she was planning to wake Zak up in just a moment – she padded barefoot across the landing. For a moment, she listened at Zak's door. There were no unnerving snoring sounds. She couldn't hear him breathing.

Gently, she lifted the latch on his door. He was in bed, but he wasn't asleep. The moon streamed in through the window, bathing his bed in its soft white light. Her friend was propped up on one arm. His chest was bare.

'I couldn't sleep,' Lauren whispered, lingering in the doorway.

'Me neither.'

Lauren felt shy, but she knew that it was now or never. 'Want some company?'

She heard Zak suck in a breath. 'If you're sure.'

Her voice had gone, so she nodded even though it was dark. Zak flicked back the duvet. She let her kimono fall from her shoulders.

'God, you're beautiful,' Zak said.

Lauren climbed into his bed and laid against him. She was relieved to find that it wasn't only Zak's chest that was bare. His skin was warm, soft – sensational against hers.

'I didn't bring you here to seduce you,' he murmured, his fingers toying with her hair. 'That was never my intention.'

Lauren stroked his face, tenderly. 'It may have escaped your notice, Mr Reynolds, but I think you'll find that *I'm* seducing *you.*'

Chapter Ninety-Five

I was supposed to be doing a car-boot sale this morning. I had my table booked and I was meant to arrive by six o'clock to display my wares – as it were. But, of course, I didn't. The selection of designer clothes that Chelsea looked out for me remain inside their posh carrier bags.

My plans were somewhat curtailed by spending until five o'clock this morning in the Accident & Emergency Department of Milton Keynes General Hospital. Never the best way to spend a night.

Now Bobby is fast asleep in bed with his hand bandaged and a ton of painkillers. It isn't broken, merely bruised – but his fingers are like sausages and his skin is black and blue, and that still looks bad enough to me.

My daughter, beige-faced, is sitting at the kitchen table in front of me, nursing a cup of camomile tea. She's wearing a pink fleece dressing-gown and a pair of zebra-print slippers. On the surface, she looks little different than when she was four years old. Except, when she was four years old, she wasn't capable of downing an entire bottle of vodka over the course of an evening.

I sigh inwardly.

'This tastes gross,' she complains.

'Drink it,' I say. 'It will do you good.'

'I don't want it to do me good,' she retorts. 'I want to die.'

I slide into the seat opposite her. 'And you might well have had your wish if Bobby hadn't turned up when that chap was molesting you and robbing you, Ellen. What else might he have done to you?'

My daughter invokes the right to remain silent.

'Why?' I ask, genuinely baffled. 'Why get so blind drunk that you don't know what you're doing?'

'It's just a bit of fun,' she insists.

'It isn't,' I tell her. 'It's potentially life-threatening.'

'Did you think about it when you did that?' She casts a disdainful glance at my foot in my big, blue boot.

'That was a one-off – a mistake. And it was all your Aunty Lauren's fault.' That's mainly true. Plus Lauren's not here to defend herself so she's fair game. 'It's not something that I do every single weekend.'

'It might stop you from going to Peru,' she points out. 'So whoever's fault it was,' my daughter's expression clearly reveals that she didn't buy into my blame-shifting techniques, 'it wasn't very bright. Okay, I was well lashed last night, but it hasn't ruined anything I was looking forward to.'

Then I seize on something that might be life-affirming for both of us. 'Come with me to Peru.'

'Get a life, Mum.'

'Mothers and daughters often do bonding things together.'

'Only mothers with daughters who don't have a life.'

'Oh, Ellen.' How can I explain to her that she's worth so much more, when she doesn't seem to have a clue what I'm talking about? 'Are you going to spend the rest of your life here, going nowhere, doing nothing?'

'*You* did.'

'Yes. And look at me now.'

'Yeah. Foot in a cast after getting pissed and a dream of doing a long walk.'

'A *very* long walk,' I correct.

'Whatever.'

'Is this all that you want for yourself – for the rest of your life?' I look around at my shabby kitchen. 'A mortgage, a husband, a couple of kids?'

'I'm sorry it's been so awful,' my daughter says sulkily. 'I thought you liked our family.'

'I do,' I say. 'It's just that I want more – for me *and* for you.'

'Well, I don't,' Ellen says. 'I like it just as it is. Stop trying to make your dreams everyone else's.'

With that, my daughter flounces upstairs. So, after I've stared blankly at the wall for a bit wondering where I've gone so wrong, I eat the toast that I made for her. The toast that she didn't want. Not only am I trying to foist my dreams on her, but also my dietary desires.

Is she right? Am I trying to make everyone else want the things that I want? Why is that? Is it because, now that I've embarked on this, I'm actually scared to death at the thought of doing it myself?

Chapter Ninety-Six

Lauren woke up still in Zak's arms. The sunlight was streaming in through the cottage window and she could see pink roses bobbing their heads in the breeze. A bird sang on the tree just outside.

She turned towards him, until they were face-to-face. Zak's eyes were open and there was a smile on his face. 'I wasn't dreaming, then,' he said.

Lauren laughed. 'No.' She snuggled closer to him. 'Have you been awake for long?'

Zak shook his head. 'A few minutes. I was just enjoying the view.' His eyes appraised her nakedness.

Lauren gave a leisurely stretch. 'I think I'd like to spend the whole day in bed.'

'That can be arranged.'

She kissed Zak's mouth, suddenly serious.

'What was that for?'

'Thank you for a great evening. And night . . .'

'I'm thinking that I'd like there to be many more of them.'

Lauren propped herself up on her arm. 'Are you?'

'Lauren,' Zak said, 'I have loved you for so long. You must surely have realised that?'

'I just thought you felt sorry for me.'

'Perhaps we need to put you in for some wiring readjust-ments,' he suggested. 'I just thought that I never had a chance with you because of . . . Well, because of *circumstances*.'

It was the first time she'd thought of Jude since yesterday. That surely was a good sign. It was also the first time that she realised that most of her relationship with her ex-lover had been based around sex – most of it rushed, frantic, guilty sex. She'd dressed it up as excitement, passion. Now she'd spent the night with Zak, she realised that it could be different. Oh, so different!

'Let's not spoil the mood,' she said. 'Let's just bask in the little glow we've created.'

'We could create another little glow,' Zak suggested.

Lauren smiled. 'We could.'

'And then you need to pay your debts, Ms Osbourne.'

She frowned.

'You're forgetting that the World Pudding-Eating Champion was promised breakfast in bed.'

'Oh yes, that's right,' she admitted. 'But then I've had a lot on my mind.'

'Me too,' he said. Zak lifted himself until he was above her. Then, with a happy sigh, he said, 'Do you realise quite how many times I've imagined you naked while I've been sitting at my desk pretending to care about websites?'

'A lot?'

'An *obscene* amount.'

They giggled like teenagers.

'And look at you,' he said wistfully. 'You're here and you're mine.' He slipped inside her, his body joined with hers and

341

she felt a wave of joy ripple through her. 'I never thought that would happen.'

'Me neither,' Lauren murmured contentedly. 'But I'm so glad that it did.'

Chapter Ninety-Seven

When they'd made love again – and again – Lauren slipped out of bed while Zak snoozed. She showered in the small bathroom and threw on her kimono before padding down to the kitchen.

In the fridge she found bacon, and there was a fresh loaf that they'd brought down with them yesterday in the bread bin. There were eggs too, but she decided against them on the grounds of practicality. They'd already made quite enough of a mess of that crisp white linen without adding egg-yolk stains to it. It made her grin to think of their crumpled sheets.

Theoretically, it was even too late for brunch. This was most definitely lunch in bed rather than breakfast.

Lauren put the bacon under the grill and four slices of bread in the toaster. She didn't know if Zak preferred tea or coffee in the mornings – even that little thought sent a thrill through her – so she plumped for coffee for him as that's what she was having.

It didn't seem a very exotic brekkie in bed – bacon sandwiches and coffee – but she knew that it would be a meal that she'd cherish for a long time. There was orange juice in the fridge too – Zak had thought of everything – and she poured them both a glass of that.

The smell of bacon drifted from the grill and Lauren slid it out before it burned. Now she just had to do the toast.

Lauren took the lid from the butter in preparation and waited, sipping her juice and gazing out of the window at the fields. It looked as if it was going to be another warm day. Perhaps they could go out for a walk this afternoon – if they could manage to drag themselves out of bed.

As she daydreamed, she thought she saw the figure of a man passing along the hedge at the side of Zak's cottage. But then he was gone. Lauren blinked. Must be imagining things.

The toast shot exuberantly out of the toaster and she turned away, but as she did so, she caught sight of a shock of dark hair again ducking down by the fence at the back. Lauren peered out of the window, but could see no one.

Turning her attention back to the toast, she buttered it liberally, slapped on the bacon and sliced each sandwich into two rather indelicate halves. She found a tray slotted down by one of the cupboards and loaded it up.

As she opened the bedroom door, Zak was just waking, rubbing his eyes, raking his hair.

'Lunch in bed,' she said.

Her boyfriend – was that what he was now? – glanced at the clock and his eyes widened. 'Is that really the time?'

'That's really the time.' Lauren plonked the tray down on the bed.

'You terrible woman,' Zak teased. 'You're leading me astray. I'm normally up with the lark.'

'I didn't know if you liked tea or coffee,' she said. 'I opted for coffee.'

'I'll drink anything as long as someone else is making it.'

'That's what I like to hear. A man who's easy to please.'

'Hey.' He caught her round the wrist. 'Come here. It must be hours since I kissed you.'

'Not even one,' she said, surrendering to his mouth before slipping into bed beside him.

'This looks great,' he said. 'I'm starving.'

'How can you be, after all those puddings?'

'I'll remind you that some of us have used up a lot of energy during the night.'

Lauren laughed. 'I'd forgotten.'

'Then I might have to remind you again in a moment.'

'We'll have to close the curtains,' she said. 'Looks like you've got some sort of prowler or Peeping Tom.'

'Really?'

'There was a guy hanging around at the back of the house. I didn't get a proper look at him though.'

Zak frowned. 'That's unusual.'

She shrugged. 'Could have been an innocent dog-walker.'

It was only later, much later, that Lauren realised that she should have known.

Chapter Ninety-Eight

Chelsea rings and asks me to meet her. Which is unusual in itself. She also sounds as if she's been crying.

'Is everything okay?'

'I'll explain when I see you.'

'Come over here,' I suggest.

'I'd rather not. Let's meet at Union Café in Campbell Park.' An outdoor café in a park? A rather downmarket one as well. That's not Chelsea's style at all.

So I bribe Bobby to take me by asking how his hand is, thus reminding him that he owes me big time after Saturday night. Oh, I can't wait to get this damn thing off my foot and am able to drive myself around again!

An hour later and Bobs drops me off at the car park nearest to the Union Café. A string of colourful narrow-boats are moored up along the water's edge. It's not that warm today, but there are still quite a few people sitting at the stainless-steel tables on the terrace which borders the Grand Union Canal. My sister is among them. Dodging all the children who are running around, out of control, I hop over to her.

She stands to greet me and air kisses both cheeks. 'Good grief, I'm sorry.' Chelsea points to my crutches. 'I forgot all about that.'

'I keep trying to.'

'I should have collected you.'

'No worries. It's out of your way. I got Bobby to bring me down here.' I don't mention the reason I was owed a favour as I'm acutely aware that my children fall way short of Chelsea's on the perfection scale, and don't want her to have another reason to feel sorry for me.

My elder sister doesn't look that great, which is also not like her. Her traditional, perfectly co-ordinated designer ensemble is not in evidence today. The immaculately coiffed hair looks lank and is pulled back in a hastily done ponytail. She's not wearing make-up. Clearly, something is terribly wrong.

'Let me get you a coffee,' Chelsea says.

'I'll have an Americano. White, two sugars, please.'

When she comes back, she's bought another one for herself – a double espresso, which she knocks back without tasting it.

'So?' I sip at mine. 'What's happened?'

At which, Chelsea starts to cry. My sister does movie-star crying – no awful hacking sobs, just gentle tears which stream silently down her cheeks in a heartbreaking way.

Budging my chair up next to hers, I put my arm round her. 'Nothing can be that bad,' I say.

She nods. 'It is.'

I wait until she's composed herself again. 'It's Rich,' she tells me, and I brace myself ready for the 'other woman' story. But no . . .

'There's some sort of fraud been going on at his company. Something to do with hedge funds. You know that I never get involved in his work.' Chelsea sniffs into her tissue. 'Rich has been implicated in it. He's lost a fortune, Annie. All our bank accounts are frozen.'

'Frozen?'

'That's why the cheque bounced.' She looks at me with frightened eyes. 'The police are investigating, and the Financial Services Authority. Until they clear it all up, Rich's hands are tied.'

'Omigod. I thought you were going to tell me he'd got another woman.'

'If only,' Chelsea says, rolling her eyes. 'That I could cope with. This . . .' she sighs unhappily. 'We're both in uncharted territory.'

'I can't believe that Richard is involved in something like this.' Not the model husband.

'He isn't,' Chelsea says determinedly. 'Of course, he isn't. He's just got caught up in the aftermath. A victim of circumstances.'

'Of course. Of course.' I echo anxiously. Fraud – Richard? I'm stunned.

'It will all come right in the end. It may just take some time. A few weeks – no more, I'm sure.'

'How can I help?' I ask. 'You know that I'll do whatever I can. You're always there for me.' I think of how she's tried to help me with my fundraising when she had all this going on.

'I need money, Annie,' she says bluntly. 'The kids' school fees are due next week and I've no idea how we're going to pay them.'

'Wow.' That's quite a big ask. I know that the kids go to one of the most expensive schools in the area when they're in England. 'I haven't got that kind of money, Chelsea.'

If only I had.

'It'll be a loan,' she says. 'Just until our bank accounts are released again.'

'And you think that'll be a few weeks?'

'I don't know,' she admits, hanging her head. 'That's what I'm hoping. Until then, I don't know what to do. That's why I came to you.'

'I'm stony broke, Chelsea. I don't have the kind of money you're talking about.'

'But you have the money for your holiday.'

Holiday? Adventure. Dream. Escape. Not holiday.

'I've worked so hard to get that. It's all I have.'

The tears start again. 'And I wouldn't ask you if I wasn't desperate. What am I to do? What else am I to do?'

What am *I* to do? I think. I can't leave my sister like this. She's frantic. I can't ask her to pull her children out of their posh school because I won't lend her the money. I know how much Henry and Sophia adore Swanleys.

I knock back my coffee. Her need is greater than mine. 'I've only got about two thousand pounds. That isn't anywhere near enough.'

'But it's a start,' Chelsea says. 'I can ask Lauren too.'

I already know that Lauren, like her impoverished twin, has no money to spare. Now that she's finally split with Jude she's going to be needing all the cash she can lay her hands on too.

'Can't you sell something? Some jewellery perhaps?'

Chelsea flashes her ring at me. 'All gone,' she admits. 'This is cheap and cheerful costume jewellery. I hoped that no one would notice.'

I certainly didn't. 'And the car?'

'Not ours to sell. It's leased by the company and I'm not sure how much longer I'll be able to hang on to it.'

'Don't you have any friends who could bail you out?' I suggest, sounding desperate even to my own ears. 'Perhaps the school could defer the payment until it's all sorted.'

'I couldn't ask that,' Chelsea says. 'What would they think of me? Our reputation would be shot to pieces. I have to keep this very quiet, Annie. No one can know.'

Ah, so that's clearly why we're meeting at this out-of-the-way place and not one of her regular haunts.

'But if you've got no money, Chelsea, won't they find out very quickly anyway?'

'Will you lend it to me or not?' my sister asks. 'I don't know where else to turn.'

I sigh because I don't know what else to do.

'We're family,' Chelsea reminds me crisply, sniffing back her tears. 'That's where people turn when they're in need. I know that you and Lauren like to keep me out of your tight-knit little twosome, but I am your sister.'

'We don't try to keep you out.'

'But you do,' my sister says. 'All of my life I've been on the outside. Do you think I don't notice?'

I feel terrible. I've let her down. Both Lauren and I have let her down.

'So,' she says, 'can I count on you?'

'Of course you can.' I see my dreams of Peru, the Inca Trail, the Nazca Lines, the pisco sour cocktails, all go up in smoke. My desire to do something daring before I die will have to be put on hold.

'I'll happily lend you the money.' I plaster a smile on my face, give Chelsea a hug and try not to howl in despair. 'What are sisters for?'

Chapter Ninety-Nine

When they finally managed to drag themselves out of bed, Zak and Lauren went for a walk.

Zak drove them through the quaint, chocolate-box countryside to the busy tourist stop of Lower Slainton. When he wasn't changing gear, they held hands.

Lauren rested her head back on the car seat, happier than she'd been in a long, long time. She'd slept so well in Zak's arms that it felt as if all the tension had melted out of her body.

Half an hour later, they pulled up beside a pretty village green. There was a posh hotel, a stream running alongside the only street, towering oaks providing dappled shade and dozens of people wielding cameras.

They climbed out of the car and headed away from the bustle, following the stream in the opposite direction into the lush, green fields. There were few people here and Zak took her hand as they strolled through the meadows that bordered the stream as it grew bolder and became a river.

'Happy?' he asked.

She leaned into his side. 'More than I ever thought possible. This is a beautiful place. It makes me wonder why on earth I live in London.'

The sound of birdsong filled the air and there was a twitcher in the opposite field to them, his binoculars to his eyes. Despite the warm weather he was wearing a big coat and had a hat pulled right down on his head. Lauren smiled to herself. A good old British eccentric.

They strolled on until they came to the picturesque village of Upper Slainton. There was a green bordered by a row of terraced cottages on one side and a small church on the other. The river meandered through the centre, water clear and sparkling in the sun. Beyond the green was a former mill house that had been converted into a tea room.

'I think it's time for some more calories,' Zak said.

'I've never known anyone eat as much as you.'

'I need to keep my strength up.' He rubbed his hands together in anticipation.

The Mill House Café was cramped inside but beyond the main room there was a welcoming garden, which stretched out along by the river. An eclectic mix of tables and chairs dressed in pastel shades were scattered about. Zak chose one in the cool shade. Lauren sat down, hot from walking, and fanned herself with the menu.

'Afternoon tea,' Zak said. 'Just what the doctor ordered.'

'I couldn't,' Lauren protested, but found herself strangely hungry. Real hunger, not the knot of anxiety that was usually there.

'You could,' Zak countered. 'What type of tea would you like?'

'Earl Grey, if they have it.'

'I'll be back in just a moment.' Zak kissed her warmly and then sighed with joy. 'Don't go away.'

Lauren squeezed his hand. 'I'm not planning on going anywhere.'

'I'll hold you to that,' he said, then disappeared into the Mill House again to order their cream teas.

An old Billie Holiday song, the name of which she couldn't remember, drifted out into the garden and Lauren closed her eyes, which were pleasantly heavy, and let the music wash over her. After a moment she became aware that she was being watched and opened her eyes, expecting to find Zak standing there.

Instead, she saw the twitcher on the other side of the river, closer now, squatting down beside a bush, his binoculars trained on her. Lauren sat up with a jolt. Her eyes strained to see in the strong sunshine and she lifted her hand to her brow to provide some shade. The man no longer wore his hat and Lauren was sure that she recognised the shock of black hair. Wasn't he the very same man who'd been lurking around behind Zak's cottage this morning?

The man stood up. Oh. Now she recognised him well enough. How could she not? And it wasn't just from this morning.

And, at that moment, Jude threw off his coat, jumped into the river and began to wade across to where she was.

Chapter One Hundred

I sit on the edge of my bed and tip out the notes and coins from my old handbag. Slowly, methodically, I count out my stash. I have one thousand, five hundred and five pounds. All spread out on the duvet before me.

There's another five hundred pounds to go to the fund which is my company contribution and which they're paying direct. Making it two thousand and five pounds in total.

How many weeks before we're due to go to Peru? How long before I have to come up with the money? I work it out on my fingers.

Am I going to have enough time to earn this all over again? Could I start from scratch now and still muster up another two grand? If we could do the car wash – yes, possibly. From sandwiches and cakes – possibly not. Unless I begin to force-feed all of my colleagues.

What with my foot and now this, I don't know why I don't just lie down, roll over and admit defeat.

I want to phone Lauren. She'd motivate me – tell me what to do. But I can't disturb her. She's gone away for a few days' peace and quiet and I can't burden her with my problems when she has more than enough of her own. Plus she would instruct me to tell Chelsea to get stuffed, and I know that I couldn't do that to my older sister, not now that she's desperate for money and, for the very first time in her life, she's come to me for help.

Making sure the door is closed, I get my travel guide out of the depths of my handbag and prop myself up against the pillows. On pages 170 to 171 there is a double-page map of the Inca Trail, and it's dirty with my fingerprints. Once again, I trace the outline of the route marked in a dotted red line. It passes more than thirty ancient Inca sites – Runkurackay, Sayacmarca, Wiñay Wayna, Phuyupatamarca. Will I ever see any of these places now? Will I ever step inside the magnificent Inca ruins? Run my hands over the smooth grey stones, so painstakingly constructed? Will my colleagues embark on this trip without me?

I close the book.

Of course they will.

How can I not give my sister this money? Chelsea has never asked me for anything before. I really want to help her out. And yet . . . I push away unkind thoughts about my sister's perfect life and how this is the first time she's ever had to endure any hardship. I will help her – of course I will. That's what family do.

But it hurts. Oh, how it hurts. There's a keening pain deep inside me and I don't know what will get rid of it.

Then I cry. I don't do dignified crying like Chelsea. I cry loud and hard and sob and sniffle and feel like the most wretched person in the entire world.

The door opens and Greg is standing there. 'I wondered where you were,' he says. 'I thought I heard a noise.'

That would be the sound of me dying inside.

'Are you all right?' He glances at the travel guide on the bed and his face darkens. 'Oh. That again.'

I try to get a grip on my tears as I say, 'I'm not going.'

'Not going?'

Shake of head. 'Chelsea needs the money. I'm lending it to her.'

'Chelsea needs money?'

I know why he looks incredulous. It's a bit like me saying the Queen or Donald Trump are short of a few quid.

'It's a long story,' I tell him, and I'll explain it all to him later – but not right now.

I start to push the money back into the old handbag. 'She promises that she'll return it. Eventually.' I'll take the cash to work tomorrow and Chelsea can come and collect it. 'But not in time for me to go to Peru.'

'I'm sorry,' Greg says. He goes to reach for my hand, but I snatch it away.

Then my anger at the injustice of it all rises to the surface. 'You're not sorry at all.' I stand up and struggle with my crutches.

'Let me help you.'

'No! You never wanted me to go.' I hop/flounce to the door. 'Now you've got your wish.'

'Annie . . .'

I slam the door as I leave.

Chapter One Hundred-One

Jude clambered out of the river, struggling up the bank. Lauren stood, hands on hips, and watched him in disbelief.

'*What*,' she asked, astonished, 'are you doing here?'

Her ex-lover was soaked through. He was dripping all over the grass. If this was supposed to be a Mr Darcy moment, it had gone horribly wrong. Jude looked distraught, and there was duckweed sticking to his shirt and in his hair. The other tea drinkers in the garden stop with cups halfway to mouths that, to a man, have fallen open.

'I might ask you the same thing,' he said breathlessly.

'How did you know I was here?'

'It was obvious who you were with, when *he* didn't turn in for work.' Jude flicked a thumb in the direction of the Mill House where Zak was currently ordering their tea. 'I saw you, Lauren. I saw you drive away with him. I was out of my mind. I had no idea where you might be going. If I'd had my car with me, I would have followed you right away. I tried to get information out of the other guys at work, but none of them knew a thing. Or pretended they didn't.'

'I didn't even know myself until just before we left,' she told him.

Jude looked unconvinced. 'Then I remembered that he'd

bought a weekend cottage in the Cotswolds. Clearly, that was my starting point. You can find out anything from the internet these days.'

'So it was you looking over the hedge this morning?'

Jude nodded bleakly.

'I don't know why you bothered,' Lauren said, sounding as hard as she could while inside, her stomach was twisting into knots.

'You're sleeping with him,' he said. His voice was laced with anguish. 'How could you?'

'You've been sleeping with your wife for the five years that we've been seeing each other,' she reminded him.

'This is totally different.' Jude raked his fingers through his wet hair. 'I had no choice.'

'You had a choice,' Lauren said quietly. 'We both did. And now I've made another choice. It's over between us, Jude. What I do and who I do it with is no longer your business.'

'I'm going to go in there and knock his head off.'

Lauren sighed. 'Don't be ridiculous. Let's at least try to be dignified about this.' Though it was hard to see how, when faced with a dripping-wet ex-lover standing in front of her and the scenes with her dressed as a pineapple still sharp in her mind.

Jude's shoulders drooped. 'I love you,' he said. 'I can't bear the thought of you with another man.'

Lauren didn't dredge up all the years that she'd been tortured by him being with another woman.

'Do you love him?' The look of pain on his face was un-bearable.

'It's too early to be talking about anything like that,' Lauren said. 'Zak's a good friend. He makes me laugh. He's *single*. Available.'

'And I'll be available too. In time.' Her lover flailed his hands. 'You can't just walk away from your family overnight. These things take time. I have to make plans.'

'We had five years, Jude. *You* had five years.'

'I'll leave,' he promised. 'Georgia knows all about us now. We can move in together.'

'Wait a minute,' Lauren said. 'You told me that you'd already moved out.'

'And I had,' Jude insisted. 'Sort of. Georgia wanted me to go home and try again. What could I do?'

'You're back at home?'

'Well, I . . .'

'Did you ever actually move out at all?'

'I, er . . . it's not that easy, Lauren. Trust me. It's not that easy.'

'Then make it easy,' she said. 'Stay with your wife. Stay with your family. Try to be a good husband and a good dad. Because I don't want you any more, Jude. It's over.'

'I love you,' he said. 'I can make this up to you. We could go back to how we were.'

'I can't do that any more. I want someone full-time in my life. Not just the scraps.'

'No.' Jude clutched her arms. 'It can't be over. It can't be. What will I do without you? We can rescue this. It's not too late.'

Her twin sister had said that this would be their year to turn their lives around, that it was never too late to start living, to go all out for what they wanted. But sometimes it *was* too late. Sometimes you had to stand back and accept that your moment had passed.

She looked at Jude and something in her demeanour must have told him that there was no going forward, no going back for them. His face crumpled and he sagged to his knees.

'I'm so sorry, Jude, but it *is* too late,' Lauren said. 'That's exactly what it is. It's just too late.'

Chapter One Hundred-Two

Zak came back bearing a tray laden with cups, an enormous teapot and a pile of cakes. 'They were rushed off their feet in there,' he said, 'but I thought I might as well wait. Did you miss me?'

Lauren was still standing, gazing out over the river, watching as the bedraggled figure of her ex-lover disappeared out of view. This time, Jude had taken the more conventional route of the small stone bridge by the café.

'What?' Zak said, following her eyes. Then he looked like he was about to drop the tray as he peered at the man retreating into the sunshine. 'Is that who I think it is?'

Lauren nodded and sat down, heavily.

'I don't need to ask what *he* was doing here.'

'No.'

Zak put the tray down. 'I'm flabbergasted.'

'Me too.'

He sat beside her and pulled her to him. 'Okay?'

'I think so.'

Zak poured her a cup of Earl Grey. 'You must need this.'

'A double brandy would be preferable.' When she lifted the cup to her lips, Lauren realised her hand was shaking. 'It was Jude who was hanging around outside your cottage this morning.'

'How did he find out?'

A shrug. 'Put two and two together.'

'I'm sorry,' Zak said. 'I didn't even think about the possibility that he'd follow us up here.'

'Me neither,' she admitted.

All those weekends when she'd begged for a morsel of his time and he'd been unable to get away from his family and yet, when it mattered to Jude, he could drop them like hot coals. It had taken her a long time – too long – but she was beginning to come to terms with the fact that her former lover wasn't a very nice man.

And she hadn't been a very nice person when she was with him, either.

'I take it that he saw us together?'

'Yes.' Lauren risked a weary smile. 'I don't think he was very impressed.'

'I can imagine.'

'He's very hurt.'

'I could say that it was no more than he deserved.'

'I know that you're right,' she agreed. 'But that doesn't make it any easier.'

'But it *is* over?' Zak's eyes were dark with concern.

'Oh, yes. It's over. Once and for all.'

Zak reached for her hand. 'Well I, for one, am very relieved to hear that.'

Lauren sighed.

'A trouble shared is a trouble halved,' Zak said. 'Or so my old gran used to say. Want to tell me what's on your mind?'

'I can't go back to work – how can I? But I don't know what else to do.'

Zak picked at the slice of cake on his plate and avoided her eyes. 'Perhaps I should have shared this with you earlier.'

'I'm not sure that I can cope with any more surprises.'

'I hope that you'll think this is a good one.' Zak put down his cup and fixed his gaze on her. 'I'm setting up my own company – with another guy from the office. We're going into business against Jude with another regional daily download. But this will be younger, funkier, aimed more at the teen market.'

'That sounds great.'

'I couldn't trust you with it until I was sure that it was definitely over between you and Jude. I'm sure that you understand why.'

'Of course I do.'

'We haven't got anyone to do the sales and marketing,' Zak said. 'I'm hoping that you might say you will.'

'I will.'

His eyes widened. 'You don't need to think about it? You don't need to know your terms and conditions? Your pay?'

'No,' Lauren said. 'You'll be fair to me. That's all I need to know.'

'We're also thinking of moving the offices out of London.'

'Even better.' She could sell the flat, split what equity there was with Jude to repay him for his past contributions, and hopefully, she'd still come out with a small sum that she could use as a deposit on another place.

It would be a blow to Jude, losing two of his best employees, but she had to put herself first from now on. Jude Taylor had been top of her list for way too long.

'There's a barn that's been partly converted, up for sale just near here,' Zak went on. 'The outbuildings would make a great office space. If I sell my London flat, I could just about afford it. Do you fancy relocating to here?'

'It would be perfect.' Annie would still be an hour away, but this was a truly idyllic location. She could imagine spending her days here.

'Want to go and look at it?'

'Do you think we have a future together, Zak?'

'I'd like to think so, Lauren,' he said. 'I love you. I've loved you for a long time.'

She leaned towards him and kissed him on the lips. 'Why was I too stupid to see it?'

'It was a question I asked myself frequently,' Zak teased.

'I will make you pay for that one day, Zak Reynolds. One day, some way, you will pay. But for now I'll forgive you because you're so damn gorgeous.'

And, saying a final goodbye in her mind to Jude, she wrapped her arms around Zak and embraced the future.

Chapter One Hundred-Three

I slept on the sofa last night and now – to add to my list of growing complaints – my back is killing me. I couldn't get into bed with Greg. I just couldn't.

I hate Mondays. Mid-morning, Chelsea comes to my office. Trying not to show that my heart is somewhere round my knees, I hand over my handbag filled with my cash. My lovely, lovely hard-earned cash that I needed so much myself.

'Thank you,' my sister breathes. 'You don't know how much this means to me.'

And you don't realise how much this is hurting me, I think. She kisses me on the cheek.

'I hope it's enough,' I say. But she doesn't answer me. Her face is drawn and she looks like she's lost weight and she didn't really have any to spare.

Then she glances at her watch. 'I'd better go.'

'You'll be fine,' I try to reassure her.

'I wish I could be so sure.' All of my sister's sparkle has evaporated overnight. I could kill Richard for putting her through this – whatever it is. All I can do is pray that they sort it out soon. 'I'm here for you, Chelsea,' I promise. 'And Lauren is too. We should all get together next week.'

My sister smiles gratefully. 'We will,' she says. 'Definitely.'

We hug each other tightly.

Then, as I watch her go back to her car – still the

top-of-the-range wotsit – Blake Chadwick comes out of the office.

'Hi,' he says. Then he frowns. 'Everything okay?'

I'd never make a poker player. Concern must be written all over my face. 'Not really,' I answer honestly. 'That was my elder sister.' I nod towards Chelsea's disappearing flash-mobile. 'She's got a few problems.'

And they've become my problems.

'You're a fine-looking family,' BC tells me with an appreciative whistle through his perfect teeth.

But I'm not in the mood for his flirting today. After spending a night on the sofa everything hurts. Not least of all my heart.

'Not long to go to Peru,' he says. 'How's the foot coming along?'

'Okay. I'm going to see the consultant after work.' Then I decide that he might as well be the first to know. 'But I won't be going to Peru, whether it's better or not.'

That stops him in his tracks. BC does comedy blinking. 'You're not going?'

'Chelsea just walked off with all the money I've raised so far,' I continue. 'Her need is greater than mine.'

'I don't believe it.'

I shrug. 'Believe it.'

'It won't be the same without you, Annie.'

And to think that a few weeks ago, I fell for all this charm. 'You *have* to go.'

'I don't have enough time left to raise the money again.'

Blake is now pacing the floor. 'It's unthinkable that you'll miss it.'

I would have said that too yesterday. Now I'm resigned to my fate.

'There must be some way . . .'

'I currently can't think of any,' I supply.

'If I had the cash to spare, I'd pay for you myself.'

'I wouldn't accept, anyway.'

'You *cannot* let this opportunity pass you by,' he insists. 'It would be a tragedy.'

But would it? One bored, frustrated housewife doesn't get her adventure. Does anyone care? Do I care? Do I *really* care any more?

I hold up my hands. 'That's the end of it. I'm not going.'

And the sooner I get used to that fact, the better.

Chapter One Hundred-Four

Greg takes me to the hospital and we wait and wait and wait. We don't speak while we're doing it.

An hour and a half after my allotted appointment time, I get an X-ray and then, after more waiting, I hobble in to see the consultant, Mr Brown. Greg follows me.

When I'm up on the couch, the consultant hums and hahs over my foot. The X-ray goes up on the wall.

Then Mr Brown takes off his glasses. 'Well,' he says, 'your foot has healed marvellously, Mrs Ashton. You have the bones of a woman half your age.'

That's a good thing, I know – but somehow I can't get excited about it. If he'd said I had the *face* of a woman half my age then I'd have been whooping.

'Have you been having physio sessions?'

'Yes.'

'Then you can start to walk on it from today,' he continues, but I'm not really listening. Who cares how long it takes to heal now?

'Take it gently at first, then gradually build it up. You'll be as right as rain before you know it.'

Mr Brown helps me off the couch and, for the first time in weeks, I can put my weight on my foot. It feels a bit weak but, other than that, not too bad at all.

'Keep one crutch,' the consultant suggests. 'It will help with the balance.'

'Thank you.' It looks as if I might have been fit enough to go to Peru, after all. A bitter taste rises to my mouth. But I'm not going. So who cares?

Outside in the corridor, Greg takes my arm. 'Need a hand?'

'I'm fine.' I limp towards the car park.

'It's good news.'

'Marvellous.'

'I thought you would be pleased,' my husband says, perplexed.

'I am,' I snap. 'Overjoyed. I might just do a happy dance in a minute.'

Now he looks alarmed. 'The consultant said to take it easy.'

'That's why I'm managing to restrain myself.'

Greg turns me to face him. 'Is this because you can't go to Peru?'

'How very perceptive of you.'

'There's no need to be like that.' He sighs at me. 'I didn't want you to go because I was worried about you. Because I didn't want you to go on your own.'

Because you don't understand my needs. Because you're happy with your life and I'm not.

'I don't want a conversation about this,' I tell my husband. 'Not now.' My disappointment is too raw, too painful, too all-encompassing.

'We could do something else instead.'

I hope that Greg has thought about this very carefully,

because if he suggests going to Cromer for the weekend as a substitute, I may just have to batter him to death with my one remaining crutch.

Chapter One Hundred-Five

'It didn't quite work out the way I planned,' Lauren says, 'but, bizarrely, I'm so glad it didn't. I never thought I'd hear myself say that.'

My twin sister is sitting at my kitchen table nursing a cup of tea. She's decided to knock the drinking on the head for the time being – maybe for good – which I think is no bad thing. I, on the other hand, am having a big glass of red wine. Or two. Or possibly even three. Let's see what two does and I'll take it from there.

'It sounds like you're making a fresh start, Lauren. And that makes me very happy.' I hug my sis warmly. I'm so glad she's got rid of that love-rat, Jude Taylor, at long last.

'Zak's so lovely,' she adds. 'I don't know why I didn't see it before.'

'Sometimes we take the people closest to us for granted.' I feel myself flush as I think guiltily of my own husband.

'We're planning on moving to the Cotswolds,' Lauren says excitedly. 'Imagine! Me, the country lady.'

'It's not too far from here. We can still see as much of each other.'

'Don't sound so desperate,' my sister says. 'Of course we can. I've ditched Jude. I've got a great new bloke and am going to start a new business, a new life. Christ, I might even go the whole hog and have a baby! Be happy for me.'

At that I burst into tears.

'What?' Lauren wants to know. 'What have I said now?'

'I'm not going to Peru,' I sob. 'I'm happy that your dream is just beginning, but mine's over.'

'Why? I thought you said your foot was okay?'

'It is.' Then I sigh. 'Promise you won't say anything.'

My sister promises.

'Chelsea is in a bit of a mess.'

'Chelsea? Never!'

'Something to do with Rich's work. Fraud or something.'

Lauren's eyes go like saucers.

'All of their bank accounts are frozen. The cheque she gave me for my fundraising bounced.'

'No way!'

'Worse than that, I had to give her the money I'd raised for my trip to Peru to help her out.'

'You did *what*?'

'I gave her the money.'

'Are you crazy?'

'She needed it.'

'Like a hole in the head,' Lauren says. 'Why didn't she sell some of her bloody diamonds? That eternity ring he bought her for her fortieth would keep them in food for a year. Or what about her big, flash motor? Why take your savings off you? What a cow.'

'Don't say that,' I chide. 'All the good stuff's gone,' I tell my sister. 'The jewellery's fake. The car isn't theirs. She really is in a mess. Let's face it, Lauren, we're her last resort. How often does Chelsea come to us for help?'

'Never.'

'Exactly.' More wine. 'What could I say?'

'Piss off? Get a job?'

'Is that really what you would have said?'

'Yes.'

I think not. Lauren may like to kid herself that she's harder than me, but I know that she's a sucker for a sob story. In my position, I'd like to bet that she would have handed over the money too. 'This –' whatever *this* turns out to be '– has hit her very hard.'

Lauren flops back in her chair and puffs out, 'I'll bet.'

'We have to help her, Lauren. Both of us. She needs us. I can go to Peru another time.'

'Yeah, right,' Lauren says. 'It's no good trying to be philosophical, Annie, when it's taken you nearly twenty years to pluck up the courage to do this.'

More wine. More crying.

'So what are you going to do?'

'Nothing,' I snivel. 'Stay here rotting away in this prison of a marriage.'

My sister makes a frantic cutting motion across her throat, but it's too late.

From behind me, my husband says, 'Thank you, Annie. That lets me know exactly where I stand.'

'Greg . . .' I spin round. My husband is standing there, hands in pockets, looking stony-faced. 'I didn't mean it. I was just being overly dramatic. I'm just disappointed that I can't go to Peru.'

'So I gather,' he says, then heads towards the back door. 'Your gaoler is going fishing. I don't know when I'll be back.'

'Greg!'

374

'Let him go,' my sister advises. 'Bloody men.'

'What shall I do now?'

'Get me a glass,' Lauren says. 'I've given up my vow of not drinking. You and I, my dear sister, need to be very, very drunk.'

I sigh inside. I'll drink to that.

Chapter One Hundred-Six

Greg couldn't face going fishing with Ray today. This was a day when he needed to be alone, to think, to wonder what had gone wrong with his marriage, why he and Annie were so far apart when once they had been so close.

He'd stayed away from the canal, because it was more than likely that Ray would be down there anyway. Instead, he'd parked up, walked for miles with a light bag of tackle and gone to a secluded bank on the River Ouse with a view to spinning for a pike.

Normally, he wouldn't head out in search of a pike, but he wanted a battle, wanted to struggle; he didn't want the ease of plucking perch one after another out of the still waters of the canal. There were some big fish lurking in this spot – twenty pounds and more – that had grown fat in relative peace, largely untroubled by the rods of anglers.

The day was overcast, the sun sulking behind the grey clouds. And it was cooler than it had been. The perfect day for his mood.

His hands were unsteady as he assembled the sections of his rod, the rod that Annie had given him all those years ago. The rod that had been steadfast and true. Greg threaded the line down through the rings and fed some small sprats he'd brought from the freezer on to the hook. He cast out and even the quiet slap of his line on the water failed to lift his spirits. After a moment he reeled the line in, smoothly, smoothly . . . easy does it. You had to be careful with pike or they could quite easily get the better of you. They were a solitary fish that would feed on any living thing in its path – even their own kind.

Greg always felt tense when he was fishing for this cunning predator. It had a coiled, explosive power that could be unleashed by one thrust from its powerful tail, which gave it a stunning turn of speed. You had to be on your toes to land one of these.

He cast again and began to reel in. Seconds later, the line snagged. He hit it quick and the fish was off with a bang that vibrated through Greg's chest. It was a big one and the reel screamed in protest as the fish took flight; the line, stretching to breaking point, went with it. He held it tight, played it, teased the fish in, slowly, slowly . . . as it fought against its constraint.

The fish thrashed in the depths of the water but Greg was immovable. He could feel it tiring, tiring, giving up the struggle as it realised that it had been beaten. He brought the fish close to the bank, finally coming face-to-face with his quarry, its mouth open to display its fearsome, needle-sharp teeth.

Greg pulled it over his net and lifted it out to the bank. It was eighteen pounds at least. He wrested the hook from its gaping mouth. The fish gasped, its muscular body heaving. The terror of the river, stranded, fighting now for its every breath. Not so frightening now, Greg thought.

For the first time, he wanted to kill a fish, to smash its skull beneath his hands, cudgel it to death. Greg sank to his knees, tears in his eyes. Was this what it had come to? Was there no other way he could get this emotion out?

He lifted the fish, cradling it to him. This would be a grinning photo opportunity for his friend Ray, but catching, defeating this fish had given Greg no joy.

Greg lowered the fish to the water and let it go, watching numbly as it quickly swam away. He'd overcome the ultimate river predator, but how would he fare against predators of the human kind? If that Blake Chadwick bloke wanted to steal his wife away, would he be able to stop him? Would Greg put up a decent fight? And, this time, would he be victorious again?

Chapter One Hundred-Seven

Four weeks have passed. The horrible blue boot is long gone. I've even been running again – but not with Blake Chadwick. I've changed my route and now run through the Linear Park, which I can do straight from my own front door. My foot ached a bit at first, but now it's fully healed and fully functioning again. Having improved my fitness, I'd like to keep it up – even though it is utterly pointless now. Maybe my cholesterol levels will thank me for it in years to come.

Relations between Greg and me are still strained. I spent a week on the sofa, but now I'm back in our 'marital' bed. I thought the fact that I'm not going away now would have helped to defrost the atmosphere between us, but it hasn't. If anything, Greg has been worse in the last few weeks and I just can't summon up the energy to extend the olive branch. We're still not touching, not communicating, not behaving at all like a couple who've been married for twenty-odd years. It saddens me, but I'm not sure how we can find our way back. At the moment, I'm too down, too depressed to be able to formulate a plan to restore our *entente cordiale*.

I've still been making sandwiches and cakes for my colleagues. A little sideline that I'm really enjoying, and which has also brought in almost a thousand pounds. It would have easily made up my fare for the trip to Peru, but I try not to think about that too much.

I also sold Chelsea's designer clothes at a car-boot sale – a hideous experience that I have no desire to repeat. Rabid hordes descended on me as I unloaded the car, all but grabbing the clothes out of my hands. However, when the scrum died down, I was pleased to see that I'd made two hundred pounds. I gave that to my sister, who is still, it seems, no nearer to sorting out what is happening in her life.

Chelsea had to take her children out of posh education after all as, even with my contribution, she was woefully short of the required money and there were no easy payment terms on offer at Swanley School. Once you haven't got the cash, you're out. No ifs, no buts. Henry and Sophia are now, by all accounts, doing very well at their local primary school. Of my money, there is still no sign.

There's a mounting air of excitement here in the offices. Everyone is getting ready for the impending trip and there's a lot of team-bonding going on. I feel desperately, desperately outside of it all. I'm going to be left on my own here for two weeks manning the offices when I still wish with all my heart that I was going too.

My colleagues are leaving on Friday and it's now Wednesday lunchtime. There's a final meeting in the boardroom so that they can all discuss their last-minute preparations, and they asked me to supply the sandwiches for it. I glance at my watch. It's just before one and that's when the gathering starts, so I need to go through and set them out now.

Picking up my heavy basket, I make my way through to the boardroom. It's all in darkness in here and I mutter to myself, fumbling for the light switch.

When the light goes on, a cry goes up and I nearly jump out of my skin, then stand there blinking like a rabbit caught in the headlights. All my colleagues are already gathered together and they're clapping and cheering and I'm sure it's not just because of the quality of my sandwiches.

'What?' I say in a manner that I'm sure sounds much more intelligent than it appears.

Blake Chadwick steps forward, all smiles, and my weak and impressionable heart flutters way too readily. He takes up a place next to me and then grins round at all the staff, who are clearly in on the joke.

I put down my basket of sandwiches and stand waiting for the punchline.

'We couldn't leave you behind, Annie,' Blake states. 'So, the company has bought your ticket.' He holds out a ticket to me, but my shaking hands won't move.

Seeing this, BC takes my fingers and folds them round the ticket.

'We couldn't have you missing out. When we get back, we'll all help you to raise the money for Dream Days.'

Everyone cheers again.

'I can't,' I say, trembling. 'I can't.'

'You can,' Blake says. 'There's nothing to stop you now.'

'But it's the day after tomorrow. I don't have time to get anything ready.'

'That's why we're giving you the afternoon off after the meeting as well so that you can go and get yourself kitted out. Minny's going to look after reception.'

My little friend grins at me.

I feel like passing out. 'I need to sit down.'

'Do it now,' someone shouts. 'There'll be no sitting down in the Andes.'

Then there's more cheering and everyone crowds round me and my back is slapped and my cheeks are kissed and my newly mended foot is trampled but, thankfully, suffers no ill-effects, and tears are rolling down my face.

I look at the ticket in my hand. London to Lima. Passenger – one Mrs Annie Ashton – bored wife and armchair adventurer, is on her way.

'Thank you,' I sob. 'Thank you so much.' I punch the air. Then we all do the same like the bloody musketeers!

'To Peru!' is the cry.

To Peru. I stroke the face of the ticket. And double-check my name so that I'm absolutely sure there's no mistake.

I'm going to Peru. And nothing – *nothing* – can stop me now!

Chapter One Hundred-Eight

Lauren went into the office. It made her heart pound with nerves just climbing the stairs. Yet, however reluctant she was to do this, she wanted to have a final look around and to clear her desk of her personal belongings. It wouldn't do for the new occupant of her job to find the pictures of her and Jude together on her computer or some of the love notes that he'd written hiding at the bottom of her drawer. Lauren sighed to herself. Those were the days.

She'd left it until eight o'clock, thinking that the offices would be deserted by then. But Lauren was surprised to see a light on in Jude's office when she opened the main door.

Sure enough he was at his desk, tapping at the keyboard with one hand, eating a carton of Chinese takeaway with the other. She had a moment when she didn't know whether to go in or to turn and bolt. But it was too late – Jude had already looked up and seen her standing there.

Lauren went over to his office and leaned on the door-frame. She tried a smile, but she didn't think that it reached her mouth. 'I've come for my stuff,' she told him. 'And to return your keys.'

Jude wiped his hands on a paper napkin that had clearly been supplied with the takeaway.

'Burning the midnight oil?' she asked.

Her ex-lover's eyes were red-rimmed and he looked terrible,

drawn and tired. 'Georgia's thrown me out,' he said. 'For good this time.'

Lauren didn't know what to say.

'I'm living here,' he told her. 'I have nowhere else to go. I've got a sleeping bag in the boardroom.'

She looked through the boardroom windows to the table where they'd made love so many times, then pushed the image away.

'I'm sorry to hear it.'

'Stay,' Jude urged. 'Have some Chinese. There's plenty here.'

'Thanks,' she said. 'I've already eaten.'

Jude laughed and it was a sound without humour. 'With him?'

'Yes.'

'You probably think I deserve all this,' he said. 'Finally got my comeuppance.'

'No. I wish you could make it up to your family.'

'Looks like that's not going to be.'

'I'm sorry,' she repeated.

'What will you do?' Jude asked.

'I'm putting the flat up for sale,' Lauren told him. 'I'll give you half of whatever profit I get. That only seems fair.'

'Oh, Lauren – there's no need for that,' Jude said sadly. 'You'll need every penny, and I just want you to be happy. You deserve it.' Then, 'Where will you go?'

'I'm moving in with Zak,' she admitted, avoiding his eyes. 'Why don't you take over the flat, Jude? Live there?'

'Too many memories.'

'You'll get over it,' Lauren said softly. 'It would make sense.'

Jude shrugged. 'Perhaps I will. Give me a couple of days to think about it. I don't know how long my back will last on that floor.' He tried to say it as a joke, but there was a sob in his voice.

'Oh, Jude,' she said. 'I'm so sorry that it's come to this.'

Her ex-lover's eyes filled with tears. 'I think you should leave now, Lauren.'

'I'll get my things.' She put the keys down on his desk.

'Can I hold you one more time before you go?'

Lauren nodded. He came forward and took her in his arms. Arms that she had waited and waited and waited for. They still felt good and strong around her. How easy it would be, to sink into his embrace.

'I still love you,' Jude whispered against her throat.

She forced herself to pull away from him. 'Be happy, Jude.'

Then Lauren walked away. To her new life, her new love. And she didn't look back. Not even one glance.

Chapter One Hundred-Nine

Once again I'm sitting on my bed. This time I'm surrounded by carrier bags laden with gear for my trip to Peru.

I've bought new hiking socks, some of those tops that you can wash out and dry within a minute, a new fleece and some hiking trousers that you can zip off at the knee to make into handy shorts. I hold them up and admire myself in the mirror.

'Nice,' Ellen says, drawling the word in an ironic manner. My daughter lounges at my bedroom door. 'You're not going to win any fashion competitions in that get-up.'

I swish to another angle. 'I think I look like a proper hiker.'

'I think you look like a proper wanker.'

'Ellen. Language.'

'What's all this for?' she wants to know as she comes and moves my carrier bags out of the way – changing lounging on the door to lounging on my bed. My child flicks through the contents of the bags.

'I'm going to Peru.' I can't help my grin.

'No way!' Ellen exclaims. 'I thought that was all off.'

'Well, it's on again. I fly the day after tomorrow.' But we're actually going down to the airport the night before and staying in a hotel on site as the flight is at ridiculous o'clock in the morning.

'What are we going to do without you?'

'Cook, clean and tidy up for yourselves.'

Ellen doesn't look very impressed by that. 'I'll end up doing everything for Dad and Bobs.'

'Only if you're stupid – as I am.'

My daughter groans. 'So you're really, like, going.'

I bite the plastic label off my trousers and fold them carefully. Probably I should travel in my jeans as they'll be heavy to pack. 'Yes, I'm really, *like*, going.'

'Where?' Now Bobby has his head round the door.

'To Peru.' I indicate my newly purchased wares.

'With that lot?'

That lot, I think, has to fit in one very small holdall. Our luggage allowance is minimal.

Bobby comes in and tries out the walking pole I've bought. The hiker's idea of a security blanket.

My son twirls it round. 'You'll look like Charlie Chaplin with this.'

'If it helps me to get up those mountains, then so be it,' I concede.

'You will be all right, won't you?' he wants to know.

'I'll be fine,' I say, touched at my son's concern. 'I'm going to take it all at my own pace. It's not a race. I don't need to be there first. I just need to finish.'

'It does sound quite exciting,' Bobs admits. 'Wish I was going now.'

'I was thinking about what you said – about changing your life and stuff.' Ellen picks at her bright blue nail varnish and avoids looking at me. 'I might go back to college. Maybe do hairdressing. I wouldn't mind my own salon one day. Or I could do a retail management course, work my way up in the shop.'

When I manage to shut my mouth again, I go over and hug my daughter. 'That sounds like a wonderful idea.'

'I gave them a bit of a ring today,' Ellen continues, clearly embarrassed by this sudden rush of ambition or by the implied admission that her aging parent might just be right. 'I've missed the September admissions date, but I could join some of the courses in January.'

I brush Ellen's hair from her forehead as I used to when she was a little girl. 'You know that Dad and I will support you in any way we can.'

She shrugs as if it doesn't matter, but she smiles gratefully. 'Thanks, Mum.'

'I've been thinking too,' Bobby says. 'I might give the Police Force a go.'

How I don't pass out in a dead faint, I don't know. 'The police?'

'There was a recruitment thing up at the city yesterday and, well, I thought it wouldn't do any harm . . .' My boy tails off, also seemingly bewildered by the glimmer of ambition that has broken through his apathy.

'No harm at all,' I say quickly. 'It's a very laudable career. You'd be good at it. You'd make a fine policeman.'

'And they give you a gun,' Ellen adds.

'Cool.'

Obviously, my son hasn't considered the fringe benefits carefully.

'We're dead proud of you, Mum,' Bobs says. 'None of our mates' mums has ever done anything like this.'

'Thanks,' I say, tearing up. I hug Bobby, and Ellen comes to join in.

'Come home safely,' she says, a bit teary herself. 'We both love you.'

'We're gonna miss you, big time,' my son adds.

'I'll be back before you know it.'

'The only downside about this Peru thing,' Bobs warns, 'is that Dad was convinced you'd never do it. Now that you're really going, he'll have a fit.'

At which point, my husband appears in the doorway and says, 'Dad will have a fit about what?'

Chapter One Hundred-Ten

My children, citing urgent matters to attend to, quite sensibly scarper.

That leaves me and Greg alone.

In lieu of speaking, my husband opens his hands and gestures at the piles of hiking-type stuff heaped on the bed.

'The company has paid for my ticket,' I explain. 'They didn't want to leave me behind. I can pay them back for it when I've earned the money.'

He still doesn't speak.

'I leave tomorrow to go to the airport.'

Greg visibly recoils. *'Tomorrow?'*

I nod. And then fight the urge to run round in a circle, screaming, 'Tomorrow!' at the top of my voice. 'We're staying at the Ramada Hotel overnight and then we fly out first thing the following morning.'

He stands and stares at my gear as if trying to work out what it is. Eventually, he speaks. 'I don't know what to say.'

That much is clear enough.

'"Good luck" would be nice,' I venture.

'I never thought you'd go,' he says. 'Not really.'

I want to ask why, but then I also don't actually want to know.

'Don't go,' he says. 'Please don't go.'

'Why not?'

'I'm worried. Worried how you'll manage. Worried that you'll be hurt or fall ill.' My husband's shoulders sag. 'Worried that you'll be so far away from me. Worried that you won't want to come home. To me.'

Now it's my turn to be taken aback.

He turns to me, eyes troubled. 'You will come home to me?'

'Of course I will,' I say, baffled. 'Why would you think otherwise?'

My husband looks round the bedroom. 'What if you like it so much that you decide that you want more than this?'

'I won't,' I say.

'How can you be so sure?'

'Because I love you. I love the kids.'

'You can't wait to get away from us.'

'It's not like that at all! I just wanted to do something for me. Something exciting. Something daring. It doesn't mean that I love any of you the less.'

Greg doesn't look convinced.

'I wanted you to come with me,' I remind him. 'I *begged* you to come with me. I'm not doing this because I want to leave you behind.'

'I'm frightened that I'm going to lose you.'

'Never,' I say.

And then Greg's face crumples and we fall into each other's arms and hold each other tightly. We both cry and kiss and cry a bit more.

I don't think that Greg will ever let me go. And now I'm beginning to wonder if I want to.

Chapter One Hundred-Eleven

My husband and I make love. Crazily, madly, passionately. Like we did when we were young. It's utterly fabulous. When we've done it once, we do it again! Then we lie in bed cuddled up together. And I wonder why I'm going to Peru at all and whether it's too late to cancel.

Chapter One Hundred-Twelve

It's the day of my departure and Lauren has come to say goodbye to me. She's all tearful too.

'Two weeks,' I say as she hugs me. 'Two tiny little weeks. That's all I'm going for.'

'But it's so far away,' my sister complains.

'And it's full of foreigners?' I grin as I say it.

'Exactly.'

Greg hangs back, saying nothing.

Throughout the day I've wondered if I'm doing the right thing. If it wasn't for the fact that the company had stumped up the money, I might well have cancelled. I'm wearing my walking boots so that they don't go missing if my luggage is lost and, despite the thickness of my hiking socks, I have the coldest feet known to man.

If Greg begged me not to go now, then I probably wouldn't. It's all very well talking about these things in theory, looking at the itinerary and the travel guides – but the reality is a lot more scary. I've only been on a plane once in my life and never on my own. Then I remember that all of my colleagues are seasoned travellers and will look after me. So I tell myself that I'm being ridiculous and it's just nerves and that this is really what I wanted. I think too of all the times I've sneakily pored over my guidebook – the exotic names, the vast, unfamiliar landscapes – all the things that have made me want to do this trip and, finally, I'll be seeing them all, I'll be among them all. I'll be breathing the air of the Andes, have my feet on Peruvian soil.

I take a deep breath. I have nothing to be afraid of. This is an experience, an adventure. This is what I wanted.

All my gear has, amazingly, fitted into my holdall. It's at my feet now and my backpack is slung over my shoulder.

There's a toot from the road and I look out of the window. My stomach lurches. 'They're here.'

The company mini-bus is outside and it appears that everyone else is packed inside.

'I could come to the airport with you,' Greg offers.

'No, no. I think that would make it worse.'

'I'm going to miss you,' he says.

I hug him. 'I'm going to miss you too.'

'Come on, come on,' Lauren urges. 'Or they'll go without you.'

Greg picks up my bag.

'I'm going to have to carry it myself for the next two weeks,' I remind him. 'I should start getting used to it.'

Nevertheless, he walks out to the bus with me, clutching it for dear life.

My colleagues cheer as I approach and I break into a smile.

'Come on, Annie,' Blake shouts. 'Get on board!'

I cling to Greg again. 'I'm going to miss you,' I whisper.

He holds me to him and I wind my arms round his neck as we kiss deeply.

'Oooo!' my colleagues shout out from the bus, teasing.

'Be safe.' My husband's fingers trail through mine as we part. 'I'll be thinking of you.'

I climb into the bus and the door is slammed. I settle in the spare seat at the front and then Blake shouts, 'Ready?'

And everyone else shouts back, 'Ready!'

Before I know it, we're off and I stare out of the window. Greg lifts his hand in a wave and I blow him a kiss. Then I watch him standing on the pavement getting smaller and smaller and smaller as we drive away from him.

Chapter One Hundred-Thirteen

Lauren put the kettle on. 'We need a brew,' she said with a heartfelt sigh.

Greg sat at the table.

'I feel like she's going away for months, not weeks,' Lauren fretted. 'Do you think she'll be okay? I'm so worried about her. Anything could happen.'

'Shut up, Lauren,' Greg said. 'You're not helping.'

His sister-in-law slapped down a mug in front of him. 'Drink that and then go fishing. That'll make you feel better.'

They both turned as they heard a vehicle pull up outside.

'That's not her back already, is it?' Lauren said. She wouldn't have put it past Annie to bottle out at the last minute.

Greg stuck his head out of the back door. 'It's Chelsea,' he said.

'Huh. We are honoured,' grunted Lauren. 'Wonder what *she* wants?'

Her eldest sister, Chelsea, slipped out of her car, wearing dark glasses and Lauren could tell that she'd lost a lot of weight.

Chelsea came into the kitchen and air-kissed them both. 'I was hoping to catch Annie,' she said. 'It is today that she's going?'

'You've just missed her,' Greg said. 'The bus came not ten minutes ago. She's on her way.'

'Oh.' Chelsea's face fell. 'I brought this for her.' She pushed an envelope towards Greg. 'It's the money I borrowed.'

The money that nearly jeopardised her trip, Lauren thought. 'It's a bit late now,' she pointed out.

'I know.' Her sister looked embarrassed. 'I didn't . . . I couldn't . . .' Behind the dark glasses it was clear that Chelsea was crying.

'Never mind,' Lauren said more softly. 'It's here for when she gets back. Does this mean that everything is sorted out?'

Their older, more perfect sister shook her head. 'It's looking bad,' she admitted. 'Richard could go to prison. The house is up for sale. One car has already gone.' She flicked a glance towards the road where her car was parked. 'I'm hanging on to this one by the skin of my teeth. I don't know what will happen.'

'Oh, Chelsea.' Lauren gave her a hug.

Her sister's tense body relaxed slightly and she cried on Lauren's shoulder while the latter patted her back soothingly.

'I'll see if there's any more tea left in that pot,' Greg said, and they both sat Chelsea down at the table while she sobbed.

'Everything I was certain about in my life has been stripped away,' she said bleakly.

Lauren closed her eyes. To think that it was Chelsea's apparent perfection that had motivated her and Annie to change their lives. Now look what had happened. She felt sorry for her sister who had seemed to have it all and yet had always been on the periphery of their lives. Well, it wasn't too late for that to change either.

'We can help you,' Lauren said. 'When Annie comes back, all three of us will get together and see what we can do.'

'I'd really like that,' Chelsea sniffed, gratefully.

'Don't worry,' Lauren said. 'We can help you to rebuild it all.'

If The Terrible Twins could turn things around, then their big sister could start all over again too.

Chapter One Hundred-Fourteen

Greg sat next to Ray on the canal bank. The day was shaping up to stay grey and overcast, the sun never quite managing to fulfil its potential.

Annie was on her way to Peru and already Greg felt as if there was a big hole in his life. He'd let her walk away, going off on the adventure of a lifetime with a bunch of people he didn't know, who might not look after her, and a bloke who definitely had designs on her. The thought knotted his stomach and all the pleasant rituals of setting up his tackle had failed to relax him.

Annie had gone and he was frightened that she might not come back.

'If I was Prime Minister—' Ray started.

'Shut up, Ray,' Greg said. 'Please shut up.'

'Hmm,' Ray said. 'Tetchy today, matey. Want to tell Uncle Raymondo what's wrong?'

'She's gone,' he said flatly.

His friend's eyes widened. 'She's left you?'

'No, no. She's on her way to Peru.' He hoped that was all, but his heart felt heavier than he'd ever known it.

His friend tsked. 'Bad,' he said. 'Bad.'

'She looked really happy.'

'You're too soft with her,' Ray intoned. 'That woman walks all over you. I told you, you need to put your foot down.'

Ray had, indeed, told him that on many occasions. But was that really the way to run things? Greg had offered a lifetime of quiet, loyal steadiness, and it had worked for many, happy years. But it wasn't working now.

What would he do if he was fishing? He wouldn't just sit there moping. He wouldn't keep on casting with the same bait, sitting in the same fruitless spot. He'd try something new, move on down the river. Anything to interest the fish in his bait. Perhaps that's what he had to do now?

Ray sucked in a breath. 'If I was you—'

Suddenly, Greg put down his rod and turned to his friend. 'Tell me, Ray, how many times have you been divorced?'

His fishing companion looked taken aback. 'Three. Four if Marla carries on the way she is.'

'Then why, exactly, am I taking my relationship advice from you?'

Ray opened and closed his mouth, rather like the perch that was testing the bait at the end of his line.

Greg snatched up his own rod, broke it in two and hurled it in the canal. 'That's what I think of your advice.'

He had things to do – he could see that now. And if he hurried, if he moved more quickly and more decisively than he'd ever done in his life, he might just manage it.

Chapter One Hundred-Fifteen

I didn't get much sleep at the hotel. It's a scuffed, well-used airport box, noisy with people coming and going all night long. Where are they going to, I wonder, with their smart wheeled cases and their scruffy backpacks? Are they feeling as anxious, as stressed, as sick to the stomach as I am now? Is their trip a big, bold adventure for any of them too?

We sat in the lounge bar until late and then I shared a twin room with Minny and, bless her, she chattered excitedly until about three o'clock before she finally fell asleep. The bed was as comfortable as lying on a pile of housebricks and I really missed Greg. One night away from him and I'm already questioning how I'll manage for the next two weeks on my own.

We were up long before dawn. It took Minny an hour to do her hair and put her make-up on. She took up gabbling again the minute her eyes opened and I wonder if I'll be sharing a tent with her on the trail. If so, I'm not going to get a minute's peace. It's like coming away with Ellen and I get a pang that my daughter has no interest in doing something like this. I smile at Minny as she preens in the mirror as she's almost beside herself with glee. With her cropped trousers, heels and oversize handbag, she does, however, look more like she's going out for a night's clubbing rather than a trekking holiday. I fight the urge to ask her if she's brought some sensible shoes with her and some warm clothes. I'm not her mother – I must remember that. To counter Minny's glamour, I went down the more native route and put on my jeans and fleece and hiking boots and no make-up to give myself a taste of what's about to come.

Now the whole group is assembled together at the airport. Blake is organising everyone, thank goodness. We've joined an enormous queue snaking through the departures area. The flight to Lima goes via Miami, and as well as us with our smattering of hiking gear – and Minny's clubwear – there's a lot of people in Hawaiian shirts and shorts who clearly aren't coming all the way with us.

There is the air of a school trip about us and everyone is completely hyper – like the kids used to be when they ate blue sweets. Except me. I feel nauseous with nerves. For two pins, I'd drop my bags and run.

My palms are sweaty as I edge forward at the far end of the line. Blake Chadwick comes to my side. He is in immaculate designer trekking gear from head to toe and looks like an advert for Davidoff aftershave. 'Feeling okay, Annie?'

'Fine,' I say tightly.

'It's natural to be a bit nervous,' he offers.

I try to stop chewing my fingernails as I look up at him. 'I'm not nervous.' I'm terrified. Utterly terrified.

He slings his arm round my shoulder. 'You'll be cool,' he assures me. 'You have me to look after you.'

But I don't want Blake Chadwick looking after me. I want Greg. I wish my husband was here, his big solid presence giving me reassurance.

We inch forward in the queue. I just want to be on my way now. I just want to be there. The mounting tension as we edge nearer and nearer to the desk is threatening to make me explode. Time is ticking away. The hour of the flight departure is getting nearer and nearer.

As we get to the desk, Blake Chadwick stands aside and ushers me in front of him. 'You go first, Annie.'

If he says, 'Age before beauty,' I'll smack him one. But he doesn't. My boss is being genuinely nice and caring and I risk a smile. 'Thanks.'

The rest of the group are standing waiting for us, shuffling about impatiently. 'Come on, you two. Get a move on,' Minny shouts. 'We've got a plane to catch!'

Blake lifts my bag on to the conveyor belt. 'Ready for this, Sexy?'

'Yes,' I say with a grin. 'Let's do it!'

Chapter One Hundred-Sixteen

After a gruelling twenty-three hours of travelling, we arrive in Lima, Peru. I'm here. I'm finally here.

The air is hot, thick and smells of diesel from the snaking traffic jams that clog the roads. Apart from the small, nut-brown, sturdy people who populate it, the outskirts of Lima look much like any cosmopolitan city.

Then we take a short orientation tour into the heart of this, the City of Kings, which blends ancient and colonial architecture with the modern, and I feel that the real Peru emerges. As we twist and turn through the squares and walk under the shade of the intricate balconies of old Lima, the city's history starts to unfold for us. The old ladies with black bowler hats sit swathed in their hand-woven red blankets smoking pipes. Young men in ponchos sell cheap alpaca hats and gloves and socks, and I think that I should have brought a bigger bag for all the souvenirs I'll want to take back. Children in brightly coloured traditional clothing, full skirts, felt jackets and flowered bonnets clutch dolls in the same attire and pose with smiling llamas and alpacas for photographs with the tourists. Music from lilting pan pipes fills the squares.

We stroll through the Plaza Mayor visiting La Catedral with its imposing twin towers then on to the striking yellow and white Spanish-Baroque church, convent and cool catacombs of San Francisco. A high proportion of Peru's population live cheek-by-jowl in Lima and the bustling streets only serve to confirm it.

That evening, tired and footsore, we check into our hotel in Miraflores on Peru's Costa Verde. It's a beautiful, Spanish-style building with white adobe walls and dark wood shutters on the windows. After dining on *rocotos rellenos* – hot red peppers stuffed with meat and tomatoes and raisins washed down with my very first pisco sour – the first of many – I sleep like the dead in my bed covered with colourful Inca blankets. In the morning, I throw open the shutters and, looking out at the ocean, I think that I'm raring to go on the other side of the world. *I'm here. I'm here. I'm here.* Let me out and at it!

Jet lag? Pah! I feel alive, zinging in every nerve cell. My incredible adventure is about to begin. This morning we're setting off on the first of our long bus journeys. This one takes us south on the Pan American Highway across the vast wastelands of the Atacama Desert and on to our ultimate destination, the incredible Nazca Lines. Before we depart, I try ringing home for about the third or fourth time since I got here. Mobile phone signals are, at best, patchy and when the line has eventually connected, I haven't yet managed to catch Greg once. At the other end, the phone rings again but no one's at home and I can't quite work out what time it should be there. Every minute, with all the wonderful sights I'm seeing, I'm wishing that he was here too.

I text my husband to tell him that I love him and I text Lauren and Chelsea to tell them that I've arrived safely and am already having a brilliant time. Then I haul my bag down-stairs and out on to the pavement. The smokers among us are having a quick drag before we leave and the others are stuffing last-minute additions into bulging backpacks. Blake Chadwick is walking up and down looking very keen to be off while Sarah Bennett – the inspiration behind this trip – is busy supervising the loading of the luggage on the bus.

Minny is bouncing with excitement. 'I can't wait,' she says.

'Me neither.' I'm itching to get going, be on our way.

'Ready, Sexy?' Blake asks me.

I nod. 'As I'll ever be.'

'You're doing great.'

'I'm loving it already,' I tell him.

'Glad you came?'

'Yes,' I say, and I know that I owe him for organising this for me. Blake might be brash and the world's biggest flirt, but I do think that he has a kind heart too. 'I wouldn't have missed it for the world.'

He hoists my bag into the luggage hold and I take one last glance at this hotel. The next time I see it will be in two weeks' time, when we spend our last night here. Then, as I go to climb on to the bus, I hear a voice call out my name.

'Annie!'

I spin round and I can't believe what my eyes are seeing. Surely, I must be hallucinating!

Running down the street towards me at warp speed is my husband. My Greg. Tourists out for an early-morning constitutional dive out of his way as he races through them, arms flailing.

'Annie!'

He's carrying a rucksack and, for a moment, my addled brain wonders exactly what he's doing here. And then I realise that my husband – my stick-in-the-mud husband, who prefers his holidays in Cromer, has travelled halfway round the world to be with me – and tears spring to my eyes.

'Greg!' I shout out and, dropping my backpack, I weave my way through my colleagues and start to run towards him, scattering the tourists going the other way.

As we get closer together, I can see that Greg looks as if he got dressed in the dark. He's wearing an ancient fleece and trekking trousers that he hasn't had on for years. The Worzel Gummidge of trekkers. By contrast, the rucksack he has over his shoulder still has the label attached to it. My heart squeezes with love for him.

'Annie!' he shouts again, and there's anguish in his voice.

'I'm here!'

Then, when he sees me, the relief on his face is palpable. He too throws his rucksack to the ground and I run full pelt into his arms. As we meet, he picks me up and spins me round, his mouth on mine. He hangs on to me tightly.

I press my face into his neck. 'What are you doing here?'

'I'm coming with you,' he says breathlessly. 'I couldn't let you go alone.'

We hug each other again.

'Why? Why now?'

'I was sitting on the canal bank with Ray and I suddenly realised what a twit I'd been. I thought, what on earth was I doing there when you were going on this adventure without me?'

I look at him again to make sure that he's really there. 'But how? How did you do it?'

'Chelsea brought the cash she borrowed back yesterday

and I raided your old handbag for the rest of the sandwich money. I just had enough so I phoned Dream Days and told them that I was a complete idiot and I needed to be with you. They fixed me a ticket at the last minute.'

'The *very* last minute.' I glance back at the bus. Everyone else is on board and Blake is standing on the step by the door.

'Come on then,' I say, excitedly. 'Or they'll go without us.'

Greg takes my hands in his and our eyes meet. 'I was so worried that I'd left it too late, Annie.'

'You nearly did, Greg,' I breathe. 'You very nearly did.'

'I'm here now,' he offers. 'Can you forgive me?'

'If you can forgive me.'

'Let's fulfil our dreams together from now on,' my husband says. 'What do you say?'

'As long as you don't want me to take up fishing,' I joke.

'No more fishing,' he says. 'Now it's just me and you. We'll do whatever you want. Travel the world, jump out of planes, swim with dolphins. I don't care as long as we're together.'

There are tears in my eyes when I tell my husband, 'I'm liking the sound of that.'

'Come on, you two lovebirds,' Blake Chadwick shouts across at us. 'You've got a bus to catch!'

'Let's do it for Team Ashton,' I say to Greg.

'This is the start of the rest of our lives,' he says.

And we both break into huge grins as we run towards the bus and the beginning of our big adventure together.

Chapter One Hundred-Seventeen

Two weeks later, we crawl on hands and knees up the Omigod Stairs – a near-vertical set of Inca stone steps that mark our final ascent to the lost city of Machu Picchu and the ultimate goal of our challenge. Fourteen long, mad, adventure-filled days after we left good old Blighty for the exotic continent of South America and we're here, we've made it. Only a few more metres to go.

My heart is pounding in my chest due to the thin air, and my thighs are burning from the long, strenuous walk. Greg takes my hand and helps me up the last step and on to the stone plateau at the top. We stand together, breathing heavily. I lean on my trekking pole and my husband's arm.

The last two weeks have been among the best of my life. Only giving birth to Ellen and Bobby can begin to compete. The sights we've seen, the places we've visited have made me cry tears of joy and it has been all the sweeter for Greg being here with me.

Hand-in-hand we've watched the giant Andean condors soaring over a landscape that's like nothing I've ever experienced before. We've bounced in a small airplane above the amazing, ancient drawings at Nazca, have come nose-to-nose with sea lions at the Ballestas Islands, have bathed in the natural hot springs at Chivay, watched a magnificent thunderstorm split the sky over Lake Titicaca. We've marvelled at the sunset over

Arequipa and, pisco sour in hand, watched the spectacular sunrise at the Inca ruins of Saqsaywaman. We've danced to the music of pan pipes more times than I care to count, have raced through the streets of Puno in bicycle taxis and have white-water rafted on the turbulent Urubamba River.

This has been, and continues to be, the trip of a lifetime.

But, of all those things, the Inca Trail has been the most exhilarating, most taxing, most punishing thing I've ever done in my life.

Despite my training, I've huffed and puffed my way up the steep Inca pathway that runs from the River Kusichaca in the east to the Urabamba in the north. The wide stone paths, which were built to accommodate llama trains, follow the rapids of the river down the Sacred Valley to Llaqtapata, one of the thirty historical Inca sites on the trail, then on to the Inca settlement of Wayllabamba. From Llulluchapampa the views of the snow-covered peaks of the Andes moved me, once again, to tears. Then we grovelled our way up Warmiwañusca – more commonly, and appropriately, called Dead Woman's Pass. This is the hardest climb due to the lack of oxygen at this height, but at the top you can look down on the Pacaymayu Valley and up to Runkurakay, the second-highest pass on the trail. From there we went down through cloud rainforest thick with vines and orchids and glossy trees. High on a ridge above the Urabamba we stopped at Puyupatamarka – another name that I remembered from my guide book – and nearly wore out our camera taking photographs of the snow-capped mountains of Veronica and Salkantay, one of the most beautiful places on the trail.

Today, before dawn has even had time to think about

breaking, we've descended to the giddily terraced ruins of Wiñay-Wayna and have wound our way to Machu Picchu itself – our final and most fabulous destination on the trail.

'Okay, guys,' Blake says, as he claps his hands. 'We've made it this far. Let's do the last push together!'

Much cheering. Greg and I exchange a glance. I don't know how I would have done this without him. He's been my rock, my angel. He's cajoled me along the trail, carried my backpack when it got too heavy, let me have his last boiled sweet when I ran out of steam.

'I want everyone to hold hands,' Blake says. We do as we're told. I think this has been an excellent team-building exercise and I'd normally spit in the eye of anyone who said the word 'team-building'. I feel that I know all of my work colleagues as friends now and I'm sure that there'll be a great atmosphere when we get back to the office, now that we've achieved so much together.

'Now trust me,' Blake continues. 'I want everyone to close their eyes and walk slowly forward together. Don't open your eyes until I count to three!'

We close our eyes and I'm not even tempted to peep. Blake leads us slowly forward and we climb the last few steps together, hands held tightly. I give Greg's an extra squeeze.

When we're all standing in a line, Blake begins to count. 'One . . .'

We all join in. 'Two! Three!'

Chapter One Hundred-Eighteen

Then we open our eyes and we're standing at IntiPunku – the Sun Gate – and we're on the edge of a sheer drop, looking down on the breathtaking ruins of Machu Picchu. The sprawling, long-lost city hacked out of the depths of the Peruvian jungle only a hundred years ago is spread below us, and the sight is more magical than I could ever have imagined. No guidebook could ever do this justice.

Everyone lifts their arms and cheers together. Then there's a group hug and happy dances. Blake breaks out two bottles of champagne that he's lugged up here.

'Oh, Greg,' I whisper when we're alone again. My husband wraps his arms round me and we hold each other tightly as the tears stream down our faces.

'We made it,' he says thickly. 'We made it, love.'

'We did.' I sob. 'We bloody well did!'

The sun peeps over the horizon and lifts the cloak of mist from Machu Picchu's ancient shoulders, showing the mountain and ruined city below it in all its glory. The pinnacle of Huayna Picchu guards the city from behind, flanked by cliffs that drop away vertically.

Blake hands us two plastic cups of champagne and we hold them up in a toast together. 'Thank you,' I say, and I know that BC understands that it's for so much more than the fizzy stuff.

412

'You're welcome,' he says with a wink and fades away to join the others.

Greg and I hold hands as we sip our bubbles together. This trip has really brought us together again, closer than we've ever been. Soon we'll walk down to the ruins and explore the sights I've memorised from my guidebook – the Temple of the Condor, the Sacred Plaza, The Royal Tomb, the Windows of the Solstices. But, for now, I just want to drink in the spectacular view.

My husband breathes out happily and I turn to him. There's a contented smile on his lips. 'It's not Cromer, is it?' he jokes.

'No,' I laugh. 'It certainly isn't.'

'Mrs Emerson's Clifftop Guest House will never seem quite the same.'

'No,' I agree. 'It won't.'

'Where shall we go next?' Greg asks.

'Not Cromer?' I venture.

'No. Not Cromer.'

'I quite fancy China,' I say. 'Or Vietnam.'

'I've always had a yearning to go to Angkor Wat.'

'You never said.'

'Oh, Annie,' Greg sighs. 'There was so much that I should have said that I never did.'

'I know.' I lean against him. 'But it doesn't matter now. None of it matters now.'

My husband turns to me. 'Thank you for making me do this,' he says. 'Thank you for shocking me out of my comfort zone. Thank you for making me see beyond the end of my own nose.'

We sit down and dangle our legs over the sheer drop.

'Let's take a picture,' I say. 'We'll send it back to the kids and to Lauren and Chelsea.'

'They won't believe that we've done it.'

'They will,' I assure him. 'They will.'

'No going back for us,' Greg says. He spreads his arms expansively and laughs out loud. 'The world is our oyster!'

Now bathed in sunshine, we sit and marvel at Machu Picchu some more.

'We could go back to Cromer,' my husband continues.

'No!'

'For the odd weekend. Just to remind us.' He squeezes my hand. 'But, you know what? Next time, Annie, I'd strip off my clothes and run into that sea with you.'

'Would you?'

Greg grins. 'I would.'

'I might just hold you to that, Mr Ashton,' I say.

And, next time, I promise to myself that I'll wear some more of that sexy underwear and let those seagulls get an eyeful of my breasts.

Read on for the beginning of Carole's delightful
Isle-of-Wight-set novel,

Sunny Days and Sea Breezes

Chapter One

The ferry slips out of the port at Southampton and heads out into the choppy, grey waters of the Solent. The sky hangs low, malevolent and brooding, as grey as the sea, the peaks of washed-out clouds mirroring the white-tipped waves. I sit outside, alone on the rear deck – the only one foolish enough to face the inclement weather. The threat of rain whips in on the sea air and I wish I'd worn a coat more appropriate for the falling temperature. This is a smart, serviceable one for popping between city meetings, not for facing down the elements. The wind is finding all the gaps around my neck, up my sleeves, and cashmere isn't known for its waterproof qualities. But I left in a hurry and the last thing on my mind was my choice of wardrobe. Maybe it should have been. As it was, I just slung as much as I could in a couple of bags and left.

It's the end of March and there are rows and rows of empty bench seats which I'm sure are better utilised in the summer crossings. Now, long before the start of the holiday season, the ferry is probably only half full, if that. A few people brave the cold and come out to look over the rails towards the dwindling view of the port behind us, but soon hurry back inside to the fuggy warmth of the onboard café. I bought a sandwich there, but it looks beyond grim and I can't face eating it. I could throw it to one of the cawing gulls that shadow the ferry, but they look huge and menacing and I feel so light, so insubstantial, so irrelevant, that they might lift me away entirely instead of just taking my disgusting sandwich.

While I further contemplate the many inadequacies of my stale-looking BLT, we pass the magnificent, floating city of the *Queen Elizabeth* – a Cunard liner in posh livery heading somewhere much more exotic than I am, no doubt. Yet, somehow, I still have the sense that I'm escaping. Perhaps there is no set distance-to-escapee ratio. A mile might be as good as a thousand, if you just want to leave everything behind you. I'm hoping less than twenty miles will do the job, as it takes in both a stretch of sea and an island destination. OK, it's not exactly Outer Mongolia, but that has to be worth something.

The Solent is a busy motorway of water, and vessels of all shapes and sizes bob, zip or lumber along beside us. The Red Jet speeds past and I know that I could have taken that, a quicker way to the Isle of Wight, but I wanted to feel the distance growing more slowly, the space opening up between me and my old life.

It sounds as if I know what I'm doing, as if there was a plan. But I don't and there wasn't. I only know that I had to get away to a place where no one knows me, where I don't keep having the same conversation over and over, where I don't have to talk at all, where no one looks at me with pity and thinks 'Poor Jodie'.

For something to do, I abandon my sandwich on the bench and cross to one of the rails, looking out to sea. I can't tell you if it's port or starboard as I'm a confirmed landlubber – but it's most definitely one or the other. The wind whips my long hair across my face and for once, I'm glad that I haven't spent money on an expensive blow-dry.

A few minutes later, the door behind me bangs and a hardy smoker joins me. Though he nods in my direction, he keeps his distance as he puffs away. I wish I smoked. It's years since I had a cigarette – a teenage flirtation – and I didn't much care for it then. Yet I'm tempted to pluck up the courage to blag one from him. I want to feel something, even if it's just burning in my lungs. However, before I can find my voice, he takes a deep drag, throws his butt into the water below and, with a theatrical shiver, disappears inside. Not as hardy as he looked, then.

Alone again, I stare down at the churning wake of the boat, mesmerised, listening to the deep thrum of the engines, feeling the vibration beneath my feet. My phone rings and I take it out of my pocket, even though I already know who it is. Sure enough, Chris's number is on the screen so I let it go straight to voicemail. I don't want to speak to my husband now. I don't want to speak to anyone. What would happen if I dropped my phone into the sea? I hold it over the rail while I think, dangling it precariously. If it sank into the depths of the ocean would I, Jodie Jackson, simply cease to exist? Would I be so off-grid that no one could find me? No more Twitter, no more Instagram, no more WhatsApp. It sounds too appealing. If my phone rings again now, I'm going to throw it into the sea. I am. But I wait and wait and my phone, for once, stays silent. I switch it to mute and, still reluctant to give it a reprieve, put it back into my pocket. I suppose that I might need it for an emergency.

I try not to think, to keep my head empty as the sea slides by below me. And it nearly works. Behind me there's a shriek and two gulls are on the bench fighting over my cast-off sandwich, having plucked it from its cardboard packet. I don't like to tell them that they'd probably be better off eating the box. The funnel belches black smoke and covers them in smuts of soot but they are too focused on the limp lettuce and the white, slimy fat on the bacon to care.

Then a sea fret rolls in and shrouds everything in mist, taking away any semblance of a view. I'm going to arrive at my destination engulfed in thick fog – both physically and metaphorically.

The ferry crossing is barely an hour long and, too soon, we're docking in Cowes. I'm sure it's usually a bustling place, but not today. The scene that greets me looks as if it's been filmed in monochrome. Even the colourful flags on the little sailing boats that line the entrance to the harbour are failing to compete with the mist, the forbidding light, and are bleached out to grey. Alabaster sand meets the silver sea, joins the battleship sky.

I came here on holiday as a child, just the once. I must have been seven or maybe eight. I remember playing on the beach with my older brother, Bill, burying our dad up to the neck in sand and sitting in deckchairs eating fish and chips from greasy paper. But that's all. After that we went to Spain every year. I don't remember much about that either. People say that the Isle of Wight is still like Britain was forty years ago. That sounds perfect to me. If only I could wind time back to then. I'd be two, would have the whole of the world ahead of me, and could make very different life choices.

Chapter Two

At the port, I take a taxi and look out of the window as we bump across the island to my destination. The driver is determinedly chatty. 'First time in the Isle of Wight, love?'

'Yes.'

'Business? Holiday?'

'Yes.' How can I explain that it's neither one nor the other?

'It's a great place. If you're looking for some tips on how to enjoy yourself, I'm your man.'

'Thanks.'

In theory, if I keep giving one-word answers, he'll stop speaking. After a few more futile attempts, he does, and I sink into my seat in silence. I'm glad he has the heater on full blast so it's cosy and warm, which thaws me out after my freezing journey.

It looks pretty enough here. Green. Lots of green. But then, compared to where I live in Inner London, so are most places. After a short while, we crest a hill and there's a rough layby marked VIEWPOINT.

'Can we stop here, please?'

The driver pulls in. 'Do you want an ice-cream?'

'No.' The lone van looks as if it has few customers today. 'I'd just like to look for a moment.'

So I climb out of the cab and go to the edge of the fields to gaze out. A meadow of rather hopeful early wildflowers spreads out in front of me. Beyond that the lush, green pastures drop away, rolling gently towards the ribbon of sparkling silver sea that stitches the land to the vast blue-white sky. It's as if I've entered a different land. The mist has gone, the sun looks like it might be struggling to come out. Even on such a dull day, it's beautiful and I take a moment to breathe in the air, to admire the view.

Sensing the driver waiting patiently behind me, I return to the car. A short while later and I'm looking at the sea again as we drop down to the coastal road on the other side of the island. I check the address again, even though I've already given it to the driver and he hasn't, thus far, looked once at his satnav. A few minutes later, the taxi turns onto the curving harbour road and a sign says WELCOME TO COCKLESHELL BAY.

He slows down as we pass a long line of smart houseboats and, eventually, he pulls up outside one that's rather smarter than the rest.

'Here you go, love.' He turns in his seat and I hand over a modest amount of cash for my journey and get out of the cab. The price of taxis is also quite different in London.

The driver joins me at the boot and flicks it open. 'Want a hand with your bags?' he asks as he lifts out my two bulging holdalls.

'I'm fine, thank you.'

'Nice place,' he observes with a nod at Bill's houseboat.

'Yes, it is.' This is the first time that I've seen it in the flesh. Although Bill's shown me enough photographs of it.

'Enjoy your holiday.' The driver jumps back into his warm car and buzzes off, leaving me standing there at the side of the harbour.

Holiday. That's not quite how I'd describe it.

I have a good long look at Bill's boat – my home for the foreseeable future. It's called *Sunny Days* and is painted cream and grey. It's not hard to tell that his lengthy and rather expensive renovations have only recently been finished. Everything looks shiny and new, even though the day is trying its best to stay dreary. My brother has clearly thrown a lot of money at his latest project, which is so typical of him. He has, of course, been too busy to visit it since it was completed, so I'm to be the first occupant. I think his plan is to use it as a weekend bolthole, but I can't see that ever happening. Bill runs his own company – the one that I work for too: WJ Design. I've been with him for years, ever since he set it up and I love working with my older bro. We lost Mum and Dad some years ago, so now it's just the two of us and, because of that, we've always been close.

Bill's company specialises in designing the interiors for hotels, office blocks, shopping centres and, though I say it myself, we're very much in demand. Which, as a result, leaves us little time for play. I'm marginally better at crafting a social life than Bill, who is a complete workaholic. My dear brother has more money than he knows what to do with and no time to spend it. At the moment, I'm feeling grateful that he has this folly as I had no idea where else to go and, when Bill suggested I escape to his houseboat, it seemed like the answer to my prayers.

The houseboat is solid, and sturdy on its moorings – I think Bill said it had been in service as a Thames Lighter. I don't even know what that is, but while the houseboat looks like it might have started out life as some kind of workaday tug there's not much evidence of that left now. Bill's team have worked their magic on it and now it's a houseboat fit for a queen – or a sister who's broken into little pieces.

Carole Matthews